The MASTER PAINTER

The MASTER PAINTER

Edwin Mullins

DOUBLEDAY

New York
London
Toronto
Sydney
Auckland

Published by Doubleday, a division of
Bantam Doubleday Dell Publishing Group, Inc.
666 Fifth Avenue, New York, New York 10103

DOUBLEDAY and the portrayal of an anchor with a dolphin
are trademarks of Doubleday, a division of
Bantam Doubleday Dell Publishing Group, Inc.

Library of Congress Cataloging-in-Publication Data

Mullins, Edwin B.
  [Lands of the sea]
  The master painter / Edwin Mullins. — 1st ed.
    p. cm.
  Original title: Lands of the sea.
  ISBN 0-385-24371-5
  1. Netherlands—History—House of Burgundy, 1384–1467—Fiction.
2. Philip, Duke of Burgundy, 1396–1467—Fiction. I. Title.
PR6063.U46L36   1989
823'.914—dc19   88-25894
                                                           CIP

This book was originally published in England by
William Collins Sons & Co., Ltd., under the title
The Lands of the Sea.

ISBN 0-385-24371-5

Book Design by Patrice Fodero

April 1989
First Edition in the United States of America

For my daughter
Frances

Preface

This novel and its predecessor, *The Golden Bird*, are intended as mirrors of one another. Between the two mirrors lies that period of history which is sometimes known as the Age of Romance—the Age of Chivalry. *The Golden Bird* was set at the dawn of that age: *The Master Painter* is set in its dusk. There are many deliberate parallels—themes and preoccupations which color the life, art and literature of the medieval world until the new sophistication of the Renaissance blew them away forever.

In this present book, Master Jan is—and is not—the first of the great painters of Northern Europe, Jan van Eyck, who was court painter to Philip, duke of Burgundy, during the second quarter of the fifteenth century and on several occasions his special ambassador. Some of Van Eyck's surviving masterpieces find their place in this novel, among them the Ghent Altarpiece and the marriage portrait of Giovanni Arnolfini. Yet I have been concerned just as much with those paintings which do not survive—if, that is, they ever existed, the omissions of history being meat and drink to the novelist: speculation is his trade.

However, such speculations must possess a measure of historical probability. It would indeed have been strange if, during sixteen years' service with the duke of Burgundy, Van Eyck was not once asked to do a portrait of his noble patron. Philip certainly posed for other artists, and he was at this time among the most powerful political figures in Europe: his image would have been in demand, not least by himself. And who better to provide it than his own court painter? As for Duke Philip's opponents in the political arena and on the battlefield, it is known that Van Eyck drew that most heroic of medieval women, the duchess Jacqueline of Hainault, and if he drew her he may well have painted her. I have Master Jan do so. Then there is that other, more celebrated, soldier-lady whom Philip also played a leading part in destroying—the Maid of Orléans, Joan of Arc. Van Eyck was in Arras in the company of the duke while Joan was briefly imprisoned there: he may very possibly have met and drawn her as part of his official duties. Master Jan does.

These are my "lost" portraits, plus one that Van Eyck never seems to have undertaken—his own face. It is an irony of history that the founder of what we now think of as "psychological portraiture" should have left us quite in the dark about who he was and what he looked like—except, that is, for one image reflected in a mirror.

Here, then, is a mirror within the mirror of the book, and I have attempted to see in it some of the people and events which that most remarkable pair of eyes could have witnessed.

E.M.

So violent and motley was life,
that it bore the mixed smell
of blood and of roses.

—J. Huizinga, *The Waning of the Middle Ages*

Chapter ♦ One

High on the prow of the leading vessel two figures were standing hooded against the cold. Their faces were invisible but it was clear from the way they were hunched forward over the gunwale that their eyes were straining to pick out the same distant objects. First one of them pointed, then the other. And across that infinite pattern of marsh and water it was possible to detect minute shapes, mere humps of darkness, spread along the rim of the horizon.

The two men glanced at one another, and in the flicker of the torches Baudouin saw an expression of joy on the face of the younger man.

"At last, Master Jan."

Baudouin's companion only nodded. His eyes seemed to feed on those distant humps. A single blade of orange cloud was growing paler as Jan looked, while around it the sky shimmered in the luminosity of dusk. Gradually the shapes took on a softness in these last moments of daylight. They became dunes; and beyond them, Jan knew, spread the flat polderland whose stubble of sea lavender was threaded by a thousand dikes raised above the watery fields, and where the arms of ten thousand windmills turned and turned against an enormous sky.

He was almost home. Flanders. She was like a face whose features one could hardly recall, so plain were they, and yet so beloved. Jan thought of the lands he had traveled since he last set eyes on those dunes. There had been white cities perched like eyries. Scarred gorges where rivers boiled under turreted bridges. Imperious ranges lifted into snow. Gardens perfumed by roses soft with the spray of fountains. Nobody could have said that Flanders possessed any such pageantry of nature;

1

nevertheless it was here he was pulled back to, where sea and land were parted only by a ripple of sand tugged by the wind. Land that the sea had lost and was hungry to reclaim.

Now, between those dunes, tall masts were passing silently from the open sea toward Sluis. They were back at last, the ships from Portugal. On this Christmas Day 1429, the duke's bride Isabella was entering Flanders in the purple of the evening.

The two men in the leading vessel still watched. Already the low outline of land had merged with the night, and there was nothing again. Then in its place there began to appear specks of fire that blinked as if it were they which moved and not the ship. Gradually, gradually as the vessel approached, the points of light appeared to disperse but only for the spaces between them to fill with countless more lights, and between them countless more, until suddenly against that wall of darkness they linked together into the pattern of an entire town and the two men saw that every building was festive with flares. At that moment a sound of cheering cut through the wind, striking the vessel in short stabs at first, then stronger and more sustained until it seemed to flood the night. And as far as they could see, along the breadth of the quay and from every ledge and window, the flames lit up faces straining, turning, grimacing, searching into the blackness where the gray ghosts of ships grew silently nearer.

There were five vessels, a little separated from each other. The men on the prow of the leading ship were surrounded now by sailors shouting and grasping hawsers and halyards, lowering sails, darting between groups of elegantly dressed figures in bright surcoats with fur sleeves and broad headdresses wound with lengths of rich cloth that swooped almost to the deck.

"At last," said Baudouin again.

He began to fumble for something in the folds of his heavy cloak.

"Fourteen months. My God, Jan. More than fourteen months. Here . . . !"

And he handed him his purse.

Jan looked at it in surprise, and then at Baudouin. He felt

too overwhelmed at being home to speak. There had been moments when he believed he was unlikely to see Flanders again. First the interminable wait in Portugal. Then illness. Storms in the Bay of Biscay. Half the fleet missing. Nearly shipwrecked off Cornwall. Why could the duke not have chosen a bride from closer to, Jan had often wondered?

"I thought you might need that," Baudouin added with a light laugh. Then he sniffed. "Buy yourself an evening to celebrate. You won't get back to Bruges till tomorrow."

Jan understood, and he threw the older man a look of gratitude. Baudouin d'Oignies had been the steward of the ducal embassy to Portugal—in charge of finances. Jan scarcely knew him. Baudouin was rather lofty, a member of the court. Yet warm, with a twinkle in his eye; he had seemed to take a fancy to the young painter. Baudouin would appear at his shoulder sometimes while he was working on the portrait of Isabella in that suffocating heat, and mutter, "I'm glad it's only head and shoulders he asked for. At least the duke won't be put off realizing how tall she is." Now he was giving him some of the money that was left over from the expedition. Generous of him. What was surprising to Jan was that there should be any money left over at all, considering the fortunes my lord of Roubaix had spent on entertaining—gifts to the king, the princes, the princess, the archbishop of Lisbon, the archbishop of Santiago, just about anybody in Granada. And the wine. Did it ever stop flowing?

"Thank you," was all Jan said, feeling the weight of the purse.

They went below to arrange their belongings. Jan could hear the creaking of ropes and the thump of the ship against the quayside.

It was Christmas Day. Tomorrow he would be in Bruges.

Jan was a slight figure of a man. Compact. He had a way of moving with a light step, head thrust a little forward, which gave him a feline air, watchful, eyes on the move, gathering. His mouth moved a lot too, puckering frequently at the corners as if amused by something no one else had noticed. There were some who felt he laughed at them, but they were on the whole the more stolid citizens whose slow thoughts Jan had already left somewhere behind, and what his expression was registering actually related to them not at all. There were some who held him to be lightly malicious, again more on account of that amused expression than through any incident of malice: it was more what he did not say that troubled them than what he did. He was a man much given to silences, and when he did speak it was with a voice so soft that it drew those he was with into a certain privacy, an intimacy even. Women had at times found this habit of softness uncomfortably flirtatious, experiencing the sensation that somehow they were being improperly disrobed: others warmed to the charm of the man for precisely the same reason, while agreeing among each other that he was a little dangerous.

When he had first arrived in Bruges the fact that Jan was already First Painter to the duke equipped him with a certain aura which his quiet and modest manner did not seem initially to suit. There was even speculation at the tavern—the Fallen Angel—that Jan might be some sort of spy, particularly as no one had ever seen him paint anything. Jan had sensed this air of suspicion and appeared at the tavern one evening with his drawing equipment. The merchant from Lucca, Giovanni Arnolfini, was there and was reluctantly persuaded by his friends to let Jan do his face. There was some laughter at the merchant's discomfort.

"A face like mine," he muttered, his Italian intonation giving his verdict a theatrical note, "should be concealed, not exposed."

He declined ever to look at the artist while he sat for him; nonetheless those who were gathered around drinking from their tankards were aware that he took some pains over the set of his mouth and the half-closing of his eyes, and adjusted his hat so.

It was noticeable how the laughter and joviality gradually subsided into silence as they watched Jan explore Giovanni's features with the finest of lines, proceeding slowly yet hardly pausing or removing the point from the soft Fabriano paper he had set before him. The high cheekbones, the heavy lids, flared nostrils, the slightly predatory upper lip—they were all there as if it were Giovanni's double. There were exclamations of astonishment as Jan produced a softer implement and proceeded to apply the gentlest of shadows to the cheek and nose until the face appeared to fill with substance before their eyes.

No one had ever seen Giovanni so confused with delight.

"Look," was all he said, passing the sheet of paper to a delectable young lady who was with him; and it was clear from the merchant's expression that Adonis could not have been made to look more handsome in his eyes.

There followed, not surprisingly, a clamor to be drawn, and the tavern was soon swelling with customers from the neighborhood who had heard that Master Jan was performing miracles at the Fallen Angel. He scarcely had room to move his drawing arm, and at times the faces of onlookers pressed so close to the paper it was as if they were anxious to partake of the miracle the very moment it was performed.

Finally Jan explained that he was too tired to draw any others that evening, but that he would willingly return tomorrow, and thereafter. To his surprise Giovanni pressed a purse of gold into his hands as he rolled up the drawing of himself, though Jan promptly made it clear to all that what he did was for pleasure, and to please his friends.

"The duke, after all, pays me to be a painter," he added, "and here I can practice my skills without having to pay the model."

They laughed, and Jan knew that he was welcome here in Bruges.

In this way Jan drew many people. Among them was the silent master jeweler De Leeuw, whose neighbor Jan was soon to become in the street of the Golden Hand. "The Lion," as he was sometimes called, sat more still than any man Jan had ever drawn, never taking his eyes off the artist and even holding a ring of his own making entirely motionless in one huge hand for the best part of an hour.

"Good," was all De Leeuw said when he saw the result. He nodded, bought Jan a flagon of beer, then resumed his customary seat in the window overlooking the canal. De Leeuw was to become one of Jan's closest friends: there was gold in him and not only in the jewelry he made.

Less pleased with his portrait was the cloth weaver Pieter van Orley. Jan drew him just as he scowled at him, with small mean eyes and downturned mouth. Van Orley had dressed fancifully for the occasion and had expected to be represented as noble, godlike almost, like one of the statues of saints on the town hall, or at least someone who looked like a master of the cloth weavers' guild—which he had ambitions to be. Disappointment and irritation masked his face when he saw the drawing. Perhaps he would have grunted something uncomplimentary if others in the tavern had not glanced inquisitively over his shoulder.

"Perfect. Everything like you," they said. Jan saw him spit in the canal as he left.

Then there was the English wool merchant, Hugo. Jan drew him as though his face were on fire, and people said you could see the ruddiness of his complexion and the yellowish mop of hair even though there was no color in Jan's drawing. Hugo, who had talked and joked continuously through the sitting between extended drafts of beer, seemed to be exploding with words as he gazed out of the Fabriano paper. It was a face creased with humor and shiny with appetite.

"Wonderful. Wonderful," he exclaimed, waving the paper about the tavern like a flag. "Could there be any lady who would not fall for such a face? Surely not. Oh, if Helen of Troy could have seen this, Paris would not have had a chance. To think, Master Jan"—and his features became tense with surprise—"that I might have caused the Trojan War."

And he laughed as if his cheeks might burst, ordered a forest of tankards for all present, and finally burst out of the door, his drawing brandished above him. From the low window onto the canal Jan followed his jubilant progress across the bridge. Hugo himself was invisible from here, but the reflection of his waving arms rippled across the water to the accompaniment of a slowly fading song.

Jan also met Bona. She came to the tavern one evening with a group of friends. Jan was at home: by then he had moved into the tall red house in the street of the Golden Hand which backed onto the canal only a short distance from the Fallen Angel. It had a garden with apple trees next to the house, hidden from the water by a wall. Jan loved the place. De Leeuw had found him a housekeeper and cook who were proudly—Jan noticed with some amusement—sprucing it into an establishment fitting for the First Painter to the duke. They were impressed by that, and marveled at one so young being so very important, as they commented to him solemnly. He feared he might be swallowed alive by their attentions: the housekeeper in particular took careful note of any young ladies he received, assessing their quality with a sharp eye as well as noting the hour they left. Jan felt she was not at all sure about Bona.

De Leeuw had brought her to see him. She had heard of his skills and begged him for a portrait—a drawing—for which she insisted she pay. And she laid a purse before him on the wooden table to leave no room for argument. She would like to sit for him now: there was surely enough light and Master Jan seemed unoccupied at this moment. Jan had in fact been working in the large room upstairs on an altarpiece which the duke intended to present to the cathedral of St. Donatian, for a chapel in honor of his father. It was taxing work, and his visitor must surely have noticed that he was in his working clothes, paint still on his hands. But if she had noticed she chose to ignore the inconvenience.

She seated herself in a place of her choice. Jan shook his head and explained that he needed more light. Bona looked surprised at being told what to do, but moved without a word toward where Jan had placed a chair. First she removed her elaborate headdress; then she peeled a long surcoat from her shoulders and let it fall, and began to untie the blue silk garment that covered her throat and neck, not looking at him at all while she did so. There was a careless, almost sulky look on her face, the mouth slightly downturned, eyes dark and distant. Jan felt he could as well not be there; she might have been removing her clothing in the presence of a maid, or no one at all. Her hand casually dropped the garment on to the floor next to the surcoat: in the same movement she seated herself on the chair and gazed directly at Jan for the first time. Above her long dress she was wearing only the lightest of bodices, cut low and quite transparent. Jan could see the entire form of her breasts.

"I want the portrait to be down as far as here," she announced, running her hand horizontally below her rib cage. "No lower. I don't like my belly."

Then she smiled at Jan. A matter-of-fact smile neither coquettish nor shy.

"But I like my breasts, don't you?" she added. "In ten years' time I shall enjoy having a reminder of what I looked like."

That was how he met Bona.

After that she returned several times, always richly dressed, never offering a reason for her visits.

"I like you," she said.

That was all. Then she would talk, about herself, about other women. It was strange. She was sensual, with fine lazy movements like a cat. Jan knew she enjoyed displaying herself in his company, but there was never any question of his becoming her lover. It was as though Bona were preparing to make love to someone else and using him to rehearse. She told him one day that she had been married. At thirteen, she said, and laughed scornfully. He was a young knight at the court of the present duke's father, John the Fearless. And she laughed again. He had been killed in a tournament: an absurd affair, she said. Why did men do these ridiculous things? Proving their manhood with their lances instead of their pricks. She had imagined all men were as useless as he until he got himself killed, and then she learned better. Bona stretched and ran her hands down her body. She had had two children since she became a widow, she explained casually: that was why her belly was too rounded.

"I don't like many men," she added.

Jan had wondered who were her lovers. And why she liked him.

Meeting Margarethe could hardly have been more of a contrast.

He had been living in Bruges almost a year when a man whose face he had drawn in the tavern—a master weaver—approached him with a courteous request that Jan make a drawing of his young cousin. It was to be for the girl's mother who lived in Louvain and sadly missed her only daughter. The woman was crippled, and it would be such a kindness, the man explained.

It was agreed that the weaver should accompany the girl to Jan's house the following afternoon in order to introduce her. He would find her rather retiring, he explained, but she was a girl of excellent character: her uncle, with whom she now lived here in Bruges, was a weaver like himself, he added with a note of self-satisfaction.

At the appointed hour the housekeeper answered the door to the master weaver and a girl who was largely invisible under a cloak and hood of an oppressive gray. Jan took her to be scarcely more than a child, and paid no attention to her while he made arrangements with the weaver about the size of the drawing, payment, and so on. Shortly the man departed, and Jan looked about him but the girl was nowhere to be seen. Then he heard the sound of footsteps overhead and realized that she had taken herself uninvited to the studio. Surprised, he climbed the stairs and caught sight of the girl peering at some drawings which lay scattered on tables about the room — studies of hands, faces, clothing, people in the streets, roofs and windows: the tools of his trade. She had removed her hood and cloak, and Jan noticed that her hair was long and fair, almost yellow, her face roundish and a little plump like girls' faces he had often seen in Holland. She was robust in appearance, comely rather than pretty, and evidently older than he had imagined.

The girl gave a start as he entered, but when he greeted her warmly she relaxed and Jan caught the look of curiosity as she kept glancing down at the drawings. He laughed and motioned her to a stool by the window, then asked her to look at him while he drew her, and to talk if she wished. She continued to say nothing, but as she turned her head toward him Jan was struck by the expression of eagerness, almost wonder, on her face, the lips slightly parted in a way that suggested there was much she was anxious to say but did not quite dare. And he noticed how fine her eyes were, wide and deep green as if they were dreaming of the sea; then as their eyes met she looked down. As he worked, every now and then that eager, fugitive look would return, and Jan found himself smiling at the girl to try to preserve it while he drew the mouth, but each time he did so she seemed embarrassed and the look had gone.

He grew intrigued by the girl's face, and by this game of pursuit—as though she were hiding herself within a thicket, bobbing up as soon as he looked elsewhere, so that he constantly felt he was being watched.

Because of this strange shyness Jan was unable to complete the drawing that afternoon. The mouth was not there. Would she be prepared to return tomorrow? he asked. She looked up at him and to his surprise the eager expression returned. Yes, she said in a voice that was just as eager. It was the first word she had uttered.

Jan knew that her name was Margarethe. He realized he was thinking about her during the morning that followed; he was unsure why. It was always that same appealing expression that rose before his eyes—as if she were making an unspoken offering.

He heard her arrive, and he showed her to the same stool. But again the face he wanted was not there when he began to draw her. He felt he could do nothing. So Jan laughed, slightly exasperated, and suggested it might be better if she drew him instead. She gazed at him for a second, puzzled, and again he noticed the fine green eyes.

"I shall try if you like," she said in a confident voice.

Jan was so surprised that he stared at her for a moment, and as he did so her lips formed that same expression of eagerness. In a few lines he had it on paper. In half an hour the drawing was finished. It was one of the best he had done. He told her so as he presented it to her. She seemed overwhelmed, and as she took it she gave him that look again in return. An offering.

Jan knew he would see her again.

"I should like to paint your portrait," he said without thinking.

It was the day after this encounter that the court arrived in Bruges, and the ducal herald Jehan Lefèvre appeared at Jan's house one morning to announce that his presence was expected at the ducal palace. For a while Lefèvre had said nothing further, but gazed about him with an air of quizzical superiority while he made small neat adjustments to his clothing.

"The duke is in a spiritual frame of mind," he added loftily after a minute or two. There was an edge to Lefèvre's words which made him sound cold and condescending. Jan felt he could easily dislike this man. His own thoughts were wandering from time to time to Margarethe and he felt intolerant of this intrusive peacock.

"That is to say," the herald continued in the same grating tone, "there are churches he wishes to befriend. You may find yourself well occupied in that spiritual capacity."

Lefèvre was still not looking at Jan, but peering closely now at the altarpiece—almost finished—for the cathedral of St. Donatian. His long pale hands were clasped softly behind his back and he was almost touching the painted panel with his nose.

"It has always seemed most unlikely to me," he went on, as if he were quietly addressing the painting rather than Jan, "that Mary was either beautiful or a virgin. I never met a carpenter with a pretty wife, nor one who wasn't handy with his drill."

The scurrilous comment seemed to float aimlessly on air. Jan looked sharply at the herald to detect any hint of a smile. But there was none. The nose was still brushing the panel.

"One of the gifts the duke proposes is to the Abbey of the Dunes."

Lefèvre's eyes had begun to roam across the surface of the altarpiece as if searching for small defects.

"A most godforsaken place, I should have thought," he added. Still the eyes of the lordly herald remained glued to the painting, lips pursed in concentration. "Perhaps the duke is of the view that your divine brush may persuade Him to visit it again. In my own opinion you would have to perform miracles.

"I shall tell you a story about the abbot," he went on. The herald's eyes had left the altarpiece and were now taking in one of Jan's unfinished portraits on a side easel. "Eustache, as you may know, is a resourceful man, a man of wide tastes. The day his election as abbot was announced his mistress gave birth to a son. He was overjoyed. 'Today,' he announced to those who had come to congratulate him, 'I have twice become a father. God's blessing on it!' "

He laughed thinly, and Jan politely.

It was some while before Jan realized that Lefèvre greatly enjoyed his visits, invariably prolonging them with irreverent tales told in that aloof disdainful manner as if they were ducal proclamations. It was hard to reconcile this languid luminary of Philip's court with the wry figure who thought nothing of accompanying the artist to the Fallen Angel on a warm evening and who was an inexhaustible well of dubious stories concerning for the most part the practices of the clergy. It was the taverner who, in his most affected French, took to addressing Lefèvre as "Monsieur Elégance," serving him without waiting for an order with his favorite Beaune.

As for the duke himself, Jan saw him only rarely. There had been the original summons of course, and how could he ever forget that meeting? At the far end of the hall lined with tapestries had stood the great duke, in black, slim, aloof, hawk-faced with a sharp nose. Jan could recall every step of that lonely walk down the length of the hall. Then the duke had smiled warmly, stepped forward to greet him, embraced him, called him a "master," invited him to be his painter—above all others, he had said.

"I am creating the greatness of Burgundy"—he spoke in a dry, intoning voice, with rather fleshy lips—"and you . . . you shall paint it. You shall have everything you may need."

It was as if a blessing were being conferred.

Then, instead of dismissing him with those quick slender fingers, Philip had requested him to stay with the court awhile, dine with him, talk together, accompany him hunting, even practice swordplay with him. He had shown the keenest interest in Jan's craft. It had been from his brother Hubert, Jan explained, that he had learned the skills of painting, of using color, layer upon layer of it until every object looked as though it were actually made of color, solid with it. Jan went on to emphasize with some pride how he had afterward taught himself to experiment with adding varnishes so as to polish the surface of things until they appeared to sparkle in the sunlight; and it was then that he had been summoned to The Hague to work for the regent of Holland and his court.

What Jan had accomplished by those painstaking layers of color, and those carefully mixed varnishes, was a bright golden world like a beautiful jewel. It was for this, he knew, that the duke had wanted him, had invited him to be First Painter. Soon Jan came to understand why. Everything about the court of Burgundy was radiant: it was so like the golden world he painted. It was as if he were living in a jewel that he had himself created. The costumes. The perfumes. The dancing. The display. The tournaments. And the women: he had never seen such women. They moved like threads of gossamer.

Then Philip's wife had died in childbirth: she was Bonne, so elegant and lovely. She just died. Jan happened to be with the duke when he heard the news, and Philip broke down. Jan had never witnessed a man grieve like that. Philip had reached out for his hand and Jan found himself clasping the duke like a friend.

After that the duke and Jan would often talk—alone. He spoke of his father's murder at Montereau by the dauphin of France—hacked to death with an ax—on a bridge where they had agreed to meet in order to discuss affairs of state. It had been the most treacherous of acts. He, Philip, had been scarcely more than a youth then; but he had sworn, he said, that he would build Burgundy to outshine France, to outshine the world. And his lips protruded angrily as if he would gobble up France and the dauphin if he could.

Jan had been dazzled by Philip. If there was a man he loved, it was him. Everything the duke undertook he did with courage, with conviction, with such splendor. Philip was the god of that golden world, and he, Jan, could imagine no nobler ambition than to place his skills in his service.

After that initial occasion Jan had seen little of the duke. Philip became engaged in the drawn-out wars in Holland and Hainault. It was through Jehan Lefèvre that Jan heard of that vixen the duchess Jacqueline, cousin to Duke Philip. Lefèvre explained how she had bigamously married the English duke Humphrey of Gloucester in order to rob Philip of his just inheritance in the Low Countries. How she had induced Humphrey to lead an English army to seize the duke's territories, even though England was a sworn ally in the wars against the French. How Philip had been compelled to raise an army to defend his own dukedom—a long and painful winter in the frozen marshes. All because of Jacqueline's pride: her lust for lands, her lust for men.

"A most evil and treacherous woman," Jehan had explained, with a flick of his silk cuff as if to brush a stinging insect away. "Dark as a raven," he continued, "and with a beak to match. The men she has pecked to death. What divine justice it was when Humphrey abandoned her for his whore—beautiful though I understand she is. Eleanor, a pretty name, I always think."

The ducal herald was launched into one of his languid soliloquies, hands folded against the small of his back, eyes scrutinizing a drawing of Margarethe which Jan had not managed to hide from Lefèvre's inquisitive sight. Later this afternoon she would be here to sit for him to begin the portrait. Jan was determined to end the herald's reminiscences as early as possible.

"Justice even more divine," he continued, "that His Holiness Pope Martin should have ruled Jacqueline's marriage to Humphrey invalid and improper. But then everything the black raven does is improper. A most loathsome creature. At least, with Humphrey rolling in the sack with his lovely whore, we shall hear no more from him. As for Jacqueline, with only a few sand dunes for territory left to her she is about as marriageable as a barrow of dung."

Lefèvre smoothed his pale hands together as though removing the stain of the duchess Jacqueline from them. To Jan's relief he then reached for his hat, wound the long strands of it around the crown until it resembled an unwieldy bird's nest.

Within the hour Margarethe was standing where the ducal herald had been pontificating. Today he would begin painting her. Jan helped her with her coat, the same gray all-enveloping garment in which she had first arrived. But to his amazement underneath she was wearing a crimson velvet robe, cut square and deep across the neck, fitting close over the breasts and waist and falling in a cascade to the floor.

She blushed a little when she saw Jan's face, and for a moment there was the softest of silences in the room.

"Is it all right?" she asked, and there again was that appealing look, the lips parted.

She was lovely, he realized. When she lowered her eyes it was not out of shyness any longer, but out of pleasure. And when he painted her mouth her lips opened slightly.

She came to pose for him many times—more than he needed her to. And between visits she began to haunt the shadows of his dreams. He was aware he knew almost nothing about her; yet he sensed he wanted her in his life—that face, that look, that feeling of something precious being offered to him. One day she came over to look at the painting of her. She was so close, and when she turned her head he leaned down and kissed her very softly. There was a look of astonishment on her face, and her eyes were as moist as the sea.

Then outside events took over like a storm. The portrait of Margarethe was finished only a week or so before that autumn day when Lefèvre appeared at Jan's door with a summons from the duke. The two men arrived at the castle to find an assembly of lords in Philip's chamber. Jan recognized the tall figure of the lord of Roubaix, the glowering chancellor Nicolas Rolin, the paymaster-general Pierre Bladelin—oily and somewhat repulsively charming—as well as the effortlessly distinguished first chamberlain Anthoine de Croy. The duke greeted the painter warmly, and in that easy and kindly manner he displayed toward his inferiors introduced Jan to the other men who were present.

It was then explained to Jan by Jehan Lefèvre, who was standing between him and the duke, that many of these gentlemen would be his companions on an embassy shortly to leave by sea for Portugal. The purpose of the voyage was to negotiate a marriage between the noble duke and Isabella, daughter of the Portuguese king, John. Jan's role, the duke interceded, was to be his special ambassador entrusted with the task of painting the princess's portrait.

"I know that Master Jan's skills will not permit him to

deceive us as to her appearance," the duke added, smiling, addressing the company. "There is no finer painter in the land, we all know that. And no one more to be trusted," he said, turning his smile toward Jan.

And with that he shook Jan's hand and wished him good luck and God's blessing.

The embassy was to depart from Sluis in one week, on the nineteenth of October, provided the winds were favorable.

Margarethe wept when he told her.

Jan awoke puzzled not to feel the sway and yaw of the ship, not to hear the creak of the masts or the thud of feet on deck. His head throbbed. Sunlight was flooding an unfamiliar room, but heaped on the floor were his traveling boxes and sea chest, unopened. Scattered over and around them was his clothing: he could see one of his boots by the far wall where he must have kicked it. His jerkin had got itself hooked over the curtain rail, he noticed. How did it get there? Fragments of the previous evening began to reassemble in his mind. He was back in Flanders: the realization of this filled him with joy and he started up on one elbow and then wished he had not as little daggers twisted behind his eyes. He remembered the ship docking at Sluis. The crowds shoving and peering. Torches everywhere. The duke waiting stiffly amid an assembly of courtiers in the half-dark—waiting for Isabella to step ashore. She had been in the second ship and he had never caught sight of her. But what had happened then? He recalled entering an inn, clutching his purse. It was crowded: Flemish was being spoken again. And it was Christmas. Two men were carrying his possessions. Suddenly—there must have been a gap but Jan could not fill it—faces he half knew were embracing him. People were shaking his hand. He was drinking with them. Laughing. So much laughter. Jan thought there was a woman with large breasts, unbuttoned. Had he unbuttoned them? She was laughing too, her breasts shaking. People seemed to be trying to keep him from falling. It was as though he were still on ship. Everything was moving. Then there was nothing. A void.

He continued to gaze over toward the window. He could

pick out a church tower and familiar Flemish roofs. His throat was parched. There was water on the washstand, he noticed. He reached for it unsteadily and raised the mug to his lips: it felt like dousing hot sand. The room was chill and he pulled the coverlet over his shoulders. An insistent bell was sounding, and he could feel it rhythmically pulling him back into sleep.

It felt like a different day when he awoke again. Cooking smells were drifting up from the street, and he remembered how all over Christmas people would set up braziers and charcoal stoves, selling mutton and ribs of pork, roasted chestnuts and hot spiced sausages. It must be nearly midday, he thought. The bed was deliciously warm. And he was back in Flanders.

Jan lay there bathed in recollections. It was as long ago as February when his portrait of the duchess had been sent back to Flanders by two ducal messengers along with a copy of the marriage agreement. Then another four months until the messengers returned with the duke's approval, and the document signed with a flourish, sealed, and the scribe's florid words, "on this day of Our Lord, et cetera et cetera, as it pleaseth the noble duke, Philip of Burgundy, et cetera et cetera." But at least in those four months he had traveled—with the lord of Roubaix, Baudouin d'Oignies, and others—to Santiago de Compostela, to Burgos, then south to Granada. So much he had seen and heard, so many faces he had drawn—and strange costumes. The women he had longed to paint: they had taken his breath away. After that it had been summer, waiting at Lisbon for the wind. The dry dead heat, everyone listless, longing for home. The ceremony of court life filled each day with nothing. How he had yearned for the bustle of Bruges, the warmth and friendship of the tavern. And how he had yearned to be able to work. He was a painter, not a piece of ducal apparatus or a chess figure moved about the world by some distant player. Jan had longed for the moment when he would see the tall towers of Flanders across those damp plains. Green plains, not chaff and dust.

Jan rose and stood staring out over the roofs at the familiar landscape he had missed so deeply. That extraordinarily clear light, sharp like flakes of crystal. Everything was distances, punctuated by dark strokes of church towers, and willows that from this far were like lines of wicker fences marking the invisible water channels. Beloved Flanders. Raised from the sea, clean-washed, tilled and tended. Jan was aware of how often he had tried to paint this very sense of reaching out to embrace horizons—all God's world within reach, here before him on his easel so that he could touch it.

He began to dress, retrieving his clothes from where he seemed to have discarded them. The smells rising from the street made him hungry, but by now he was too impatient to eat. The journey to Bruges would be no more than a couple of hours, and Jan felt a thrill as he imagined the ride he had so often taken along the banks of the broad waterway under a huge translucent sky. The innkeeper soon obtained him a horse, and Jan stood watching for a moment as his belongings were stacked onto a cart that would follow him that afternoon. A small crowd was gathering, and he waved to them as he mounted; then he was off.

How familiar, and yet wonderfully new. And how quiet it was, and still. After the unending creak and shudder of the ship, and the cramped conditions, Jan could scarcely believe himself to be alone, with just the rhythmic clip of hooves on frozen ground and the steady passage of horse and rider along the riverbank. Tree after tree passed by at their careful distances—measured strides stretching toward Bruges.

Even in the afternoon the marshlands wore a silvering of frost so that it was impossible to distinguish which was meadow and which was water. It was only when Jan crossed the bridge at Damme and turned his horse to follow the long ridge of dike southward that suddenly the low sun picked out a maze of channels hitherto invisible, as though a brush were trailing patterns of gold across the landscape only to dissolve them the instant it passed. Jan rode on through this ever-shifting web of golden water. Wherever he looked windmills turned slowly against the sky, while scattered irregularly between them the bowed skeletons of willows kept sentinel. Now and again a heron would rise from some hidden pool and flap heavily a brief distance before settling stiffly again. A streak of copper marked the intent scamper of a fox.

It surprised Jan to realize he was thinking about Margarethe. He had been so far from her and had often imagined the thread which had spun itself between them to have withered. There had been other women who had caught his gaze: emboldened Portuguese in brilliant headscarves lining a rooftop —sallow Galicians bending to the rhythm of a scythe—proud inquisitive faces of Burgos—gypsies wreathing dangerous fingers as they danced. Yet it had always been Margarethe who stood waiting at the next turning of the road, eyes raised to him suddenly, that hint of eagerness in the mouth, fair hair blown across the cheek. She was like Flanders itself—a landscape you might pass by until it stirred something unexpected in you, and you sought out the magic in it. Margarethe was like that.

As Jan pondered over his feelings for Margarethe the last blades of the sun suddenly held in silhouette a crown of dark ramparts on the skyline ahead; and as he drew closer he could see that the crown was bejeweled with mill sails.

Bruges. He was home.

And while the lone figure of Jan rode toward the gates of Bruges, from the farther side of the city there approached a sight which, had he been aware of it, would have dispersed those thoughts about the stillness and emptiness of Flanders. For stretching southward several miles in the direction of Lille and Dijon was a line of more than three hundred carts of all descriptions, each heavily laden and each accompanied by an escort of mounted men. And concealed within those carts lay a cargo from every corner of the earth—tapestries, silken furnishings, armor, ensigns, lances, silver goblets, gold, jewels, damasks, furs, the most wonderful of costumes; and at least one hundred of those wagons contained barrels of the finest Burgundian wine from Beaune.

It was a caravan of treasures such as few had seen. For Duke Philip, as all of Bruges knew, was about to be married to the princess of Portugal.

Chapter ◆ Two

To be back in Bruges was like a rebirth. There she lay, the city. Girdled by water. And girdled a second time by ramparts. Five miles of stone, no less, and from those ramparts rose up nine great gates, each facing a land which fed this city with the good life. There was wool from England. Wine from southern Burgundy. Tapestries from Arras. Silks and cloth of silver from Venice. Oil and iron from Spain. Furs and timber from the Baltic ports. Spices and damasks from the Orient. Ivories from Africa. And so much more, not forgetting the brand of wealth they liked best here, making the Florentines so especially welcome, and that was banking: the soft reassuring clink of gold. Those nine gates, they stood like double teeth along the jawbone of the city, sucking in the pleasures of the world.

Jan had risen early. He walked through the wakening streets, anxious to savor the city alone. He felt radiant, reborn, and the city reborn around him. Serene, secure within those ramparts, how lovely Bruges looked on so much rich fare. Her element was water, and wherever Jan looked she seemed to be admiring her face in it. Towers. Trellises. Tracery. Sharp spires in the early sun. Wooden gables painted bright for the festive season. Steep-pitched roofs orange as flames in the winter light. Balconies. Bridges. Statues. Belfries. Banners. Awnings. All these were mirrored softly in the canals which veined the city, their reflections rippled by passing water birds, then settling again like tired limbs. At this hour Bruges seemed overcome by a languor of self-love.

He had forgotten how the morning always came on bells. The sounds clattered and stumbled into one another, lurching along the narrow streets between the leaning houses. Jan smiled. God was never in unison in the early mornings. The

21

cathedral of St. Donatian possessed the oldest bell but it was showing its age now with a bad-tempered croak. Once it must have been a lone voice, but now there were upstarts wherever you turned your ear. The church of Our Lady clamored arrogantly from the highest perch in the city. St. Saviour's squatted more gloomily nearby, gutted by fire so often though no flames had ever extinguished the bells. Then on through the apostles, saints, and martyrs, major and minor. St. James's church. St. Anne's. St. Giles's. St. John's. St. Jacob's. The church of Our Lady of Blindekens. The church of Our Lady of the Potterie. The chapel of the Beguines. The new church of Jerusalem, modeled on the Holy Sepulcher as if to persuade Our Lord to swell here more closely. And in front of Jan in the main square the chapel of the Holy Blood, tinkling with confidence as though knowing that a relic of Our Lord's Passion was infinitely superior to a few bones of a local martyr, which was all the cathedral opposite could boast.

The air was awash with sound. No one could possibly sleep through this cacophony. And as if the bells were not enough to rouse the people of Bruges to honest toil and moneymaking, there were the twelve trumpeters commanded by the duke to blast him awake each morning from beneath his windows in the palace—though they were silent today, the duke being still at Sluis preparing for his wedding.

Jan gazed up at the grim hulk of the ducal palace. How lumpen in appearance—so unlike the duke: it always frowned. And how little it compared in splendor with the adjacent town hall. Oh, the money that had gone into it. But then it was money that ruled this city. Money that bought pleasure. Money that bought love. Money that the merchants paid the duke to overlord the place while making it quite clear where the roots of his wealth lay—in their pockets. The new town hall was their cathedral and their palace. What ostentation. Those pinnacles and finials. Lacelike. Exuberant arches, thin-bladed, drawing the windows up into frail webs of stone. And between the windows forty-eight niches each holding a statue more than lifesize. Painting these, Jan remembered dolefully, was another task awaiting him now that he had returned from Portugal. The burghers had insisted on him, fearing that any lesser hand might coarsen their temple of Midas. But at least he would not be expected to color the huge statue of a bear that stood before the entrance—the bear being a symbol of Bruges, having apparently been the only living creature encountered here by Baldwyn Iron Arm when he founded the city against the Norsemen six hundred years ago. Some, Jan reflected, would say that bears were still the most common form of life in this place.

And there, across the face of the town hall, were the coats of arms he would have to paint too. These told the story of Bruges louder than any bells or the duke's trumpeters. It was power that was emblazoned up there. They were the crests of the city guilds, symbols of the craftsmen's right to share in the running of this city, share it with the merchants whom they so mistrusted. The guildsmen had shed their blood for that right here in Bruges. They had no noble names and houses but they were proud of their crests. Rather pompous they might seem, with their tools of trade elevated to heraldic status—chisels, saws, shuttles, hammers, and the like—but woe betide anyone who raised a sneer. They were a haughty and belligerent lot, the guildsmen, not exactly brimming with human kindness even toward each other. The weavers loathed the fullers. The archers of St. Sebastian's guild were forever quarreling with the crossbowmen of St. George's guild, even though they formed part of the same city militia. As for their counterparts in Ghent or Tournai or Antwerp, one might imagine it to be a holy war, so self-righteous were they on either side.

It was the meanness of new men, in this city of new men. And yet, whatever the currents of parsimony, it was a city to be proud of. Jan was making his way homeward now toward the street of the Golden Hand. How alive it all was after the slothful heat of Portugal. The houses were beginning to spill open onto the streets—shoemakers, barbers, weavers, butchers, fishmongers, cutlers, saddlers, locksmiths, blacksmiths, joiners: even on this winter day they were setting up their stalls and workbenches in the open to catch more trade and shout their wares and their skills among the passersby amid the spank of hot iron, the whine of saws and the delectable smells of baking bread, smoking pork, spices, and fresh leather. It was a daily fairground, and even the snow when it came would do no more than lay a white carpet to muffle the racket and brighten the color of it.

What conviviality there was in this city. It could be no accident that it was the Flemings who proclaimed there to be an eighth Deadly Sin—*tristitia*— sadness: surely, Jan thought, it was the only Deadly Sin they did not make a habit of committing.

And could there be anywhere which possessed taverns like those in Bruges? Ahead of him Jan caught sight of the familiar sign of the Angel suspended somewhat tipsily over the canal. Here, it was said, you could hear more languages spoken than in Babel, and just as many halting versions of Flemish—which was a spluttering language when spoken purely but quite extraordinary from the mouths of Scotsmen, Portuguese, Lucchese, and the rest. For this was the traders' and craftsmen's district around the street of the Golden Hand—so called because of the prevalence of goldsmiths and jewelers living there. And the tavern was where they met. Sometimes it could seem as if the whole world came to the Angel, among them a great many ladies as well as many who were not ladies, which was why the place was widely known as the Fallen Angel.

Jan stood on the little bridge over the canal on that sharp winter morning. Bruges. He could not remember when he had felt so contented.

News of his return brought friends crowding into the house on the street of the Golden Hand: everyone, that is, except Margarethe, who was spending Christmas with her mother in Louvain, as Jan learned to his dismay from her uncle the master weaver. But yes, the good man informed him with a grin of welcome, Margarethe was well, in fair spirits, a little thinner perhaps, he said with a laugh, but she had grown so lovely, he assured Jan; and she would be lovelier still when she saw him, which would be in two days, he added.

"She has talked of nothing but you. Most tedious." And he clapped Jan jovially on the shoulder.

Jan felt a surge of longing to see her.

All those who came to visit him seemed intent on recounting the strangest of stories. At first Jan paid little attention: it sounded unlikely and farfetched. But as one visitor after another repeated the tale he grew intrigued. During his absence in Portugal it appeared that a girl—a mere girl—had put on armor and led the armies of France against the English and Burgundians. Triumphantly, everyone said. She had even persuaded the French dauphin to be crowned king at Reims, standing by his side throughout the ceremony, holding her personal standard painted with the image of Our Lord. The girl was guided by the voices of angels, she claimed, and called herself "the Maiden." Her name was Joan of Arc. Duke Philip was much perturbed, explained the ducal herald Jehan Lefèvre. More perturbed than by the long delay in the arrival of his own bride from Portugal.

Lefèvre was peering about him seemingly surprised by the emptiness of Jan's studio. It was the first time the two men had met for fifteen months, yet the herald had arrived with his normal elevated air as if the passage of time were a mere speck on his velvet surcoat to be flicked away with an elegant hand.

"The duke is amazed that your portrait of his bride should be so exactly like her," he went on, picking his phrases like fine polished grapes. He seemed leaner than ever, Jan thought, and even more haughty.

"And as a result he talks of requesting from you a portrait of himself. Some kind of state portrait, it seems. Robes, orders, jewels. You know how he loves to dress up, and you're good at all that." Lefèvre flapped a hand almost dismissively as if nothing could be simpler. Jan restrained a smile as he tried to imagine the ducal herald turning his proud talents to painting a lace cuff or a ruby set in a fret of gold. Oh, the arrogance of courtiers.

Lefèvre was beginning the lengthy adjustment of his clothing which was always the first sign that he was contemplating departure. Jan knew the herald well enough to expect some final quip before the parting bow.

"If you want my opinion," he said, carefully entwining the trailing loops of his hat until it resembled a black velvet nest, "if you do the portrait satisfactorily there'll be no end to it.

He'll want another and another and another . . . Well!"—and a small smile came to his lips. "At least it'll free you from painting all those Virgins and martyrs: I've never known such people as the Flemish for worshipping virginity while seeking to steal it at every opportunity. I don't know how you can keep a straight face; but perhaps you don't and it just doesn't show in your pictures."

The herald took his leave in the best of spirits, promising to let Jan know when he might expect a summons from the duke. It would be some time after the wedding, naturally. Jan felt proud and somewhat daunted. How did one paint so incomparably elevated a man as the duke? he wondered. From his window Jan watched the tall figure of the herald swirl his surcoat about him and proceed in a lordly fashion down the very center of the street of the Golden Hand. A few flakes of snow were falling, but from the windows at the rear of the house Jan saw that the clouds had parted, and a blur of cold winter sunlight slanted across the steep-pitched roofs and glimmered weakly in the dark canal.

He was home. It was a joy to be able to wander through the rooms of his house and to know that they were his rooms. He wanted to pull the walls around his shoulders and feel warmed.

The next day Jan heard excited voices downstairs and the sound of running feet. As he opened the studio door Margarethe threw herself into his arms. Words and laughter stumbled over each other and Jan could feel her tears on his cheeks. Fifteen months of separation seemed to drain away, and when she drew back to gaze at him the look in those green eyes washed over him like a warm sea. Yes, she was lovelier, as her uncle had promised. There was a radiance about her, a bloom on her skin, and the eager mouth when it moved formed delightful patterns as if her whole body spoke through her lips.

"You're back, you're back," was all she could say at first.

Then she wanted to know everything, and to tell him everything. Were the storms at sea as terrible as she had been told? She had been terrified for him, she said. And were there monsters and flying fish and lights that danced on the water? And as her fancy began to take over now that Jan was safe her face took on a child's look of wonder. Tell me, tell me, she would say, rarely allowing Jan space to reply before the next question. And Portugal? Was it burning hot, with lions and snakes? Margarethe's knowledge of places was somewhat confused by travelers' tales, and Jan would laugh. She grew petulant. Why was he making fun of her? Not telling her things? And the women? Did they wear no clothes like the savages she had heard about, with black skin and rings in their noses? Margarethe was enjoying the flow of her own imagination, and all the time gazing at Jan with those appealing green eyes. He took her hands, which were wonderfully cool: Yes, he reassured her, she was just as beautiful as any lady in Portugal, where no one had hair like hers or eyes like hers; and no, they did not go around naked with rings in their noses, and he had not been in love with any of them. She looked at him searchingly.

How she had grown up. How lovely she was. Such vigor and passion in that face. When he kissed her she pressed her body against his.

"You won't leave again, will you?" she whispered.

The duke and Isabella were married at Sluis on the seventh of January. And the following day the couple made their entry into Bruges.

They came by water. The thousands lining the city ramparts craned their necks to catch sight of the ducal barge as it approached serenely under the clearest of afternoon skies through that expanse of polderland now polished white with snow. The barge was decked with flags and banners like a garment of brilliant colors that ripped in the wind. Gradually, silently, it slipped into the shadow of the city gate; then as the duke and his bride stepped onto the stone quay a fanfare of silver trumpets rose above the cheering of the crowds and a knot of city councillors in black robes hastened forward to greet the pair. Accompanying them more sedately, in scarlet, was the archbishop, and by his side in their robes of office walked the squat chancellor of Burgundy, Nicolas Rolin, and the lean figure of the bailiff of Bruges, Lodewijk van Haverskerke. The duke embraced them all and introduced them one by one to the duchess Isabella. As best they could in their finery they bowed and bowed. Finally the ducal couple mounted the waiting carriage and the procession began to edge its way through the throng of citizens toward the palace.

Evening was now closing in, and along every street a blaze of torches lit up the tall wooden gables of the houses and smeared the canals with gold. And from the cathedral of St. Donatian, from St. Saviour's, from the church of Our Lady, from the chapel of the Holy Blood, and from the church of every parish spread across the city, rose a tremendous clamor of bells.

The days following were swamped in color and carnival. Throughout the city of Bruges people were drawn into a festive world in which for once the hard business of manufacture and trade yielded to the spell of make-believe. As the snow continued to fall, everywhere the streets became haunted by dark figures in masks, their faces and their laughter anonymous under veils and long cloaks as they passed from torchlight to torchlight as if the snow itself were a mask of the city's dreams.

The heart of the festivities was of course the ducal palace, whose gates were now forever open to the flow of citizens and the exodus of courtiers in elaborate disguises. It was said that the duke and his bride were seen here in the street of the leather workers or there by the bridge of the Rosary, but the tall figure dressed as a stag and his lady veiled in white and crowned with the helmet of Minerva might have been any couple at all passing through that curtain of snow between the orange light of the torches. No theme or pattern of disguise was predominant: people dressed according to their fancy, and during these days of celebration there was no constraint on what those fancies might be. One evening as dusk was falling there processed across the marketplace crowded with revelers an unusual trail of figures, and those close by enjoyed the view of what appeared to be Abbot Eustache, trundling a loaf of penis before him on a barrow and pursued by thirty children chanting "Papa" to the tune of a well-known psalm.

Among the women there were few extravagances quite so robust as this—even in Bruges certain proprieties were expected of the female sex, at least in public. A few nuns were to be seen whose behavior might have reddened a Mother Superior, and there were several well-known ladies of the ducal court whose husbands would have been amazed by what they saw. But on the whole the imagination of the women was quite poetical by comparison, and whereas so many of the men strived for excesses of heavy laughter, those women who were blessed with good looks generally sought to make the very best of them now that such a golden opportunity was here. So there were glorious Snow Maidens and Ice Queens; goddesses who advanced in threes inviting any passing Paris to make his judgment; and along one torchlit street near the church of St. Saviour the snow fell so very gently about the face of Diana the Huntress. Her hair glowed deep auburn in a cascade over her bow and quiver, and in either hand she grasped a long cord to which were attached two wolfhounds quietly following behind her. There were many invitations that evening to be the victim of her arrow, but nobody knew who she was.

On the fourth evening of the wedding festivities there was not a murmur of wind and the snow floated like feathers turned black against the torchlight, muffling the footsteps of masked revelers as they made their way to and from the square of the ducal palace and the cathedral of St. Donatian.

A little before midnight Jan crossed the little bridge of St. John over the inner canal behind the market hall. By his side was Margarethe, muffled in furs against the cold. On the bridge they stopped, and Jan wiped the snow from his face and pointed. Three people on horseback were approaching along the far side of the canal. The riders themselves were all but lost in shadow, but from the bellow of song it was obvious that they were exceedingly drunk. As the leading rider passed within the torchlight that lit up the bridge he turned to stare uncertainly at Jan and Margarethe, and halted. Then he yelled out their names and as he did so he raised his hat in an extravagant gesture of greeting, swaying perilously on his horse. There was no mistaking the pale hair and hot complexion of the Englishman Hugo, and Jan saw that he was dressed in a ludicrous imitation of an English squire, his surcoat vastly padded in the front and a hat set so far on one side that the goose feathers which were stuck into it drooped over his shoulder like a bedraggled bird's wing. The snow that covered him made his face look even redder than his breeches, and he removed his hat and waved it round and round and round with each outburst of song.

"I have two prisoners," he shouted. "Behold the Maid and the king of France." His words spilled and tumbled over each other; and as he spoke he gestured to the two riders behind him, whereupon they advanced into the torchlight and Jan saw that they were attached to Hugo's horse by two ropes.

An absurd sight met Jan's eyes. The woman armed to represent Joan of Arc he recognized as a celebrated whore from the seamen's brothel near the harbor, who was celebrated mainly because she was certainly the fattest woman in Bruges and catered—it was said—to largely Germanic tastes. Her face was hidden now by a mask shaped like a soldier's visor, and in her right hand she carried a standard with the image of Christ crudely painted upon it—his hand raised in judgment and beside him the figure of an angel among the clouds holding the royal fleur-de-lis of France. She rolled about on the horse like an armored bun, from time to time letting out incoherent snatches of song. And by her side her companion, tittering like a girl, wore the mask of an idiot, a crown of what appeared to be a wood saw tied in a circle, and a scepter which Jan could see was actually a fire poker impaling a large bread roll. From the hairy hand that grasped it Jan knew him to be the silversmith Michaut Pontin.

Jan could only stand and laugh. The three riders were halted there bellowing in the gently falling snow.

"See my prisoners?" Hugo was shouting. "One king and one virgin." He produced a tankard of beer from the folds of his surcoat and took a draft, much of which slithered down his chin and left a stain of melted snow around his collar. "About as much a virgin as the Maid," he roared, "and as much of a soldier." And he laughed and laughed.

Jan could feel Margarethe stiffen. Then she turned halfway from the riders.

"He's dishonorable, the Englishman," she said with feeling.

Jan's laughter died away and he gave her a startled glance.

"It's a joke," he said. "What does it matter?"

Margarethe was looking at him with a fierceness he had never seen from her.

"It would matter if you were a woman," she said almost angrily. And she looked away toward the three figures on horseback who were still singing and shouting obscenities, their horses impatiently pawing the snow.

"There are women who would rather be virgins than give themselves to men like Hugo," she went on with a firmness that made Jan feel quite uncomfortable. "Joan is brave," Margarethe continued in a quiet voice, "and a finer soldier than anyone here. She's defeated the English, which is something no man has managed to do . . . And she hears the voices of angels. The only angels in this city are those in the tavern."

Jan was aware of feeling humbled and withdrawn. His eyes wandered toward the canal—billowing with ghostly snow beyond the torchlight. And as he looked he noticed another figure on horseback approaching through the shadows. The horse was almost white as it passed within the glare of the torches—white with a flowing mane and tail unbound, though Jan saw that the crupper glistened with jewels that were red and golden in the flickering light. The rider was another woman. She was robed all in scarlet and her boots shone black against the ivory flank of her horse. Her hair was black too—it fell in a shining cascade down the scarlet of her robe and was studded with snow like pearls. He had never seen such hair; and then he noticed that across her forehead rested a slender coronet set with bright stones. At that moment the woman turned her head toward the group of other riders and the two figures standing on the bridge, and Jan made out a face of extraordinary majesty, as if carved softly in white marble. But across that face there was a mask covering the eyes, and he saw that the mask consisted only of painted eyes—huge, staring, malevolent.

Margarethe gently plucked Jan's sleeve.

"Don't you recognize who she's meant to be?" she whispered. "Those eyes. That hair. There's no one else who looks like that." Margarethe's voice sounded breathless. "Jacqueline . . . duchess of Hainault, until Philip . . ."

Her words were cut short by a raucous shout from Hugo.

"Ha!" he cried, pointing to the masked figure on horseback. "Another enemy of Burgundy." And he waved his hat with one hand and his beer tankard with the other. "Jacqueline the whore. Bravo!"

But instead of the smile and the wave Hugo anticipated, the dark lady turned on him a look of withering contempt. Hugo's laughter faltered into an uneasy snigger and his tankard was lowered as if it was suddenly too heavy.

The lady gave a twitch of the reins; then, as she rode past, she raised her mask and to Jan's astonishment he saw that her eyes were as dark and almost as large as those she had painted. She threw him a glare so piercing Jan felt he had been physically struck. He could feel Margarethe pull back. And together they watched as the mounted figure receded into the shadows of the canal.

With an awkward silence Hugo, Pontin, and the whore departed in the direction from which they had come. Jan and Margarethe walked back silently through the snow.

The duke was in his splendor.

It was a matter of pride as well as politics that the court of Burgundy should outshine all other courts of Europe; and the occasion of the duke's wedding was one that all who witnessed it—from whatever country they came as guests—felt sure could never be matched for invention and spectacle. Indeed, who but Duke Philip would have been able to expend such wealth on so much temporary magnificence?

No one had ever seen the duke happier. He took part in all the festivities. When a duck-hunting party set out from the Minnewater the lean, lithe figure was there watchful in the prow, feathered cap set jauntily on one side of his head, water spaniel on a short leash by his side. Or he would ride out of the city on the leading horse, falcon on his shoulder attached to a gloved wrist by a golden chain, an eager smile on his face as he galloped through the white landscape. Or there would be jousting, archery contests, swordsmanship, tennis: the snow and the cold posed no barrier to the duke's pleasure or his skill. And his new duchess accompanied him wherever he went with a look of genuine, if well-practiced, devotion.

Those close to Isabella were aware how relieved she was that she had not married a beer-filled barbarian, as she had feared. She was agreeably surprised to discover that her husband played the harp most expertly, often singing in a pleasant high voice trained, she learned, by that celebrated Englishman Robert Morton. Isabella was impressed, too, by the duke's library: she had known nothing of those lengthy epics and romances of which the Burgundians seemed so fond, and admitted to being a little perplexed by the accounts of astonishing feats of arms which Philip read to her, not liking to ask the purpose of such elaborate trials and tourneys for the love of ladies who were either unavailable or entirely indifferent, as it appeared to her. Nonetheless the poetry, she had to admit, was very finely phrased, as far as she could understand it: and her pleasure was increased when her husband read to her his own verses, composed, she understood, in the manner taught him by his handsome court poet, Michault de Caron. The duke, in short, was a cultivated man with the most becoming manner imaginable, especially toward women. There were stories, it was true, of other women in Philip's life, but then a man who had already been twice married could hardly be expected to lack experience, and to have been twice widowed was pain enough for anyone to feel in need of solace. Besides, love was an art, and to have married someone who was accomplished at such an art was surely a benefit to any marriage—in fact, it was a delight.

His clothing she found especially impressive. Isabella had never encountered a man who paid such rich attention to his appearance, and she felt a surge of pride when he reappeared many times in a single day wearing different and ever more splendid apparel. Philip's preference was for black, she noticed, which suited him well, though the reason for it she understood was the duke's grief over his father's murder at the hands of the man who now had the audacity to call himself king of France. A feeble and deceitful man by comparison, so she had heard. But if black was out of respect for the dead, the duke wore it as if no color could be so becoming to one so noble. His satin robes she particularly admired, lined as they were with ermine or with cloth of gold, often worn with a hat so heavily studded with jewels that it resembled a royal crown, and Isabella found it hard not to think of her husband as a king like her own father. He looked magnificent, a god perhaps or the Emperor Solomon, and when he leaned over to kiss her she felt that truly there could be no other man on earth more worthy of love.

Then there were the festivities which Philip had arranged to celebrate their marriage: these were such as she had never imagined could be devised by man. Accustomed to the modest and formal processions which accompanied events of this nature in Lisbon, Isabella could scarcely believe it when it was pointed out to her by the ducal herald, Jehan Lefèvre, that the main courtyard of the palace had been specially covered over by a wooden structure vast enough to incorporate three entire kitchens, six larders, and numerous ovens, all of them set around the fringe of a banqueting hall that was itself more than fifty paces long and almost as wide.

On her fourth evening in Bruges the duke threw a banquet in her honor for the entire court and innumerable visiting nobles and churchmen from as far afield as Scotland, Venice, and Castile. She had never seen such a gathering or heard so many languages spoken. Gazing around her at the banqueting hall, she found herself weak at the thought that all this—the throng of guests, the feast, the hall itself—had been assembled especially for her.

At that moment a fanfare of trumpets announced the arrival of the first array of dishes from the kitchens, led by a rubicund figure all in white whom she understood to be the chief pantler, and who proceeded to taste a morsel of each dish before personally serving Isabella and then the duke seated next to her. She was pleased to feel the duke's hand on hers, and turned to be greeted by the most tender of smiles. She felt a surge of gratitude that after the interminable procedures of diplomacy the man marked out for her to marry should be a man she felt sure she could love. He had said that he found her beautiful—even more beautiful than in Master Jan's portrait.

From that moment everything had seemed filled with sunshine.

The evening progressed from spectacle to spectacle, each course more extravagant and elaborate than its predecessor, and accompanied by a fresh tableau of the rarest invention. The duke rose and applauded each appearance with the enthusiasm of a youth. After a procession of peacocks the chefs advanced with the traditional wedding-day swans, each dish decorated with fruits and sweetmeats to represent the colors of one of the duke's territories. Then, after further music and singing, in which the duke joined most heartily and encouraged Isabella to do the same, a colossal pie was borne slowly up the hall until the four bearers stood directly in front of the duchess. They carefully lowered the vast confection until it rested on the floor, whereupon one of them produced a carving knife and slowly cut away a slice of piecrust almost as large as himself. Before Isabella had time to feel horror at the prospect of such a gargantuan portion a tremendous cheer rose from the hall and a man stepped out of the pie. He was of remarkable physique and dressed only in a loincloth, and in his right hand he carried a club.

Further cheering echoed around the banqueting hall as the athletic figure advanced and bowed to Isabella, laying his club submissively at her feet before retrieving from the interior of the pie a golden key as large as his arm which he likewise lay before the duchess.

"The key to the heart of Burgundy," the man said to even louder cheering.

Isabella turned to Philip with a look of bewilderment, whereupon he explained to her, grasping her hand, which she realized was trembling, that the athletic figure represented Hercules, who, according to legend, had stopped in Burgundy on his journey to Spain and was considered to have been the father of the noble house into which she had now married.

"And the heart of Burgundy is my heart," he added with the most gentle of smiles.

There was one final surprise that evening. The trumpets again sounded a fanfare and Isabella saw a huge model ship being wheeled into the hall to the accompaniment of women's voices singing. And as the strange vessel moved within the torchlight Isabella saw that all around the ship, moving as if they were swimming, were sirens with strands of seaweed in their hair but otherwise entirely naked. At first she was shocked, having never seen another woman naked, but then she noticed that no one else in the hall, men or women, seemed in the slightest perturbed; and at that moment from the vessel a man emerged and began to climb the mast to the crow's nest high above the torches and the sirens and the figures seated at the tables. The man wore a quiver at his side and a bow at his shoulder, and when he reached the crow's nest he raised his bow and drew a red rose from his quiver which he shot in the direction of the duke and herself: then another and another until the floor and table around her were strewn with flowers.

Isabella rose delighted to her feet and applauded, before turning to Philip and leaning over to embrace him. She felt his arms curl around her, and heard the loudest applause of the evening resounding in her ears. What marvelous kind of man was he, she wondered, who could have created all this for her?

Late the following morning they rode together. Isabella gazed at her husband, who was riding a few paces ahead of her, the ducal bodyguard keeping a discreet distance behind them. How gracefully he rode, she thought; and how effortlessly his clothing became him whatever he did. Today over his hunting tunic he was draped in a surcoat of white ermine, and at his wrist she caught a glimpse of the gold bracelet studded with rubies which had been a gift to him from her father, the king. A sable hat covered his short dark hair. He looked—quite simply—magnificent. Suddenly he turned to her with those rather prominent eyes and that curious smile of the lower lip only.

"This evening I have another surprise for you," he said.

"Yet another!" she answered, laughing. "More sirens?" she added teasingly. Isabella could hear him chuckle. His eyes were scanning the white landscape.

"Tell me now," she said in a soft voice.

He reined his horse and kissed her. Isabella wanted him to make love to her—here in the snow in his ermine coat. The

thought made her laugh and she glanced back at the bodyguard of soldiers waiting some twenty paces behind them pre-
tending not to be looking.

The duke talked as they rode. Burgundy, he explained, la-
bored under a disadvantage: it was separated into two regions.
Here in the north were the cities of Flanders, also of Holland,
Brabant, Hainault, Artois, Limbourg. Much of the wealth of
the dukedom lay here. But there was also southern Burgundy.
A beautiful region. He would take her there. The winelands of
all Europe. But the two regions were divided—it was two days'
ride to reach one from the other. Before he died he was set on
making them a single dukedom: he had sworn to himself to do
this. The "surprise" he had promised her was a new order of
knighthood, and it would unite the nobility of northern and
southern Burgundy in a bond of loyalty to himself. It would
be the proudest order of knighthood in Europe. Twenty-four
men. No more than twenty-four, he emphasized. And they
would all of them be Burgundians. So many other orders had
lost their meaning and their strength because membership was
offered to foreign kings and princes, bishops, popes, bastards,
heaven knows who—on whim, just to please: so what did such
an order mean? And he mentioned the English Order of the
Garter—it had been offered to him, he said, and he had refused.

"Why should I bind my loyalties to a foreign crown?" he
added. "And if I did, what would that mean? I hardly imagine
the king of France would become a faithful ally just because I
awarded him a golden insignia and a beautiful robe." There
was a look of pride and disdain on the duke's face. The thin
nose reminded Isabella of a blade, and she felt almost frightened by the sternness of that face, again looking far away from
her.

"The Order of the Golden Fleece." Philip's words were
pronounced slowly, as if he were engraving them on a tablet of
history.

"The Golden Fleece," he repeated, this time as though
wrapping himself in it. Then he reined his horse and placed
both hands on hers.

"Isabella," he said, "everything will come of this."

The banqueting hall that evening was as crowded and as splendid as before. This was the last evening of the wedding festivities, and tomorrow the guests would disperse—on horseback east, south, and west, or by ship to England, Scotland, the Baltic ports, to Brittany, Spain, Naples, Genoa, Venice. Vessels would slide away from Sluis on the winter tide laden with gifts, with letters of greeting, with wine, tapestries, crimson cloth, silver and gold, jewels, enamels—all the largesse of Burgundy sailing to the corners of the world.

But tonight was Philip's triumph.

He rose to his feet toward the end of the feasting and the banqueting hall fell quiet. He stood silent for a few moments, and all eyes were on the tall figure in the black velvet robe of state, lined with ermine and bordered so richly with jewels that in the torchlight he glittered like so many points of fire. The face was impassive, severe, until suddenly he smiled, looking down on Isabella; and she raised her hand and laid it in his.

And then he spoke, still holding her hand. His voice was soft and precise: people had to strain to listen, and this intensified the silence and the stillness around the hall.

At first Isabella did not understand the strangeness of her own response to him as he spoke. He was describing to the gathering lords his purpose in founding this new order—just as he had explained it to her while they were riding in the snow that morning: except that he was not describing it in the same way. He was speaking of the beauty of chivalry and his devotion to its ideals; how the world would fall into disarray without the steadfastness of those to whom it had been given to rule it. He swore with God as his witness that he would choose death rather than betray that trust. He had decided, he said, on the insignia of the Golden Fleece because he wished the patron of the order to be the Greek hero Jason, whose voyages in search of the fleece in ancient times offered the noblest antecedent of the crusading spirit which he knew all Burgundians nurtured. And with that he extended his arm eastward and made a vow that he would lead a crusade against the tyranny of the pagan Turks who—he reminded his guests —had once captured and held to high ransom his own father at Nicopolis. To man's shame the birthplace of Our Lord remained in the hands of the infidel, he went on, and what comfort could there be in the soft pleasures of this life when the fountainhead of life itself remained soiled by Satan? And if, he continued in a voice now raised to a stirring pitch, he should be any means discover during this crusade that the Grand Turk would be willing to do battle with him in single combat, then for love of the Christian faith he would fight him with the aid of God and the Virgin Mother.

The duke paused. There was utter silence. The embassies of all Europe remained seated as though chained by his words. Then, like an unannounced storm, cheering burst from the crowded hall. It continued on and on. There were cries that they all of them would follow him. And as the voices echoed around him the duke signaled to a steward who hurried forward bearing a large folded garment. Philip took it and in a single flourish shook it open and threw it around his shoulders. It was a gown of brilliant scarlet lined with ermine, and around it lay a mantle embroidered all in gold. Next the steward handed him a heavy golden collar studded with precious stones to which was attached a glistening pendant, and even those furthest from the duke would see that it represented a fleece. The Golden Fleece. Philip raised the insignia to his lips and kissed it. Then he bowed his head.

"To this I pledge my life," he said.

The applause continued wave after wave as the duke stood there, head still bowed. Then once again he reached out his hand and very gently took the fingers of Isabella in his own.

Instead of strangeness she now felt overwhelmed. Listening to her husband, she had heard a new voice. On this morning he had described his ambitions to her, and his reasons for founding the new order, but he had described things only as politics, just as she knew that his marriage to her had been politics. Suddenly she had heard a different man speak. Now as she listened she understood that for Philip politics was no more than a device, a means. She had married a man who looked far, far beyond the grasp of wealth and the flattery of power. He possessed a vision as noble as anyone could conceive. Isabella saw it as a bright star above him. And as she stood there facing that sea of torches and those waves of cheering voices, with his fingers grasping hers before the ranks of Europe, she understood that her marriage to this man would also be a bright star. The brightest star.

Isabella looked at Philip and knew, with a sense of shock and delight, that she loved him.

In Bruges the festivities ended as the snow ended. Once again the vessels bringing wool and spices, timber and silks, furs and iron, lay jostled in the harbor off the canal of St. Anne amid the creaking of winches and the shouting of so many languages. And people stopped thinking about their duke—as they were already ready to do once the daily business of money and pleasure replaced such carnivals of dreams.

Not that everyone in Bruges was permitted to forget him. Closeted in a room within the town hall sat an enormous man of fascinating ugliness, heavily groaning. Godscalc Oom was one of the ducal rentmasters, a clever and normally genial man to whom the chancellor Nicolas Rolin had entrusted the finances of the ducal wedding.

Never had such uncontrolled expenditure passed before Godscalc's shrewd gaze, and his meetings with the court treasurer, whom he despised as a lordly buffoon, were passed extracting exorbitant sums from the ducal purse for such whims as twenty-five plucked bitterns, fifty roses transported from Spain in order that they might be shot from Cupid's bow, as well as the payment which most surprised Godscalc—namely, six pieces of silver to each of six young women who had acted as naked sirens during some ducal extravagance or other. Godscalc's imagination stretched itself to the limit trying to understand how such delightful mythology could have been made to embellish a wedding; and being a man educated in the classics, he could not help wondering if it was quite tactful of the duke to have presented himself to his young bride as the storm-tossed Odysseus heroically resisting temptations of the flesh for her sake. And in addition, he felt as he grumpily passed the coins over to the secretary who had obtained the girls' services from one of the city's bathhouses, he was certain they had already been more than adequately rewarded for their display by those embassies from stricter countries like Scotland and Pomerania. Godscalc was a generous man, but there was a difference in his view between giving money to a good cause and throwing it in the direction of a cause already lost.

He sighed, thankful that the duke was unlikely—God willing—to be married again, at least not in his own lifetime.

It was while Godscalc was engaged in these labors that the ducal herald was again seen stepping warily over the icy cobbles of the street of the Golden Hand. Those in the Fallen Angel noticed him pass and remarked that his head seem stretched more loftily than ever, doubtless due to his appointment as King-of-Arms of the new order. There was some laughter. De Leeuw also noticed him from his window and was relieved to see him go by. It could only be that he had some instruction for Master Jan.

The ducal herald was holding a letter between thin fingers as he entered Jan's studio.

"The duke wishes you to begin his portrait on the first of February," he announced. "That is in ten days' time."

There was a pause while the herald scrutinized a small drawing of Bruges rooftops which Jan had made from his window that morning. Then Lefèvre explained the delay without removing his nose from the drawing.

"Tomorrow the duke leaves on urgent matters. Matters concerning the French—the Maid. It seems she is recovered and is raising an army again."

Jan was sure that by now Lefèvre's eyes had peered into every window in the drawing. He resolved to make a larger drawing of the same subject, and in each window to depict tiny figures of naked women in inviting postures. Next time the herald called he would have it ready.

The duke wanted a true portrait, Lefèvre informed Jan; a picture that would be his splendid living presence permanently here in Bruges even though he, the duke, might be elsewhere—at war, or in counsel at Dijon, or hunting. It was to be a true likeness—nothing wooden. With life in it. A portrait of the duke as he really was. The whole man.

"I may tell you, Jan, that the duke feels you know him,

understand him. He is aware from your portrait of the duchess Isabella that when you paint a face you also paint what is beneath the face. A man's nature. His ideals. His nobility. His soul, you might say." Lefèvre paused, and Jan looked at him in some astonishment. "Philip expects you to do that for him, so that when the world looks at his portrait they will understand him, perceive his greatness."

There was another pause. "He says you have a mind skilled in all knowledge as well as painting, and this is what makes you the painter you are. Meanwhile the duke wishes you to have this." And he handed Jan the letter he had been holding.

The letter was unsealed. It was in a large, ungainly script, and addressed to Philip, duke of Burgundy, from his loyal and devoted servant Jodocus Vyt, burgomaster of the city of Ghent, after which the compliments unfolded, as ungainly as the script. Jan's eyes scanned the parchment until to his surprise he saw his own name.

He proceeded to read it studiously. To his further surprise the letter drew the duke's attention to Jan's late brother Hubert, who had lived and worked in Ghent. Hubert had been the elder of the two brothers by a good many years, and it was from him that Jan had learned much of his art. At the time of his death more than three years earlier Hubert had been engaged on the largest church altarpiece ever commissioned in this country. It was for the cathedral of St. Bavon, in Ghent, and Jan recalled that the donor of this painting had been a wealthy alderman by the name of Vyt—Hubert used to refer to him as Joos but his full name was undoubtedly Jodocus. Vyt was not at that time burgomaster of the city but a shrewd, pious gentleman, Jan remembered Hubert saying, who had made his fortune constructing dikes and reclaiming land from the sea, and who was anxious to repay some of that wealth to the city which had rewarded him so richly. The painting—Jan could recall it now—was on a great many separate panels: these folded in on each other and it had been Hubert's intention to depict on these folded panels the Annunciation of the Messiah as predicted by the prophets Micah and Zachariah; but when unfolded they revealed the most wonderful and spacious landscape with the towers of the holy city radiant in the sunlight and, in the very center, a fountain and nearby an altar on which stood the Holy Lamb. Across the floral meadows were groups of figures gathered in adoration—martyrs, Old Testament kings, knights in armor, holy maidens, men famous in history, pilgrims, heaven knows who else besides. Hubert had almost completed this marvelous scene, as he had the panel of God the Father above it and a number of the smaller panels, when the tragedy occurred. It had been so sudden— Hubert was killed in an accident. A messenger had brought the news to Jan, who was then at Lille. This had been in September—the loneliest autumn of his life. Hubert had been both a brother and a father to him.

As Jan read the letter from Jodocus Vyt the memory of it all flooded over him. And now Vyt had written to the duke asking whether his court painter, Jan, brother of the celebrated Hubert, might be permitted to complete the great altarpiece. Vyt had delayed writing before, he explained, since he understood Master Jan was on a ducal embassy to Portugal. There was no one, the donor continued, to whom he would rather entrust so godly a work, and should the duke accede to his request he would be happy to receive Master Jan in Ghent in order that the artist might inspect the work so far achieved, and to discuss with him Jan's proposal for its completion. He was confident, Vyt concluded, that no example of a painter's art would ever bring greater glory to Christendom or more honor to the dukedom of Burgundy. The faithful would flock to the cathedral of Ghent and bend their knee in awe and in worship.

"The duke is happy for you to undertake this task," Lefèvre added as soon as Jan had raised his eyes from the letter. Then, his official function over, he went on with the palest of smiles, "I suppose this means that your head will be full of virgins again. I fear, Jan, you may have to travel much further than Ghent before you find any to paint, after the visitation of all those foreign embassies for the ducal wedding."

He paused before adding as a well-considered afterthought, "I'm told Luxembourg still has a few."

Brightened by his favorite subject, Lefèvre departed almost jauntily. Jan was left feeling moved by the thought of completing his brother's masterpiece. Events were suddenly hurrying apace after the seemingly interminable journey to Portugal and back. First the ducal portrait, and now the altarpiece for the cathedral at Ghent. Jan felt a flush of pride and ambition.

It was a while since he had called in at the Fallen Angel. The Englishman Hugo was there, with Bona, and they were talking with the rentmaster Godscalc Oom, who had clearly just arrived and was gesturing hugely about the sums he had been compelled to pay out for the ducal excesses, his face appearing to expand in size at each item of extravagance he named. Jan noticed a minute glass held between his gigantic fingers. Godscalc was rarely seen in the tavern without his modest dose of hippocras, having many years ago instructed the taverner on exactly how to mix the wine with the right sticky maceration of sugar and honey, wormwood and hyssop, rosemary and myrtle. Jan liked this mountain of a man.

"There'll be taxes all around by the spring—you wait," Godscalc boomed. "Weavers. Fullers. Dyers. Even bankers and merchants."

The conversation turned to the portrait Jan was to make of the duke. Most of them gathered there by the blazing fire on that early winter evening had themselves been drawn or painted by Jan before his departure with the embassy to Portugal; and the experience of seeing their own features and their own nature caught so precisely sharpened their curiosity about the way the painter might portray their duke.

"Well, I'm glad my job was only to make the plate and goblets for the wedding," announced the silversmith Michaut Pontin, a tankard of beer held before him in an amazingly hairy hand. Those who had seen Pontin in the public bathhouse swore he had even more hair on his body than the bear encountered by Baldwyn Iron Arm. His wife, a meticulous lady, was said to shear him every so often in order to find his cock.

"Only the ducal crest to worry about, not his face," Pontin went on. "And you, Giovanni"—he turned to the sallow figure of the Italian merchant Arnolfini, who was with the prettiest girl yet—"you were better off supplying the silks and tapestries."

The jovial Englishman, Hugo, was the one member of the company not at that moment engaged in speculating about the duke's portrait. He had been distracted by some very fetching glances from the enchanting girl who was with Arnolfini. How on earth does he do it? he wondered. Where does he find them? Giovanni was unmarried. But then so was he, reflected Hugo, and yet all the women he wanted were invariably inaccessible. He must inquire about this one: he knew only that Giovanni called her Lysbet—a name as pretty as she was. And such hair, like liquid gold.

There was laughter which brought Hugo back from his dreams of golden hair.

"If it were me I should have preferred a caricature," Godscalc was announcing with a cavernous smile that added a further chin to those already slung below his face. "It would have to be more truthful than any portrait." There was further laughter.

"Ah!" added Giovanni, his small eyes crinkling. "Ugly men like you and me need to be flattered, Godscalc," whereupon he placed a pale hand on Lysbet's bare neck and slid the dress a little with bejeweled fingers so that it exposed the skin of one shoulder. "To be flattered and to flatter—or at least to take liberties. That's the privilege of being ugly."

"Or rich," suggested the court poet Michault de Caron, his voice betraying his envy of the Italian merchant, who was of course very rich. The jewels in Lysbet's hair undoubtedly explained her choice of companion.

"Oh, flattery comes easily to you, Michault." Arnolfini's long lugubrious face had broken into a reptilian smile. "It's your job. Perhaps you should teach it to Jan when he comes to paint the duke."

"I think he'll never learn that," commented Bona, who had slipped into the tavern unseen while the others were talking. "If he only could, then I'd ask him to paint me naked."

"I should have thought he could have done that from memory," came the sour voice of Pieter van Orley from the background.

Bona looked up and awarded the master weaver a dismissive smile. Everyone knew that Jan had never been her lover and never would be. Bona preferred lovers who were very young and whom she could dismiss in the morning. She enjoyed being the initiator, she freely admitted: there was nothing quite like knowing that when they entered you it was for the first time. They were so eager, and grateful. They explored a new world in her body. Alas, she would add, they invariably wanted her to be *their* world ever after, and that could not be. She was a free spirit.

There was more beer, and hippocras for Bona and Arnolfini's girl. Hugo drank more than most. Still the conversation kept returning to Jan's portrait. These men and women who had themselves been portrayed by Jan—as they talked it became clear that each had learned something unexpected from the experience, which made them wish to talk about it out of a need for reassurance that they were not unique in this. Jan paid such attention, De Caron observed, to minute details which another artist might not even have noticed—Jan understood that it was precisely these little things about a face which made it different from other faces. Sometimes, added the goldsmith De Leeuw, who had remained taciturn until now, friends who looked at Jan's portrait of him commented on a sense of shock as if they were meeting him for the first time. Not everyone, he suspected, enjoyed this kind of exposure—Pieter van Orley was an obvious case; they felt betrayed, cheated, as though Jan had acquired unfair access to information nobody was supposed to know.

There was no one in that company at the Fallen Angel who knew Jan better than De Leeuw.

"Well, I'm happy that I only had to make the wedding rings," the goldsmith went on, unusually talkative. "A ring flatters a man without your having to flatter him yourself. And the duke, after all, has some reason for believing he's the most powerful man in Europe. Certainly the wealthiest."

It was late when the party split into the snow-covered street, and the sounds of revelry echoed across the black canal. In a patch of moonlight the vast silhouette of Godscalc Oom could be seen supporting the outline of Hugo on one side and Master Jan on the other, like two unstable ladders resting against a barrel.

Chapter ♦ Three

Jan rode to Ghent across frozen meadows. The wind was bitter off the sea and the moisture from his breath formed a comb of icicles on the rim of the fur hat low over his eyes.

There was no difficulty finding the house of Jodocus Vyt. The gabled mansion almost in the shadow of the old ducal castle was taller and noticeably grander than the merchants' houses that kept a respectful distance from it along the banks of the river Lys. Even if Jan had not known that Vyt was burgomaster of Ghent he might have imagined that only the burgomaster could possibly live here. And the way, he thought, that its reflection filled the river from bank to bank; how appropriate for a man grown to wealth on squeezing that river until it yielded up its rich lands.

Jan had never met Vyt during the year or so when Hubert was working on the great altarpiece for the cathedral. He had an image in his mind of a massive figure—rather like Godscalc Oom—and he was quite unprepared for the small rotund figure with a gentle meekness of air who greeted him in the warm, handsomely furnished room that faced the river with a distant view of the cathedral. Jan noticed the soft watery eyes and the broad cheeks which seemed to push his ears almost to the back of his head. His hands were incongruously delicate and slim, and he wore no hat. Jan imagined him to be about sixty.

He shook Jan's hand warmly. Then the moist eyes gazed at him for a moment.

"Yes, you are very like your brother," he said. His voice was soft. "I loved him," Vyt added. Jan was surprised and pleased. It felt as if Vyt was saying he wished to love Jan too.

"His death was a shock," he went on, smoothing a hand

47

across the few remaining hairs on his pate. "For you, too, I'm sure: even more so."

Jan found himself warming to this soft-spoken old man.

"Yes," he replied. "I loved him. He was my only family."

Vyt nodded sadly. Then he looked at Jan. "Hubert often said you were a better painter than he. I used to think he was being modest. But he insisted. And do you know why he thought that?"

Jan said nothing and shook his head. Vyt shuffled over to a tall cupboard on the far side of the room: he opened it and took down a dark bottle, and with his other hand two large green goblets with thick bulbs of glass protruding from the stem. He laid these on the table before them and filled each to the brim with a rich dark wine.

"Your brother and I used to drink from these same glasses," he went on, without answering his own question. "I miss him. And I miss talking to him about the altarpiece. He would call here, you know, when the light became too dim to work—almost every evening. I learned a lot about painting—and he learned a lot about wine."

Vyt gave a smile and took a sip from his goblet.

"He used to love painting landscapes. I'd tell him he was fortunate to have people like me without whom the land would all be under the sea." And Vyt chuckled. "Much more difficult to make a landscape than to paint it, I'd say to him. Hubert didn't agree—he only admitted that there was certainly more money in it than painting. And I would say to him that he should consider himself lucky, then, that I could afford to pay him to paint it. All that gold he liked to use: it cost a fortune."

How agreeable those evenings must have been, Jan thought, drinking excellent Burgundy with this acute and kindly man.

"Now I'll show you why your brother believed you were better than he."

Vyt took a gulp of wine, which left a purple stain on his upper lip. He placed his goblet on the table and grasped Jan by the arm; then they walked slowly toward a small door at the far end of the room. Jan noticed that here and there on the paneling around them hung diminutive paintings of saints, and, to Jan's astonishment, there before him in an otherwise empty room stood Hubert's altarpiece, exactly as he remembered it in his brother's house more than three years earlier. It almost filled the room, and the midday light fell on that miraculous landscape with the fountain and the altar of the Holy Lamb, the aura of an evening sun bathing far hills and cities with a light as clear as crystal. And all around the central scene with the fountain and the lamb were smaller panels, some of them painted or partly so, some with a few lines drawn on them only, others entirely blank.

"You see, Hubert did first what he did best," Vyt explained. "Whereas these"—and he pointed to the unpainted panels—"he told me he intended to ask you to help him with because you were the one, he said, who understood how to paint people; and that was what painting should be about."

Vyt looked at Jan earnestly with those pale moist eyes.

"He said that no one had ever painted people so that you knew them just from looking at them. Knew all about them. He said that," Vyt added firmly. "I assure you."

Jan was too touched to know how to reply. He remembered that the duke had said much the same thing. So had some of the people he had drawn in the tavern. And now to hear that his own revered brother had said it too. Jan looked at his own hands. He had always thought of himself as a craftsman. Hubert more than anyone else had equipped him with those skills. Later Jan had taught himself to experiment with varnishes so that whatever he painted would appear more vivid, lifelike: it would sparkle. Now it was if a mere manual skill struck others as something extraordinary, occult almost—like an extra eye which could see into people. Jan felt proud, and at the same time he felt uneasy.

Vyt was explaining that Hubert had completed those areas of the altarpiece in which the figures were small. Groups. Crowds. He was wonderfully good at all that. And Vyt pointed to the apostles in the foreground, and the holy martyrs in red, the gathering of pilgrims, of knights, bishops, hermits. The only large-size figure Hubert painted, Vyt went on, was that of God the Father—there in the center, in scarlet and gold. Hubert had explained to him that you did not have to know how to paint people to paint God the Father because God was not a person—and in any case you could hide the divine presence behind a great beard and a massive crown. That was one of the tricks of the trade, Hubert had admitted. Artists invariably painted God like that. Vyt was chuckling irreverently as he indicated to Jan the majestic figure of the Deity, who was indeed so shrouded in beard and ornament that there was hardly a recognizable figure visible.

"Besides," said Vyt, his round face beaming, "you can't imagine someone sitting for a portrait of God, can you?"

Jan smiled. He liked the old burgomaster more the longer he was with him.

"But the others," Vyt continued, his hand sweeping over the unpainted panels, "they were intended for you. The Virgin. John the Baptist. The heavenly choir. Adam and Eve. The angel of the Annunciation." Then he pointed to a vacant panel as he listed each name. "And"—Vyt suddenly looked awkward, his fingers tapping another of the unpainted panels— "also myself."

Then he laughed loudly as if to clear his own embarrassment.

"The donor, you see," he explained. "I'm vain enough to feel entitled to a modest place, together with my wife. In an attitude of prayer, of course. Do you think you can make me look humble and devout?"

And with that the old man descended carefully to his knees, placed his hands together before him, and raised his eyes upward.

"Like this?" he said inquiringly.

"Exactly like that," Jan answered, laughing. "I promise. Even the stain of Burgundy on your lips."

Vyt looked momentarily startled; then he wiped his mouth with the back of his hand and gave a childlike giggle.

"I think I shall like you as much as your brother," he said as he led Jan from the room and refilled their goblets. "Where will you paint it, Jan?" he asked, taking another sip of wine.

Jan paused.

"In Bruges," he answered.

Jan thought he detected a look of disappointment cloud Vyt's face.

"You see, I shall need people I can paint—people I know," he explained. Vyt nodded. Then the smile returned to his face.

"And how on earth will you choose them? I wonder. The Virgin Mary. John the Baptist. The angel of the Annunciation." He gazed at Jan with mock solemnity. "Perhaps you should find a way to ask Joan the Maid: I understand she is acquainted with angels and she might tell you what they are like." Vyt's eyebrows were raised so high his forehead resembled a plowed field.

"But for all I know, you hear voices too," he went on, much enjoying the meander of his own thoughts. "The only voice I ever hear in this house is my wife's telling me I've drunk quite enough of this." And he raised the large green goblet to his lips once more. "She'll enjoy being painted by you, though she'll pretend she hates it, I warn you. Not like me: I shall love it." And Vyt's face broke into a beatific smile. "You must let me know when you wish to return and do the deed. Stay with us. We should enjoy that. And I shall prepare myself to look very pious indeed. No wine stains, I assure you."

To Jan's surprise the burgomaster gave him a bearlike hug as he left. Vyt was still standing at the open door as Jan rode across the bridge and glanced back—a small rotund figure surveying the city he ruled.

Jan looked forward to painting Joos Vyt: perhaps more, he realized, than painting the duke.

The absence of the duke in Lille was scarcely noticed at the Fallen Angel, where beer and gossip were consumed much as before, but it left its mark on the ducal palace and on no one more than the duchess Isabella. She felt prematurely widowed. Her husband, her companion, her lover, the man she loved— Philip had suddenly gone only a few weeks after he had entered and taken over her life. Isabella had always fancied she would enjoy being alone, never in her life having been so. She had imagined it to be a delicious opportunity to muse and wander, do little things, and to untie in her mind those rich packages of thought she had shelved there during the course of her sociable days, waiting for just such a time when she could return to them. It was therefore to her dismay to discover now that actually there was very little there at all: ideas that had appeared so vibrant as they crossed her mind at a crowded ball seemed on close acquaintance to be trivial matters hardly worth a second thought—after which there remained the long, long day stretching ahead. Besides, it was winter, and never had she imagined weather could be so interminably disagreeable. She gazed from her window onto what looked at this moment like something Master Jan might have painted as a background to the penitence of St. Jerome. A wilderness of Flanders.

Daily life at court without the duke to shield her was like a sequence of penitential ordeals. She was formally woken, formally served breakfast, formally greeted by secretaries and chamberlains, chaplains and dressmakers, formally escorted to dinner to be bowed and mumbled at and royally overfed until she was almost asleep with boredom, to be escorted at last with the final formalities of the day to her rooms—by which time she longed to scream some healthy abuse, or laugh aloud, or toss her clothing in a disordered trail wherever she felt like it. She had even tried all these things. But her modest flow of abuse had been met within minutes by a culprit dragged before her for a sentence of punishment. An outburst of laughter about nothing at all had received a polite echo around the room behind gloved hands. And as soon as she hurled any article of clothing there appeared some handmaiden to pick it up again.

Worst of all, at night she was alone. There was no Philip to make love to her.

Isabella felt like some rare creature in the ducal menagerie—segregated for fear of contamination or damage. Oh, that she could have been a falcon on Philip's wrist, let to fly, skim free, and return again to his outstretched arm.

She came to realize, also, that the few attracting and entertaining members of the ducal court either accompanied the duke when he traveled or absented themselves the moment he departed—presumably to lead the kind of normal life denied to her. Michault de Caron, the court poet, for example: where was he? Her lady-in-waiting Louise gave a laugh and suggested that he preferred the taverns where the singing was not of a courtly nature and where the ladies were likewise not of a courtly nature.

And what about Master Jan, the painter? He had been her frequent companion in Portugal, but here in Bruges she had set eyes on him scarcely at all. Jan, Louise explained, was not a member of the ducal court but lived in the craftsmen's district of Bruges, and in any case was heavily committed to a young lady called Margarethe, an innocent creature. The duchess would of course see more of him, Louise added, while he was engaged in painting the ducal portrait. Indeed Louise much hoped that she would see more of him herself: she rather took to Jan, she said, with a tilt of her pretty face. He had a mischievous eye and she would like to catch it.

"So what do people do at court?" Isabella asked fretfully. "What is there?"

Louise laughed, glancing down at her low bodice as she did so.

"Love," she said. "That's all there is to do."

Isabella looked surprised. Then she smiled. Louise was the only bright spark in her day.

"And what if your husband is away?"

It was Louise's turn to look surprised.

"Oh, my lady, I wasn't talking about husbands; I was talking about love."

Isabella did not understand.

"But I love my husband."

Louise looked awkward. It was difficult enough coping with the duchess's uncertain French without having to explain the human heart. She liked Isabella but felt herself to be on fragile ground.

"Forgive me, my lady, but you are only just married," she said tentatively.

"But I shall always love my husband," came the forceful reply.

Louise was silent. How could she explain? Isabella knew nothing.

"Don't you love your husband?" the duchess went on.
Louise looked startled.

"I hardly know him," she said. Isabella gazed at her incredulously.

"How can that be so? You're so young, so pretty."

Louise did her best. It was hard to know how frank she
could be. Isabella was, after all, the duchess. She tried to explain that she had been married six years, since she was thirteen. He was a knight, from Namur. Her father had drawn up
the contract, and she had been delivered—like a package—but
only for the wedding. After that she had become part of the
ducal court. He was forever away. Tournaments. Jousting. Always traveling. Sometimes it was England or Scotland. Or
Spain. Italy. France. That was his life. She scarcely saw him.

"But after your wedding . . . ?" Isabella was looking at
her slightly embarrassed. Louise shook her head.

"No!"

"Didn't you want to . . . ?"

"No! I was too young."

"And didn't he . . . ?"

Louise gave a little laugh.

"He respected me, he said. And then he went away."

The duchess was shaking her head in astonishment. She
gazed at this beautiful creature, so warm, so lively, with the
body of Venus. Was it possible that a husband should not
want such a woman? And yet she talked about love.

"But why?" Isabella went on. Again the girl laughed.

"There are men," she said, and suddenly she sounded so
much older than Isabella, "who love to champion women,
fight for them, worship them, but don't actually want them."

Isabella was still looking at Louise in amazement.

"And your husband is like that?"

Louise nodded. "Oh, he likes women, but only harlots.
They're a man's sport. He's a knight, you see. And what a
knight really admires is virtue, purity. The Virgin Mary, not
Eve." And she laughed again. "The Burgundians are like that.
And the French. In love with chivalry. Why do you imagine
the Maid of Orléans is so successful?"

Isabella was surprised by the sudden mention of Joan.

"Tell me."

"To have a spotless maiden lead them into battle: my lady, that's the dream of every French knight."

Isabella had never imagined a young woman could say such things. She remembered the fine vows of chivalry she had heard Philip make before the assembled lords of Europe. The Golden Fleece. The plight of Christendom. The pledge to defeat the Grand Turk. Isabella shook her head, bemused. The man who had declared those vows was her own husband—who loved her, who made love to her, who was at this very moment preparing for battle against the Maid of Orléans with his brave general, Jehan de Luxembourg. And she smiled at Louise, who was, after all, she decided, just a girl disappointed in love.

"Perhaps," said Isabella, laughing, "the duke should consider appointing a Flemish peasant girl to lead his army instead of the lord of Luxembourg." Then she added, more seriously, "Philip is quite sure he will defeat Joan just as convincingly as he defeated Jacqueline of Hainault. He certainly doesn't believe in her holy voices and her visions. Joan is just a girl who's been clever enough to show the French that the English army is tired and weak."

Her lady-in-waiting said nothing. There were many things, she thought, that the duchess would learn before long about the dukedom of Burgundy.

The consensus view at the Fallen Angel was that it was a pity Hubert had already painted God the Father, since there was no doubt in anyone's mind that there was only one man fit to be painted in such an elevated role, and that was the ducal rentmaster Godscalc Oom. Even his name fitted.

Godscalc beamed benevolently at the suggestion, and even looked a trifle sad that the honor of being the supreme deity in the cathedral of Ghent had been withheld from him by Master Jan's late brother. Might there not still be a place for him? he suggested. There was, after all, a Trinity. God the Father. God the Son. God the Holy Ghost.

Michaut Pontin took the view that the three divine persons were supposed to be one, theologically speaking, and to represent them separately was certainly blasphemous. That sounded unanswerable.

Jan de Leeuw lowered his flagon of beer and suggested without a flicker of a smile that in any case Godscalc would make a poor Holy Dove.

"So who remains to be painted?" asked Michault de Caron.

Jan explained that he had yet to study Hubert's drawing of the altarpiece carefully, but there would certainly have to be large-scale figures of Adam and Eve, the Virgin Mary, John the Baptist, and the angel of the Annunciation. Also various choirs of angels.

"Well now, you must think of your friends," said the jovial Englishman, Hugo. "We have our reputations to consider."

Bona wanted to know what reputation he had in mind. She thought that nobody who drank as heavily as Hugo deserved a place in the company of John the Baptist, who was an ascetic accustomed to asses' milk and wild honey.

"He was also a very hairy man," added the Italian merchant Arnolfini. "At least so he is always represented in paintings in Italy. As the hairiest man in Bruges, Pontin, it has to be you," he said, nodding toward the silversmith.

Pontin looked pleased, and Jan agreed that he would make an admirable John the Baptist. Further drinks were produced by the taverner, and the group standing around the large open fire continued to paint Jan's altarpiece in their fertile minds.

"I see myself as Adam," ventured Michault de Caron.

Jan explained that he would have to pose naked, in a state of primal innocence. But Arnolfini, whose knowledge of these things surprised everyone, pointed out that in the paintings which he supplied to many courts of Europe, Adam was invariably represented after the Temptation and therefore already fallen: hence Michault should be allowed to cover his loins. There was much laughter.

Bona disagreed with Arnolfini. Since she fully intended to pose for Eve, she said, she wanted an opportunity to gaze at Adam *in toto*. She had been told that the court poet had more than adequate parts, not to be hidden in shame. There was even more laughter.

"Do you really want to pose as Eve?" Jan asked, surprised.

"Jan, I *am* Eve," Bona replied with a sly laugh. "And now I shall be immortal as well. Besides, I always wanted an excuse for you to paint me naked—provided Margarethe doesn't object, of course," she added with a slight smirk.

It was Bona, standing there looking almost beautiful in the firelight, who supplied Jan with the last two figures he needed for the altarpiece—the Virgin Mary (to be seated on the right hand of God) and the angel of the Annunciation (on the folded wing of the altarpiece above the figure of Joos Vyt).

"Of course," she announced, "the heavenly twins."

Arnolfini looked startled. For a man of taste such as himself it was uncomfortable to envisage his current mistress as the Virgin Mother or as any kind of angel, though in terms of beauty—certainly—Lysbet would look perfect. As for her twin sister, the virtuous Marie, well, she would of course make the ideal Virgin. There Bona was right.

"Don't be anxious, Giovanni," said Bona reassuringly, "neither of them will need to be painted in the flesh."

There was further laughter except from Hugo, whose knowledge of the Bible was sketchy and who had already been entertaining a glimpse of the divine Lysbet as nature intended.

"There!" said Michault de Caron, summoning the taverner to bring more beer and wine. "We've assembled your picture for you, Jan. When do we begin?"

It was scarcely a reverent way to be setting about such a task, Jan thought, as he closed the door of the Fallen Angel on an unusually boisterous chorus of song. And yet, had not John the Baptist, the Virgin Mary, Christ himself, been real people —as real as Joos Vyt and Jan's own friends at the tavern? What was more, in a Passion play did not people from the streets and the taverns perform the roles of Mary, of Joseph, of Christ, of Judas? Why then should painting be any different?

Margarethe was waiting for him and she threw herself into his arms. He did not tell her about Bona but he described the others he would paint, hoping when he said the court poet was to pose for Adam that she would not inquire who was to pose for Eve. Margarethe was not so stupid.

"And Eve?" she asked straightaway. "Who will be Eve?"

Jan wished he had been forthright from the outset. It was more difficult now.

"Bona," he said, aware that he had cleared his throat several times.

Margarethe was silent, looking at him with uncertain eyes.

"Tell me what it means to you to be a painter," she asked unexpectedly.

At first he did not know what to answer. But she was waiting, looking at him for an answer. Thoughts Jan had never really formulated came to the surface as he gazed at her. He had no understanding, he said, of the world as other artists saw it. To him it was neither the black of hell nor the gold of heaven. There was only the actual world and it was beautiful in every flower, every leaf, every imperfection even. His delight was to observe it, and in observing it to understand it. Margarethe was nodding her head as he said this. It was the same with people, he went on. God had made a world of infinite richness and complexity in which every person was different, and to observe each person was also to understand them. They were not merely sinners or saints, young or old, fair or ugly, as painters invariably portrayed them: to do this was to reduce them to puppets, masks. Perhaps, Jan added, he was led to see complexities in people—doubts too—where they themselves might see only single-mindedness and certainty of purpose.

She was looking at him so intently while he spoke that suddenly he stopped. The warm flicker of the lamp painted minute points of light on those green eyes, and there was just the slightest movement of her lips. Jan reached out toward her and slowly ran his fingers down her face and neck. He began to unfasten her bodice and slipped her dress very gently down over her shoulders and arms. The lamplight cast a deep shadow under the fullness of her breasts and he cupped his hands where the shadows fell. She let out a soft gasp and he could feel her nipples grow hard against the palms of his hands.

"Jan," was all she said, almost inaudibly, and she pressed her own hands over his against her breasts.

They stood in silence until he felt her body begin to shiver with the cold. She did not look at him as she fastened her dress, but as he accompanied her home, their chins muffled against the cold, she buried her head in his shoulder, their breath billowing about them. The canals were frozen over now, and the occasional lamplight from the houses threw pallid stains across the ice. Her face was cold to his lips as he kissed her good night.

"Tomorrow," she whispered, and Jan could just make out the dark pools of her eyes. For a few seconds longer she looked at him, then one hand touched his cheek and she turned into the doorway.

Margarethe watched him walk away beside the black canal in which a huge moon lay frozen. She could still feel the gentle roughness of his hands holding her breasts. She wanted those hands everywhere, and his body everywhere. There would never be anybody else about whom she could feel that: from the first it had been only Jan. Before him she had never imagined there could be anyone, or that she could ever risk so much. Even now, watching that figure recede into the night, she imagined he was walking away from her, and she felt bereft. It was a shock to be aware of such vulnerability, to know that the man you love walks in so dangerous a world ready to pluck him at any minute. Margarethe did not know what those dangers might be, but she feared they would always be there. Hold back, a frail voice told her. And yet she wanted him. She wanted him.

The moon was hidden by the time Jan crossed the bridge over the canal and turned into the street of the Golden Hand. The night was like a cold shawl around him, yet he walked on air with the warmth of Margarethe's body around him. He could see lights glowing from De Leeuw's windows, and hear the laughter of children. His own house was in darkness, but as he entered, his housekeeper hurried forward, her face flustered and a little disapproving. There was a lady here, she said. A different lady, she emphasized, with a sharp glance at him.

It was Bona. She was reclining majestically on a couch in her long surcoat trimmed with fur. She turned her head as he greeted her, and took Jan's hand affectionately.

"There was something I wanted to tell you earlier," she said, "but there was no opportunity in the tavern."

Bona was looking at him a little mischievously, Jan thought. He was intrigued, but he knew that Bona liked to intrigue.

"I wish you well with your portrait of the duke," she went on, and there was a hint of archness in her voice. "It must be an important moment in your life." She paused for a moment, a quizzical smile on her face. What an infuriating woman she could be, he realized. "But I have another offer for you— which you may find even more exciting. A lady. A great lady. You know of her."

Bona was still looking at him strangely. Then she gave just the smallest laugh through her nose, and stretched languorously like a cat in the sun.

"She has asked for the best painter in Flanders to do a portrait of her. Naturally I suggested you. She would like you to visit her—when you are not needed by the duke, of course. Bona gave another little laugh. "She lives in Zeeland—in Goes —two days' ride. She will reward you well."

Jan was puzzled.

"And who is she?" he asked.

Bona rose from the couch as if to leave, pausing for a moment to glance at some drawings of Margarethe's hands which were lying on the table. Then she looked at her own hands as if to compare them.

"The duchess Jacqueline," Bona said, without looking up.

It was the first of February. The duke greeted Jan like a friend. The two men had not met since before the departure of the embassy for Portugal, and Philip was immediately anxious to know whether he had profited from his stay in that country— if he had been respectfully treated; if he had found other ladies as beautiful as Isabella to draw (here he clapped Jan warmly on the shoulder); if the storms on the return journey had really been as appalling as the duchess had described; and if he had found Bruges a welcoming place to return to. He hoped so.

Jan was reminded of the graciousness and charm of this

man. The apprehensions he had felt appearing at the ducal palace were quite dispelled, and Jan was conscious—as he had been often in the past—of Philip's knack of seeming to have no business in the world except that of exchanging gentle courtesies with whoever he was with at that moment. He certainly appeared to be in no hurry to begin the portrait. The duke was keen to talk about his falcons, and promised to show them to Jan. He was delighted to hear only this morning, he said, that his favorite saker falcon which had been missing for a month had been found safe in Austria: the margrave of Brandenburg, himself a keen falconer, had undertaken to return the bird to him and to send with it as a gift a pair of goshawks. The duke looked inordinately pleased, and went on to express his delight that the duchess Isabella shared his passion for the noble sport. They had been hunting several times together, though in this inclement season there had been little to hunt beyond a few miserable water rats. When the court moved to Lille, and later to Dijon, there would be more fruitful opportunities: perhaps Jan would care to join them: the duchess would find it a pleasure to have his company again. She had often spoken warmly of the conversations they had enjoyed in Lisbon.

Jan imagined that the subject of the portrait might be introduced any moment, since he suspected it had been at Isabella's prompting that the duke had decided on it. But now Philip was describing the remarkable epithalamion which the poet Michault de Caron had composed for their marriage. He found it hard to believe, he said with a laugh, that either he or the duchess were quite the paragons of virtue and upholders of perfect justice—or the Zeus and Hera—that the poet claimed; nonetheless, no more harmonious words could possibly have been found for such an occasion. It was his third marriage, he reminded Jan; he trusted that it would be his last. To have been widowed twice was more than enough for any man. And when, he inquired, did Jan intend to marry? A most desirable state, he added, though of course there were delightful compensations in being single, and he had heard that Jan's house was not noted for being deprived of pretty women.

But then virginity, the duke suggested with a light laugh,

was not a precondition of moral excellence, whatever the church might preach on the matter.

"Are there not some exceptions, my lord?" Jan ventured. "The Maid of Orléans would seem to have prospered through moral excellence." His own boldness in answering the duke rather surprised him, and he noticed Philip's face take on a stern appearance.

"Jan, you have been my ambassador; you must know something of the world," he replied firmly. "Only an army as feeble as that of France would seek to be led by a peasant girl who claims to be a virgin and claims to hear the voices of angels."

There was contempt in the duke's voice but no apparent resentment at being challenged. Rather, he seemed to enjoy the chance to air his superior wisdom. Jan decided to risk probing the matter further.

"And yet, my lord, Joan seems to have got the better of the English."

Again no irritation showed on the duke's face. He appeared to be lost in thought for a moment. Then he turned a firm gaze onto Jan and his mouth was set hard.

"The English are not what they were when King Henry was alive," he said quietly. And after a further pause he added, "But it will not last."

Jan wanted to ask why, if the English were now so weak, the army of Burgundy had not been set against the Maid, since Burgundy and England were allies in the war with France. But he thought it prudent not to pursue the argument further.

Then, as if he had been reading Jan's mind, the duke went on. "The wise general, Jan, is the one who waits. Hotheads destroy themselves without your having to risk your own soldiers' lives."

And he described how only in September Joan had ignominiously failed to take the city of Paris. She had hopelessly overstretched herself, he explained. Her own army had suffered terrible loss of life. Joan herself was severely wounded. The French had retreated in disorder.

"A soldier who takes military orders from angels may all

too soon find himself among them," Philip said with a rough laugh.

The duke had recovered his good humor. At this moment the duchess Isabella appeared, and Philip embraced her delightedly. She gave a cry of pleasure as she caught sight of Jan, but instantly remembered her dignity and extended her hand for Jan to kiss. He was smiling and saw that she was smiling too. It was a moment of gentle complicity. He had enjoyed the company of Isabella in Portugal even though they had been compelled to communicate in French, in which neither was fluent. The duke of course spoke Flemish and French with equal ease, and was taking pains—Isabella was now explaining —to learn a little Portuguese. Her own French, she added, was improving rapidly thanks to the duke and to her lady-in-waiting Louise, who never stopped talking and was telling her all manner of things about the ducal court that she was sure were not intended for her ears. Jan thought the duke's smile of pleasure faltered for an instant, but she did not appear to notice.

"And your portrait of the duke," Isabella exclaimed. "I await it with impatience."

Jan had begun to imagine the duke had entirely forgotten the purpose of his visit. But he was wrong, because at that very moment Philip rang a small bell and instantly a secretary appeared with servile haste. The duke spoke a few quick words to him, and then turned to Jan.

"And now I shall dress for you."

The duke's face was that of a man who acknowledged himself to be vain and deemed it to be a virtue—at least in a duke.

Isabella departed with her husband and Jan was left alone in that handsome chamber lined with tapestries. Everywhere he looked the winter sun glinted on golden objects whose only function appeared to be to display the jewels set into them. Jan realized that he was already imagining himself painting those jeweled and golden ornaments in his portrait of the duke: Philip would certainly wish to have himself portrayed as a man whose splendor was reflected in the wealth at his disposal. And Jan felt proud that no painter possessed his skill at trapping the glitter of a ruby in dull pigment. Perhaps it was this, he reflected more ruefully, rather than any skill with faces, that made him First Painter to the court of Burgundy. And yet the duke wanted him to paint "the whole man." That would be difficult.

Another thought troubled Jan more deeply: Jacqueline, and her request that he paint her portrait too. She was the duke's cousin—but she was the duke's enemy. Jan knew he needed to tell Philip, and maybe he would refuse to allow it. In fact it seemed likely that he would. The black raven, as Lefèvre had described her. And yet Bona had called her a great lady.

The door opened and Philip entered, followed by the sallow figure of Jehan Lefèvre. The duke stood in his robes of the Golden Fleece—the bright scarlet gown lined with ermine, the mantle embroidered in gold, the black hood with its long band, the golden collar studded with rubies and the insignia of the fleece suspended across his chest. He had the air of an emperor.

The duke was smiling. Jan sensed that he had been carefully rehearsing his pose and position, for he appeared unwilling to move except to extend a gloved hand in which was held a small scroll.

"Read it," he said in a matter-of-fact voice.

Jan took the scroll, glancing inquiringly at the duke, who remained statuesque before the window in the sun.

"The articles of foundation—they'll be read out at the first solemn Chapter of the Order, on St. Andrew's Day. Read it," he repeated. "Aloud, so I can hear what it sounds like."

Jan began to unroll the parchment and began to read out what he saw—and it seemed to go on forever.

" 'From the great love which we bear to the noble order of chivalry, whose honor and prosperity are our only concern, to the end that the true Catholic Faith, the Faith of the Holy Church, our Mother, as well as the peace and welfare of the realm, may be defended, preserved, and maintained to the glory and praise of Almighty God our Creator and Saviour, in honor of his glorious Mother, the Virgin Mary, and of our Lord, St. Andrew, Apostle and Martyr, and for the furtherance of virtue . . .' "

"Enough!" The duke raised his hand.

Jan returned the scroll to the duke, who in turn passed it to the ducal herald. Lefèvre bowed stiffly and took his leave.

"I wanted you to understand something of the purpose of this portrait," the duke went on. Then the suggestion of a smile crossed his face. "I didn't want you to imagine that you were to paint me in these robes just because everybody tells you I love to dress up." And he laughed. "Which I do, of course."

Jan was relieved to see the duke in such good humor. His eyes were bright and he was gazing with curiosity at the drawing materials which Jan had placed on the floor.

"So we can begin. You must tell me how you wish to set about it. Any other artist I would have told *him*"—the duke laughed again—"but you, you must tell *me.*"

He looked hard at the painter, and waited.

Jan explained that today he wished only to draw the duke. The drawing was the essential thing—the face, the figure, the poise. Then he would like to return, he said, when he had studied that drawing, lived with it, seen whether he had captured a living face, the real person. There would certainly need to be some corrections, some aspects of the duke's expression and presence which very likely he would not have entirely grasped. It was important to get it absolutely right. If all this were permitted. He hoped he would not absorb too much of the duke's time, but for such an important occasion . . . Then, once he was satisfied—and he hoped his lordship too— he would like to apply the first colors again in the duke's presence, in order to obtain exactly the correct tone, shading, texture. After that, Jan went on, he would not need to bother the duke further: the robes, once drawn, he could color in his absence provided it might be possible to borrow them for a period of time. Not the duke's own, naturally, but perhaps those of some other lord, if this could be arranged. Likewise the jewels and the insignia of the Golden Fleece. These would require a great many layers of glaze and special varnishes in order that they should sparkle as intensely as they did in life, or even more so. Then all that remained, Jan explained, was the setting and the background. Perhaps the duke would express his wishes on the matter. If he might himself offer a suggestion, the portrait should be in an imaginary setting—of a religious nature since the aims of the Order were of that kind: a chapel with an altar, but beyond it a handsome colonnade of marble through which a wide vista of the dukedom might be glimpsed, and in the distance a city of spires and domes that would suggest the holy city of Jerusalem.

Jan paused. The duke had been gazing at him intently all the while. Now he nodded.

"Now I know why I appointed you First Painter of Burgundy," he said. "You are a master, Jan. And if you truly achieve all that you will be the greatest of masters."

So great was the duke's delight that Jan felt fearful lest he had painted in words a picture far more beautiful than he would ever be able to achieve. He said as much to the duke, who, to Jan's relief, only laughed.

"Now you must tell me what you want me to do," he said.

Jan suggested that he sit: not that the final portrait would be of the duke seated, he explained, but in order to capture the face it would be better if he were in a relaxed pose. He would draw him standing later, perhaps on his second visit.

"And must I stay absolutely still? May I talk? I don't want to go to sleep, or look bored."

Jan could see that the duke was enjoying himself like a child, which was a good beginning.

"I should like you to be thinking," he answered.

The duke looked surprised.

"It's a man's thoughts that count most in a face," Jan explained. "They are what bring the features to life."

The duke nodded.

"I see," he said. "You mean you can *see* me thinking. How very dangerous. And what would you like me to think about?"

"I suggest that since you are wearing the robes of the Golden Fleece you might think about everything it means; your ambitions, your hopes, plans. The glory of it."

The duke seemed already lost in thought as he spoke, exactly as Jan wanted. He had been preparing his drawing materials while they had been talking, and now he fixed before him a sheet of paper that he had already prepared with Chinese white; then in his right hand he took up a slender rod of silver and began the first slow sharp lines of the duke's half-profile. Jan loved drawing in silverpoint; it gave that fineness of outline, that attention to the barely perceptible crinkling around the eyes and mouth; nothing blurred, uncertain. There was nothing quite like the sense of precise concentration with which his hand guided that needle of metal, and his eye guided his hand; the feeling of risk lest his perception falter for a second and the expression grow vague, impersonal. If this happened he would lose it.

The mind. The eye. The hand. It was as if they were interlocked, messages passing to and fro continuously, obliterating all else. There was this face in front of him—he was hardly aware now who it was. The needle probed it piece by piece, hand/mind/eye gathering grains of information, adding them to the store. The slightly pinched mouth, strained, determined, humorous. That blade of a nose, tense around the nostrils, dark hairs bristling. The rather flat ears set far back, almost fleshless. Skin sagging a little beneath the eyes—distant eyes, gray-blue. (Jan noted the colors on the edge of the paper.) Thin eyebrows unusually high: it was these that gave the face a surprised look. But the heavy eyelids contradicted the surprise with weariness. Both were deceptive; the gaze itself was cool and firm. It was a face which acquired many such contradictions the longer Jan peered: the upper lip tense, the lower one full and loose; firm chin but haggard jawline; brow smooth on one side, lightly furrowed on the other; fine cheekbones but with small muscles flickering. It was not an easy face to draw, not a face entirely at ease.

Jan's concentration was becoming strained: he would need to let go of it for a period. The duke's face looked as though the thinking had ceased and a daydream had taken over. It was becoming a lifeless face. Jan would need to return.

"My lord duke, I suggest that may be enough for today."

The duke's face gathered an awareness of things around him slowly as if awakening.

"How long have I been sitting here?" he asked.

Jan said he thought it was perhaps an hour. Long enough, he added, for both of them. He explained that the drawing was still unfinished and that he would require a further session if the duke could spare the time. And he would draw the standing pose on the same occasion: that would be much briefer.

"It's the face that is the hardest, because it's the seat of a man's thoughts and of his nature," Jan said.

"And do you believe you have discovered mine?" asked the duke with a laugh. "Show me."

Jan unfixed the sheet of paper and handed it to the duke. He knew the drawing to be good, but as Philip took the paper Jan felt a wave of unease: the way that he, Jan, saw the duke's face might not at all be how he himself saw it, or how he wished to see it; besides, how often had Philip seen his face as others saw it? Perhaps never.

The duke gazed at it for a long time without an expression. Finally he laid it in front of him and, still gazing at it, made a muttering sound. Jan strained to hear whether it was a sound of disapproval or dismay. It occurred to him that at this moment his own career was held precariously in the balance.

Then the duke made a strange remark.

"It's like my ghost," he said. "My own spirit haunting me." Then, after a pause: "You've seen so much that I thought I had well hidden." Quite suddenly he laughed. "But how vain I am."

And as if to prove it, he rose and, straightening his scarlet robe and golden collar, he strode to the window and turned so that the sun blazed on him from his forehead to his thighs.

Within seconds the artist had fixed a second sheet of paper, and as the duke stood gazing haughtily at him in his splendor Jan drew a series of rapid silver lines which exactly caught the pose. Nothing could have been more vivid. Jan could feel the excitement again in his fingers as he drew. He was aware at that moment how disappointed he had felt by the duke's ambivalent response. Now he would catch him by surprise. Quickly he proffered the second sheet to the duke—who took it. His face filled with astonishment, and he ran his fingers over the lines as if to touch the form of his own body that was not there.

This time he said nothing. But a slow smile spread across his face. Still not saying anything, he crossed the room and pulled on a bell cord by the fireplace. A servant entered almost immediately and Jan heard the duke give an order which he could not catch.

There followed an uncertain few minutes, with the duke apparently unaware of Jan's presence as he took the two drawings one in each hand. His eyes moved from one to the other. Jan felt uncomfortable and his own eyes strayed to the window. A long skein of geese was passing low over the ramparts of the city between the turning mill sails. Jan followed them in their flight, wishing at this moment that he were out there in the white landscape—with Margarethe, with Michault, with Bona, with Godscalc, with anybody just so long as he was not here in this silent room with the most powerful man in Europe weighing his future in his hands.

The geese had passed out of sight; the servant had returned; on the table before the duke stood two tall glasses and a bottle dusty with age. He was pouring dark wine into each glass. He passed one to Jan—who took it, bewildered. Then the duke raised his own glass, and all at once his face broke into the most radiant of smiles.

"A man of rare skills," he said, "deserves the rarest of wines. Let's drink to your portrait, and to us both."

For a while the duke said nothing further about the drawings. The two men stood before the great fireplace carved with all the crests of the ducal lands, drinking fine Burgundy and enjoying the warmth of the flames. Jan was filled with a quiet elation, conscious of having passed the hardest test of his life. He wanted to rush away and tell his friends, tell Margarethe, especially Margarethe. Meanwhile the wine was soothing and delicious, and the duke appeared to have all the time in the world to share it with him.

Then, quite casually, the duke picked up the drawings from the table. He looked at them closely again, his eyes roaming from one to the other. After a moment he shook his head.

"Uncanny," he said, more to himself than to Jan. Still shaking his head, he added, "I love skills. What intrigues me, Jan, is how you can work like a jeweler one moment and like a swordsman the next."

Jan felt complimented. He had never thought of it like that, but the duke was right. Those were the two ways he liked to work: the closest study of nature, and the swift grasp of it in flight.

The duke poured more wine and began to talk of other things. The court would be leaving again soon for Lille, he explained. He hoped that he could invite Jan to return and complete the drawings before he departed, but that would depend on—he hesitated for a moment—on the war. The French would be reassembling an army as soon as the winter passed. The Maid was restless for battle, he said with just the hint of a laugh. After her failure to gain Paris she was in need of a victory—even a small one; otherwise the French would soon cease to believe in her angels and her voices. Perhaps in her virginity too, he added with a further laugh. It was time to put an end to her little triumphs. Then the duke turned to Jan with a wry look. He had never expected, he said, that as a man of battle he would find himself taking up arms against women. What was happening to men that they needed women to become soldiers? Now there was Joan: before that there was Jacqueline.

Jan waited for an opportunity to raise the subject of Jacqueline's portrait.

"She's my cousin," the duke continued, as his voice sounded sad. "Her grandfather, Philip the Bold, was my grandfather; her mother was my father's sister. People shouldn't take up arms against their own family. It's treacherous."

There was a pause, and Philip's thoughts seemed far away. Jan knew that this was the moment.

"My lord duke," he said quietly, "I have received a request from her to paint her portrait."

Philip turned his head and looked at Jan impassively.

"Yes, I know. And when will you do it?"

Jan was dumbfounded. How did the duke know? Could Bona have told him? It seemed unlikely. Jan was disturbed to realize that of course the duke would make it his business to know such things. He would have spies everywhere. Then, once again, the duke surprised him.

"I understand you, Jan," he said, and his voice was warm, almost fatherly. "When I look at the drawings you made of me I see myself more sharply than in a mirror. Yours is a rare gift. You're fascinated by people—their natures, their thoughts, what makes them different from others—and you see them more deeply than others. That's why you're a fine painter—the finest. Why I respect you. Why I like you."

He paused, and then walked slowly toward the window and looked out over the roofs and ramparts of his city.

"I well understand," he went on without turning to face Jan, "why you should be intrigued at the thought of painting Jacqueline. How could you not be? You're young; you're full of curiosity. And you like a touch of danger, as I do."

The duke turned to face Jan as he said this, and there was a smile on his face.

"You see, I like you and I trust you. If I didn't I wouldn't let you go." The duke returned to the blazing fire, wineglass in one hand, the other casually fingering the insignia of the Golden Fleece. "The black raven; you'll paint her well," he said; then in the same calm voice, "It would be useful to me if you undertook to do it."

A fresh wave of astonishment overtook Jan. He stood there speechless as the duke refilled their goblets.

"Let me put something to you, Jan. You have been my ambassador more than once, and most ably." Philip handed him a full goblet and took a sip from his own, reflectively. "People talk to you when you're painting them. I know that—even though you requested *me* not to talk." The duke gave a light laugh. "Isabella tells me she unfolded almost everything about her life while sitting for her portrait. I felt quite jealous." A smile creased his face. "Others have said the same. I have another letter from the burgomaster of Ghent singing your praises: he swears he has seldom met a man to whom he felt more able to entrust his thoughts. That's praise indeed from Vyt. A fine man."

Jan began to understand what the duke was proposing. He felt flattered and uneasy. He wondered if he should simply refuse, but then he realized he was probably not in a position to refuse if he wanted to remain First Painter to the duke of Burgundy.

"So, Jacqueline will talk to you—because of what you are and because of what she is," the duke went on. Jan was puzzled by what he meant by that last remark. "Jacqueline is dangerous. She is defeated but she is still dangerous. She hates me, though I do not hate her. She is my cousin, after all. But I need to know what plans she may have."

The duke gazed into the fire for a moment; then he looked at Jan quizzically out of the corner of his eye.

"You will be *her* painter and *my* ambassador."

The duke emptied his goblet and without a further word crossed the room and gave another tug at the bell cord. The session was over.

Jan's last image of Philip as he departed was of a slim, graceful figure in his robes of splendor once more gazing out over the winter landscape. As he walked back through the crowded streets of the city, Jan felt disturbed. He had been awarded his freedom. At the same time it was as though a light but strong chain had been placed invisibly around him.

Chapter • Four

It was the longest winter anyone could remember. For months nothing moved except the wind—neither farmers, nor beggars, nor armies: even the rivers remained sealed within the clamp of the relentless ice. It was said that to the north the sea froze. Many people froze. And their livestock. But then overnight, as it seemed, it was spring. There were fresh sounds—birds at dawn, children playing, laughter, and running water. People hung furs and animal skins on the outside of their cottages to freshen them after the stench of winter. They mourned their dead, watched the mill sails swiftly turning, and felt their own strength stir. And from the dead ground suddenly there were primroses and coltsfoots staining the slopes of the dikes, and under the ragged trees violets, wood sorrel, and daffodils. Storks returned to the belfries with a clatter of wings, and cranes to the swamplands. The air felt soft.

On one such spring afternoon a horseman in the service of the duke of Burgundy was riding hard from the direction of Paris eastward toward the city of Lille. And on the same afternoon another horseman in the duke's service was riding more thoughtfully northward from Flanders along a lonely dike which divided a broad stretch of polderland from the sea.

The first horseman was delivering a simple message contained in a letter which he carried in his wallet. It was from the captain of the Burgundian army, Jehan de Luxembourg, to Duke Philip in his palace at Lille. The letter, in Jehan's own hasty hand, gave a single piece of information: the Maid had entered Compiègne. There was no need to say more since the plan had already been agreed. The letter was signed the thirteenth of May 1430.

The second rider carried no letter, but in his saddlebag was a box of materials which included colors, chalks, inks, small knives, brushes of various thicknesses, rods of silver, sheets of paper from Troyes and Fabriano, fixatives and other gadgets of the artist's trade. He was singing, and a group of men who were ditching the sodden polderland some distance to his right leaned on their tall spades and hailed him as he passed. He raised his fur hat in salute.

Jan was singing because the day seemed specially beautiful after the interminable winter. The pale sky veined white. Purple of the marshes. Pallor of the sea. The whistle of the wind through the dune grass. The steady jingle of the bridle. Ahead of him Jan could see how the dike veered to the left across open salt flats speckled with seabirds, and at the far end of that thread of land he could pick out the island—or what had been an island until the intrepid Zeelanders humped this long link of causeway across the marsh. Perhaps in his own lifetime there would be fields here just as there were around Bruges.

Zeeland. The lands of the sea. The land, more particularly, of the duchess Jacqueline, or all that was now left to her since the loss of Hainault, Holland, and Brabant to Philip. Jan felt no little apprehension at the thought of meeting her. The black raven. Jacqueline of Zeeland. Jacqueline of the lands of the sea.

Above the dunes far beyond the causeway Jan thought he could make out the walls of the town of Goes, her fortress. He was riding westward now, along the narrow spine that rose above the gray tide, the sun stretching veils of crimson over the water and the approaching island. It seemed a desolate place to be; around him nothing but marsh and patterns of the sea—lone gulls, the sucking of the wind, colors of the evening. He heard a distant bell. It would be dusk before he reached Goes.

The message from Jacqueline had come once again through Bona—the mysterious Bona.

"The duchess will be glad to see you," was all Bona said. Jan noticed that she referred to Jacqueline as "the duchess" even though she was no longer that. Again he could not help wondering how it happened that Bona was in this role; but when he had tactfully inquired she had replied with a shrug—"I know her."

It had been a strange period of waiting. First for the duke—until the entire court had departed for Lille and still there had been no summons to complete the drawing of him. Then waiting for Jacqueline. Meanwhile Jan had begun work on the huge altarpiece for Joos Vyt—completing Hubert's majestic landscape with here and there some plants and trees Jan had sketched in Portugal (palms, pomegranates, vines), and which he thought would make it more closely suggest the landscape of the holy city of Jerusalem. Margarethe had been constantly with him like a warm shadow. The scale of the altarpiece, she said, overwhelmed her; and he noticed that her eyes invariably traveled to the empty panels each time she entered the room to see if there were any signs that he had begun to paint Eve, or the Virgin Mary, or the angel of the Annunciation. And he would tease her by promising that she could be present when he painted Adam.

"He's handsome, Michault de Caron, don't you think? There are plenty of ladies who would like to see him naked in front of them. You'll be the envy of Bruges."

Margarethe laughed.

When the summons finally came from Jacqueline he had just completed the figure of Adam. On one occasion Margarethe had decided that she *would* watch—through the partition of a screen; and afterwards she had blushed, but her eyes were bright. She had never seen a naked man, she said, and . . . she paused in some embarrassment . . . she kept wondering what it might be like to be looking at Jan. Margarethe gazed at him with those deep green eyes, and he kissed her.

"How long will you be away?" she had asked, quite breathless.

"I don't know," he had replied. "Perhaps a week. It's two days' ride. I'll be safe."

She had waved him goodbye from the town gate. He turned several times and she was still there, smaller and smaller, still waving. Jan loved her; he hated riding away.

It was a luminous evening gradually deepening into dusk. The bell was still ringing, closer now. Jan could not entirely understand the apprehension he felt approaching Jacqueline's fortress. All around him were tall dunes like waves rising between the dark pines, with occasional glimpses of the sea through a trough in the dunes. Then the wind tore a plume of sand from a ridge ahead of him, scattering it around him like snow; and in that instant Jan remembered the masked figure of the woman in the snow dressed as Jacqueline—with that cascade of black hair and eyes as large as the eyes painted on her mask, turned on him with an imperious glare. And the laughter of Hugo stifled by that look of contempt.

Why had she sent for him?

It was a portrait—only a portrait—he told himself. He was merely a painter of faces: figures and faces. They seemed to stand before him, those people he was painting. Before him and all around him. The duke. Jacqueline. Vyt. Bona. The Maid. (Why was she there? Would he paint her too?) Jan felt trapped in a crowd of faces; they were sweeping him along; he was at their mercy. They all wanted something from him. It was as if what he saw in the faces he painted was a truth which they could not see themselves; as if he were painting what they would become. That was what they needed: to see with his eyes.

A thrill of fear ran through Jan. Then he laughed. It was an absurd thought. He dismissed the faces around him and summoned up instead the face of Margarethe. She was smiling at him with those open eager lips. She was naked and he desired her. He could see the pale hair loose over her skin, and the deep shadow beneath her breasts. But as he approached her, suddenly she turned and walked away. Instead, standing before him was that masked, staring figure in the snow. The black raven.

The walls rose huge above him as a guard held back the gate for Jan to ride through. Goes was a small town, scarcely more than a village huddled between those formidable outer walls and the castle in the center to which he made his way. A plain chunk of a church overlooked a small square to his left, and Jan could see from the open belfry the solitary bell that he had heard from far across the marshes. It was still tolling, and above it on what seemed the flimsiest of platforms a pair of storks were preening and prodding at their nest. A flight of swifts sped screaming around and around the square against the darkening sky, then vanished over the walls of the castle.

The duchess was expecting him, said a voice as he entered: Jan could hardly see the man's face in the near-darkness of the castle gateway. He could hear the jangle of a distant bell. Then his horse was led away, and at the same moment a young page appeared. The boy bowed and indicated to Jan that he should accompany him. He found himself in a chill stone corridor lit by torches. Then there was another corridor. Not a soul appeared to be about in the castle and the only sound was the echo of his own boots as he followed the small figure in red moving between the torches. At the end of the corridor he noticed a large door, above which hung a shield painted with a coat of arms. Jan could make out a mailed fist and above it a bird with its wings outspread and a sword in its beak. Was it a raven? he wondered.

"The duchess is waiting for you," the boy said quietly as he reached for the handle of the door. He opened it, bowed, and stood back to let Jan enter.

He found himself in a spacious hall deep in shadow under its roof of ancient beams. Here and there along the stone walls torches lit up further shields painted with crests and mottoes in Latin; but the principal source of light came from the far end of the hall, where a fireplace blazed with logs that were almost as massive as the beams. Even from where Jan stood near the door he could feel its heat, and the brightness of the fire threw all around it into even heavier darkness.

The hall seemed empty, and for a moment or two he stood there hypnotized by the dance of the flames. There was no sound except the crackling of the wood. Then he began to walk slowly toward the fire, relishing the warmth on his face and hands after the chill of the evening wind from the sea. In the shadows Jan could just make out the same image of a bird with a sword in its beak carved in stone all around the fringes of the fire. But as he peered closer he gave a start, and his hand flew to the dagger in his belt. There was unmistakable movement in the darkness beyond the glare of the flames—and there it was again. Jan stepped back in a sweat of fear. A figure was emerging into the half-shadow. It was the figure of a woman. Jan could scarcely see her, but she must have been waiting there, watching him. He could see that she was dressed all in white, partly silhouetted now on the fringes of the firelight. She was tall and slender, and, even in the half-light, strikingly beautiful. To his amazement Jan saw that the white robe fitted her body like a delicate glove from the low bodice to the belted waist, hips, and thighs, before falling in a ripple of folds around her feet. Her neck and shoulders were quite bare and, as she approached, the firelight threw an amber sheen on the upper part of her breasts and cast a deep shadow between them. Jan gazed at her transfixed as if by an apparition. And then suddenly she turned her head a little toward the fire so that the light caught her features, and in that second Jan knew he was gazing at the very same face he had seen on that evening of the carnival in the falling snow.

It had been Jacqueline. And this was Jacqueline. He could see the same cascade of black hair. The majestic face, as if carved softly in white marble. And the extraordinary eyes—bright pools of darkness.

The eyes were gazing at him. He was speechless. He managed to collect his senses sufficiently to make a deep bow.

"Your ladyship," Jan heard himself say in more of a croak than a voice.

The reply was warm, surprisingly deep.

"You're very welcome, Jan," she said, and with that she gave him her hand. "Very welcome."

He kissed it, and perhaps held it a little longer than he should have. As he did so Jan found himself trying to believe that the cool hand in his had carried a sword, directed knights in battle, a hand that maybe had killed. He released it and she stepped back with a smile.

"I don't often invite strangers here," she went on. "But then of course you're not entirely a stranger."

She was looking at him with those dark, inquiring eyes. Was it possible that she recognized him from that one chance meeting? Jan wondered.

"But it's a pleasure," she added. "I'm alone here." Jan thought she emphasized the last remark slightly. "So I'm free to do whatever I want. And this evening I decided I would dress for you as I would like you to paint me."

She smiled again, and her lips as she smiled seemed to invite and to taunt at the same time.

"So we'll dine together, you and I."

Jan felt a wave of pleasure. He wondered if he had ever seen a more handsome face. The proud Roman nose. The high brow. Heavy eyelids. And those hooded eyes. She was younger than he had imagined, perhaps no more than his own age. Yet, he thought, there had been two marriages, battles, years of war; and still she was as young and beautiful as a goddess. Or Circe perhaps. "Dangerous," the duke had called her. "But you like a touch of danger," he had added.

Jan bowed a second time.

"Thank you," he said.

She laughed—a rich deep laugh. Again that inviting, taunting smile.

"You must not be too polite. This is not the court."

And for a second time she placed her hand on his forearm. Jan was aware of the scent of her body and the smoothness of her skin.

She was asking about his journey, talking more lightly now, but still with that deep voice that seemed to caress what it spoke of—just as she had touched his arm. Had he known, she asked, that she lived on an island? When the seas were high the causeway he had crossed could be dangerous. Throughout much of the winter she had been marooned here. Not entirely, Jan recalled to himself, thinking of the rider in the snow. He longed to ask her why she had been there: was it not a risk? He hoped he would have the chance to inquire. He would find it quiet here after Bruges, she went on. And after Portugal, she added. She wanted to know what it had been like in Lisbon, and so long at sea. As for herself she loved the sea, which was just as well, living in this place, was it not? She laughed again. She used to sail with her own navy, she explained. Again Jan was astonished, trying to imagine this goddess in white on board a warship.

"I had power in those days." Jacqueline's deep voice took on a hard note, and Jan could see the Roman features grow tense, almost arrogant. "Now I live in retreat—except for special visitors"; and she squeezed his forearm, gently. "I'm vain enough to enjoy that," she added, and the smile had returned. "I think we shall have much to say to each other."

She had walked over to a table that Jan had not noticed in the shadows close to the fire.

"I should have offered you some wine."

Jan's eyes caught the long slim curve of her back as she reached for a flask on the table. He could hear the delicate clink of glass and the sound of wine being poured.

At that moment the door opened and in the half-light Jan could make out the figure of an elderly man standing there. Jacqueline raised her head and called him over. He was carrying a small sheaf of papers, which he presented to her, saying something in a low voice which Jan did not catch. He saw her look gravely at the man, and nod. Jan noticed that he was holding writing materials in his other hand. She took a quill from him and he promptly fetched a second, smaller table from the shadows and placed it near the fire, then a chair, which he held while Jacqueline seated herself. For a minute or two she read the document in front of her before dipping the quill into the small phial of ink and writing something at the foot of the paper. Jan presumed it to be a signature. The elderly man took the document, dusted the signature meticulously, and with a slight bow walked in a stately fashion down the hall, closing the door behind him. Jacqueline rose from the table, handed Jan a glass of wine, and took one of her own. She took a sip of the wine and suddenly laughed.

"Can't you see he's an Englishman?" she said.

Jan must have looked surprised, for Jacqueline laughed again and explained.

"You knew of course that my last husband was an Englishman." Then her voice trailed off into a mocking recitation: "Humphrey, duke of Gloucester, brother of King Henry, hero of Agincourt, a great lecher and a perfect swine." Her face brightened again and the lovely eyes took on an amused glint. "When Humphrey left me for his trollop this gentleman left *him* for me. Not as a lover, you understand." She gave Jan a glance of mock outrage, then broke it with a smile. "All the same, I think I got the better bargain. He was the duke's valet at Agincourt. A fine man."

Then with scarcely a break, she went on.

"Speaking of lechers, I've just signed the banishment of one. That document," she explained, "it was one of the trustiest knights I had—at least, not so trusty—he raped one of my serving girls. Now he's forfeited his titles and his lands."

There was a pause. Jacqueline's face was grave and severe. Jan waited.

"A most chivalrous knight," she went on. "A champion of ladies in the lists. What nonsense it all is," she said vehemently, and then added wistfully, "All for the honor of love on the battlefield, and all brute lust in the sack. Such hypocrisy. Well, there's one who won't abuse a woman again in my lands."

Jan was astonished to hear her speak like this. Her mouth was set, the eyes downcast, nostrils tensed. Jan could feel the depth of scorn and anger in Jacqueline. An extraordinary lady, he thought. First the beauty, the serene vanity, the seductiveness, charm; now this moral fierceness and fury. Already he was beginning to draw that face in his mind.

"The worst is," she went on, and her face acquired a weary look, "I can't spare men like that. I'm unprotected enough. He'll go and join my enemies." She looked hard at Jan again. "And I have many enemies, Jan . . . as you well know."

As she delayed the last few words the faintest of smiles crept over her lips. Jan wondered if she was suspicious of him. How could she not be? he thought. He had an impulse to confess that the duke had only allowed him here on condition that Jan report back to him: then as he looked at the expression on her face he understood that she knew already. There were no innocent encounters in her world, and this made her warm response to him the more puzzling. *Was* it a response to him, or was he a shuttlecock between two combatants? Why had she summoned him here? "But you like a touch of danger," the duke had said.

Then her mood changed again. Her whole face appeared to relax, and her body regained that beguiling consciousness of itself which she had shown earlier. Again she laid her hand on his arm: there was silence for a few seconds as the hand lingered where it rested. Jan wanted to touch it, but did not dare.

Suddenly, with that knack of hers which Jan had already noticed of deflecting intimacy into the gentlest of taunts, she remarked how alluring it was to be with a man who spoke so little; this must be, she imagined, because he was a painter accustomed to observing and listening, and she found herself wondering—she said—what he must be thinking about her. She laughed, and Jan himself wondered what she might be thinking about him.

They dined together in a smaller room and by another fire: wild duck with quinces, pastries, apples, white cheese, dark wine. Servants brought dishes silently, and Jan could detect in their manner the respect they felt for her. There was no false subservience, no stiffness: Jacqueline addressed each of them by name, and to one she inquired about the health of his child. Jan could see the pleasure on the servant's face. Then they were alone. He was gazing at her in that slender white dress, her shoulders and neck exposed to the firelight and the caressing shadows. This was the duchess Jacqueline, Jan reminded himself, enemy of Burgundy, soldier, a "dangerous" woman. It was hard to comprehend. He had known her only a few hours. What would it be like to have known her a few days, months, years? Jan felt an extraordinary happiness.

From beyond the window as they dined by the firelight, he could just make out the regular thud and drag of the sea.

Jacqueline was ready for him punctually at the hour she had appointed. She was wearing the same dress as the previous evening—not that she liked to do this, she explained with that lovely deep laugh, but she wanted him to paint her like this. She wanted to be remembered as . . . Her smile completed the sentence.

The room where they stood looked out over the marshes and the water. The light was clear as crystal. Jan could already envisage the portrait of her, stately and beautiful in white, the window with the sky and the sea behind her. A portrait of Jacqueline of the lands of the sea. White skin. White dress.

Red tapestries on the wall. A vase with flowers. Stone columns between the windows. An expanse of blue and gray beyond. Air and light. And that wonderful face in silhouette against the sea. It had been before his eyes ever since they parted after dinner the previous night. She had rested her hand once more on his arm as she rose. For a second he had wondered if he should accompany her: but he could not, he thought. A lady such as she: he a mere painter. But she disturbed his sleep like a fire.

He was to paint the portrait entirely here in Goes, Jacqueline made it clear. Jan was relieved: this meant he would have to spend longer with her, would have to return a number of times. Besides—and she laughed as she said it—he could scarcely paint her portrait in Bruges, in the same room as his portrait of the duke. So she knew about that, Jan thought. Bona must have told her, or maybe someone else. He wondered who her other spies were.

It was thrilling to draw her. The touch of the silver point on paper was like touching her. The lips, nose, eyes, brow, shoulders, neck, breasts. She looked at him intently as he worked, and it seemed to Jan that her eyes were aware of precisely which detail he was drawing, and that her body responded to his touch with each line he drew.

For a while he worked silently, and she too was silent. The light carved her face, her expression far away, and he saw how that distant expression would be mirrored in the background of ocean and sky that he would give the portrait: a humming shell of space and far horizons.

After some time, when the ghost of her features had already taken possession of the paper in front of him, he noticed that she was gazing at him with curiosity, and he sensed there was a question on her lips. She had said nothing for perhaps an hour. The sun was high and streamed across her face.

"Do you see me as I am or as I was?" she asked in that low, appealing voice.

"I never knew you as you were," he replied, aware that it was a banal reply. He had been concentrating on drawing her, had answered almost without thinking. "Who were you?" he added. He wondered if his question was impudent.

She smiled, a sad and lovely smile: Jan remembered what the duke had said about Isabella telling him everything about her own life while he painted her.

"I must seem like a hermit to you here," she started. "And sometimes it does feel as though the world has banished me." There was a pause, and she looked away toward the window. "It's curious to think that my great-grandfather was a king." Jan knew this but it was strange to hear her say so. "The king of France. My grandfather was the duke of Burgundy. My father a count. I was twice a duchess through my two husbands." There was another pause. "Now I am the lady of a few islands. That's all."

With a minute correction of line Jan caught the petulant hardening of the upper lip.

"When my father died I was sixteen. I was his only child. When my mother held me, crying, she told me I now ruled more lands than I had ever seen. I think she expected me to be surprised, but I had known it already. Because I had no brother I was brought up to be my father's son and daughter. He never treated me as a frail thing. I rode better than most men. I could shoot. I could run. I could hunt. Oh, I read books and poems, sung, dreamed, gathered flowers, wondered about love: all those things. But I never thought of men as better than me. That was *his* doing." She paused for a moment, and Jan went on looking at her, not drawing any longer. "And then he died."

There was a look of grief on her face. Then she laughed: it was a mocking laugh.

"Suddenly all Holland, Hainault, and Zeeland were mine," she said, "for a little over a month." And she gave the same bitter laugh. "It was the duke of Burgundy who ended it—Duke Philip's father. John 'the Fearless' he was called, but he was frightened of me. He married me to his nephew, the duke of Brabant. His nephew and his slave." Her voice carried a sneer of contempt. "I found myself the slave of a slave, and I wasn't good at that." Again Jacqueline turned to gaze out over the sea. "And so I left him."

Jan had begun to shade Jacqueline's high cheekbones and the tired line of shadow beneath her eyes. Now he lowered the silver point. He wondered why she was telling him this. What was there about being drawn that compelled people to talk?

"Bona warned me that you painted more than you saw," she went on. This time the laugh was warm with that slightly mocking note again. "It's better that you hear it from me than from my enemies. While you're painting my portrait I'll tell you in stages how I've come to be here—then we'll see how much of what I've told you is visible in my face. That should test your skill."

She looked at him slightly awry. And as she did so Jan added a touch of the crinkle of amusement that lingered at the corners of her mouth.

"And so I left him," she repeated as if to remind herself where she had reached in her tale.

For three days Jacqueline came to sit for Jan in that sunlit room high above the sea. By the end of that time the drawing was finished in every detail, the silver lines as fine and taut as so many threads: she was alive on the paper. Furthermore, in Jan's mind the painted portrait he was now about to begin was already more than half complete, suffused with the light of that room in late spring and colored by the extraordinary tale she was unfolding before him. It was hard to reconcile those wild and terrible things she was telling him with this beguiling creature who would reappear to dine with him each evening, reaching out with cool fingers to touch his arm from time to time and awarding him that inviting, melting smile. Her half-exposed breast and bare shoulders would stir as if the firelight were stroking her with its hands.

"And so I left him," she had begun.

She was sixteen then, she said. A beautiful colt of a girl, all vigor and laughter. She had known simply by her own instincts what she wanted in a man, Jacqueline went on, and after only a few months she recognized with the conviction of a passionate creature that it was certainly not John, duke of Brabant. At first in her well-bred childishness she had imagined the fault must lie in her, and had tried inventive ways of approaching her husband. She undressed in front of him, reclined most fetchingly, touched him where he was supposed to respond: all to no avail. She wept, and after hating herself hated him more, especially when she discovered that his fair-haired page boy had achieved considerably more success than she had done.

Even then the high-spirited girl might not have left him—he was, after all, her master—had it not been for the manner in which Duke John proceeded to deal with her own inheritance. Slumped melancholically in his chair at his palace in Brussels, he entrusted the administration of Holland (of which Jacqueline was countess, no less) to her own uncle, the bishop of Liège, her late father's brother and a weaker man even than her own husband.

The day before she departed from him—fleeing with a handful of servants one summer dawn through the forests to her own duchy of Hainault—Jacqueline learned of a worse crime committed by her loathsome pederast of a husband. She discovered that the feckless bishop had been persuaded by John of Brabant to claim Holland as his own; furthermore to name as his heir none other than the duke of Burgundy, again without any reference to herself, the rightful heiress. The reason: this was revealed to the enraged Jacqueline's eyes by her faithful chamberlain—a chest heavy with gold and jewels, and (as a crowning insult to her) brought to Brussels from Dijon by two boys each as fair as Adonis. The duke of Burgundy had simply bribed him.

They took the quiet forest tracks to avoid detection. Jacqueline alternately wept and railed furiously against her husband. Her servants tried to comfort her but she was inconsolable: a storm of rage lay behind those huge dark eyes. Once in Hainault she delayed only long enough to dispatch an embassy to the Pope in Avignon, appealing for the marriage to be annulled. She remained untouched, she declared, even after six months of marriage; meanwhile her husband indulged in all the wantoness of Sodom and had sold her birthright for a chest of gold.

Before her husband could be roused from his sodomite bed to pursue her, Jacqueline equipped herself with what jewels and finery remained to her and, with a company of some fifty followers, fled to Calais, and thence to England, where a messenger rode with haste to announce her arrival to the court of the king. Jacqueline waited, her anger cooling slowly into an icy will to harness the power of England to her cause. But when the messenger returned it was with the news that the great King Henry of Lancaster, victor of Agincourt and conqueror of France, was dead. Her hopes seemed dead too.

The company proceeded slowly and disconsolately to London. As she rode by people stared at the young duchess with the sad, lovely face. News of her beauty proceeded her, and at the gates of London the party was met by an ambassador from the regent of England, Humphrey, duke of Gloucester, the late king's brother. The duke welcomed Jacqueline with all the ceremony due to a ruler, and it was the first time since her father's death that any man had greeted her as an equal. England was like a home in exile. And because she already knew what she wanted in a man Jacqueline saw in Humphrey of Gloucester all that she might ever hope for. She had never set eyes on a man so handsome or so gracious. There were banquets for her at which he paid her the most intimate of courtesies. They hunted together in the royal forests, the duke a dashing figure in red embroidered with the lion of England. They walked in the park of the palace on summer evenings, his words full of compliments, his voice so very manly. She fell in love; he became her first lover; and he married her.

And he became her true champion. Imagine her pride one autumn morning as she gazed around her from the foredeck of her ship and saw everywhere she looked a fleet carrying the English army to Calais, and next to her the man she loved in glorious armor, his eyes bright with confidence, his hand holding hers.

It was October—a day that sparkled like his sword—when Humphrey and Jacqueline led that great army from Calais and across Flanders into Hainault, Duke John's hopeless soldiers scattering before them like rabbits. Hainault was hers again, and next it was the turn of Holland to bow the knee.

She had fled in misery and anger. Now she had returned in triumph and in love.

Jan worked and listened, stirred by the tale Jacqueline was unfolding. The woman whose face was emerging into life on the paper before him would always be as he perceived her now. She would decay, as he would, yet his portrait would bestow upon her a kind of immortality. This, he knew, was what she was asking him—perhaps he was the only man capable of rendering her such a service; and in this lay his own pride in the skill of his hand and of his eye. Jan experienced a sensation of gratification and power. To listen to her history as he portrayed her was to portray her as history. No other painter, he believed, had ever done this—imbued the image he was creating with a sense of its own past and its own future.

Jan wondered how the tale would progress, and when the storm would break. For the moment the horizons were bright.

The long May evenings stretched out across the lands of the sea—across a thousand waterways and twenty thousand mill sails turning. To the southward spread Flanders, Hainault, Artois, with never a hill to ruffle the carpet of green embroidered now with the blossom of spring. The lands of Burgundy and the lands of France merged imperceptibly somewhere in that landscape of forest and river; and it was here amid this garden of springtime that at this moment the army of the duke of Burgundy was on the move southward—from Lille, past Douai, Cambrai, St.-Quentin, Noyon, and steadily southwest along the bank of the river Oise. At Cambrai, Duke Philip, in his splendor of black and ermine, summoned Enguerrand de Monstrelet—his faithful chronicler—to accompany him. Soon there would be great matters of history to be recorded, and Monsieur Monstrelet of Cambrai must be there to witness them and to note each triumph of the glorious dukedom. Within a day now the Burgundians, led by their captain, Jehan de Luxembourg, would have the city of Compiègne within the range of their cannon. Philip himself, together with the duchess Isabella and a company of knights of the Golden Fleece, halted and prepared their proud camp close to the banks of the Oise; and in the morning they stood watching as Jehan de Luxembourg led the army cautiously toward the city where the Maid had raised the fleur-de-lis of France. Before long they would see it fluttering over Compiègne.

The air seemed to Philip almost too sweet for a sword to spill the blood of France. But there was a smile of triumph on his face. Fresh in his memory lay his victory over Jacqueline. Before long he would crush the Maid, he said to Monstrelet standing beside him. A lesser women, he added.

And the meticulous chronicler noticed a look almost of regret over the duke's face as he said it. Jacqueline had been the bravest of all tigresses.

Her champion, her love, her husband—Humphrey of Gloucester—brought Jacqueline all she had ever wished. Her eyes never left him: she followed him in his glittering armor, she accompanied him hunting, she took him naked to her bed. It seemed to Jacqueline that her happiness could never end.

Then, one day, word came to her of an army moving into Hainault to oppose him. It was not her ex-husband who led it, but his brother, the lord of St. Pol, whom she had known as a quiet, treacherous man. Her suspicions were well founded: Jacqueline never saw the chests of gold, but she knew that the man who had paid for his army, and paid for St. Pol to lead it, was Philip, duke of Burgundy, son of John the Fearless. Jacqueline watched with awe as her champion and lover rode out at the head of the English army to do battle on that bright winter morning: but in the evening, to her grief, Humphrey returned amid the rabble of that army. He said nothing to her, barely looked at her. It had not been so much a defeat as a disarray, she learned. The English had struck at the ranks of the enemy without plan or preparation, so confident was Humphrey that he would sweep them aside as he had the army of her former husband; but St. Pol had kept his finest knights waiting out of sight in the forests on either side of the English advance, and when Humphrey rode with his own knights across the open battlefield they found themselves caught on all sides, trapped in the muddy ground. It was strange, Jacqueline heard, that the duke who had witnessed the French knights destroying themselves in precisely this fashion at Agincourt should have fallen for the same trap. Thanks to the English bowmen, who had come to Humphrey's aid and forced back the Burgundian knights, there was no massacre. But there was no honor either: the men Jacqueline spoke to looked away, ill at ease. The English lords had just seemed to lose heart for the fight, as if it were not their fight, some said. They simply dispersed—shamefully, others added. Behind their uneasy expressions Jacqueline suspected there was something she did not know. No one would tell her. And they departed as quickly as they could.

Humphrey never came to her that night. Jacqueline was heartbroken: she could never have believed he would abandon her—her knight, her true lover, champion. In the morning she learned of a truce with the duke of Burgundy. And still Humphrey never appeared to her. It was Gloucester's valet who visited her one day as she sat alone. He pledged his loyalty to her, he said; then he told her of a letter that her husband had received the evening before the battle. It was from his brother the duke of Bedford, regent of France since the death of King Henry. Bedford was perturbed, the letter said, that an English army should be fighting the forces of Burgundy who were their allies. Humphrey should make his peace and return to England. Immediately after the battle a second letter had reached him—from the duke of Burgundy, offering terms for a truce. These were that his trusted "ally" Humphrey of Gloucester would be given safe-conduct to Calais, along with the entire English army, on the condition that he abandon his support of Jacqueline's claims to Hainault and Holland. If Humphrey should choose to disagree to these terms, continued the letter, then a Burgundian army led by that fine captain Jehan de Luxembourg would assist Jacqueline's uncle, the regent of Holland, and the lord of St. Pol to drive the English to the sea. The letter was accompanied, vouched the valet, by the gift of a gold and ruby ring of great price as a token of Burgundian respect for the noble English house of Lancaster.

Jacqueline was dumbfounded. She determined that she would see her husband. The valet declined to accompany her: he had left the duke's service out of shame, he said. Jacqueline did not know the full reason for the man's shame until late that evening when she angrily swept aside the English guards and flung open the door of Humphrey's room. There on the marriage bed lay two naked figures intertwined: her husband

and a lady with long golden hair into which Humphrey's face was buried. Jacqueline thought she would die.

She never saw him again. From that moment it was as if she had lost everything in which she had ever believed. Humphrey fled to England with his golden-haired mistress: she had been Jacqueline's own lady-in-waiting, Eleanor Cobham, beautiful as a rose. A plucked rose.

Now she was alone with only the remnants of an army to protect her: a prisoner in her own lands, besieged in her own capital of Mons. Beyond the walls of the city the army of Burgundy waited. She vowed to die rather than surrender. Then one day a messenger reached her in her solitary room high in the ducal palace: her uncle, whom her first husband had made regent of Holland without her consent, had been found murdered. He had been a weak man but a devout man, and beside his body lay a prayer book, its pages drenched in poison. The prayer book had been a gift from the duke of Burgundy, it was said. Her late uncle, she also learned from the messenger, had made the duke the sole heir to his estates. Philip of Burgundy was now the ruler of Holland.

Jacqueline did not know she had so much anger in her. She had lost her husband, she had lost her dukedom, but she had not lost her strength of will. The siege had lasted four months. Before her lay an ultimatum from Jehan de Luxembourg: if she surrendered she would be allowed to return unmolested to Zeeland, though without an army. She must renounce her claims to Hainault and to Holland. That night Jacqueline called her maid and together they dressed her as a boy page. She knew the quiet ways out of the city, and by dawn she was riding through the forests accompanied only by the cry of wolves. She made for Antwerp, where she raised a guard of soldiers; then for Holland, where she raised an army. The people rallied to her—the lady they had known as a beautiful girl was now a beautiful lady in armor, with eyes that burned black with anger. And on her ensign flew the image of a raven, black with revenge.

People marveled at her courage and her skill. The Burgundians marched against her, and she routed them by the banks of the Rhine at Alphen; her own sword cut down Jehan de

Luxembourg's lieutenant as he rode at her laughing. He lay on the frozen ground, his face cut almost into two where the laugh had turned to blood.

For more than two years Jacqueline's army held the Burgundians at bay. There was not an ally who did not receive the most bountiful gifts from Duke Philip—gold, jewels, the most beautiful books from Limbourg, lace and silks from Venice; where there were unmarried sons he made the most eligible heiresses available to them if they chose; daughters received suitors with titles and lands far above their expectations. And if these methods did not weaken support for Jacqueline, then the duke was adept at more vivid kinds of persuasion. The lord of Zwolle's lands suffered unaccountable fires at harvesttime, relatives of the bishop of Leiden encountered a series of robberies in the street in broad daylight, the countess of Friesland was raped—it was said by a party of bandits, but the men seen hanging from the town gibbet in Leeuwarden were not thought to be those who committed the crime.

Jacqueline fought on, year after year. Gradually her small army, weakened by defection and disease, was pressed back by the forces of Jehan de Luxembourg until only one stronghold on the mainland remained in her hands. And here at Zevenbergen, throughout the bitter winter of 1426, she held out.

There was scarcely a rat uneaten that winter, and more people died than rats.

The careful glazes of ocher and white, carmine and blue, which Jan was applying to the primed surface of the panel were more subtle and more rich than the fine lines of silver he had employed for the preliminary drawing. Now he could work on the portrait even when Jacqueline was absent, and the sunlit room high over the sea was quiet. Perhaps it was no accident that he should be concerning himself more closely with the shadows of her face: her story had grown dark with shadow. It was hard to believe that those bitter events she had recounted, her face taut with feeling, were little more than three years ago. She had not finished, she said; there was more.

Jan rose at dawn: a castle watchman saw to it that the town gate was opened for him, and he walked for an hour along the sea. The shock of meeting Jacqueline had calmed; what remained was the sensation of having encountered a woman whose qualities were as deep and rich as a mine: they dazzled when brought to the light. Her anger. Her remorse. Courage. Womanliness. None of the tragedies she described to him had impaired her intoxicating femininity. He felt enchanted. There was no question of loving her: his heart was with Margarethe, and in any case how could a man like himself love someone so out of reach? At the same time Jacqueline could appear so beguilingly accessible in that slender white dress, her bosom partly exposed, her hand on his arm, huge eyes looking at him, mouth in the most inviting of smiles. One evening her hand had lingered even longer on his arm, and there was the slightest pressure of soft fingers. He had looked at her, and at that moment if her smile had said yes he knew he would have accompanied her. But the eyes were suddenly downcast and the face sad.

Another day she asked teasingly about the women he knew. Were they beautiful? Were they as beautiful as she? she added; and there was such an awareness of her own body as she said it that Jan felt his heart beat loud enough, he felt sure, for her to hear, and for a while he could think of nothing he desired more than to possess her. Perhaps, he thought later when he was alone, she wanted that too, wanted him to step lightly across all those barriers as though they did not exist, and make love to her; and yet there was one barrier he was sure she would never cross, because if she loved she would love totally, and something in her face told him she would be destroyed by it. Jan did not know what had stirred that premonition: he wondered if he would ever know.

Jan gazed back across the long curve of the bay. Tiny plovers were scuttling along the ripple of the tide. A flock of sandpipers swept past him low over the water, then turned on the wing all together as if at an unseen signal, and as they turned they flashed silver in the early sunlight before turning once again and becoming a moving cluster of black dots, growing fainter as they skimmed toward the castle beyond the bay.

There rose the castle of Jacqueline. Jan could just make out the emblem of the black raven fluttering above the lone tower.

It was the twentieth of May. An hour after dawn.

Above the castle of Compiègne on that same morning shone the fleur-de-lis of France. The mounted figure of a young woman in full armor was riding on a dapple-gray horse into the city across the lowered drawbridge. By her side was her standard-bearer, the image of Christ fluttering above, hand raised in judgment. With her rode a party of soldiers who had just accompanied the Maid on one of those surprise sorties on the enemy camp which were the mark of her presence among the armies of France. They were like a goad, and invariably they drew blood. But this time the Burgundians were watching for her, and she had been compelled to retreat swiftly.

Soon the Maid would report to her fellow commanders the news which a messenger from Jehan de Luxembourg was already hastening to report to the duke of Burgundy at his camp upstream—namely, that the city of Compiègne was now under siege.

Throughout that savage winter of the siege of Zevenbergen, Jacqueline continued to believe that she could win. If the bastion could hold out until the spring the army of Duke Philip would have to disperse. There was land to be tilled, crops planted, boats, plows, roofs, nets to be mended. The cost to Duke Philip of so large an army for so long was one he would be loath to pay. In the spring the people of Holland would rally round their duchess: they detested the "foreigner" from Burgundy, from the soft winelands of the south, French-speaking. Jacqueline gazed from her high window over the frozen army encamped below the walls, and prayed for courage; prayed that the soul of Humphrey of Gloucester would roast in hell; prayed that his trollop would die of the palsy or the plague. Jacqueline's fierce jealousy was stoked by the cold and starvation of that helpless winter. Her knight had betrayed her for a golden girl with a pretty laugh. Courage. She vowed she would not give in. Over and over again she told herself that it was she who was in the right, and that there were others—her own people—who stood behind her.

The shock came, not from Philip's army, but from a delegation of burgesses and merchants admitted to her presence one morning. They stood before her in the cold damp room she had scarcely left for three months: their breath veiled their uneasy faces; their eyes avoided hers. There was betrayal in the slump of their gait. They had come to tell her, they said, that they had agreed to favor the duke of Burgundy as ruler of Holland rather than herself. Yes, she had some claims, they conceded, and they expressed fulsome respect for her as a lady: but she was nonetheless . . . a lady. They hesitated as they said it, and looked away unable to meet the fury of her glare.

There was silence for a few moments.

"I am a woman, and more of a man than any of you," she spat; but they only looked more awkward, their faces stubborn.

Jacqueline knew that there was more than this: she seized the spokesman of the party by the throat with one hand, and grasped his hair with the other.

"Tell me. Tell me."

The terrified man squirmed and spluttered pitifully until Jacqueline felled him with a blow in the groin from her knee. The others drew back in horror. No one dared lay a hand on her. She rushed at the next man who doubled up in terror, his hands darting between face and his genitals.

Then he told. It was trade, he said. The duke had promised terms. Very favorable terms. They could market their wares freely throughout Flanders, Hainault, Artois, Brabant, Limbourg. No taxes.

So the moneymen had betrayed her. She had been sold for a cargo of cheese and a barrel of fish.

Jacqueline dismissed them with a nod. She gazed out over her lands that were no longer her lands. Clean, snow-white fields soiled by the treachery of the house of Burgundy. She threw open the window and felt the sting of frost on her face. She tore off her dress and bared herself to the knife of winter, hands clasped below her breast.

"I am a woman," she cried. "And I am beautiful. There is not one man in that army who would not desire me, flatter me, promise to honor me, long for these arms around them and these breasts against their breast. And there is not one man among you who would not betray me." And she wept.

Her lady-in-waiting found her half conscious, her face frozen with tears. They carried Jacqueline to her bed and for many days they feared for her life. After the shivering came the heat—the fever, the delirium. Head turning fretfully on the pillow, she talked, but always to those who were not there. To her father—and her voice was gentle and sweet, as a little girl, and her maids sobbed when they heard her. And she talked to Humphrey as her first lover; her face grew radiant and her body moved as if he were caressing her. "Sweet love," she kept repeating: "take me." Then she would cry—a long, long cry of such weariness trailing into a silence so complete that the maids bent forward fearfully to hear if she was still breathing.

Then one day her face grew calm and her eyes seemed to take in the room and those attending on her. Suddenly she looked toward the window and gave a flicker of a smile, a weak hand pointing.

"A swallow," she murmured in a half-whisper. "It is spring."

A few days later she was strong enough to sit in her chair, and all day she scarcely took her eyes off the window, as if exploring the sky.

"Tell me, what should I do?" she asked her valet.

There was a long pause: then the old man told her what had occurred during the weeks she had been ill. He told her as gently as he could. Her first husband, the duke of Brabant, was dead. The lord of St. Pol, his brother, had succeeded him. The valet paused again before telling her the sequel—that St. Pol had made Philip of Burgundy his heir.

Jacqueline seemed hardly to move a muscle. It was as if she knew already. Nor did she flinch when he told her the remainder. That Philip had taken over Holland and Hainault: only Zeeland was now left to her. That Philip, aided by the duke of Bedford, Humphrey's brother, had persuaded Pope Martin in Rome to rule that Jacqueline's marriage of John of Brabant had been the only valid one. The ruling of the Pope in Avignon was disregarded. In other words, her marriage to Duke Humphrey had never officially existed.

Still Jacqueline's pallid face remained unmoved. Only when her valet informed her that Duke Humphrey intended to marry her former lady-in-waiting, Eleanor Cobham, did she raise her eyes, and the valet saw that they swam with tears.

"Leave me alone now," she whispered.

Jacqueline surrendered to Philip of Burgundy on the eleventh of April 1427. She was permitted to return to the castle of Goes amid the few lands that were still hers. The lands of the sea. Zeeland. It was more than a year before Philip summoned her to the city of Delft and compelled her to sign a treaty recognizing Philip's possession of almost all her former lands. She would be allowed to keep the title of countess, he assured her, but she must recognize him as her heir to those lands remaining to her.

There was a final indignity. The chancellor of Burgundy, Nicolas Rolin, read it out to her in the great hall where Philip and his lords were assembled on that day in July 1428. "If the countess Jacqueline marry again"—ran the decree—"without the consent of Philip, duke of Burgundy, and of the estates of the three lands of Holland, Hainault, and Zeeland, or of any one of them, her subjects shall withdraw their obedience to her and give allegiance instead to Duke Philip."

The pen Jacqueline was handed by the chancellor felt heavier than any sword she had raised against Burgundy. After she had signed she gazed down the hall at the ranks of lords assembled before her in their composure and their solemnity; then without even a glance at Duke Philip she made her way out of that place, piercing each of them as she passed with a dark eye and a thin smile of contempt. And there was not one of them who did not lower his gaze.

How well Jan knew that piercing look. As she said it he again recalled his first encounter with Jacqueline in the lamplight and the swirling snow as she rode by. He could imagine the courtiers of Burgundy shriveling beneath her stare. "I am a woman," she had said, "and more of a man than any of you."

"You may understand now, Jan, why the duke was so anxious to marry a princess."

Jacqueline had risen and was standing with her back to the window, looking at him. It was nearly midday. Jan put down his brush as she spoke. The painted portrait was half finished and already very different from the silverpoint drawing by his side. The triumphant Jacqueline had become a beautiful, tragic figure with downcast eyes—proud, unyielding, unhumiliated in defeat. Jan waited for her to continue.

"You see," she went on, turning her lovely head into the sunlight, "Philip now possessed all the Low Countries as well as Burgundy. It was like a kingdom. He was like a king. And kings marry princesses. And that's where you entered."

She looked at Jan and smiled. It was as though she had been describing part of his own life he did not know was there; as though she held his brushes and were painting him. It was true, what she had said. In July 1428 Jacqueline had signed away her birthright. Less than two years ago. It had been in the autumn of that same year when Jan had set sail for Portugal to make a portrait of the princess Isabella. And he had never known any of this, only that there was a war in Holland —a long, bitter war. He had been far away, working for the duke in Lille, then in Bruges. Distant echoes of it had reached him, and how different they had sounded from the tale she had been telling him.

"So the duke won his kingdom and his princess," she was saying. "And the one who paid the price was me."

Again she was gazing at him, but there was no smile now. Then she raised one hand to her bare shoulder and gently slid it across her collarbone and deep neck until her fingers rested against the curve of her breasts. The hand rose and fell as she breathed, and still she gazed at him.

"I lost my husband, my lands, my happiness. I even lost the right to be a woman." As she spoke her fingers closed over her breast and she lowered her eyes as if in shame. "I lost the right to take a man of my choice. My father would have died to defend that. No one else did."

Jan did not see her again until that evening.

"You must leave tomorrow. I have many things to attend

to," she said quietly, her hand again pressed against his forearm, her dark eyes gleaming in the firelight. She was her enigmatic self once more.

Jan felt a pang of sadness. Jacqueline seemed to read it in his face, for she placed her other hand in his and smiled, her eyes searching his face.

"But you'll come back. I've made sure the portrait is unfinished." She laughed, and again the firelight caught her lovely face and burnished her bare shoulder and breast. Jan longed to touch her. "In the summer here," she added, "we can walk along the sea. I love the sea: it's almost all I have. And I'll tell you about your good duke." Again she gave a laugh, but it was hollow with scorn. "And what will you tell *him* about me?"

Jan looked at her for a moment. She felt very close.

"If I was truthful I should tell him that I was captivated by you."

Her expression did not change, but Jan heard her let out a deep breath. When she got up to leave she led him through a small door, and Jan found himself in a small twilit garden. He could make out a circular pool with rushes and irises rising from the water, and a stone sundial between twin trees clipped into the shape of two birds facing one another. The sky was deep violet above the black walls of the castle, and there was not a sound.

"This is my place of peace," she said, still gripping him by the arm. "Where I am most happy. And where I dream."

With that she turned to face him, and raising her head, leaned forward and kissed him on the mouth. A long kiss, lips a little parted. He drew her to him and could feel her whole body against his. Then, just as suddenly, he felt her draw back, and as she did so she took his hands and placed them on her breast.

"Thank you" was all she said, and her voice was as soft as dark water. He kissed her again, and she held him close against her.

"You must go," she whispered.

They parted at the door of the castle and he watched her make her way down the stone corridor between the flickering lamps, her hair glistening black where the light fell.

Jan knew it was an adventure of the heart that he would never make, and neither would she. He felt numb, and sad, yet at the same time strangely fulfilled, almost relieved. He understood, as she did, what lay there to be loved and taken; and he understood, as she did, what dangers and what pain they would embrace, would never embrace. In his room he closed his eyes and listened to the sea. A gentle swish and murmur on the shore. The ocean soft as sleep moving only as a dreamer breathes. And yet such a bed of storms. He could not set a frail craft on that water.

Jan slept peacefully.

Jacqueline accompanied him some distance from the town gate the following morning—a figure of majesty in her flowing surcoat and bejeweled headdress, riding beside him along that lone dike between marsh and sea. There was no word of the intimacy of the previous evening, only an air of warmth about the silence as they rode and the richness of her smile as she halted after a few miles and bade him goodbye. This time Jan reached out his hand to touch *her* arm, and her own hand closed over it. From the look that passed between them you might have believed them to be lovers; and in a sense, Jan reflected, they were. She looked back just once, and seemed to hesitate, as if she had forgotten to say something. Jan hoped she would return: instead she wheeled her horse and broke into a gallop. He watched the figure silhouetted against the sea recede into a tiny moving shape, and felt suddenly alone. All around him lay marsh and scattered seabirds: not a living soul. She would send word, she had said, for his return. "Before the paint is too dry," she had added with her irresistible laugh. He had wanted to kiss her again then.

There were many things on Jan's mind during that journey home, and they appeared to him with puzzling extremes of clarity and confusion, not at all as he expected. His feelings for Jacqueline had swept him along like a storm: in other circumstances he could imagine himself devoting his life to such a woman, serenading her, adoring her, never wishing to leave her. But those were not the circumstances, and much to his surprise Jan felt the relationship to be complete as it was— complete and separate. He had imagined, with some dread and some guilt, that the image of Margarethe might grow blurred and pale in his mind. Far from it: he longed to see her and hold her. He would tell her about Jacqueline: she would be jealous but she would have him whole, and she would know that. There were kinds of loving. There was love for the living and love for some kind of dream of heaven; and Jan was a man of this earth.

Of this he was quite sure. He would marry Margarethe.

About the duke he was no longer sure at all. Over and again on his journey Jan placed side by side in his mind the two faces of Philip: the one he had drawn and was shortly to paint, and the one painted for him by Jacqueline's words. How could they be the same man? He recalled the duke's warmth to him, his kindness of chivalry and love, his splendor. This could not be the man who robbed Jacqueline of her inheritance, who bribed and flattered, who denied her even the right to marry without his own consent.

Jan was deep in thought as he rode through the spring woodlands of northern Flanders—in an hour he would be in Atwerp at the inn where he had stayed more than a week earlier, and already the trees seemed richer, greener, heavier. He found himself trying to see Jacqueline as the duke saw her. Supposing she was indeed a dangerous woman. Was it not true that her flight to England and marriage to Humphrey of Gloucester were a threat to Burgundy? After all, Jacqueline had been heir to Hainault, Brabant, Holland, and Zeeland. Such wealth. And yet she was the duke's vassal. And supposing Humphrey never loved her, but only wanted her so that he could claim all those lands for himself—for England. An ally but nonetheless a foreign country. How could he have done other than he did? Jacqueline—his own cousin—was the price *he* had to pay; otherwise the greater price would have been Burgundy itself, that vision of a great land stretching from the Alps to the sea.

And yet . . . what she had told him could scarcely be untrue. Jacqueline *had* been married against her will to a pederast for nothing other than Philip's personal gain. She *had* fallen in love with Humphrey of Gloucester and had married him. She *had* been betrayed, deprived of her rightful lands, besieged, defeated, forbidden to marry again without the duke's consent. These facts could not be denied.

So what, Jan wondered, might be her motive for using her charms to win him over? He a mere painter, albeit the duke's court painter, yet a painter only, with no power, no influence, position, wealth. How could he, Jan, damage the duke of Burgundy?

Or was it, maybe, none of these things at all? Might it not be that this lone and loveless woman simply grasped for a moment at a man who would listen attentively to her grief while he painted her, who affirmed to her with his brush and with his eyes that she was still beautiful, still capable of desire and of arousing desire? But oh, Jan reflected, how much more than all these little motives she was. A great lady, Bona had said. She seemed to Jan like someone the gods had sent from Olympus to rule the lands of the sea.

It was amid this turmoil of thoughts that Jan rode out of Antwerp the following morning. Only gradually did he set himself at a calm distance from Jacqueline. He would be in Ghent by midday, in Bruges by evening. He would be in his house in the street of the Golden Hand. He would see Margarethe, the lovely Margarethe.

It was a warm, windless afternoon as he followed the familiar riverbank westward toward Bruges. Ducks rose noisily from the water as he passed. A pair of swans were nesting at the very tip of an island, prodding the twigs around them and gazing aggressively at him as he rode by. Before long he could hear the sounds of bells. So many bells, even though it was not Sunday. Could it be that the duke had returned? He listened to the clamor of sound growing louder. Jan could see the distant ramparts now, with the mill sails turning: and the broad city gates rising above the walls between the mills. Every bell in the city must be ringing, he thought. And then beneath the bells he heard another sound, more indistinct, like the roaring of a wind rising and falling. It was the sound of human voices, thousands of them. They were cheering, shouting, singing.

At the city gate he halted. What was the sound, what was happening? he asked the guard. The man looked at him and grinned. He looked flushed with beer and waved an arm extravagantly in no particular direction.

"The Maid," he called out hoarsely. "The Maid. She's taken!"

Chapter ♦ Five

The news spread like a fire in the wind.

Across the green carpet of Europe during those early summer days messengers rode from Compiègne reporting the capture of the Maid—to the winelands of southern Burgundy, the perched castles of the Loire, the northern lands of the sea, to Dijon, Toulouse, Reims, Rouen, Paris, London, Madrid, Rome.

So she was only a girl after all, people said, who had the temerity to wear men's clothing and men's armor. In the end the deception had failed her; she fell like any other weak mortal; the duke of Burgundy was once again too strong. At the same time there were more astute listeners who remarked that if Joan was a mere girl, then why was joy so unbounded, why did everyone talk of her, why was her capture such a prize? And why did France weep?

One question was on everyone's lips—what was to be done with her?

Joan's captor, Jehan de Luxembourg, was nothing if not a good soldier. The captain of the duke's army scarcely left the house where she was guarded day or night. He gazed at her as though she might vanish if he averted his eyes: he did not believe the story of her divine voices, but good soldiers do not take risks, and from time to time he would glance around him —in that simple house outside Compiègne—as if suspicious of some unnatural interference. She seemed to him such an ordinary girl, so young, almost beautiful in spite of the clothing and the cropped hair, and with a manner that appeared mild until he noticed the hard eyes and the tautness of the mouth. The gold-and-scarlet surcoat by which she had been dragged from her horse suggested to Luxembourg that she might not be so totally immune to human vanities after all. But she would

105

not look at him. He spoke to her a number of times, as gently as the tough old soldier knew how; he could not help but feel sorry for her. But she would not respond: only once did she turn an angry glare on him and said—more to herself than to him—that she had been betrayed by the Burgundians. Luxembourg did not understand what she might mean. Then after a few days something happened which surprised and affected him. He had returned from a brief visit to the duke to find Joan quivering with fury. When he questioned her she thrust a finger toward one of the men guarding her. The man looked awkward and sniggered. He had tried to assault her, she said; to tear off her clothes. She found difficulty in saying it. Luxembourg was furious and had the guard publicly whipped until he bled. Any man laying a hand on Joan in the future would be hanged, he announced in front of her. She was a woman, and a soldier, and she should be honored as such.

The look Joan gave him was haughty, but there was curiosity in that face, and Luxembourg was surprised to find himself moved. From that moment he began to feel strangely protective toward his captive, responsible for her almost as an equal. Still she would not talk to him but the hostility had softened. Whatever was to be done with Joan, the duke's captain determined to do his best to see that she was treated with respect.

The question of what to do with Joan was in the forefront of the duke's mind. As soon as he heard the news of her capture he hastened to the Burgundian camp to see Jehan de Luxembourg, and prepared himself to meet the Maid just as soon as he felt clear in his mind what he intended to ask her and what he intended to tell her.

These matters were less straightforward than he had imagined. She was no ordinary prisoner. Already there had been approaches from the English—the duke of Bedford—suggesting that Joan be handed over to them. The letter had been almost casual in tone, from which Philip was shrewd enough to detect an intense irritation that it was not the English who had captured her, as well as an awareness of precisely how much money they might have to pay him if he did agree to hand Joan over. He would consider it very carefully.

Then there had been approaches from the Church Inquisitor—not so much a request as a demand that the Maid, "vehemently suspect of several crimes smacking of heresy," should be brought to trial. In this Philip detected the loathsome hand of the bishop of Beauvais, whom the wars had virtually reduced to being a bishop without a diocese, and who sorely needed an opportunity to retrieve some authority. A trial of so notorious a figure as Joan, with himself presiding, would gain him the self-esteem he sought if not the glory he sought more —though Philip found himself confused as to what the charges could be. He was not a man who had found much time for defining heresies: indeed he was not a man who found much time for the Church, as his own chaplain, Guillaume Gilastre, had sadly commented. Let the Church abide by its own rules: he would abide by his.

Flickers of evening campfires lit up the dusk.

The duke would not see her tonight, he decided. Joan was the captive he wanted, yet there was much on his mind and doubts ruffled his thoughts. He even found himself wondering why he was fighting this war—which could actually win him little except the humiliation of the French and the greater gain of the English. Philip could see nothing appealing in either. It had begun as a war of revenge against Charles of France for the murder of his father on the bridge at Montereau. The shock and pain of that loss to him as a young man had fired his blood, his hatred of Charles, his determination to crush France. But that was now more than ten years ago, and much had happened. Two things above all rested uncomfortably in his mind. The alliance with the English felt unnatural to him in every respect but one: it brought him money—trade with England, gold for the splendors of his own court, gold for his battles against Jacqueline to win the Low Countries for Burgundy: nothing else. Then there was the scar of that murder. He had loved his father blindly, beyond reason: how painful it had been to understand that the murder had been in retaliation for another murder—that his own father had been responsible for the killing of the royal favorite, Louis of Orléans. Philip himself had been a mere child then: he had known nothing of it. Now it troubled him.

This war seemed a hollow thing to be fighting. But for the moment there was the question of the Maid. What should he do with her?

"My lord Duke." Jehan de Luxembourg was surprised to come across him alone in the half-dark, just standing there staring out over the landscape of France and the long stretch of the river. "You wished to see the Maid."

Philip turned to look at the scarred, weathered face even more roughened by the firelight—a face he had relied on for so many years.

"Not tonight."

In Lille, Isabella heard the news from her lady-in-waiting Louise.

As usual, the duchess was walking alone in the park of the palace, where she was free of the suffocating attentions of the ducal court. It was evening, and Isabella was watching a pair of swans proudly escorting their brown balls of young across the lake between the water lilies, one parent at the front like the prow of a ship, the other at the stern. Isabella was amused to realize how regularly her attention was drawn to such scenes of motherhood: even young sparrows caught her attention. She could not help wondering if the child she was carrying would be the son her husband craved for.

Louise blew down the path toward her like a blossom of summer. Prettier than ever, Isabella thought, aware that her own body no longer had the girl's shapeliness. Not that it had ever been much of a match. She could not help feeling a twinge of envy: what was more, Isabella was sure from the radiance of Louise as she stopped breathless before her that she had been making love. The girl never spoke about her lovers—only about love, as if it were a disembodied thing, a delicacy you tasted when you felt hunger for it. Isabella wondered whom she favored with that beauty and those lovely limbs. With her own husband away, and so often away, Isabella felt ugly and cast off, a mere womb waiting to breed.

"Where have you been?" Isabella realized as she said it that her voice was hard and admonitory.

Louise either did not notice or did not care. But the way

she laughed confirmed Isabella's view of what she had been up to.

"Have you heard, your ladyship?" the girl asked. And seeing the face of the duchess register only puzzlement, she went on: "The Maid is captured. At Compiègne. Yesterday."

Isabella did not understand why she felt a sense of shock. Anger almost. She became aware of the child moving inside her. And she thought of the Maid, the same age as this radiant creature standing before her in silks and velvet and her body warm from love, but instead a soldier in men's clothes and armor, in prison perhaps, her own body never given to anyone and maybe never would be; no lover, no children, only her voices and her God and her pure cause.

"Where is the duke now?" she asked.

"At Compiègne," Louise replied, "with the lord of Luxembourg."

"And who else?"

Even as she said it Isabella could not understand what had made her do so. It had slipped out in a spark of jealousy—something that had lain deep in her mind for many months without her fully realizing it. Perhaps it was those half-heard stories of the women Philip had known; the averted glances; the doors suddenly closing; the distant laughter; Philip's ever-increasing absences. All the same she was horrified to have exposed her feelings so nakedly to Louise, and she heard herself mumble something about the foolish fears aroused by pregnancy. And as she did so Isabella noticed that Louise was blushing; and in that moment she was convinced that the duke had been this girl's lover.

Isabella burst into tears. Louise placed her arms around her, but she shrugged her away.

"My ladyship, what is it? What has upset you?"

There was such pain in her that Isabella sought the only possible fragment of relief, which was to ask the question hurting her most.

"Louise, has the duke made love to you?"

The girl's face took on a look of horror: in her misery Isabella could not tell whether it was guilt, or embarrassment, or disbelief. It was such a young face, how could you tell? As well look at a peach and know if a maggot lay within it. Louise was shaking her head helplessly, saying nothing. Then, still shaking her head, tears in her eyes, she rushed away.

Isabella stood in utter misery in the silence of the park, her eyes resting on the young swans bobbing and spinning in the water but hardly knowing what she was seeing. She had humiliated herself, cast accusations at the one woman in the ducal court she could talk to, given way to quite unfounded fears. She had not realized how unhappy she felt here; how lonely; how vulnerable. It seemed so long ago, those few months since the duke had welcomed her to Flanders, courted her, entertained her, dazzled her, made love to her, filled her ears with his dreams and ideals. Isabella did not know even now what had gone wrong, or indeed if anything had gone wrong. Perhaps it *was* just the child in her belly. But there was no one, no one to talk to.

After a while she felt a yearning to seek out Louise—speak to her and confide her fears. If only there were someone she loved in this alien place. But her only lover was not here, was hardly ever here. It was growing dark now. A slight chill was creeping up from the lake. The swans had gone, and small insects pricked the silver surface of the water. What a fool I am, she thought; how will I ever know anything? About Philip. About this country. About Louise. Of course the girl would shake her head in horror at being asked such a question —whether it was true or untrue. But if it was not Louise, who else? And how many? Perhaps none. How would she discover? Nobody told all the truth, even lovers. She was learning much since leaving the simplicity of Portugal: a great deal but never enough. If only she could learn not to care, to withdraw to a safe place within herself.

She felt calmer now: weak, but the pain had eased. Then, with a surge of spirit she knew that she must trust Philip: without that she could not support life here. She would crumble. And with this resolve she imagined him with his army at Compiègne, so many great things on his mind, so much larger than herself. The struggle for Burgundy. The war with France, and now, of course, the Maid. Whatever Philip did, Isabella knew that he would treat Joan honorably. This was her husband, she repeated to herself. One of the greatest of men.

Isabella heard someone calling her out of the darkness. To her relief she recognized the voice of Louise, and she called back. When they met there were tears on Louise's cheeks as they embraced.

"My lady, my lady . . . the duke loves you: that's all I was going to say."

In Zeeland, a maidservant woke Jacqueline at dawn with news of a messenger who had ridden to Goes through the night. The man was unknown to her but she knew who had sent him and why he had traveled under cover of darkness. Recently the duke of Burgundy watched everything.

The splendid eyes of Jacqueline widened as she read the letter. Finally she looked up at the man with a look so intense that he stepped back frightened. Then she smiled and extended her hand.

"Thank you," she said. "You're a brave man." The voice was deep, smooth as velvet, the smile warm and generous. She touched his arm affectionately with her fingers and he averted his eyes from her gaze.

"Stay. They'll look after you here. And tomorrow I'll give you a reply for your lord. But you must leave at night as you came. Do you understand?"

He nodded. Then he bowed and left the room rather awkwardly. Her smile followed him and remained with him long after he had closed the door.

So the Maid was captured. Jacqueline had expected it for several months. Joan had grown too rash: her failures had made her so. She winced at the thought of another victim for Philip, duke of Burgundy; and yet it was to her relief that the Burgundians had taken her, not the English. As though it were a fledgling in her hand, she warmed the slender chance this gave her: slender, but her only chance.

Jacqueline spent much of that day alone in the room high over the sea and the gray spread of mud flats which swelled and shrank her little domain with each greedy tide. The wind had swept the sky clean, and Jacqueline's eyes followed the long broken shoreline until it melted into the horizon that was Flanders. Then she crossed the room to the other window. There, somewhere beyond those purple marshes, lay Brabant. Far to the left and beyond was Holland: far to the right, Hainault. All of them hers—stolen from her. There was anger in Jacqueline's eyes.

But on her lips there was a shadow of a smile. Joan, captive, could be her savior.

There was a turmoil of thoughts in Jacqueline's mind on that windswept morning. She was like a cornered animal—so long trapped that the most slim avenue of escape drew her body tense, ready to spring. It was a measure of her despair that the small bright hope at the end of that avenue rested on the two men she hated most, Philip of Burgundy and Humphrey of Gloucester. Her calculation was a simple one. Philip was holding the Maid prisoner. For the English, Joan would be the most valuable prize if they could obtain her. Philip would be torn: the English were his allies and the ransom would be enormous. But he saw himself as a man of honor: had he not founded the Order of the Golden Fleece to demonstrate to all the world his devotion to chivalry and to Christendom? He would not find it easy to release Joan—unless pressure could be brought to bear. There was only one way this could be done, and that was an invasion by the English. She would write to John, duke of Bedford, reminding him of his brother Humphrey's claims to Hainault, Brabant, and Holland through her marriage to him—even though Humphrey had abandoned her. What did it matter that the Pope had annulled the marriage? Gloucester would not find this a barrier to his greed, she was sure of that.

It wounded Jacqueline to invoke the name of Humphrey, who had knifed her soul. And it wounded her to treat the Maid in this way, as a mere pawn. But she had no other claws to fight with: affairs of this world had caught her in their tempests and beached her on these lonely islands of dune and marsh which she surveyed from this high room braced against the wind. The view was always a wilderness from which no help came.

Now there was just this glimmer. Even a slender hope felt

like a breath of love. If it failed, then there would be nothing
—a cold life and a cold tomb.

She wrote the letter to Bedford, and after a while a calm-
ness settled on her spirit. Jacqueline's eyes caught her own
eyes looking at her from Jan's half-finished portrait, and it was
as if another self were present in that room—a person Jacqueline had forgotten she ever was. She was gazing at herself
responding to a man. She rose from the table and stood before
the portrait, and as she did so she could feel her body grow
tense and vibrant. Her eyes followed the sure lines of Jan's
brush over her shoulders and breast, and it was as if his hands
touched her where she looked. She felt herself to be a woman
again. Then, like a feather that was drifting by almost out of
reach, she became aware of the most magical conjunction of
advantage and desire, and she knew that she would seize it.
Suddenly everything around her felt like a burgeoning of summer, her own body breathing the scent of warm grass and
blossom, her limbs and heart alive, laughter on her lips. Jan,
the duke's ambassador, would be her good messenger to still
his fears. This time it was self-indulgence in her eyes as they
traced the line of Jan's brush over her body. She could feel his
slender, clever hands. It was as if a blade of lightning passed
through her.

Jacqueline sealed the letter.

In Bruges the city hummed with talk of the Maid's capture. In
the taverns, in the cloth hall, the marketplace, the streets, the
public bathhouse, in the churches, the name of Joan was on
the lips of everyone. Even those who railed against the duke's
interminable wars, and at the taxes levied to pay for them,
were surprised to find themselves drawn into the general debate about "la Pucelle"—"the Virgin." The choice of that name
by which to describe her was not only an inquisitive fascina-
tion for Joan's immaculate state: the solid burghers of Bruges,
in their less than subtle grasp of religious matters, had grown
accustomed to there being only one notable Virgin in history,
synonymous with Virtue, and could not so easily come to
terms with there being another who was supposed to be synonymous with Heresy. Besides, it was widely known that the

Maid referred to herself as Jehanne la Pucelle, as though in defiance of those Englishmen and Burgundians who expressed a bawdy disbelief that this could be so. It was strange how important it appeared to be to the craftsmen and traders of Bruges that Joan should have been well and truly deflowered: you might have imagined that her magic and her power rested on that fragile membrane alone, without which she became reduced to mere hotheaded mortality. And such was that power, and the clamor to discredit it, that listening to the more bluff guildsmen in the Fallen Angel it would have been easy to believe she had lain with the entire French army, pausing only to don her armor and dash off to capture a city or two from the English. That, at least, was the expressed opinion of the cloth weaver Pieter van Orley, his eyes agleam as if he personally had made the first breach in her defenses. Quaffing his beer noisily, he referred to Joan unceremoniously as "the whore," that being the only kind of woman—Bona pointed out—Van Orley was capable of understanding.

"She was on her black stallion," explained the ducal herald, Jehan Lefèvre. His customary lofty gaze was lowered somewhat in the relish of such attentive company. Monsieur Elégance found himself for once the bearer of news all were eager to hear about, and he sipped his excellent Beaune amid dramatic pauses in his tale, savoring the eagerness about him. Arnolfini was there along with Michaut Pontin, Jan de Leeuw, Bona, Van Orley, Godscalc Oom, Michault de Caron, Master Jan, and the Englishman Hugo. It was a warm, early summer evening, and the doors of the tavern were thrown open onto the small terrace by the canal. The company was slouched or seated in the doorway enjoying the last moments of sunlight and savoring the downfall of the Maid.

"Yes, she was on her black stallion, proud as ever," continued Lefèvre. "Until suddenly that brave knight Guillaume de Wandonne challenged her. She was no match for him, I assure you. And after a few blows she surrendered—just surrendered ignominiously." The herald gave a haughty sneer, nodding his head toward the taverner for a further glass of Beaune while he prepared to resume his tale.

"As it happens, her horse was dapple-gray." The voice was

Michault de Caron's, the court poet. Eyes turned toward him in surprise. "She did not surrender," he went on. "She was trapped by the drawbridge raised before she could cross it."

Lefèvre's well-practiced air of superiority showed not a flicker of irritation.

"And then she surrendered," he proceeded, leapfrogging Caron's contradictory report as if it were so much clutter.

"As a matter of fact she was trapped in boggy ground by the river," Caron continued with a gentle smile of satisfaction, "whereupon a Picard archer dragged her from her horse."

"It was a dastardly thing to do after Wandonne had already compelled her to submit," Lefèvre went on, still surveying his audience with unruffled composure. "These men of Picardy, they have no sense of honor."

And he turned to Caron with a thin smile, taking a further sip of wine and hoping that was the end of the dispute. He was anxious to proceed with his tale.

"Guillaume de Wandonne was not present at the time," corrected the poet almost apologetically, his expression eliciting a ripple of laughter from the company. "The news of Joan's capture reached him very shortly, and he received the Maid's sword on behalf of his captain, Jehan de Luxembourg."

"Perhaps Lefèvre is referring to a different Maid," Godecalc Oom was heard to suggest with ponderous solemnity.

At this point the ducal herald seemed to find his glass of Beaune no longer to his taste and departed, carefully enfolding himself in the dignity of his black tunic. The laughter rose as they watched him make his way with exaggerated nonchalance across the little bridge in the direction of the ducal palace.

It emerged that whereas Lefèvre had returned to Bruges on some other ducal business, Michault de Caron was with the court in Lille when the messengers arrived from Compiègne with the news of the Maid's capture. He had spoken with them himself at some length, knowing that he would shortly be required to compose suitable verses on the triumphant occasion. The messengers had remained in Lille, and knowledge of Joan's defeat and captivity had only reached Bruges through secondhand reports. Lefèvre's claim to have received the sole official account of these events was more to do with his own self-esteem than it was with the truth.

No one expected to see him at the Fallen Angel for a while —which was a pity, it was agreed: they liked the ducal herald for all his absurdities and could easily have forgiven him his little vanities. But Lefèvre, they surmised, would find it harder to forgive those vanities being exposed.

Michault then regaled them with the story in full, as far as he knew it. The duke, it seemed, had hastened to Compiègne as soon as he heard the news, and on the following day had spent several hours in the company of the Maid. A surprising length of time, Michault suggested: it was not known what transpired between them, though it was said that the duke emerged from their meeting with a grave face, refusing to speak even to Jehan de Luxembourg. It was strange that a mere encounter between victor and captive should have been so protracted and have produced such a strained effect on Philip. Why? Michault wondered. No doubt all would soon be known since the duke had ensured that the court chronicler Enguerrand de Monstrelet was with him to record the historic exchange of words, whatever these may have been.

And what was to be done with Joan? Van Orley's throaty laugh left no one in doubt as to what he would do. The others were mostly silent and thoughtful. From Hugo's faraway look you might have imagined the Maid to be another unobtainable love. De Leeuw's huge hand clasped a pot of beer a few inches from his handsome, sturdy face, and he said nothing as usual, though there was a look almost of sadness in his eyes. Pontin pulled at the crop of hair on his fingers and likewise said nothing. Jan gazed out at the canal, on which slivers of sunlight floated, convinced now that he would very soon meet and draw the Maid. Godscalc Oom emitted one of his grumbling sounds from somewhere deep in the barrel of his body, then ventured that there would surely be a very high ransom on Joan's life. Bona gave an affectionate snort and suggested that of course a rentmaster would think like that.

"So, I suspect, may the duke," Godscalc replied.

Giovanni Arnolfini was seen to nod in agreement, but he made no comment.

"One thing I know," added Michault de Caron. "Within two days of her capture the duke had received a letter from the vicar-general to the inquisitor."

At this everyone who was assembled on the sunlit terrace looked attentively at the poet.

"It was a demand—no less—that Joan be sent for trial. Crimes of heresy, as I understand."

"Is it heresy to hear divine voices?" Bona inquired laconically. "If so, then all the Old Testament prophets were heretics, and most of the apostles as well."

This brought a languid smile from Arnolfini.

"Pontius Pilate would certainly have agreed with that," he suggested. And they all laughed except De Leeuw, who was reflecting perhaps on the comparison between Pilate and their own duke.

"It seems," Caron went on, "that the bishop of Beauvais is already pressing to have her turned over to the English so that he can preside over the trial in person. For myself, I cannot see the duke doing that."

It was Jan's turn to look interested.

"The bishop of Beauvais!" There was surprise in Jan's voice. "I've met him. Pierre Cauchon is his name. An unscrupulous man. In the pay of the English. Certainly not in the service of God."

Bona laughed.

"And how many men of the church have you met who are?"

There was more laughter.

"Perhaps the lord bishop is like our own Abbot Eustache," suggested Arnolfini, draining his glass and signaling the taverner for another. "Seventeen illegitimate children in one village at the most recent count, I understand. In which case all the Maid will have to do is offer her services and the inquisitor will pronounce her a true and loyal servant of God."

This time there were several who did not join in the laughter. Jan knew well how Giovanni's cynicism could grate. But Arnolfini did not seem to notice.

"Mind you," he continued, "it takes an Italian abbot to do that sort of thing in style. We have one in Lucca who keeps seventy concubines. I know this because he told me. In fact he has several times asked me to supply him."

"And did you?" There was a touch of acid in Bona's voice.

"No. It's not my trade. Besides, I prefer to keep my women for myself." Arnolfini gave a meaningful look at Hugo. Bona turned away and decided to depart.

"I've no doubt," she said over her shoulder as she left, "it would be your trade if there was enough money in it."

Arnolfini ignored the barb and continued to smile content-edly in the last of the sun, fingering the heavy ring on his right hand and thinking of the lucrative set of tapestries ordered by Cardinal Octavianni, and then of the lovely Lysbet.

Jan grew weary of the banter and followed Bona out of the tavern into the street of the Golden Hand. He saw her turn her head when she saw him, and pause. She looked graceful and handsome in her light summer clothing, and there was a sug-gestion of a smile on her lips.

"You certainly made an impression on the duchess Jacque-line," she said as he approached. And as she spoke Bona placed a hand on his arm precisely as Jacqueline used to do. Jan was intrigued by the coincidence; but then he was invari-ably intrigued by Bona.

"Are you going to tell me how you know?" he asked.

Bona gazed at him with amused eyes. The light was just beginning to fade into dusk, and her features appeared soft and young.

"Perhaps I'll tell you while you're painting me as Eve," she replied. "How would you like that? There are a lot of things I could tell you, though some of them will have to wait."

Jan arranged for Bona to pose for him some weeks hence. The idea, he admitted to her, rather excited him.

"Aren't men supposed to be excited by Eve?" she added. "That's what she's there for: to hold out the apple and then be rejected so you can all feel good."

There was a quizzical look on her face.

"Mind you," she added. "I don't imagine Margarethe will feel as excited as you. I notice you haven't asked her to be your Eve. But then, ambitious men like to marry good girls, don't they? I warn you, though, good girls can be very jealous."

Bona was laughing as she left.

The capture of the Maid preyed on Jan's mind. Joan was no longer a distant legend but someone he was even more strongly convinced he would soon meet and draw. He tried to picture her in his mind: he even imagined her talking to him while he drew her, though he found it impossible to think what she might say.

Jan was also aware that Joan's presence in the hands of Burgundy cast a further shadow over his perception of the duke, much as the presence of Jacqueline did. He looked at the two drawings he had made of Philip many months earlier—still waiting to be completed. They occupied a corner of the studio otherwise almost filled with the huge altarpiece of Joos Vyt, and yet they appeared to dominate the room. Progress on the altarpiece was exasperatingly slow because Jan's attention kept slipping toward them.

As he stared at the drawings he tried to envisage the duke's finished portrait, but whenever he did so the proud figure standing before the broad landscape of Flanders became flanked in Jan's mind by these two women gazing at Philip: Jacqueline and Joan. The picture before his eyes became not one, but three—a triptych: when the two wings of the painting were unfolded there they stood, these two figures, staring, questioning, accusing. It was as if the duke were trapped between them; the two women he had crushed were crushing him. The figure of Philip seemed to shrink, become weaker, and the radiance of Flanders grow blurred.

It was an uneasy period of waiting. Around him summer in Bruges blossomed into languid evenings filled with the sounds of laughter and lovemaking, and the canal beyond Jan's garden glimmered with the lights of boat parties: meanwhile, when Margarethe was not with him he generally preferred to be alone—wondering when the duke might return, when there would be a further summons from Jacqueline, when he might hear further news about the fate of the Maid.

During the day he concentrated as best he could on the

altarpiece for Vyt. From time to time messages arrived from the burgomaster inquiring after Jan's progress, concluding always with the invitation to return to Ghent in order to paint the portrait of the donor and his wife, Elizabeth. He was looking forward to that, Vyt said. Jan could still see the neat, rotund figure of Joos on his knees with his hands pressed together and eyes raised: he smiled at the thought of the old man practicing his expression of suitable devotion, and when he replied Jan would end his report on the altarpiece with warm assurances of the pleasure a prolonged visit to Ghent would certainly give him. He would like to paint the portraits of Vyt and his wife last of all, he explained, after he had the chance to assemble the nearly completed altarpiece where the burgomaster could see it. He hoped Vyt would be pleased, and that his pleasure might be reflected in his face as Jan painted him.

"Don't be too long or you'll have to paint my corpse," the burgomaster scrawled at the end of one message; and Jan remembered the delight he had felt in the old man's company. Vyt's was a face he would enjoy painting. The humor. The shrewd, twinkling expression.

Gradually, as the huge altarpiece absorbed him, Jan's peace of mind returned, and the specter of the duke's portrait haunted by the twin figures of Jacqueline and the Maid troubled him less. A routine of work began to govern each day. Margarethe came to visit him regularly—a bright shy figure in red slipping quietly into the studio—and Jan sensed in the eagerness of her face the pride she felt in watching the great painting steadily fill the empty spaces around the room. He was working harder. Much of the time he was engaged in the drapery of the figures, the embroidery and the jewels: painstaking layers of color that were needed in order to achieve that richness and sparkle Jan loved. And because each glaze took so long to dry he was constantly having to move from figure to figure, and back again. Jan was especially proud of the two figures of John the Baptist and the apostle John, both painted so as to look as if they were sculpture. This was just himself being clever. He was pleased that Margarethe tried to touch them, drawing back with a cry of astonishment.

"Perhaps I'm not real either," he teased her.

She laughed delightfully and ran over to him. When he touched her bare shoulders she gave him her lips and her body pressed against his.

There were long and peaceful days as the summer ripened. Now there were no more than seven panels unpainted out of the twenty which made up the altarpiece. Two were the portraits of Vyt and his wife; there was a view of Ghent which he would paint from the burgomaster's window; a choir of angels, provided Jan could find children angelic enough; the panel of the Virgin Mary (Marie); the angel of the Annunciation (Lysbet); and of course there was Eve (Bona). Margarethe would sometimes fix her eyes on that tall slender panel, already primed and given several coats of dark background; Jan knew she was imagining the naked form of Bona standing there, and trying not to be jealous. At first Margarethe had inquired almost daily when Bona was due to pose. Finally Jan had suggested that if she was concerned she should watch from behind a screen just as she had watched Michault. Margarethe looked sulky for a while and fell silent.

"Has she got a better body than mine?" she asked suddenly one morning, surveying the blank panel as if Bona were standing before her.

"How should I know?" Jan answered truthfully. He gazed at Margarethe's gentle, passionate face. She had never shown him all her body, he reminded her mischievously. As for Bona, she had yet to pose for him.

Margarethe looked at him questioningly. He was wearing that shadow of a smile which always made her desire him. She watched the light, agile way he moved about the studio; the lean, compact body, catlike, eyes on the move, mouth puckering slightly at the corners as if unseen images were appearing before him and amusing him lightly as they passed—amusing him and perhaps attracting him. Margarethe did not know how to stifle the jealousies she felt. It had taken her quite by surprise to discover that there was only Jan in her world; she wanted only to be with him. She longed to sleep with him, marry him, keep him. But she was in love with an ambitious man, a restless man: he belonged to so much wider a world that she knew, and each time he moved into that world she wanted to pull him back for fear he would never return. Part of Jan was always somewhere else, and she could never reach that far.

Margarethe's were not the only tremors of anxiety to fill the house on the street of the Golden Hand. The great altarpiece invited a host of small intrigues and suspicions which frequently rendered Jan's days anything by peaceful. He was compelled to resign himself to the thought that, since the huge undertaking had been adopted from the outset by the customers of the Fallen Angel, it was unreasonable to expect them to allow him privacy in which to paint it.

Their curiosity haunted him like a pack of hungry dogs. The Englishman Hugo, who had never before exhibited the least sensibility toward Jan's profession, or toward religion, all at once became devoted to the cult of the Virgin Mary, and in particular to how the Mother of Our Lord should be represented in paint. He appeared to know as if by divine guidance when the pious girl Marie was visiting Jan's studio: Hugo's hopeless and pining adoration filled the house like ooze. But Marie's expression remained as unmoved as a lovely shell, and her eyes never left her holy book.

"Hugo, leave us now; I have to work," Jan would say as patiently as he was able.

He enjoyed painting Marie, but it was like painting a jewel. The pearls she wore, the rubies in their settings of gold and silver, were no cooler or more still than she. The petals of her mouth opened only to breathe the Latin verses held before her in such little hands. There were hours of silence while he painted her. She would forever be—Jan reflected—perhaps the loveliest of all Virgins ever painted; his name might be famous because of her; all people would worship her and call her perfect; and yet in Jan's mind rose the thought that if the real Virgin had been so uncorporeal even God might have had to plant his seed elsewhere. He tried not to let the thought show on his face.

But at least—except when Hugo was around—there was tranquillity. It was not so with the other heavenly twin, Lysbet. Arnolfini would bring her, complacently as if he were lending Jan his property, and he would look on while the girl donned the pale robe Jan had tought suitable for the angel of the Annunciation. And the slim gold coronet, and a lily in her hand. Then Giovanni would talk.

"In my country the angel Gabriel is a man. Is he not described so in the Bible?"

Jan would explain that this was indeed so, but that in art Gabriel was frequently given the features of a girl since they were regarded as more beautiful, and in any case this was what the cathedral had requested.

Next there would be a question about the wings. Where were they? What would they be made of? Then it was—why had Jan chosen for the coronet the cross of St. John, when this was created by the Crusaders, the Knights Hospitalers, many centuries later? Jan pointed out, somewhat wearily, that *any* cross would strictly speaking be inaccurate since at the annunciation Our Lord had not yet been born, let alone been crucified. Christian symbols transcend time.

"Even in Italy," he added acidly. But Giovanni was not put off.

"In that case why leave poor Adam naked? Does his fig leaf transcend time?"

"Yes, Giovanni. And now I must work."

But this was not so easy. After Arnolfini's departure Lysbet talked almost as much as her lover, and her hands and eyes were never still. Then suddenly Jan saw a look of wonder on her face as she caught sight of the crown which her sister Marie had worn earlier that day. Her lips parted in amazement and she signaled with one finger crooked for him to bring it to her. Jan did not; instead, with a few rapid lines on paper he caught the look and the gesture.

And so it was that Lysbet, astonished at the sight of so many desirable gems, became the archangel Gabriel announcing to the Virgin Mary the gladdest tidings on earth. Such, Jan reflected, was a painter's artifice. He did not think a truly pious artist—like the monks who had taught him in Limbourg— could possibly have done such a thing. Nor, he believed proudly, could they ever have done it so convincingly.

When it was finished, he stood back and considered the painting of the archangel. What goodness in that lovely face—

an expression of the purest Christian joy—her hair threads of the gold of heaven. Yet she was Lysbet, Giovanni's mistress, who had sold herself for gold, and whom even now Giovanni was begging him to paint naked for Cardinal Octavianni, for more gold.

What a dirty, beautiful world, he thought.

He was waiting for Bona. It seemed appropriate to be painting the temptress, the serpent. Jan was curious to know what Bona would say about Jacqueline, and was glad Margarethe would not be there.

Jan heard the jangle of a bell downstairs. But it was not Bona. Michault de Caron was let into the studio. He had come, he said, in order to inspect the finished portrait of himself as Adam. Jan liked the poet too much to be irritated at the subterfuge. He knew that Michault hoped Bona might be here posing as Eve. There was a look of disappointment on the visitor's face.

"Michault, my dear friend, will you please leave?" The poet's face took on an expression of injured righteousness.

"Don't you think I have a right to set eyes on the woman who was made from my own rib?" he retorted.

Jan could only laugh. Then he watched Michault peer attentively at the fig leaf which Jan had selected most carefully from his own garden, bearing in mind the poet's vanities: not so small a leaf as to suggest that Adam might be ashamed of what he was concealing, nor so large that he might be accused of an idle boast.

From the look on his face Michault seemed satisfied that justice had been done to his manliness. Jan smiled.

"Do you think I've managed to suggest, Michault, that what lies beneath that leaf is responsible for the entire human race?"

It was Michault's turn to laugh, and he clapped the painter on the shoulder. Jan decided not to repeat what the peeping Margarethe had commented earlier, never having set eyes on a male organ before—namely, that it seemed to her a rather shriveled thing.

Bona arrived at precisely the hour she had suggested, not long after Jan had managed to dispose of Michault de Caron. It was a warm summer afternoon, and without a word she proceeded to remove her clothing as casually—Jan thought—as though she were peeling an apple: and immediately he smiled as he realized the aptness of the comparison.

"Well, do I make a suitable Eve?" she asked, holding her left hand over her genitals to match the painting of Adam which was facing her across the room.

Jan was too surprised to do more than nod. He admired the high breasts, still firm, and the long muscular legs. Her belly, as she had complained, was rather rounded: Jan could make out the stretch marks on either side of the smudge of hair rising to her navel. No, she was not beautiful, and her nakedness somehow made her face appear less serene than usual. She wore an almost sulky look, the hair straggly over the fine shoulders, the hint of a double chin emphasized by the pout of her lips. The eyes, just as when she had posed for him the first time, appeared distant: she seemed hardly aware of Jan, or even aware of herself. It was as if she had posed herself there, and gone away.

This time Jan made no preliminary drawing in silverpoint. He had drawn her before and knew precisely the oval smoothness of her face, the shallow pits of shadow, the flat eyelids and forehead, full lips, nose a little bulbous at the end. And the fine neck and shoulders. The firm feet. He traced the form of her body confidently on the dark background of the panel, shading in the long muscle of her thigh, the boniness of the knee and ankle. He asked her to raise her right hand, imagining that she was holding up an apple. Bona did so with the most tempting of looks. Jan chuckled.

"Tell me," he said, noticing the cunning shifts of expression on her face as she listened, "why did you say you had to be Eve because you *were* Eve?"

Bona gazed at him, her mouth gradually forming the hint of a smile so knowing that Jan could imagine what it must be like to be her lover. She would demand silently, and give silently; then her energies would explode like a cat's.

"Because I like to corrupt," she replied nonchalantly. "Women always feel the need to corrupt a man or save him: didn't you know?" Then, still with no expression on her face, she looked down at her own nakedness and slowly ran one hand over her breasts and belly. "Also, I like my own body. I shall enjoy being able to go and look at it when I'm old." And, glancing at Jan, she laughed. "Besides," she went on, "I cherish the idea of a cathedral congregation on their knees before me as a sinner—which I am."

She laughed again, and then the face in front of him retreated once more into its own thoughts. With the finest of brushes Jan shadowed in the slight puckering in the corners of the mouth, and the girlish dimple on the chin. He loved painting this face. There was a stubbornness about it, and a sadness in those eyes, the mouth voracious but with a hint of anger. He was curious to know whether she had ever loved anybody. He imagined her to be a woman of appetites: hungry, she would gobble a man; sated she would spit him out and forget him.

For a while there was silence while he worked intensely. Every so often he wanted to ask her about Jacqueline: how it was that Bona knew her so well. She had even promised to tell him and then had added that there were things she could not tell him. So what, Jan wondered, was the secret the two women shared? She described herself in the role of Eve as though it were a vain joke, yet he could not help suspecting there was more to it, and when she said she wanted to corrupt him she was not altogether joking. He would be on his guard for the serpent; perhaps there too he might find the clue to Bona's secret.

Jan realized that he was rather enjoying the double game. Suddenly, in a spirit of mischief, he said, "So, were you thinking of corrupting me?"

"Of course," she said without hesitation. "Every woman would like to corrupt you." There was a taunting look in Bona's eyes. "Except the lovely Margarethe perhaps," she added. "She would like to keep you safely in a little box, and guard the key."

And she laughed.

You could never be sure with Bona whether she believed what she said or was being provocative. She was scornful of Margarethe; he knew that. But she was also envious—envious of her youth, her bloom, perhaps most of all her ability to love.

"Do you imagine I would allow myself to be locked up?" he asked.

Bona said nothing for a moment, but looked at him as if she were trying to make up her mind.

"Yes, I believe you might," she said after a while. Then she gave him that same knowing smile. "But only if you made sure you had a spare key." She fingered a stray strand of hair and flicked it casually back over her shoulder. "I think you like people who are more dangerous than Margarethe."

Jan noticed that word again. Dangerous! The duke had used it. And now Bona. He wondered whom she might have in mind. It was hard not to believe that Bona was thinking of Jacqueline; except that the idea seemed absurd. Jacqueline was a noblewoman, a duchess, cousin of the duke, great-granddaughter of a king; whereas he, Jan, was just the duke's court painter with no titles, estates, ancestry. Two quiet separate worlds, Jacqueline's and his. There were relationships that you could only play with in the mind, that remained forever in the ether, beautiful colors and shapes in the sky of a man's dreams. Even during those beguiling evenings by the huge fire when Jacqueline had rested her hand on his arm and the shadows had modeled her body; even then what passed between them was not a reality, nor ever could it be.

So what did Bona mean?

Outside the window the late afternoon sun was low above the rooftops across the canal. Jan could hear the squabble of ducks on the water, and laughter from an unseen boat. Someone was playing a flute. A dog was barking. Sounds of summer. How normal it all seemed—and serene. Yet inside this room the atmosphere was taut, the silence loaded with questions, unasked and unanswered, flying between them.

"Jacqueline likes you," Bona said quietly. "She hopes you'll return soon."

Jan felt startled: it seemed such a coincidence that Jacqueline should have been in Bona's thoughts too. But then he laughed to himself at his own vanity. What could be more natural than that Bona should talk about Jacqueline's portrait?

It was through Bona, after all, that he would receive his summons to return.

"I'm waiting to hear," Jan said.

He went on painting her eyes. Bona was not looking at him, but seemed to be gazing absentmindedly across the room to where the picture of Michault de Caron stood gazing at her. Eve staring at Adam, Jan thought, and laughed again to himself.

"It'll be soon now, Jan." Suddenly Bona sounded open and warm. "Jacqueline has had much on her mind, and it's not so easy to get messages from her now. You may know," she went on, "the duke has thrown a cordon of informers round Zeeland. He's suspicious of her—still fears her. Messengers have to travel by night." Then she added, glancing at Jan, "Of course, you're all right: you're the duke's ambassador."

Jan thought he detected the shadow of a smile, though the impassive face was once more staring across the room. He had never seen Bona so inscrutable: she was naked in front of him, yet it was as if her nakedness concealed her like a veil. He decided to remind her of what she had promised.

"You said you'd tell me how you know her." Jan longed to know much more than this, but he sensed that Bona would only tell him so much. Still she did not look at him.

"There's no secret," she replied, this time more to herself than to him. "I've known Jacqueline since I was very young. We were children together. Jacqueline's father was Count William of Hainault: my father was his chamberlain." For a moment Bona looked at Jan almost angrily. "And then he died. My mother had died when I was born. So I was alone. Jacqueline and I were like sisters. Her father was a father to me—until he died too. And then, within six months, we were both found husbands by the duke of Burgundy—the present duke's father."

Suddenly Bona laughed loudly, and there was scorn in that laugh.

"And what husbands!" she went on. "One a pederast, the other a knight of honor." Contempt clouded Bona's face. "But I must remember, mustn't I?" she added, and there was a mocking sharpness in her voice. "You admire knights of honor. You even believe the duke to be one."

Jan was puzzled by the change of tone.

"I have thought so," he replied.

As he said it he was aware of a hesitancy in his own voice. She noticed it too, and without altering her pose she lifted her left hand and slowly ran her fingers through her lank hair without once taking her eyes off the painter. He felt those eyes searching him. Jan raised his brush and added tiny points of light to the eyes, sharpening the gaze. That, he realized, was the look of Eve he wanted. At the same time, as he painted that look, he understood why she was Eve. She wanted to test his loyalty to Philip: she wanted to know how undivided that loyalty was. Here lay the clue he was searching for. He would need to be very, very careful.

"Don't you admire him still?" she inquired very quietly.

There was silence. Bona's eyes never left his own. For a moment Jan did not answer. Since Jacqueline had recounted her story to him there were many things he no longer admired about the duke; but he was nonetheless Philip's painter and his ambassador. The duke had never treated him anything but well. Jan thought of the portrait he was preparing. The duke in his robes of the Golden Fleece. The articles of foundation which Philip had asked him to read out aloud. The pledge to defend Christendom. And he remembered the duke's vision of a great Burgundy stretching from the Alps to the sea.

Bona's silence was still interrogating him. She had not once taken her eyes off him, and there was no expression on her face.

"I think the duke has his ideals," Jan said at last. "And I admire him for that."

He could hear Bona draw a deep breath.

"And I believe he has none," she replied.

Now there was a challenging look on Bona's face. Her denial of what he had said came as no surprise: neither she nor Jacqueline could be expected to admire what the duke stood for, or share his dream of Burgundy. It was, after all, at their cost.

"He has no ideals," she said again. "Only ambitions." Jan looked at her sternly.

"I believe the duke loves chivalry, and believes in it, as he believes in God," he said.

Bona laughed.

"So how do you imagine, Jan, that the chivalrous duke will treat the Maid now he has her in his power? Tell me."

"With honor," he replied.

Again Bona laughed.

"I tell you, he will sell her to the English—when the price is right. Philip's honor always has a price."

But Jan was shaking his head.

"No, Bona. He will not do that."

Jan was certain. If the duke were to hand Joan to the English, they would kill her. She had been his enemy in battle but he would never want her death on his hands. His honor would forbid that. Nor would the duke wish to invite the hatred of all France.

"You're quite wrong," he said.

Bona looked irritated. Then she crossed the room and began to dress—carelessly. Suddenly she turned to him with exasperation in her face.

"You sound exactly like Jacqueline," she blurted out angrily. "Trusting Philip's honor. Trusting England. Trusting Gloucester of all people. Good God!"

The outburst was cut short because even as she spoke Bona knew from Jan's face that she had said too much. She had let slip the word "Gloucester." She could not believe she could have mentioned the name of Gloucester in front of Jan, who had been the duke's ambassador and who knew precisely how to listen and how to hear the things that people only hinted at. This was what everyone said about Jan; it was what made him the painter he was; he "read" people as if he were inside their heads. Jan had never seen fear in Bona's eyes before. In that instant he understood what it was Jacqueline needed from him. It seemed incredible—but then as he remembered Jacqueline's despair Jan could see that her hopes might indeed be pinned upon it since there was nothing else. Jacqueline, for all her hatred, yet trusted Philip's honor not to release Joan to the

English. So much was clear from what Bona had said. But Gloucester! Why should she trust him too—the husband who had abandoned her and whom she loathed as deeply as she loathed Philip?

There could be only one reason. Jacqueline was inviting Gloucester to return. The incentive? To reclaim his lands from Philip by force. And the pretext? To try to compel Philip to hand over the Maid.

And Jan's own role? Such a simple one. To be the dupe: to know nothing of all this, and to reassure the duke that all was well in Zeeland by saying nothing. To be Jacqueline's good ambassador. So very simple, and a trap from which Jan could see no way out. From what he now knew, either he betrayed Jacqueline or he betrayed the duke.

Jan looked at Bona, and he recalled the duke saying—half jokingly he had thought at the time—how people always said more than they should when he painted them; more than was wise.

And do, Jan thought, it was the temptress who had allowed herself to be tempted. Bona was hurriedly preparing herself to leave. There was unhappiness in her face and her eyes avoided his. He was aware of further sounds of music and laughter drifting up from the canal through the open window, and shadows of the evening were creeping over the surface of the huge altarpiece in front of him against the wall. And here by the side of him was Eve, her right hand just sketched in with the fingers outstretched to hold the apple.

Bona was looking at her own naked figure too—mortified. She ached at the thought that she might have betrayed Jacqueline: Jan had only to tell the duke and that would be the end.

There followed one of those silences in which nothing needed to be said. Bona was standing there hesitant, uncertain whether any explanation would only make it worse, and yet unwilling to leave in case some repair was possible.

After a few moments her face took on a bewildered, pleading look.

"If you only knew, Jan," she managed to say; "if you only knew."

She laid her hands in his, and he held them for a while as she recovered her composure.

"I'm so very sorry," she went on. "I realize I've placed you in an impossible position. I should never have done that. You're a friend. A good friend. There's no one I like more in Bruges than you." Then she looked at him appealingly. "It's just that . . . forgive me . . . what can you do when you love someone who's been like a sister to you?"

Bona walked to the door, but again hesitated a moment.

"If you only knew how Jacqueline had suffered. I've bled for her." Her voice was firm again, almost defiant. "Jan," she went on more gently; "they cannot both be right, the duke and Jacqueline. You have to choose which. But please remember, it's Jacqueline's life that is on the scales."

The absurdity of the situation was not lost on Jan: that he should be engaged in painting the portraits of two people, each of whom expected him to betray the other. And a third painting, what was more, which had brought the situation about. Eve. Jan gazed at the picture of Bona: just the face, the raised hand, the outline of the naked body. She had done her work, he reflected ruefully. The Tree of Knowledge—he had bitten the fruit without even being aware. It seemed an unkind twist of justice that he, who always searched to know about those he painted, should now know too much.

Jan's gaze shifted to the great central panel of the altarpiece which his brother Hubert had painted in honor of the Holy Lamb. That image of purity there on its sacrificial altar in a summer landscape raked by golden rays of sunlight, with all around it the martyrs and saints, knights and pilgrims: what a serene world, so resolved in its acceptance of man's sin, so hopeful in its vision of the new Jerusalem. Jan longed for his dead brother to be alive and explain to him that vision, to convince him of the truth of it; because with his own eyes he could not see those golden rays of goodness when he looked out at the world he knew.

It was as the light began to fade that Jan crossed the city eastward to where the ramparts rose against the evening sky. He climbed into the wind and stood gazing over the green polderlands where ten thousand mill sails turned and turned between a thousand silver threads of water; and his eyes felt like a bird gliding toward Damme and beyond, toward Sluis, where pale hills of dune lined the estuary, and even further beyond to where—somewhere across those hungry tides—lay the lands of the sea. Jacqueline's domain. And suddenly he imagined the swell of that great ocean scuffed by the prows of English ships as Humphrey of Gloucester returned to claim his marriage and his titles. Would it all begin again, the story she had told him?

Strangely Jan felt no fear for himself. When the time came he would do whatever he needed to do, and if he had to flee, then he would flee. There were other lords besides the duke of Burgundy, other patrons—France, Italy, England; and there were other enchantresses besides the duchess Jacqueline. No, it was not fear; only an enormous sadness. Everywhere he looked in this world he saw people striving for unobtainable things—fame or kingdoms or love. Everyone he knew seemed caught in this struggling web—while the spider waited, laughing. But where was the joy?

Jan looked around him. The sky was luminous now: the haze of summer heat was being pulled aside like curtains to the farthest horizons. There was such promise in this lovely land; but "Oh!" Jan found himself saying aloud. "Hubert, where are your golden rays?"

He turned and looked back over the city, its dark spires spiking the twilit sky. And as his eyes surveyed this city that was his home Jan knew that there was only one ray of gold in the life he had found here. Margarethe.

He hastened back to her house. Jan took her by the arm and they walked quietly through the dusk.

"I've missed you," she whispered.

And in the secluded garden Jan held her in his arms, and the night held them both. She felt like a small bird that had been lost and was slowly finding its strength. After a while she raised her head, and he knew from touching her face that she was absorbing him with those green eyes, her lips parted, inviting him. And as he kissed her again the gentle rippling sounds from the canal accompanied their bodies into the night.

They did not speak, but touched and listened, lips and hair close, each aware only of the other under the silent stars. The night excluded all the world beyond their arms, beyond the discovery of skin against skin, the nakedness of thighs and breasts, the waves of hunger and need which neither of them any longer wanted to resist. Then the numb half-slumber on the cool grass, the reborn desire, the slow and longer lovemaking, more deliberate and more sure, her mind fixed on the strong lithe rhythm of his body, his on the softness and eagerness of hers. The storm of love when it broke washed away all thoughts, and they lay breathing each other's hair, each other's breath.

It was almost dawn when he said, "Marry me."

There was not enough light for Jan to see the love in her eyes as she said, "Yes."

Chapter ♦ Six

It was almost midsummer when the duke returned to Bruges, and his return was staged to be a triumph unmatched by Alexander the Great or Julius Caesar. There were those in the Fallen Angel who complained that such preparations were excessive, considering that the triumph was nothing more than the capture of a girl in men's clothing: what was more, it was learned, the duke was not even bringing the Maid with him so that the townspeople might line the streets and gape at this phenomenon; there would only be the duke as usual in his swaggering black, with his chancellor and lesser dignitaries in fawning attendance. The view in the tavern was that the forthcoming celebrations were likely to cost as much as the war they celebrated, and there was the massive presence of the rentmaster Godscalc Oom to reassure them—over his tiny glass of hippocras—of the taxes they would all be contributing as a result. The indignant figure of Pieter van Orley, the master weaver, was to be heard thumping his fist and declaring he would watch none of the pageantry. The silversmith Michaut Pontin retorted that since he understood many of the tableaux were to feature naked ladies, he was quite certain Van Orley would be craning his neck along with everybody else.

And so it was.

The duke processed sedately on horseback through the southern gate of the city and along the Minnewater toward the church of Our Lady, and as he did so his eyes were greeted by numerous scenes of great enchantment enacted on platforms that had been erected at intervals along the route. The duchess Isabella (who had joyfully met the duke at the city gates) was not the only one to comment that these tableaux did not appear to bear much relevance to the ducal triumph against the French: nonetheless she noticed that they gave evident pleasure to the admiring crowds and even more evident pleasure to her husband the duke. On one stage she saw a figure dressed as a serpent who writhed most energetically between Adam and Eve. On another stood the hugely bearded figure of what she took to be Moses solemnly presenting the tablets of the law to his people. A third displayed a naked and chained Andromeda about to be rescued by Perseus from a dragon; while almost outside the church of Our Lady stood a stage upon which three further maidens, dressed in nothing but jeweled necklaces, were engaged in inviting Paris to judge their loveliness—no hard task, Isabella thought, considering the remarkable proportions of the young lady who represented Aphrodite.

Further on, to her amazement she saw another maiden seated quite unperturbed as it seemed between a lion and a leopard—both, she presumed, from the ducal menagerie which Philip had yet to show her. Then, as the procession crossed the little bridge over the Diyver canal her attention was drawn to an extraordinary scene in the water: at least six or eight young ladies were to be seen swimming under and around the bridge uttering wordless cries of greeting. Isabella recollected from her marriage festivities the court of Burgundy's fondness for the legend of Odysseus tempted by the sirens. Altogether she could not help reflecting on the prevailing theme of female nakedness in these celebrations, and she recalled how her lady-in-waiting Louise had talked of the Burgundian obsession with love. In spite of this she decided she would ask Louise, who knew all about these things, why such immodest displays were thought suitable for welcoming their triumphant duke, and where the girls were to be found who were happy to disport themselves in this way. The duke was waving his ermine hat with vigorous enthusiasm. She herself rode more quietly, feeling it improper for a duchess to approve too openly, and conscious of the child nestling within her. But her more sedate course allowed Isabella the pleasure of observing the councillors in their flowing black robes, and how their elderly eyes were forever darting from their respected duke to glimpse a pretty breast momentarily raised from the water.

Godscalc Oom considered himself too old for such frivolities, though he knew he would enjoy hearing about them from Master Jan or whoever else might be at the Fallen Angel later in the day. Meanwhile he found himself once again charged with the finances of the ducal banquet that evening, seated heavily in the small room high in the town hall where only a few months earlier he had groaned over the excesses of the wedding festivities. Several bags of coins lay on the table before him, close to the lamp, and his secretary stood nearby, quill and paper at the ready.

Godscalc was muttering, reading from a list before him:

"Seventy-four dozen rolls of bread, sixteen joints of beef, forty-three pounds of lard, twenty-one shoulders of mutton, two hundred sausages, three pigs, three geese, twelve water birds, fourteen rabbits, twenty-two partridges, one hundred and fifty-nine chickens, sixteen pairs of pigeons, six cranes, eighteen cheeses, three hundred and fifty eggs, tripe and calves' feet for making jellies, sixteen pounds of butter, one bittern" . . . he paused with a long groan, incredulous eyebrows hoisted like trophies, before hastening through the remainder of the kitchen list, "cress, lettuce, pastries, flour, cabbages, peas, parsley, onions, morels, cream, vinegar, oranges, lemons, wines" . . . and on noticing the quantity of wines specified, he gave another groan, and stopped.

"We shall sink beneath the sea," said Godscalc wearily. And turning to the secretary, he added, "All this because of the capture of the Maid. Can you imagine what it would be like if the duke had defeated the Grand Turk and liberated Jerusalem? . . . Well, you draw up the due list of expense, and whom we should pay. Thank God, at least I'm not responsible for cooking it too."

The secretary returned the bags of coins to the iron chest, locked it, then gathered up the papers from the table. He could not help thinking, as he watched Godscalc take his small, widely spread legs toward the door, that from his appearance you could have imagined the ducal rentmaster to have already dined on the very foodstuffs he had been bemoaning. The old man, he felt sure, was now heading for his favorite tavern. The victualers would be lucky to be paid inside a month.

After the banquet there was a sumptuous ball, bathed in the magic of a summer night. The doors of the ducal palace were flung open to music and song, and everyone in Bruges who served the duke was present in whatever finery they possessed, or could borrow. And if, as had often been said, the special gift of the duke was to tap that Flemish gift for enjoyment, then at no other time had it been more liberally displayed. As was the custom people wore masks, both men and women; and as was also the custom, concealment afforded a thousand pretexts for indulgence—trysts, declarations of passion, exhibition of delicious secrets, and all manner of displays of true feeling which would no doubt become as untrue and unfelt as a trickster's tale by the morning.

Those dancers from among the court wore white. On the embroidered mantles of the men shone the most intricate clusters of pearls, sapphires, and rubies. The duke himself displayed a gorgeous necklace of gold and precious stones, and on his hat shone so many diamonds that there was not a space for more. Among the women, white became them like swans floating in the lamplight, their gowns billowing as they turned, hair looped with pearls entwined with threads of silver, arms and shoulders and breasts all but bare beneath webs of gossamer. Beneath the privacy of the mask the eyes of Jan and Margarethe fed on one another, while the eyes of many a ducal courtier noted the shapely girl with pale flaxen hair who moved with her lithe companion as though the dance were a mime of love and the lamps were the starlight in which they lay.

As Jan and Margarethe departed late that evening, their heads swimming with wine and dance, Jehan Lefèvre glided toward them and intimated in his most confidential manner that within a day or so the duke would summon Master Jan to proceed with the ducal portrait. Lefèvre had been scarcely inconspicuous at the ball: even if his lean, willowy figure had not betrayed his identity there was no mistaking the predatory thrust of the neck and chin whenever bare limbs passed within range. His eyes blazed through the peepholes of his mask, and while he imparted his precious information to Jan his sight veered not for one moment from Margarethe's bosom, still heaving from the exertions of the dance.

"I've never seen Lefèvre with a woman," commented Jan as they strolled homeward beside the dark canal. "And I've hardly ever seen him not staring at one."

He heard Margarethe chuckle as she pressed even closer to him. Her hair about his face smelled sweet.

"Don't you think he has a secret life?" she asked. "Don't they all have secret lives at the court?"

"In his case it's a secret I'd prefer not to know."

She stopped and turned to gaze at him.

"If *you* had a secret life I'd want to know about it," she said earnestly. It was almost dawn, and Jan could just make out the brightness of her eyes fixed on him. He knew that she was thinking of Jacqueline; that she was dreading his return to Zeeland. He had said perhaps too little to reassure her, and too much not to arouse her fears. Jan did not know what more he could do.

"Make love to me." There was urgency in her voice, and Jan desired her with that delicious sense of delay of one who knows he is about to spend the remainder of the night with the girl he loves.

For Margarethe, making love with Jan was her newfound land. Soon they would be married, and she would live with him in that house by the canal. She wanted his love, his children, his old age, all of him. Always. Each time he took her he took all of her, and before her eyes it was as though a curtain blacked out all the world beyond their love. And within that cocoon of two bodies she felt safe.

At the same time she glowed in the radiance of the wider world Jan inhabited. The man she loved was the most accomplished painter north of Italy, First Painter of Burgundy; everyone requested his services, paid court to him, honored him, and there was a fire of young pride in her that she was to become part of all this. And oh, if she were Jacqueline how she would want her painter, her prince, to come riding across the marshlands at her summons; how she would want to dress specially for him, entertain him, watch him watching her, and finally to receive from him an image of her own beauty such as no one else could have created. And then perhaps to offer as a sweet favor in return . . . herself. What luxury. But she was not Jacqueline. She was not the duchess Isabella. She was not even Bona. She was only a girl called Margarethe who had discovered love.

Jan marveled at how the shyness of the girl he first knew had quite melted. Margarethe had begun to glory in her own body in a way that amazed and delighted him. He would watch her washing, doing her hair, turning her face and her nakedness to the light in the mornings as if she were giving herself to the sun. She was so young and so lovely; each day she seemed to grow more beautiful to his eyes and to his own.

It was two days after the ball at the ducal palace. Knowing that Lefèvre would be calling any day now with the summons from the duke, Jan told Margarethe with a laugh how the herald invariably peered minutely at some drawing while delivering whatever message had been entrusted to him; and how on one occasion the drawing had been of the roofs and houses of Bruges seen from his own studio. Lefèvre had pressed his nose against the paper and scrutinized every window as if to uncover dark secrets within, and Jan had decided that he would make a similar drawing but with tiny figures of naked women within each window. Now, Jan decided, was the moment. And he took out a sheet of paper and settled himself to draw the familiar roofline exactly as he had done before.

"And the women?" Margarethe inquired, standing behind him while he worked, her hands on his shoulders and her head lowered occasionally to press her face into his hair. "Who will they be?"

"They'll be too small to be anybody," Jan replied, anxious not to arouse her jealousies.

"In that case they can all be me."

Jan turned and gazed at her in astonishment.

"You!"

"Why not? I don't want another woman naked in this place. Nor do I want you remembering other women you've drawn naked before. And anyway"—and she laughed delightedly—"we could have fun. And no one will ever know."

And with that she began to remove her clothing, indicating

as she did so that Jan should draw her. There was a mischievous look on her face, and she gave a little laugh from time to time.

"And now," she said, after Jan had covered several sheets of paper with sketches of her in various stages of undress, "I shall do all sorts of things women normally do about the house." And just as if she were fully dressed Margarethe proceeded to enact a pantomime of domestic life, pausing just long enough to enable Jan to sketch her in every pose.

By the end of the day Jan's innocent drawing of the houses of Bruges was complete. But in every window, if you looked close, was Margarethe pouring water, Margarethe sweeping the floor, Margarethe drawing the curtains, Margarethe combing her hair, and so on; and all the tiny figures were as naked as Eve—and so much prettier, Jan thought, than the Eve he had painted for Jodocus Vyt. It was altogether an enchanted day, and at the end of it they made love as though all their days would forever be just as enchanted.

Lefèvre arrived the following morning. Margarethe had already departed for her uncle's house. A broad-minded man, she assured Jan as she kissed him goodbye.

"He knows I love you. He knows we shall be married. That's enough."

Jan watched her make her way down the street of the Golden Hand. She wore the lightest cloak of blue, and her fair hair shone in the sunlight around the fringes of her hood. He admired the relaxed flexing of her body as she moved.

Lefèvre could scarcely miss the drawing: Jan had placed it prominently next to the panel of Michault de Caron as Adam, which he knew would be unlikely to distract the herald's eye.

"Jan, the duke will be ready for you tomorrow at nine," he announced.

Lefèvre was not customarily so quick to the point, but Jan recollected that since his humiliation at the Fallen Angel over the story of the Maid's capture he was passing as little time as possible in the company of vulgar merchants and craftsmen.

The ducal herald was standing gazing around him at the panels of the Ghent altarpiece, now only a few months from completion, Jan hoped.

"So the great work progresses," he went on, managing to suggest by his manner that the work was neither great nor had it progressed very far. As ever, there were two Jehan Lefèvres, the contemptuous courtier and the shrewd eccentric, and they announced themselves in that order.

Jan merely nodded. The herald swiveled theatrically on his heels as his eyes took in Hubert's landscape with the Holy Lamb, the portrait of Adam (Jan had hidden Eve), the Virgin Mary, and the angel of the Annunciation (Jan wondered if Lefèvre would recognize Arnolfini's mistress Lysbet). Then inevitably he began to lean like some dark insect toward the drawing Jan had placed there for the purpose, nose sharpening, nostrils flared, his eyes beginning to scan the gabled roofline of Bruges. Jan pretended to be occupied with other matters, but watched Lefèvre out of the corner of his eye. The herald's fingers were scraping against each other behind his back like fine twigs. At length there came a long sigh, and Lefèvre turned to Jan and his face wore the most fragile of smiles.

"What a very absorbing life a painter must have, I often think, Jan," he said. Still smiling, he leaned forward again toward the drawing and Jan could follow his eyes moving from window to window. "And for a painter to have a girl—so shapely and beautiful a girl—to draw over and over again: myself, I would never tire of it. You very evidently don't."

Jan could only laugh.

"But I don't imagine," Lefèvre went on, "that these little observations of domestic life will find their place in the cathedral of Ghent—even though I feel sure burgomaster Vyt would enjoy it."

Then with unusual haste Lefèvre replaced his hat and turned toward the door, throwing Jan a wry smile that was almost a wink.

"At nine o'clock then, tomorrow."

In the splendor of his robes of the Golden Fleece the duke was standing in the same sunlit room lined with tapestries in which he had received Jan almost five months earlier. Philip greeted him warmly, as always, but this time there were no preliminaries: the duke was here to be painted. There was a briskness about Philip's manner on this summer morning, as of a man who knew there was work to be done, and done promptly. Jan explained that he would complete the drawing he had made on his previous visit and straightaway begin the portrait itself.

"How long?"

Jan was taken aback by the curtness of the question. He explained that once the drawings could give him what he needed, all that was required then was that he should establish the outline of the portrait on the panel: the remainder, if the duke so wished, could be done without his presence.

Philip nodded. Without a word he assumed the noble pose he had adopted many months earlier, and Jan began to work in silence. At first he made a large rapid drawing of the duke standing before the bright latticed window, noting the exact position of the legs in their fine black hose, the hands clasped before him holding the charter of the Order of the Golden Fleece between long fingers; also the exact angle of the broad hat, the position of the insignia dangling from the golden collar, the folds of the scarlet gown lined with ermine and of the richly embroidered mantle. This done, Jan made careful studies and color notes of the duke's rings and necklace, and of the pearl brooch in his hat. He worked with speed and accuracy. Then he took out the almost completed silverpoint drawing of the duke's face and head, which he had looked at so often in his studio while planning in his mind the form which the finished portrait was to take. Jan placed this in front of him, peering at it sharply, switching his gaze from time to time toward the face of the duke standing before him—from one to the other, back and forth.

He found himself making small alterations to the mouth and the eyes, and for a time he was puzzled why this should be so. He wondered if perhaps in his initial nervousness he had overlooked certain characteristics of the duke's face—a slight watering and reddishness of the lower eyelids; a habit of tensing the muscles below the corners of the mouth, combined with a barely perceptible faraway smile; more than anything a curious blankness of feature, as if he had loaned his presence to this noble regalia but in spirit and in mind he were somewhere else.

But after a while Jan grew certain that he had not been unobservant. The duke had changed. It was as though he had aged several years in a matter of months: his face wore an air of frailty and fatigue, and even as these thoughts came to Jan's mind he realized that he read another quality in that face. It was cruelty.

It shocked Jan to recognize this. Indeed, as soon as he did so the duke appeared to blink back to life and became his former self again.

"I remember you telling me I should think while you draw my portrait," he said laughingly. "Well, I've tried. I'm not always good at it; sometimes the mind drifts away." Then he added more seriously, "I have many things that preoccupy me at the moment."

Jan knew that Philip was referring to the Maid, and what was to become of her; and he remembered his own conversation with Bona—again while he was painting her—and Bona's certainty that the duke would hand Joan over to the English. Jan now had before him the prepared panel on which he was to paint the duke's portrait, and he could see so clearly on that smooth dark surface how the noble figure would stand there in the glory of his regalia, an altar supporting a crucifix to his left, with behind him like a carpet of summer the lands of Burgundy stretching as far as dreams would carry to the glittering domes of the Holy City. There lay Philip's vision of the mightiest of all kingdoms of Christendom built in the service of chivalry, of honor, and of God. Philip "the Good"—as he wished to be known in times to come.

Boldly and with a sure hand Jan drew in the outline of the duke's standing form, and his eyes created around that form the exact position of the altar and the colonnade behind opening onto the vault of sky and the huge spread of cities, river, and forest. It was there in his mind already, all of it; and as he gazed almost hypnotized into the landscape that he would paint, his sight flew like a falcon to the farthest borders of Burgundy where the wind raked the dunes and the marshes— the lands of the sea. And suddenly through Jan's mind flashed an image of Jacqueline, dark-haired, all in white, barefoot on the shore, and a sword raised in her hand—bloodstained. She was weeping, and her tears stained her face and her white clothing until she stood there like a siren naked from the sea. Jan shuddered. The image faded. The duke was standing before him in the majesty of his robes, looking at him. He was smiling.

"And what news has my ambassador to Zeeland for me?" For a second Jan imagined the duke must have seen that image of Jacqueline reflected in his eyes, or else had read his mind. "How did you find my cousin?" Philip continued. "That is, if I may be permitted to talk now, master painter. I'm tired of thinking." And he gave a warm laugh. He looked his old self again.

Jan told him of his visit to Goes; how Jacqueline had received him with hospitality, how he had remained there more than a week, and would return to complete the portrait. "She is a beautiful lady," he added.

"You find her so?" There was a smile of curiosity on the duke's face. "And so of course did the lord of Gloucester," he went on, "unfortunately for her. But I imagine she told you of that." Jan nodded.

"Yes, she did, my lord," replied Jan somewhat hesitantly. "She talked a great deal while I painted her—as you predicted. But only of the past. . . . Hers has been a sad life."

"Of her own doing." Philip's voice sounded regretful. "She could have had everything."

For awhile nothing further was said, and Jan continued to work. The outline was complete, as well as the exact position of the hands, the feet, the angle of the head. He was concentrating now on the duke's face, aware that he might have no other chance. Suddenly Philip gave a short laugh.

"I can just imagine, Jan, you painting her while she so to speak painted me—as a villain, of course. Isn't that so?"

Jan looked at the duke, uncertain quite what to say. Then Philip laughed again.

"Come, you don't need to be afraid. I told you she hates me. I know it."

"Yes, that's so, my lord duke," Jan replied. "I think she

feels she was married against her will, and then robbed of her inheritance."

The duke's face became grave all of a sudden, and his eyes wandered toward the open window.

"Robbed!" he repeated. "Jacqueline could never see that the real robber was Humphrey of Gloucester. She was an infatuated girl. He took her to his bed to take her lands, and the moment I opposed him he ran away with his mistress. And now she's alone. She brought it on herself." There was a pause for several moments, and then he turned back from the window. "I wished better things for her."

The duke's voice was sad.

"But Jacqueline is a dangerous woman," he went on, "as I told you." He looked at Jan intently now. "What did you think was going on in her head?" he asked. Jan put down his brush.

"Anger, regrets, failure, loneliness perhaps," Jan replied.

"And revenge?"

Jan sensed he was gradually being cornered. The conversation with Bona came sharply into his mind. He felt he was walking a tightrope. It was a profound relief to him that Bona had not actually spoken a word to him about Jacqueline's appeal to the English. All he had was his own intuition, and he was not obliged to confess that.

"She said nothing about revenge, my lord," he replied; "nor did she hint at it, I assure you. As far as I could tell she sees no one. She lives alone."

The duke was still staring at him with hard, intelligent eyes, searching Jan's face.

"And when is it you return, Jan?"

"I wait to hear," he replied. "I shall let you know."

"Good," was all the duke said.

It was an uneasy time, and Jan was happy to become absorbed again in the portrait. It was going well. Jan felt relieved that he would not need to come back. Soon he would be able to finish the portrait at home. He could sense that the duke's mind had already drifted away on to other things. Then to Jan's surprise the duke suddenly said, "The Maid. I should like you to draw her portrait."

So Jan had been right.

"I shall accompany you," Philip went on. "She's at Beaurevoir."

Jan wondered why the duke should want a portrait of her. Again Philip surprised him.

"She's a noble creature," he said in that same sad voice in which he had talked of Jacqueline. "And grave. But she lives on dreams—like Jacqueline."

"And what will become of her, my lord?" Jan inquired. The duke's face took on a look of weariness.

"The English want her—Humphrey's brother, the lord Bedford—but they shall not have her," he said without hesitation.

So Bona was wrong: the duke's honor would prevail. But this meant, Jan realized, that if Jacqueline had her way the English would invade Holland and Brabant to put pressure on Philip to release the Maid. On this warm midsummer morning Jan could feel a chill of perspiration bind his brow. Here was a trap he could not avoid: he must return to Goes to complete Jacqueline's portrait and to be Philip's ambassador; then if he should get wind of any plot he was obliged to report the fact to the duke. At the same time there was Jacqueline—wronged, beautiful, enchanting—how could he betray her? It was as if the path he trod were a gorge narrowing on either side, and before long the rocks would press at him: there was no way through.

The duke was smiling.

"So it's not only me whose mind drifts," he said. And Jan realized he had been staring at the open window, for how long he did not know. He apologized.

"Perhaps you were thinking of another beautiful woman," Philip went on. "I hear you are to be married, and that she is as lovely as summer. Tell me about her: it's my turn to listen. You've worked enough, and I not at all."

Falteringly Jan described Margarethe to him: that when he left for Portugal she had been young—scarcely more than a child; that she had blossomed like a pale rose; that she loved him; that her father was dead and she living with her uncle in

Bruges, a master weaver; that she was everything he could ever wish for.

"And she enjoys domestic things," added the duke with the broadest of smiles. He pulled the bell rope by the unlit fireplace and a servant appeared carrying a silver tray with two glasses of wine. "And you practice your art while she does so, as I understand."

Jan did not know what to say as he realized to his horror that everything Lefèvre saw and heard was reported instantly to the duke. His little joke at the herald's expense was becoming an embarrassment.

"I understand she is as shapely as Venus. I'm pleased for you," Philip continued, still smiling broadly. "A lovely woman keeps a man young." And he handed Jan a silver goblet gleaming golden with wine. "And when you marry, Jan, I'll make you a handsome gift, and for your first child another. Meanwhile please give your lady my compliments. Let us drink to her."

And the two men raised their glasses to the absent Margarethe.

Then, as Jan was gathering his materials and preparing to leave, the duke added with a seriousness only lightly veiled by a laugh: "If her guardian and uncle is a master weaver, then maybe he can influence those guildsmen to temper their complaints. The weavers grow rich through my protection, yet they throw me looks of hate whenever I ask for money to protect them. They want everything, and give nothing." He paused before adding, "I fear there may be trouble one day."

Jan thought of Pieter van Orley and his grumbling anger against the ducal court, and he thought of Godscalc Oom's prophecies of further taxes to pay for the wars with France; and he felt uneasy.

The duke embraced Jan warmly as he left, commanding a servant to assist him with his materials and the portrait that was now carefully covered with a cloth.

"When I see that again it will be finished, I trust," he said in the doorway; "though I shall see you before that—after your return from Goes." The duke's eyes bore into Jan like a gimlet. "Goodbye now, my First Painter and my ambassador."

Jan's last image of Philip was of a stately figure in his robes of the Golden Fleece, his face set in a kindly but cunning smile. Jan made his way along the cool stone corridors of the palace thinking of the many things the duke had said. Only once were his thoughts interrupted: from an open door near the stairway he heard the sound of a woman crying, and the beseeching tones of another voice, also a woman's. One of them Jan did not recognize, but the woman in tears he knew instantly. It was the duchess Isabella. Jan felt a sense of shock: there was such anger and grief in those tears.

Then the door closed, and Jan continued his way down the stone staircase and across the courtyard toward the square and the clamor of midday bells.

The summer heat shimmered like waves over the flat land. To Jan it seemed sometimes like an augury of fire—a tremor, a warning that disturbed the languor of those long days.

He had taken to riding out of the city with Margarethe in the cool of the early morning. They would take the forest paths and she would canter on ahead, then turn and wait for him, tossing her fair hair into the sunbeams and laughing with that wonderful abandon to the senses which she invariably displayed now when they were alone. He loved her, and he loved watching the movements of her strong body as she controlled the friskiness of the chestnut mare. He would spur his own horse into a gallop and they would speed together through the curtains of sun-dust and shadow, leaping fallen trees and ducking branches heavy with the green of summer. And as the sun rose higher they would head for the broad river near Damme to water their horses and cool their own brows; or else make their way to a stream deep in the woods where dark pools held the reflection of a thousand branches combing the sunlight into veins of gold. They would undress and plunge into the gasping water, then make love on the moist carpet of green; and if he made a move to break the idyll Margarethe would press Jan's shoulders onto the grass with strong arms and kneel above him, her pale hair cascading about his face, her body lowered so that her breasts brushed his belly and chest.

"You shan't work this morning," she would whisper, her green eyes gazing down at him. "You shan't." He would roll her over, laughing, and another hour would pass.

Other distractions Jan succumbed to less willingly. The council of city guildsmen had been pressing him ever since his return from Portugal to paint the statues on the outside of the town hall, along with the fretted stone tabernacles which held them. It was a task any competent artisan could have accomplished with ease, but the burghers would have none other than Jan. Finally he concluded it was better to carry out the tedious work while the weather was favorable rather than find himself perched on windswept scaffolding amid the autumn rains. So now, after mornings of lovemaking in the forest, Jan's afternoons were spent perched on wooden planks daubing stone apostles and city fathers with garish colors.

The leaders of each craft guild had clearly posed for some workaday stonemason who had condemned them to expressions of eternal lifelessness; nonetheless, he had perfectly captured their pomposity, Jan thought. Only considerable self-restraint dissuaded him from reddening the nose of the chief fishmonger and endowing the master cutler with a majestic squint. However, Jan did permit himself a discreet joke at the expense of the chief butcher, whose squeaky voice had hectored him from below for more than an hour while he was painting his effigy. Next to the large carving knife which the mason had awarded the man as his tool of office Jan carefully added a legend, quite invisible from the ground, but which anyone who levitated thirty feet and understood Latin would have read as "By the Will of God with this knife I did remove my balls." Jan was rash enough after several goblets of wine that evening to confide his prank to several occupants of the Fallen Angel, all more drunk than he, with the result that he received further suggestions for embellishing the town hall which made his own contribution appear quite decorous. The court poet Michault de Caron then proceeded to devise an impromptu song about the master locksmith which rather strained the imagination; this over, he told of a solemn theological treatise he had seen in the duke's own library which he swore ended with the phrase *"Scriptori por pena sua datur pulchra puella"*—meaning, Michault explained, "For his trouble may this copyist be granted a beautiful girl." The conversation then slid—as it usually did on scabrous occasions—to the misdeeds of Abbot Eustache and the debauchery that accompanied the annual procession of holy relics between Bruges and the Abbey of the Dunes.

"Ah, but it brings revenues to the Church," commented Godscalc Oom solemnly between small sips of hippocras. "God is very forgiving. Think of Mary Magdalene."

It was the goldsmith Jan de Leeuw who sobered the evening with tales of unrest and rebellion in the countryside of Flanders. The others looked at him and there was silence in the Fallen Angel until De Leeuw expanded his story. His brother, it transpired, had arrived from Tournai in the south of the county, and reported that the countryside was lit by what appeared to be beacons of fire; except that they were not beacons, they were the houses of the bailiff's agents. Many of them had been killed: his brother had himself witnessed one man thrown naked into the river with a stone around his neck, and in another village a corpse hung from a gibbet with its eyes gouged out. Everywhere there were bands of men armed with swords and scythes: he had been compelled to seek the shelter of the forest to avoid them. It was taxes, he said, the burden of tolls and impositions. (Godscalc nodded knowingly.) Some men he had spoken to in the fields talked of starvation in this rich land—their children dying because their crops were stolen by the duke's men to feed his armies and his court. Or else bands of soldiers would descend on a village and rape every woman in sight. Left alone, the peasants could be comfortable, wealthy even, but year after year the weight of demands grew, while the bailiff's agents lined their own pockets and their own stomachs. The country people wanted Flanders to be free of the oppression of Burgundy: what did it matter to the peasants that the duke should have dreams of glory, that he should have captured the Maid, that he should long to stretch his dukedom from the Alps to the sea? Just let us be, they said. Soon, De Leeuw added, the unrest would surely spread to the guild workers in the towns. The bailiff of Bruges, Lodewijk van Haverskerke, was already alerting the militia. The duke, he thought, would want to end this war with France; and yet if he chose he could of course pay his army from his own pocket instead of milking the peasants and the traders. They were angry and they were desperate, and they would fight with their bare hands. Supposing this were to happen here?

It was rare to hear De Leeuw speak at such length and they all looked at the goldsmith uneasily, though his own face never once lost its expression of handsome calm, and the large tankard of beer remained steady in his hand.

Jan thought about all the things De Leeuw had said, reflecting that not so very far from those burning houses and gouged eyes he had that very morning been bathing in the tranquillity of the countryside in Margarethe's arms. Again it felt as though his own life of peace were being marched inexorably toward the thrash of a storm. He could imagine Margarethe's eyes filled with fear; yet for himself he was not afraid. Something told him he could ride whatever storm burst around him: it would sweep him along but he would survive unscathed, and Margarethe with him. But how could he persuade her of that?

Before stories of the unrest reached her, Jan decided that he would take her to Ghent. They would stay with Joos Vyt, whom she would surely grow to love; he would paint the portrait of the donor and his wife for the altarpiece; there would be calm and companionship; and there would be time to talk and be together. They would even plan the wedding.

She was overjoyed when he told her. Jan immediately wrote a letter to Joos and dispatched a messenger to Ghent; and while awaiting the reply he hastened to complete the work on the outside of the town hall. Now there were no more early rides through the countryside, no more bathing and lovemaking in the forest: shortly after dawn each day Jan clambered up the wooden scaffolding and prepared to color the garments of yet another apostle or yet another leading burgher. He began to paint them alternately, finding the banalities of the stonemason more tolerable if he switched from St. James with his scallop shell one day to the chief fishmonger with his herrings the next. St. Peter, he recognized, was only a fisherman and Joseph a carpenter, yet Jan found it hard to imagine any of these quarrelsome guildsmen abandoning the profits of their trade to follow a messiah; and should twelve apostles by chance be found among them they would be Judas to a man.

Such uncharitable thoughts sustained Jan in his labors, and within a week the task was complete and the scaffolding removed. A delegation of city fathers gathered in the square and made lengthy speeches to which Jan was compelled to reply. Much gratitude was voiced, and a great deal made of the extraordinary services of so eminent a painter. Jan endeavored to look as if this was indeed the case, careful to avoid any hint of the fact that the work could have been done by the least gifted boy apprentice. Margarethe blushed prettily throughout the ceremony, and Jan received a sum of gold appropriate to his elevated status.

That evening came a welcoming reply from Joos Vyt, and the following morning Jan and Margarethe rode through the southern gate of the city bound for Ghent.

Margarethe had by now heard rumors of the violence in the Flemish countryside, and had a frightened look on her face. Jan assured her that they had nothing to fear—they were not agents of the duke's bailiff but simple travelers visiting Ghent—and as they rode through the summer meadows her anxieties began to disperse in the sun. They followed the same track Jan had taken during the winter on his first visit to Joos Vyt, and Margarethe was soon enchanted by everything around her. It seemed impossible to believe that these sighing forests and quietly flowing rivers could ever be the scene of bloodshed and death, or that anyone could starve here. There was hardly a soul to be seen except occasional laborers in the fields who greeted them as they passed by, their eyes lingering on Margarethe's radiant face and flaxen hair. She waved to them and threw them the loveliest of smiles.

They reached Vyt's house at midday, and the distant jangle of a bell brought servants who relieved them of their luggage and led away their horses. They stood in the long empty hall Jan remembered, looking about them until suddenly the burgomaster appeared at the head of the stairs, his face beaming and his arms outstretched in welcome. He seemed even shorter in stature than Jan recalled, and more rotund: as he descended the stairs one foot reached cautiously for the next step and then his body swiveled until the other foot joined the first. All the while his smile never wavered and he made short excited exhalations of breath.

On reaching the hall he embraced Jan like a son before stepping back almost ceremoniously as he turned to face Margarethe. For a moment Vyt's expression appeared blank, but then his eyebrows began to push his forehead upward into a maze of furrows and at the same time he slowly raised his hands before him as if all were controlled by a single invisible string from above.

"My dear," he said to Margarethe, in a tone of astonishment, and Jan could see beads of water in the reddish corners of his eyes, "I have to say this is almost too much for me. Can it be that Jan really deserves someone so lovely?" Whereupon he laughed. "Margarethe," he went on, his face assuming an expression of such gentleness, "you are very, very welcome in this house." And he embraced her too.

A moment later Vyt's wife appeared, and Joos introduced her. She was a shy, watchful woman with a kindly face, who murmured rather than spoke and concerned herself immediately with showing Jan and Margarethe their rooms, her face turning anxiously toward her visitors from time to time to make sure her hospitality was considered suitable. And when Margarethe smiled appreciatively pleasure spread awkwardly over the old woman's face.

"I like them," said Margarethe when they were alone. "And he likes you so much," she added proudly, and kissed him. "And so do I." Her deep green eyes were very close. "But I suppose we shall have to be very proper for a few days, shan't we?" She gave that lovely, hungry laugh Jan loved, and he ran his fingers slowly down her body.

"We'll see," he said.

The next few days were some of the happiest they had ever spent. While Jan worked on the drawing of Joos, Vyt's wife took Margarethe busily under her wing, visiting countless members of the Vyt family, to whom she was introduced—to her deep pride—as the future wife of the First Painter of Burgundy. They were cloth merchants, most of them, and they lived in houses along the banks of the river Lys that were only a little less splendid than the one inhabited by Joos and his wife. It was Margarethe's first experience of the ease of wealth, and she loved it. There was a sturdiness about these people, and an ease of manner, which warmed Margarethe to them. They went about their lives at a confident and unhurried pace, sharply attending things without fuss, effortlessly in control as if the world functioned solely for them to take charge of it. This was how it should be, she reflected, and how she wanted it to be for Jan and herself. She pictured herself with a large family of her own presiding over just such an unshakable kingdom.

After three days Jan had completed two silverpoint drawings, one each of Vyt and his wife. She had quite naturally slipped into the attitude of piety appropriate to the donor's wife: Joos on the other hand, hands clasped before him, kept recalling incidents of an irreverent nature which would crinkle his heavy face into a smile, and Jan would have to pause while the old man recomposed his features.

"I'm sorry, Jan," he said after the tenth or fifteenth pause. "I am a God-fearing man—you must believe me. It's just that when I assume this attitude of prayer all sorts of godless thoughts come into my mind."

Jan did his best to obtain an image of sincere devotion, yet he feared that however hard he tried Vyt's eyes retained a certain relentless gleam, as if contemplation of the better life had in that very instant been distracted by the sight of a good bottle of Beaune.

This, Jan realized, was not so far from the truth. The moment each sitting was over Vyt would gleefully make his way to the tall oak cupboard by the wall and lay on the table the same two glasses he had produced for Jan on his first visit here, together with a venerable bottle of his choice.

"Enjoy this while you can," he said after the third day. "This evening I fear there will be none."

Jan's heart fell when Joos informed him of the reason. There was nothing he could do about it, Joos explained wearily, but their guest for dinner was none other than the bishop of Ghent, Bishop Denis. A man of ferocious religious ardor, Vyt went on, who partook of wine only for the sacrament—and indeed partook of any other worldly pleasure only to comprehend more painfully man's state of sin.

"Not a man to my taste, Jan; nonetheless, a man with whom I have to deal. He is my bishop and I am his burgomaster. And he will be the recipient of your painting, which is why he wishes to meet you." Jan's spirits sank even lower. Seeing his face, Joos chuckled and filled Jan's glass generously. "One saving grace," he went on, "the bishop will leave early in order to pray, perhaps for us." And Joos laughed heartily. "He told me only yesterday that I should pray to God daily so that I might experience the daily baptism of tears. I told him I did not imagine the Lord God would waste his tears on me, but I fear the bishop is not a man blessed with humor. Among the clergy in Ghent he is known, by the way, as Dr. Ecstaticus. He is also reputed to converse with the dead—I do not know why, nor with whom. And I'm told that he sleeps next to women in order to test his own chastity—but that may just be gossip. . . . Let me give you a flavor of the man."

And with that Joos went over to a low cupboard at the far end of the room and returned bearing a volume bound in vellum.

"Bishop Denis presented me with this on my appointment as burgomaster. It is his own writings. A treatise. Sample it."

Jan took the volume and opened it. "Concerning the four states of man," he read. The Latin text that followed was not lengthy, ample space being allowed in the margins for annotation and comment. Jan noticed that Joos had made no such additions, only a number of soiled thumb marks. He turned the pages.

"Just read something out," urged Joos. "It's all much the same."

Jan read at random. The passage was on hell.

" 'Let us imagine a white-hot oven and in this oven a naked man, never to be released from such a torment. Does not the mere sight of it appear insupportable? How miserable this man would seem to us! Let us think how he would sprawl in the oven, how he would yell and roar: in short, how he would *live*, and what would be his agony and his sorrow when he understood that this unbearable punishment was never to end.' "

Jan closed the book and looked at Joos.

"And this man is coming to dine this evening?"

"I fear so. I promise you, I shall have a bottle of something special for us after he departs. Meanwhile I fear it is up to you to explain to the bishop how you have set about the altarpiece for his cathedral."

At that moment Jan bitterly regretted ever having agreed to paint it.

By the time the bishop arrived at six Jan had composed the situation in his mind. His experience of zealous churchmen had taught him that invariably their public zeal was in equal proportion to their private vanity, one masking the other. As the painter of a huge altarpiece for Bishop Denis's cathedral, Jan's task as he saw it was to seem to appeal to the former while liberally sweetening the latter. Above all, he must support Joos, whose gift to his native city was—beneath the playfulness of his manner—something dear to his heart. Perhaps more than his place in heaven, it was his place in history. At the same time Jan decided to be in no way daunted by this dreadful occasion. And Margarethe looked enchanting: he would feast his eyes on her during dark moments of the evening.

The bishop was a tall, emaciated man of about fifty. His black robes hung loosely from his body and his remaining hairs just as loosely from the scalp. His eyes were dark-rimmed, perhaps from the long habit of sleep interrupted by prayer, and his mouth receded into the loose parchment of his cheeks. There was not a ray of enjoyment on his face, except maybe that of perceiving how his own presence daunted those around him. He peered critically at the large pitcher of water laid before him on the table as though suspicious that some alchemy of Vyt's might cunningly turn it into wine.

If there was any grain of good humor in the man it was instantly expunged by the sight of Margarethe as she entered the room dressed, as she had resolutely decided to be, as lovely as possible—which to Jan's delight meant a close-fitting robe of white satin that made flattering emphasis of the softness of her shoulders and the fullness of her breasts. It would have needed a reptile not to be warmed by her presence, and Dr. Ecstaticus was just such a creature.

"Is she not beautiful, my lord bishop?" announced Joos, seating himself comfortably at the table and glancing appreciatively at Margarethe. Clearly Vyt had decided to make no concessions to the bishop's stern tastes and to pretend he was a man like any other.

Jan could see Bishop Denis stiffen as his eyes rested on Margarethe.

"True beauty," came the cool reply, his eyes still on Margarethe, "appertains only to God." He drew breath deeply and began to survey the company as though it were his congregation. "All beauties of creation," he went on, "are but brooks flowing from the source of supreme beauty."

The bishop awarded Vyt a coldly reproachful look.

"But are such things not beautiful nonetheless?" asked Jan calmly. The bishop turned a surprised face toward him.

"Master Jan," he replied firmly after a little cough, "true beauty is spiritual, not material. It is visible to us only as light."

Jan noticed a look of gentle enjoyment begin to cross Vyt's face as his eyes moved from one to the other. His wife was gazing resolutely downward, wishing this entire evening would disappear, while Margarethe was looking uncomfortably aware of her own nakedness.

"My lord bishop," Jan went on, speaking softly, "I am a painter, not a theologian. Your knowledge of course far exceeds mine." Jan could see a glimmer of satisfaction in the bishop's eyes. "But as a painter I have observed that we perceive light only by what it illuminates—even small particles of dust as in a sunbeam. It seems to me that there are two kinds of knowledge available to us, the physical and the divine, and that it is through the first that we may obtain access to the second."

He paused, seeing beads of perspiration begin to form on the bishop's face.

"As a humble painter," Jan continued in as gentle a voice as he could muster, "this is what I feel I am here to do—to paint the world I know since I cannot paint the one I do not know."

There was a look not so much of anger as of lofty reproach on the bishop's face.

"If you were a churchman, Master Jan, I should accuse you of heresy. As a mere craftsman your folly may perhaps be excused as ignorance. I must point out to you that the divine doctor, the revered Thomas Aquinas, established beyond question that there is but one indivisible system in this world: everything is dependent upon God. It stands to reason therefore that you cannot find images from your earthly life to describe God; rather should you be seeking an absence of images corresponding to eternity."

The bishop looked about him to observe the effect of his enlightenment upon those at the table. The two women were gazing studiously elsewhere. Vyt's expression remained one of eager silence. Jan was controlling his irritation with some difficulty.

"In that case, my lord bishop," he said, "would you have me paint your altarpiece with nothing on it at all except light? And what would that mean to your congregation?"

Jan was unsure whether the bishop's mouth fell open with disbelief or with anger, but he was too aggravated by this pompous prelate to stay silent now.

"My lord," he continued, "permit me to say that I have thought much about what I do, and have discussed my profession widely with men of the church. As I see it, I paint for ordinary people who do not have the benefit of theology; nor can they read holy books, or indeed read at all. So what I paint are things that people can see and touch and understand. Personally, I cannot imagine how God's design and purpose may be comprehended by anybody except through what we know of the world we live in: I cannot paint prayers or visions. If I am wrong then I have been wasting my life."

Jan saw that Denis was shaking. The bishop took a rapid sip of water and appeared to make an effort to calm himself. But there was no stemming the torrent Jan had released.

"You may indeed have wasted your life," he began, the measured words uttered with a tremor of rage. White hands clawed at the table as he spoke and the tall forehead glistened with moisture.

"Let me tell you about the world you live in and which you have the temerity to offer to God on his altar," he went on, his voice growing louder and more shrill. "It is a cesspool. A dunghill. A rotting corpse on which maggots feed. It is a place given over to every practice of the devil and where Satan himself reigns. And you have the effrontery to tell me you paint it in order that people shall understand heaven!"

There was a pause while the bishop's rage erupted in a wordless explosion of sound as if he were expelling Jan's foul person from his body. Then his eyes seemed to glow like torches and he began to speak as though another voice were speaking through him and a vision of the world were unrolling before him. He spoke of fields of severed limbs plucked by kites and crows, of heads impaled on trees, rivers bubbling with blood, mountains erupting into fire, houses, villages, cities engulfed by torrents of molten flame. And everywhere on earth the cries of the damned, and everywhere in the livid sky the relentless beat of a drum.

Jan sat horrified by what he heard. He was watching a madman dressed as a servant of God. Margarethe was looking pale, Vyt's wife numb. Yet Vyt himself sat apparently unconcerned, his moist eyes fixed on the bishop and his mouth set quite calmly.

Then it was as though the vision passed, and Denis was looking at the three of them round the table with the lofty scorn of a man addressing them from the pulpit. Everywhere, he explained, the world was punished by war—Flanders, Burgundy, France. People rose against their masters, brother killed brother, the devil's servants wielded their bloodied swords. He spoke of Joan the Witch whom the voices of Satan had commanded to don men's armor and to strike at the lawful crown of France. And he spoke of the adulteress Jacqueline whose insatiable appetites seized men's lands and men's bodies. Our land, he said, is no better than a garden of lust: the world was ruled by harlots offering their perfumed bodies shamelessly to men's eyes and succoring the Lord's children with the poison of their drugs.

The bishop's eyes blazed accusingly first in the direction of the burgomaster, and then Jan, before directing their heat on the loveliness of Margarethe. Jan felt incensed by the lascivious hatred of that gaze.

"My lord bishop," he said, aware that his own voice trembled with suppressed anger, "you talk of the divine doctor; but it was the view of Aquinas that all things on earth have been created in and through God. How, then, is it possible that a good and benign God could have created such corruption?"

The bishop's eyes turned their inquisition from Margarethe's flesh back to Jan, and succulent noises could be heard from within his mouth.

"Young man," he answered, his voice thin with disdain, "do I have to point out to you that the Creation preceded the Fall of Man? Corruption of the flesh was not God's doing, it was Adam's. And who tempted him? Woman. 'She gave me of the tree, and I did eat': so did Adam answer God. To which God replied, 'In sorrow shalt thou eat of it all the days of thy life.' And so he drove Adam and Eve from the Garden. *That* is what you ignore in your blindness. *That* is the cause of man's corruption." The bishop's bony finger spiked the air before Jan's face. Then the finger turned on a note of triumphant loathing. "It was women who corrupted Adam; woman who turned this world into a stinking dunghill."

There was the scraping of a chair against the floor, and Margarethe rose. Without a word she left the room. Jan threw a glance at the bishop and hurried after her. She was sobbing on her bed, deep gulps of misery, her hands tense against the white linen. He held her and could feel her whole body heaving. Her head was turning from side to side.

"No! No! No! No!" she was saying, over and over again.

After a while he could feel her body begin to relax, and he kissed her very gently. Her crying was calmer now, and before long he knew from her breathing that she had fallen asleep. Jan pulled a blanket over her bare shoulders, smoothed the strands of hair from her damp face, and kissed her again on her closed eyelids. It was still daylight but he lit a lamp and placed it on the table by her bed; then he quietly left the room and closed the door. He could hear no sound from downstairs.

The bishop had gone. To Jan's surprise Vyt was smiling as he entered the room, and holding out to him a tall glass of wine. Jan drank it gratefully and Vyt refilled the glass and his own.

"So now you have heard the voice of God in this city," he said with no note of concern or dismay. "I don't believe the Almighty would recognize that voice as his own, do you?" he added. "Jan, you did extremely well."

Jan grunted. It seemed to him quite clear that if he had done well it was certainly at the expense of Vyt's altarpiece.

"I'm sorry," he said.

"Whatever for?" replied Joos with a look of surprise.

"About the painting."

"What's wrong with the painting? Did I not look devotional enough today?"

"I assume," Jan explained, "that after what I said, and what the bishop said, there can be no question of his wanting it."

Vyt laughed, again refilling their two glasses.

"Rubbish!" he retorted. "You don't know the bishop as I do. He will want it even more." Seeing Jan's perplexed look, Joos explained. "You must understand the power of remorse in a man of extreme passions. Remember, he is Dr. Ecstaticus. Ecstasy of fury is always followed by an ecstasy of regret. He loves to play the sinner who repents: he believes that brings him closer to God. The bishop will be here tomorrow begging my forgiveness, I assure you."

"But I shall not be here, Joos. I could not meet him again." Jan shuddered at the thought and comforted himself with Vyt's excellent wine.

"That will be a sadness for me," Joos replied. "But I fear you will have to meet him again when the painting is unveiled. Meanwhile, Jan, please return soon when you've painted my devout self. I've so enjoyed it." And Vyt placed both hands affectionately on Jan's shoulders. "But tell me, is Margarethe all right?"

Jan nodded. He explained that she was sleeping.

"I'm glad," Vyt went on, smiling. "I fear it was the sight of so much pulchritude that set the bishop going. Those who are tempted always blame the tempter. I've always felt it was hard on Eve to have taken the blame for Adam's weakness. If you'll forgive my saying so, your lovely Margarethe will be disturbing the bishop's dreams tonight. Never mind. Let us drink to her—and to your happiness."

Joos called his wife to join them, and the three of them raised their glasses to Margarethe, who lay asleep in her tears.

But happiness did not seem to be Margarethe's destination in the days that followed.

She awoke in the early dawn in a silent house, alone with her thoughts. She remembered Jan cradling her the evening before, but now he was not here. Why should it feel significant that he was not here? Why should she feel abandoned? It was not only loneliness that wrapped itself around her; it was as though her body had been soiled by the bishop's eyes and words. Then Margarethe realized that she was still fully dressed. She rose and went over to the mirror, remembering how the previous evening she had prepared herself for Jan so lovingly, how it had excited her to dab the scent of lily of the valley between her breasts, knowing that his eyes would rest there and later his lips and tongue would furrow there. She let her dress fall to the floor and stood examining her reflection, and as she did so she saw before her in the mirror, not a woman who was to be Jan's wife, but the bishop's whore. Margarethe shuddered. She was too confused to understand the effect of the bishop's words and of his relentless eyes; but she remembered his voice thundering across that room, speaking of a garden of lust, a world ruled by harlots offering their perfumed bodies to men's eyes. She did not know why she felt so afraid, or why it was that she was overcome by a sickening of guilt, of shame, that she should have given herself so totally to Jan, her whole body his. Was she his whore? And might there be others?

She wrapped a blanket around her body and felt warmed by it. As a young girl she had imagined she would never give herself to any man. She had watched her growing body with distaste, and when men's eyes lingered on her she would retreat into herself, wrap herself around in gray just like the blanket now about her. She had been safe then; no one could hurt her.

When Jan appeared in her room to inquire how she was, she found herself recoiling from him, crossing her arms over her breast. His hurt look wounded her, yet she could do nothing: she did not want him to touch her. He knew she was upset by the bishop's outburst and suggested they ride back to Bruges a quieter way, along the riverbank of the Lys where there were flowers and sweet meadows, and they could talk at ease. He was upset, he said, that she had been subjected to such foul thoughts. There were churchmen with sick minds who raved against what they lusted for most, and their choked lust turned to poison.

They said farewell to Vyt and his wife. And perhaps Margarethe's fears would have melted among the summer flowers, as she would have loved them to do, had worse events not overtaken them.

By midmorning the two riders were approaching the village of Deurle on a rise above a sharp bend of the river. They could see the church above the clustered roofs, and before them meadows swept down to the quiet water. Jan was riding a little ahead. Suddenly she saw him rein his horse vigorously and turn toward her.

"Go back!"

But they could not go back. In a minute there were soldiers all around them. From their caps and cuirasses Jan knew them to be Burgundians: there must have been nine or ten of them, and they were drunk. Jan grasped Margarethe's bridle and tried to ride through them, but two of the soldiers seized the horse's head: the animal shied violently, nearly throwing him and tearing his grip from the other horse's bridle. He drew his dagger and struck out at one of the men, but the soldier had reeled out of range, laughing, while Jan's horse continued to buck and rear. The other soldiers gathered around Margarethe. They were jeering and pulling at her. Jan tried to drive his horse at them but the terrified creature jerked away and its flailing hooves lifted one of the soldiers into a ditch. Then he saw Margarethe was falling. Rough hands were seizing her, pressing her to the ground. The soldiers were jeering. She was half naked, a soldier's hand on one breast. Another was unbuckling his belt. She was screaming. Jan flung himself from his horse and plunged a dagger deep into the back of the nearest soldier. His yell as he collapsed caused the others to turn their heads and gave Jan just time to thrust his hand into his wallet and brandish the bright red seal he always kept with him—the seal of Burgundy given to him by the duke. The soldiers slunk back the instant they saw it: they began to run in all directions, the slowest of them hitching his clothing with one hand. In a surge of fury Jan leapt at him and sank the dagger into the man's back.

Suddenly there was silence. Two soldiers were lying dead: he had killed them, Jan realized with no more than a passing sense of surprise. Margarethe was on her knees, her garment pressed to her bare torso. She was shaking, but made no sound until he held her, and then she began to sob uncontrollably from the deepest well of anguish. All around her the beautiful world seemed a hateful place and she thought she would go mad. There was so much pain within her that nothing from outside could find access to her mind. She was scarcely aware of being lifted onto Jan's horse, of his holding her while they rode, her own horse following behind. The day passed by in a dark dream: she heard his words, comforting her, but they brought no comfort: she did not know who she was, but she knew that she must go somewhere—away, away, away.

Places passed before Margarethe like shadows—places she recognized but did not know. She heard her own voice but did not know that either. She was in Bruges, in Jan's house. There were people—helping her, holding her arm, peering anxiously. One of them was Jan, and she did not want him.

Chapter Seven

She was gone.

Jan did not know that he could feel such pain. He moved about the house as if he were his own ghost. In the streets he imagined her at every corner and on every bridge, and on his return he would urge himself not to hope she would be there; but he always did hope and then the pain of his empty studio was almost unbearable. He would wake at dawn at the hour when only a few weeks before they would rise and go riding in the forests, and for a few half-awake moments Jan would forget this was not one of those mornings; and then the emptiness of his bed and his room was like a cell. It was impossible to work: he would walk the streets aimlessly, often finding himself gazing out from the ramparts southward, his eyes purposelessly following the turning and turning of the mill sails across the summer plain. Sometimes it would grow dark before he moved.

He did not count how many days passed like that.

At first Jan did not know where Margarethe had gone. Her uncle's house was locked, empty. Through the window he could see so many unused familiar things, and when he returned to his own house in the street of the Golden Hand there too were so many unused familiar things.

But one day there was a message. A young man Jan did not know brought a letter—from his father, he said, who was in Louvain. Jan hastily broke the seal: the letter was from Margarethe's uncle, the master weaver, written in an awkward careful hand. Before he even read it Jan wanted to seize the young man and order him to lead him to Margarethe; but the man had already slipped away.

The letter numbed him. It said so little, and with such finality. Margarethe was unwell in her mind and could see no one. The master weaver and his wife had taken her to Louvain and were taking care of her and of her mother, who was dying. Margarethe wished him to say that she would always love Jan, but that she could not go through with it: it would destroy her. Then the weaver added, as though he felt the need to stress how critically Margarethe felt this, that he had narrowly restrained her from throwing herself from the window. It was then that he and his wife had decided to take her away from Bruges immediately. He was heartbroken, he said, but he feared for the girl. She must be looked after.

Jan put down the letter, bewildered.

It was Bona, her hand on his arm, who helped him understand.

"Jan, Margarethe's young, so very young," she said. "Too much has happened too quickly—too much that has terrified her. Can you imagine what it must be like almost to be raped? A gang of soldiers?"

Jan nodded. The thought brought back the pain, and Margarethe's pain.

"She's always been frightened of the world," Bona went on. "And now she wants to shut it away. I always told you she wanted to lock you in a box. But you're not like that, and she knows it."

"And what should I do?" Jan asked emptily.

"There's nothing you can do," replied Bona. "Except wait. She has to find her own strength. And if she does, she'll come back."

"And if she doesn't?"

"Then she'd be no use to you anyway."

"And she'd become a nun?"

"Maybe—if that's what she needs." Bona walked across the studio and pulled back the sheet covering the painting of herself as Eve. "Or maybe," she went on without turning to look at Jan, "she needs to marry someone very ordinary and very safe."

It wounded Jan to think of Margarethe living with someone else, giving her body to him—her laughter, those green eyes, that eager look.

"She's not your property, Jan," Bona added, turning and noticing the flicker of jealousy in his face. "And neither are you hers."

Bona's visit restored some normality to his mind. She was right: too much had happened too quickly. Their lovemaking together—such a beckoning fire. Her vulnerability. Then the bishop's terrible words about harlots and perfumed nakedness. The assault by the soldiers—to be half stripped, imagining what was about to happen, the man unbuckling himself above her. Jan shuddered as he remembered it: and he had killed two men to save her. A double murderer: he would have killed them all if he could, he would kill anyone for her.

After that it had been as though everything became a confirmation of her terrors. The news that the duchess Isabella had lost her child. The message from Jacqueline requesting Jan to return to Zeeland. And then—strangest of all—the news that Joan the Maid had tried to escape by hurling herself from the prison tower at Beaurevoir. Was that why, by some strange connection, Margarethe had tried to throw herself from her own window? Jan remembered her fierce championing of Joan during that evening in the snow during the winter carnival, and her anger at Hugo's mockery of the Maid.

There was a mystery about the Maid which seemed to hold the clue to so many things. Jacqueline's desperate bid for her lost lands. The change in the duke (Jan still could not forget that hard, absent look). And now Margarethe.

She had gone. So suddenly. So many flowers trampled on before his eyes.

After the pain, Jan felt a surge of inexplicable anger.

Lefèvre led Jan to the duke on the morning of his departure. Philip looked grave, and again there was that empty, distant look on his face which Jan had noticed at their last meeting.

"So, you're returning to Zeeland," he said quietly. Jan nodded. The duke seemed lost in thought for a while; then his face brightened a little and briefly something of the old warmth returned. "Don't let it delay my own portrait too long, Jan," he went on, with just the shadow of a smile. "I know Jacqueline is more exciting to paint than I am: nonetheless, you are *my* painter . . . and of course *my* ambassador, don't forget."

Jan noticed a sharpness in the duke's eyes as he said this, and felt a little uncomfortable.

"Of course," he replied.

Then Philip let out a deep breath and turned toward the window.

"Forgive me, Jan, my low spirits today," he said, his eyes still fixed on some distant point. "As you know, I have many troubles. I had not hoped it would be like this," he added, and his voice sounded weary again.

Then he spoke, quite without anger, of the unrest in Flanders and the killing of the bailiff's agents, the burning of houses, and the belligerence of the guildsmen here in Bruges. And he spoke of Joan: her attempt to escape from the tower at Beaurevoir, his need to guard her more securely.

"But for what?" He sounded exasperated for a moment, and began to pace the room restlessly. "The duke of Bedford keeps pressing me to turn her over to the English. And I refuse: I don't want Joan hunted as a witch by that self-seeking bishop, Cauchon. But it's not easy, Jan. Remember, Bedford's wife, Anne, is my own sister."

So the issue of Joan was not a matter of honor or money, it was ties of blood. Jan's mind turned to Jacqueline, and again he felt deeply torn. He longed for the "black raven" to regain her inheritance—such a woman, wronged, desperate, majestic; but how he dreaded having to decide if he should betray her. It was a choice of evils: if only fate would enable him to choose neither.

The duke had stopped pacing the room and was standing once again by the window. Suddenly he turned, and Jan saw that there was pain in his eyes.

"I've lost a child, Jan, and you have lost a bride," he said. Jan felt moved. Philip's grief was almost naked, and yet his consideration for Jan rose from the heart. Then with a frail smile he added, "But we have to believe that your Margarethe will come back, and that Isabella will bear me another child. Think of that while you're riding northward . . . and take care."

Jan reached Antwerp at dusk on that late summer evening, and in the morning headed north for the lands of the sea. Margarethe lived in his thoughts like a pool of sadness all this time. Was she thinking of him? And what did he really think about her now?

It disturbed him to realize that he no longer knew. He loved her. Yes, he would always love her. But perhaps Bona was right: she was so very young, and she wanted to lock him safely from the world; whereas he needed to explore that world, embrace it, feel its dangers in his veins.

The sky appeared to spread over the lands of the sea. Before Jan lay that familiar wilderness of marsh and dunes, dry now under the heat of the evening. A flock of cranes rose from beyond a dike, their long necks and legs stretched like spears as they followed a line of dark mills whose sails barely turned against the windless blue of the horizon. Such vastness of nothing: Zeeland.

From time to time—nervously—Jan felt for the seal of Burgundy in his wallet, and each time he did so he remembered that moment of horror by the riverbank. This seal, and his dagger—only these had saved her. He had killed for her. Again Jan felt the weight of the seal. No one had approached him on his journey, but he knew there were eyes within the woods where he had ridden and even now there would be eyes in the hidden creeks of this wilderness. Of course they knew who he was: that was why they left him to ride by. He was the duke's ambassador.

At the gate of the castle Jan was met by the same young page in red, who smiled in recognition and led him without a word to the bedroom high over the sea which he had occupied before, only now Jan noticed there were fresh flowers arranged in vases about the room, and by the bed a sprig of lavender. The windows were open onto the warm silence of the evening.

The duchess, the boy said, would join him in the garden: meanwhile he was to have this. And the page handed Jan a small package wrapped in black silk. Jan followed him along the cool stone corridors and narrow stairways: they passed the large door which Jan remembered led to the hall where he had first met Jacqueline in the shadows by the fire, and again he noticed the shield above the entrance painted with a mailed fist and the bird with outspread wings and a sword in its beak. The black raven.

Jan remembered the garden, too, with its circular pool of rushes and irises, and the stone sundial set between twin trees clipped into the shape of two birds facing one another. Jacqueline's place of peace, she had called it. There was no one in the garden, and the page bowed and departed. Jan looked at the package in the palm of his hand: puzzled, he pulled at the fine thread which bound it and carefully unfolded the black silk. There was enough light from the evening sky to make out what lay in his open hand. It was a gold locket, and across the face of it was embossed that same emblem of the bird and the sword. Why had Jacqueline given him this? Jan turned it over; he could see a small indentation where the lid opened, and with his fingernail gently pulled at it. There was a cavity inside, quiet empty. Jan closed it again and stood puzzled as the evening darkened around him.

He still had it in his hand, feeling the smooth gold with his fingers, when behind him Jan heard the soft creak of a door, and turning around, he saw Jacqueline standing in the twilight.

"Welcome, Jan." The voice was deeper, softer, than he remembered. And she extended both hands for him to grasp; then she noticed his awkwardness as he tried to take her left hand while at the same time holding the locket, and she laughed and withdrew it. "A small gift for a friend," she added. "I've given you nothing."

Jan thanked her, not knowing what more he should say. She just looked at him, smiling. Jan saw that she was wearing the same slim white dress she had worn on the last evening of his visit three months earlier; and there was something about the way she said little and smiled at him that told him she had deliberately done this, as if to banish the passage of time.

It was exactly as it had been before. They dined alone at a table by the fire. Servants quietly brought in dishes, and a flask of dark wine. Jacqueline hardly spoke, but from time to time she would seem to feel his attention wander to her shoulders and neck and the caressing shadows from the fire on her breasts, and her black eyes would fix curiously on him, the firelight catching them like small lanterns in the dark. He longed to know what she was thinking, what she was planning, what if anything she would have to say to him. She had promised to tell him about the duke. He wondered if she would speak about Humphrey of Gloucester, and if so what she would say.

Through the evening, in the silence between them drifted the soft drag and whisper of the sea. The enchantment was just as Jan remembered, and the touch of her fingers on his arm was that same naked gesture, and later it reached out into his sleep as he lay in the room filled with her flowers.

In the morning she was there in the same room overlooking the marshes and the sea. Smiling. The radiant Jacqueline, as Jan had first seen her. He pulled back the cloth from the portrait where he had left it three months before and was astonished to see the proud, tragic figure with downcast eyes he had painted such a short time ago. The dark tale she had told him flooded back into his mind: Jacqueline married against her will —her flight to England—her love for Humphrey of Gloucester —his betrayal of her—the defeat and capture by Philip—her escape dressed as a page—the long final siege—the humiliating treaty—the loss of the right even to marry without the duke's consent.

Jan recalled the rage with which she had spoken, and the terrible calm with which she had added, "I even lost the right to be a woman."

He began to paint her again—exactly where he had left off. And as he did so, the fine brush touching the shadows of her face, that same intimacy returned. There was silence for a while, the silence of reacquaintance. Then, as he began to paint the heavy eyelids, she looked up at him with that inviting, teasing smile.

"Do you enjoy painting me?" she asked.

Jan looked surprised.

"Yes, I do," he said.

"More than you enjoy painting the duke?"

Jan smiled. "The duke is not a beautiful woman."

"But he is a flatterer . . . like his court painter," Jacqueline added with a slight laugh. Jan said nothing for a moment, and saw that she was watching him questioningly.

"I thought I was just telling the truth," he said eventually. "You are a beautiful woman, and I love painting you."

She looked pleased, then lowered her eyes.

"I'm glad," she answered softly, and Jan noticed a slight movement of her shoulders and neck as if she were readjusting them more to her liking, and perhaps to his. Yes, she was vain, he thought, but no more vain than she had a right to be.

Another quarter of an hour or so passed. The portrait was progressing too quickly. He wanted time in Jacqueline's company; he did not want to return to Bruges. He was beginning to feel at peace here after the pain and dramas of the past month. Jan began to pay unnecessary attention to background details which he could perfectly well have done in her absence; but even this did not work—his eyes kept returning to the face, and to the lovely neck, and the deepening shadow between her breasts.

Suddenly she asked him, "Have you noticed how all the women in the duke's life come to grief?"

Jan remembered that Jacqueline had promised to tell him about the duke, and increasingly he came to realize how obsessed she was by him: the victim's obsession with its tyrant. And the duke, too, Jan reflected, was obsessed by her—hurt by her, it often sounded, as if it were he who was the victim. But who was Jacqueline thinking of besides herself? he wondered. "You mean the Maid," he asked. "Who else?"

"His wives," she answered with a look almost of surprise that Jan should not have mentioned them. "To be twice widowed," she went on; and then after a short pause, "I wonder what will happen to Isabella."

Jan was puzzled. What was Jacqueline trying to tell him?

"She has lost her child," he replied, "but I believe she loves him."

"Do you?" Jacqueline's expression was touched with mockery. "Would you love a woman who kept thirty lovers?"

Jan realized he had never given any thought to the duke's

life. He was more surprised than shocked, and he waited for Jacqueline to go on.

"Do you know why Isabella lost her child?" she asked in that same almost disdainful voice. Jan did not know, and again he waited. "She discovered that one of Philip's mistresses in Bruges was her own lady-in-waiting, Louise."

Jan remembered the cries of anger he had heard in the ducal palace, and the second woman's voice he had not known. He felt hurt for Isabella.

"Of course, all dukes and princes take the women they want," Jacqueline went on. "They buy them like apples, and spit out the core. But to preach chivalry, a love of honor, a love of love"—Jacqueline's face broke into a bitter smile—"Oh, Jan, I despise men like that."

Then her voice changed.

"When I love, I love," she said. "All of me—my body and my thoughts and my hunger. I want him and I want him. No one else."

Jan was silent. It was like being in the presence of a fire that had suddenly flared and caught him in its heat. She said nothing for a moment, still breathing deeply. Finally a smile passed across Jacqueline's face and she reached out for his hand.

"Jan, forgive me. Too much has happened."

He thought she was about to go on speaking. Instead she shook her head, her eyes lowered. And when she raised her face Jan saw it was bathed in tears. He held her hand firmly in his own and she seemed calmed by his grasp.

"Thank you," she said after a moment, and her voice was the faintest of whispers.

Always in the evenings she would meet him in the enclosed garden. And always she would be a little later than she said. He would look about him, watching the small birds squabbling in the foliage of the trees clipped to resemble themselves, the fish sending gentle ripples across the surface of the circular pool, and the fading light drawing hidden colors from the dark stone of the castle above him. The swifts would scream above his head for a moment, then vanish on their circuit of the walls as if an invisible thread whirled them round and round until the thread broke and the swifts would scatter afar.

One evening Jan took paper and materials with him and sat quietly drawing the pool and the twin trees. He thought he might include them in the portrait of Jacqueline: besides, it would prolong the work now nearing completion. He became so absorbed that he was unaware of Jacqueline entering the garden until he felt a hand rest on his shoulder.

"Don't stop," she said quietly.

Jan found it difficult to work with that hand pressed lightly there, one finger resting on the skin of his neck.

"I don't normally have a chance to see how you do it," she added. He was drawing details of the flowering rushes, and she leaned forward to peer more closely. Jan felt the pressure of her breasts against his shoulder, and her hair carried the faintest scent of roses. He was aware beside him of that long, serene profile, and of one dark eye that was fixed on his right hand as he drew. "How clever you are," she said softly.

There was an intimacy about their days and evenings which seemed to establish exactly the closeness and the distance between them. He remembered that he had once kissed her, and she had softly placed his hand against her breast; but there were never any hints of that. She would touch his arm, as before, sometimes turn that deep gaze on him, and often there were moments as he painted her, or as she sat close to him near the fire, when her awareness of her own body was like a perfume that embraced him. But that was always the distance, just a little out of reach, inviting, enchanting, not to be trespassed upon.

From time to time she talked while he painted her in that high room overlooking the calm of the sea. Almost casually she told him of the death of Philip of St. Pol, who had ruled Brabant since the death of her first husband, Duke John. It was St. Pol, Jacqueline reminded him, who had led the Burgundian army against Humphrey of Gloucester, and Humphrey had retreated in ignominy: she had found him the following evening on their own marriage bed in the arms of his mistress, Eleanor Cobham. Each time Jacqueline mentioned Humphrey's name Jan wondered if he was about to return—at her own invitation; and if she knew when, and if she would ever tell him. How would she receive him—her champion who had betrayed her but who was now her only hope? Jan remembered Jacqueline's words: "When I love, I love . . . all of me." In her heart did she still love Humphrey? Would she take him back if he could win back her lands?

"So now St. Pol is dead," she went on, "and Duke Philip will have Brabant. I wonder if he poisoned him."

There was no bitterness in her voice.

"Might he have done that?" Jan inquired, surprised.

"Why not?" she answered in the same casual tone. "It's one way. It won't be the first time."

She did not expound, nor did Jan ask.

"So, he's nearly got it all," Jacqueline went on reflectively. "Flanders. Artois. Hainault. Namur. Limbourg. Brabant. Holland." She listed Philip's possessions slowly, as if she were handing the duke each one of them in turn. "Only my few islands are left to me," she added, and to Jan's surprise Jacqueline gave a slight laugh. "My empire of sand. My kingdom of the dunes. My marshes·and seabirds and sky."

There was a long silence. Jan was painting her hands. Elegant, strong hands that had held a sword, had killed, had clung to Gloucester in joy and in pain; hands that had wiped away more tears than he, Jan, had ever shed; hands that now rested softly before her. He was painting the rings and wondering whose they were: the huge ruby—might that be Humphrey's gift on their wedding, or perhaps her own father's? Even the duke wore no larger stone. Then on her forefinger she wore a sapphire set in silver and small diamonds; Jan made a record of the precise color, but he would need hours of work and many glazes mixed to obtain the sparkle of those stones. And on the little finger of the right hand there was a plain gold ring with lettering inscribed—he could not read it, and did not like to ask. He was fascinated by her hands—the long fingers, pronounced knuckles, the unusually large thumb; on the right hand he noticed the thumb had a slight callus, and there was a corresponding callus on the forefinger next to it. Her sword hand, Jan realized: after more than two years the marks of battle remained. If he could have seen her heart, the scars would have made Jan wince, he imagined.

On another morning Jacqueline talked almost jokingly of the duke's political scheming. How sad it was for him, she explained, that he had no legitimate children to marry off for territorial gain. They would have been so useful. Instead Philip had to make do with the children of his vassals, as she knew to her cost; but they tended to lack the loyalty of his own blood relatives, she added with a scornful laugh. Of course, he had no lack of illegitimate offspring, male and female, and these had their uses as bishops, abbots, abbesses, and as marriage partners for lesser nobles and minor heiresses, except that they were also more expensive since a lack of legitimacy invariably had to be compensated in gold. And Philip liked to keep gold for himself. Jacqueline smiled as she said this, and Jan noticed that she looked down at her own sapphire ring.

The English, of course, she continued, paid the duke handsomely for being their ally against France—tens of thousands of gold saluts each month, so she understood, as well as the promise of the county of Champagne, which would also improve his wine cellar, she added with another laugh. She often doubted, though, she said, whether the English felt satisfied with the support they paid for so heavily, since a great many of Philip's military excursions against the French were a mockery. And Jacqueline described how a number of the campaigns Philip claimed to have waged were entirely fictitious, while there were other battles in which the Burgundians advanced without armor, pausing to chase hares and partridges and then running for shelter at the first sight of the enemy.

"I sometimes wonder what the lord of Bedford thinks about the prowess of his expensive ally when he hears such reports." There was a note of scornful amusement in Jacqueline's voice.

"Of course," she added, "when Philip really wants something, then he fights—as I well know. And he will stop at nothing." Jacqueline fell silent and Jan saw her face take on a look of weariness. Then she shook her head and her gaze moved toward the open window. Jan put down his brush and waited for her to resume her pose.

"And all for a dream of Burgundy," she said after a while. This time the laugh sounded hollow and disdainful. "You know, Jan," she went on, turning to him and placing a hand lightly on his arm, "there's no such thing as Burgundy except in Philip's mind."

Then as if a map of Europe were lying before her eyes she talked of the duke's vision of a nation stretching from the Alps to the sea—a nation that was to be like the proudest ship of Europe, beating down the Turks, sailing for Jerusalem, itself a new Jerusalem.

"I'm sure you've heard all that," she said. "But it's a dream —a dangerous dream for those who get in its way."

Her eyes fell on Jan's drawing materials, and unhurriedly Jacqueline walked over and took up a sheet of white paper and a piece of charcoal; then she laid the paper on the table and with the charcoal drew a single black line down the center of it.

"Think of this paper as Burgundy. And now this line . . ." Her hand swept across the area to the left. "All this is really France, and the duke holds it only in the name of the king of France—with whom he happens to be at war." Again she gave the suggestion of a laugh. "And here"—she indicated the right-hand side of the paper—"it's not merely a dream of Burgundy, it's theft: the true ruler is the Holy Roman Emperor, who happens to be too preoccupied, too weak, and too drunk to do anything about it."

Jan had said nothing all this time. He had ceased painting her: the many faces of Jacqueline left him feeling bewildered. The enchantress. The soldier. The victim. And now the politician. Who was she, and why was she telling him all this?

Suddenly she surprised him once more.

"Shall I tell you, Jan, why I fought Philip?" Her expression was soft and appealing again, the large eyes filled with warmth. "You must think it was pride," she went on, "because he had seized what was mine. But there was something else. I fought him because I was a woman."

There was a pause. Jan did not think he had ever seen her looking so intent, as if what she was telling him mattered more to her at this moment than all the tales of disastrous battles, desertion by Humphrey of Gloucester, loss of almost everything that had been hers.

"It's because I'm not a man that I don't have men's dreams. Glory. Chivalry. Building nations to outshine the world. I wanted to rule justly, I wanted to protect, I wanted my lands to prosper in peace. To be left alone; and to marry a man I could love." Then she added, almost to herself, "I was never allowed any of those things—because of him."

There was silence in the high room overlooking the sea. She was gazing away from him out of the window, and when eventually she turned her head toward him Jan saw that she was in tears. She made no attempt to hide them.

"I must go now," she said quickly, squeezing his arm as she left.

From the window Jan could make out the mottled pattern of dune and marsh which was Jacqueline's last domain. Here and there in the distance a village was clustered by the water's edge, and before it fields like scraps of carpets lay spread between the dikes and channels and the reed beds bronzed with summer and patterned by the wind. A few cows. Scattered fishermen in flatboats. A tiny harbor. A wooden church. Red roofs. Specks of children playing. The sound of dogs. None of it seemed to Jan to have much to do with the splendors of the Golden Fleece.

Jacqueline had told him so much that cast into doubt his estimation of the duke. He felt oppressed, besieged. So many of the props that shored his life were being knocked away. His happiness with Margarethe. His faith in the just humility of churchmen. The benign authority of the duke. It was as if the world were corrupting before his eyes, and that clear, bright vision of the truth he loved to paint seemed clouded with a pall of darkness. There was no luster in the heavens: he should be painting the light of God in grays and browns, lit only by the flecked intimations of fire. It was another vision Jan had never contemplated.

That evening it was again as if Jacqueline had never talked as she did—as if what she said while he painted her belonged only to those hours and only to that room. She was dressed even more gorgeously—in red velvet with a diamond necklace

sweeping across her bare neck and shoulders, and in her dark
blaze of hair was set a coronet of emeralds. The scent of roses
filled the space between them, and her eyes seemed gently to
be hunting that space for his response to her presence.

It was Jan's turn, she said, to say what was on his mind.
Why was it he spoke so little? Did every woman he knew say
this, or was his silence reserved for her? She remembered that
she had asked this before, and that Jan had answered with
another silence. And all the time her eyes were scanning his
face as if in search of some secret she sensed lay there, and
now and then her mouth moved into that inviting, taunting
smile.

She asked him about love. How many women had Jan
loved? And did he fall in love with the women he painted? If
they were beautiful? she added with a delightful laugh. Or
was plainness no barrier?

"So tell me about the other women you've painted," she
asked.

Jan spoke, a little unwillingly, about Isabella—her sitting
for him in the long white room at Cintra with her maids-of-
honor giggling behind delicate fans until the princess dismissed them after a few days because she wanted to talk more
freely; what she really wanted was to ask Jan as discreetly as
she could about the duke she was about to marry. He had
loved her smile, he explained, and her fondness for enormous
hats. How protected her life had been, and how little she knew
of the world.

And then he talked of the women he had painted in
Bruges. Bona—how she had demanded to be included in the
altarpiece for the cathedral at Ghent. Jacqueline wanted to
know if Bona had made a convincing Eve, and Jan wondered
how much she knew of what had taken place, whether Bona
had told Jacqueline of what she had let slip about Humphrey
of Gloucester coming to her aid. And then Jan mentioned the
heavenly twins, and Jacqueline laughed. Who were they? she
wanted to know. Was it exciting painting a beautiful woman
who was another man's mistress, or did Jan prefer the lovely
purity of the twin sister? She herself, Jacqueline explained,
could not imagine being enamored of that kind of innocent

purity—how entirely unappealing it would be in a man; she always found it hard to understand the male adoration of the Virgin Mary—her own sympathies went out to Joseph, who was cuckolded by God.

Jacqueline was enjoying herself, leaning intimately across the table and allowing the scent of roses to embrace Jan while he talked. Her eyes never left him, and her expression was never far from that inviting, teasing smile.

"Tell me about Margarethe," she asked in the same unhurried voice.

Jan was surprised. Bona must have told her, he realized. But how had Bona told her when the duke's spies made it impossible for any messenger to reach Jacqueline? And in any case, why should she have told her?

It pained him to think of Margarethe, and as he explained what had occurred Jacqueline must have noticed the sadness in his voice, because her face grew concerned and the smile faded. He told her of his happiness with Margarethe, that they were lovers, that they were to have been married; and he told her of Margarethe's terrors of the outer world, the bishop's terrible words, and the attack by the drunken soldiers.

"You killed for her?" Jacqueline's face was tense with astonishment.

"I killed to save her."

There was a pause, and it was impossible for Jan to guess what was going through her mind. After a while she reached out an arm and took his hand in hers.

"You're a good man, Jan," she said quietly.

At that she rose to her feet and went over to the small open window where dusk was falling. The silence was broken only by the cry of gulls and the occasional thud of the sea. When she spoke again her voice sounded distant.

"Men don't often say things like that."

There was another pause. Then as if she felt the need to explain she told Jan how often she had heard men talk of laying down their lives for a woman's sake; of staking their honor in her cause; of composing poems, enduring sacrifices, making perilous journeys, all for the love of a woman. And how they would fight one another for her love as though she were a trophy. But to kill to save a woman, she said, her face brightening with a look almost of wonder. She turned to look at Jan. Suddenly she lowered her eyes.

"I believe Humphrey would have done that once," she added.

Again Jan wondered what was stirring in her mind. Then, with another of those surprising shifts of mood she added with the suggestion of a smile, "Do you think you would kill a man to save me?"

Jan tried to swallow his astonishment, but her laughter rescued him.

"My lady," he replied with just a touch of lightness, "I'm your painter not your savior, but I would try."

Jacqueline was watching him intently.

"Then you should be my knight, Jan; I have few others," she said. "And if you're to be my knight," she went on, "tomorrow you must ride with me. I shall show you my kingdom and you shall rescue me from dragons." She laughed again.

Her velvet gown rustled as Jacqueline made her way to the door, and as she reached it she turned and gave him her hand. He kissed it very formally.

"You're learning," she said. "Good night."

She fascinated and confused him the longer he knew her. She was like a many-sided jewel: as it turned each facet showed a new face of her. And it was never still, one face was forever losing another and becoming another; her anger held tears, her tears laughter, her laughter compassion, her compassion cunning. She could love and she could destroy. Jan waited for Jacqueline on that early morning, his horse restless in the sunlight, and he wondered where he was being led and to what purpose. In his wallet was the locket she had given him: his fingers felt the surface of the gold, tracing the insignia of the raven with a sword in its beak. With his other hand Jan felt the blade of his own dagger at his belt: as a last thought he had slipped it there as he left his room.

People gathered and cheered her as they left the gate of the town. She was dressed simply, in linen and pale buckskin, and a hat of red cloth like a man's—with a feather in it. She rode easily, holding the reins in one hand as they turned away from the long dike leading to the mainland and followed the shore of the marsh, cracked into dry flakes at this season, their horses' hooves flailing the purple sea lavender and the stranded tussocks of reed. There were perhaps twenty of them in the party, the guard of mounted soldiers riding some ten paces behind Jacqueline and Jan.

She talked as they rode, and she looked as happy as Jan had ever seen her.

"I love this land," she said, her eyes surveying the huge spread of dry marsh and dune around them. "It feels like the rim of the world. No one comes here."

She explained how she had spent years of her childhood here, riding like a wild thing alone, or sometimes with Bona. There was always supposed to be a bodyguard with her, she said; but she knew there was no danger in this place then. A wilderness with a child on a horse. She would let her hair flow in the wind as she rode, and strap her boots to the saddle so that she could feel the horse's warm flank against her bare feet. Sometimes on a hot summer day she made her way to a deserted creek where an old jetty rose and fell on the tide. She would tether her horse to a post and plunged naked into the water. The mud was soft as down between her toes, and the salt stung her eyes. She would watch her hair floating like weed and run her fingers through it, lifting strands of it so that it shone dark in the sunlight. If the tide was low there would be a strip of island she could swim to, and there she felt happiest of all, like the first woman on earth naked on the cool sand. Once, only once, she turned and saw a boy standing on the jetty staring at her. At first she had wanted to hide, but there was nowhere to hide and his face looked full of wonder. So she stood there in the sun, her hair over her young breasts. The boy went on staring for a while; then he turned and ran away, and she felt disappointed—she realized she had wanted him to join her on her island. She had wanted to touch him naked, and he would never have known who she was. She told only Bona, who frowned, but Jacqueline knew that she was envious and would have done the same.

"I'm telling you all these things and you're not even painting me," she said, laughing. "You see, as a child I was a mermaid. I always loved the sea. And sometimes in these last years I've wished I could dive into it and live there without anyone knowing."

For two hours or more they rode between the dunes and the dried marshes. Gradually a few signs of human habitation came into view. A low dike held back the marsh, and beyond it lay fields veined with thin water channels where cows grazed. Geese screeched at the riders as they passed, heads thrust angrily toward the horses' legs. A child in rags ran stumbling over the farther dike and disappeared without a backward glance. A line of mills, their sails furled on this windless summer morning, thrust their arms like giant scarecrows into the sky, and flat reed boats lay along the bank of a hidden creek. The village when they reached it rose hardly higher than the reeds, its roofs reed-thatched, its mud walls barely visible beneath. There were perhaps twenty such huts, and as they drew closer Jan could see that each was raised on a low mound, and even in this long dry season the spaces between each hut glistened with water. Pigs and hens scattered as the party of riders approached, dogs barked, but there was no hint of human life.

"They're frightened," Jacqueline explained.

Without another word she dismounted, and throwing the reins to the nearest soldier, made her way toward one of the huts.

"Toos," Jan heard Jacqueline call out.

For a while nothing happened. Then gradually he became aware of small movements within the darkness of each doorway, and he could sense invisible eyes everywhere around them.

Jacqueline called out a second time: "Toos." And as she did so a young woman appeared cautiously at the doorway of the hut closest to them. She was barefooted and dressed only in sacking, and she was holding a naked child to her breast. Her hair was pale and lank, and her face sullen with fear.

"Toos," said Jacqueline, her voice welcoming now. Suddenly the woman's face broke into a generous smile. Clasping the child closely to her bare breast she hurried toward Jacqueline and the two women embraced. Excited words were exchanged in a language Jan could not understand.

Then it was as if the empty village exploded with human life. There were cries of children, women, old men, all around them as Jan and the soldiers dismounted. More than fifty people surrounded Jacqueline, and she embraced them in turn. With one arm she held Toos's child, who was gazing at her curiously; the other arm grasped shoulder after shoulder, and as she processed slowly through the village people followed her with excited voices. "Jacqueline," Jan heard again and again amid a babble of words which meant nothing to him. He saw they were making for what appeared to be the only house in the village larger than a hut, and as they approached it an old man emerged slowly, dressed like the others in clogs and sacking except that he wore an embroidered waistcoat over the top, its colors faded together into a universal bleached brown. His whiskers were silver and the hands resting on his stick were knobbed like the roots of an oak.

"Jacob," Jacqueline called out.

For a moment the old man did not seem to recognize her, and Jan realized that he was blind.

"Jacob," she said again. "It's Jacqueline."

The old man's face creased into a hundred furrows and he opened his crooked arms to her.

"Jacqueline. Jacqueline," was all he said in a voice that was little more than a squeak.

Jan saw her take his hand and fold his fingers carefully around a purse, closing them like a clasp. Then she embraced him again.

The soldiers gathered silently around, except for two or three who were led away by excited clusters of villagers: Jan watched them being greeted by children who hurried out of doorways, and by uncles, cousins, grandparents, their rags contrasting with the bright swords and handsome jerkins of the soldiers.

Suddenly there were tables being set out in front of the old man's house; wooden benches beside them. Women were bringing broad flat disks of bread dusted white, round cheeses, pitchers of water and milk, wooden goblets. The visitors ate and drank as the villagers stood about awkwardly, excitedly, chattering in low voices.

Afterward Jacqueline gave a final hug to Toos, the child, and the old man, and the villagers lined the low dike as the riders departed; and glancing back, Jan could see a hundred small silhouettes between the silent mills, the village itself already vanished below the tall plumes of the reeds.

It was early afternoon. There was such contentment on Jacqueline's face as she rode beside Jan ahead of the soldiers. Beyond them the dike seemed to extend endlessly until the sky leveled it into the horizon, and again there was no sign of life around them except flights of marsh birds whose cries rippled across the wasteland. But after a while Jacqueline roused herself from her thoughts and began to talk. There were a hundred villages like that one in Zeeland, she said. It was all there was in Zeeland, she added wryly. She herself tried to visit them all once a year, though there were so many islands that sometimes the weather hindred it. That particular village she visited more often because it was among the closest; also she knew them well. The old man, Jacob, had been a friend all her life: his daughter was her nurse as a child, and it was his granddaughter Toos whose child she had carried in her arms. She was the child's godmother. She was godmother to a child in every village in Zeeland, she explained.

"They are my family, my only family. I love them." Then she added, with a quizzical glance at Jan, "It's a long way from the duke's pageants in Bruges, isn't it?"

They rode on through the hot afternoon. Perspiration glued Jan's clothing to him: Jacqueline, on the other hand, looked fresh in her pale linen. Her skin, already a little darkened by the sun, showed no mark of the day's heat, and when she guided her horse to water she leaped to the ground as lightly as if she had rested all day in the shade.

The long chain of dikes had given way now to sandy tracks along the verges of the marsh. The riders followed Jacqueline, leading their horses across the brittle crust of mud to a freshwater stream where the animals drank thirstily, stamping puffs of dust and stirring clouds of flies with their tails. Small purple herons rose lazily from the water's edge and flapped low across the flats before dropping one by one into unseen creeks. Jan quenched his own thirst, then he unlaced his shirt and dashed the cool water gratefully onto his face and chest. Behind him he heard a soft laugh from Jacqueline.

"So you find it warmer riding through the Garden of Eden than painting it."

There was that familiar amused smile on her face as she watched him remount, and while he mopped his body with a cloth he was aware of her eyes searching him; but when he looked at her she lowered them. It was almost the first time Jan had seen her uncomposed, and again he was conscious of those unaccountable changes of mood in her. She was very still and elegant seated there with the reins held in her lap, the faintest breeze brushing a few strands of black hair across her cheek.

"Do you imagine they had flies in the Garden of Eden?" he asked. She made no reply, but another gentle smile passed across her face.

The sandy track soon lost itself in a forest of coarse dune grass, and the sound of their hooves became muffled as they made their way through a wilderness of dry hillocks. Around them hills of sand rose higher and higher, ridged sharply by the wind, until in a while they reached the shoulder of a dune and suddenly beyond them stretched a rolling desert of sand hills and, further beyond, the ocean.

"There," Jacqueline pointed. "Do you see?"

Jan's eyes followed the direction of her arm, and in the distance far to the left he caught sight of a dark mass hunched above the shore. He could just make out the shape of towers and spires jutting into the shimmer of heat.

"Goes," she added. "Another hour, that's all."

The dunes rose and fell like giant waves around them, and the horses' hooves left craters which the sliding sand gradually filled behind them, smoothing away all signs of their existence as if this wild place denied any presence except what the sea and the wind had thrown here. These were the dead lands of the sea, Jan thought, the very boundary of the world before it expired into eternal water.

The party of horsemen was halted along the ridge of a high dune as though silenced by the vast emptiness of the place.

"There's nowhere else I like to feel so alone." Jacqueline's voice was quiet as if she were in a small empty room. "Perhaps you should paint me with these dunes around me," she added; "because it's what I am." Jan turned to look at her, and her face wore an expression of deep contentment as she looked out over the desert of sand hills and sleeping ocean. "Can you understand that?"

Jan nodded. He had begun to realize that this woman who had led armies, who had held courts, held power, ruled cities and nations, in some part of her heart wanted none of it; that she longed for the kind of peace no man had ever offered her and yet from which her own ambitions would always drive her. She was gazing, Jan knew, at a dream just as powerful and just as unobtainable as Philip's vision of a glorious Burgundy spreading its bright banners across Europe.

"Yes, I do understand," he said truthfully. She turned to look at him, and her face was soft as a child's.

"You may be the only man who does, Jan. But then you would understand, my painter, wouldn't you?" And after a moment she added, "I should like to stay here a while with you."

She turned her horse and rode slowly over to the soldiers, who were waiting along the ridge. Jan saw Jacqueline speak to one of them: then he beckoned to the others and the men began to lead their horses down the long flank of the dune. Jan watched them wind their way, gradually growing smaller as they descended toward the sea. Once on the hard sand they glanced back before setting off at a canter along the fringe of the tide, heading toward Goes. In a few minutes they were minute specks moving along the far haze of shoreline.

Jacqueline had dismounted and was seated gazing out toward the sea, her arms around her knees and her chin resting on her hands. As he joined her she said nothing, but her hand took his. It was cool and soft, and her fingers entwined in his own.

"There's no other man I could be with here," she said after a moment, still gazing out over the far dunes. "No one."

Jan felt surprised and pleased. Then, even as he sensed the thrill of knowing what might happen, she turned her head and her face invited him to kiss her. Her lips were warm and yielding, and she clung to him, her body pressed against his. He could hear her breathing. Her face was lowered toward his chest, her hair against his mouth.

"Yes," was all she said.

She undressed without haste and lay back on the warm sand while he removed his own clothes, his eyes feeding on the dark hair spread about her head, on the deep breasts, on the long thighs parted. He lay on her and in her, mouth hungry against his, fingers dug into his naked back. Her cry was like the release of a thousand joys, and as he took her there was no other world or moment beyond the thrill of his own hunger spilled into her body. Then they lay in the stunned sunlight and the warm cradle of the sand; and after a while when he looked at her the dark eyes which met his drew his lips to her neck and breasts, and his hands and tongue to every part of her until she whimpered as he entered her again, left her, entered her, the unending play of lust while the day lingered over their two bodies in that vast summer bed of the dunes.

"My painter; my lover," she whispered almost inaudibly.

He watched her dress slowly, turning her body in the last of the sun. Then, with her blouse still open and her breasts bare, she gazed down at Jan.

"I'll tell you," she said, "when I first saw you from the shadows of the hall as you entered, I wanted to be like this for you; and when I took your arm I wanted to lay your hands here." Her own hands reached up and touched the dark nipples of each breast. "And when you were painting me that first morning I wanted you inside me. . . . You see, I've waited a long time." Then she looked away with a sad expression suddenly. "I wish I were not who I am," she added quietly.

There was something final about those last few words, Jan realized. He dressed in silence and they prepared to leave, but before they mounted their waiting horses she kissed him once again, and he knew it was a kiss of goodbye, and perhaps of regret that it was goodbye.

Then, to Jan's surprise, she said, "Give me your dagger."

Hesitantly he took it from his belt and handed it to her. Jan watched, fearful, as Jacqueline held the dagger close to her bare shoulder. She took a strand of hair between her fingers and sliced through it with the dagger.

"The locket I gave you?" she asked very quietly.

Jan reached for it in his wallet and again handed it to her. She opened the back of it and carefully wound the strand of black glossy hair into the cavity. She closed it, and with a smile almost shy returned it to him.

"From me."

He held her hand. There was something overwhelming about that little gift. Nothing she could ever give him for the portrait would match that piece of herself. Jan looked at her.

"I wanted you that evening . . . and ever since," he said. "Thank you for bringing me here—to the place where you're most what you are. Sea and sand and Jacqueline." He kissed her very lightly on the lips, and looked at her. "Jacqueline of the lands of the sea," he added.

Her lips opened as if she were about to speak; then they shut quickly and she looked away.

They rode back almost in silence. The sun stained the sea orange, becoming purple, finally deep violet turning iron gray. The swifts screamed around the walls of the castle in the dusk as they entered the gates of the town.

Jacqueline excused herself for the evening, not looking at him. She was tired, she said, but she grasped his hand almost urgently as she left, and kissed it.

"Thank you, Jan," she said under her breath, still without raising her eyes. And she was gone.

A servant brought him food and wine but he could feel no hunger. He sipped the wine and nibbled bread. From the window he could just make out the shoreline bending toward the dark horizon, and a blur of dunes. Was he in love with Jacqueline? he kept asking himself. He did not know the answer. And she with him? No, he thought, though perhaps she would have liked to be. "I wish I were not who I am," she had said. No, she could never love him; there could be no place for love in her life now, since Humphrey of Gloucester. He had taken all there was from her, and now there was solitude, a sweet solitude sometimes—and he thought of her hunger and her cries. Yes, he could love her if living were only loving, and if the magic of this woman were never broken under the rough heel of the world. To love her would be paradise, and paradise was another dream. Dreams were everywhere, like halos, like the perfumes of summer, like the tears and longings of lost people.

He felt too restless to remain in his room. The guard opened the gate for him with a nod, and he made his way through the dark town in the direction of the sea. He was drawn to the sea as if it were a figment of Jacqueline. Lamps glowed in the windows here and there, and between the leaning roofs bats spun and darted against the deep translucent sky. Shafts of moonlight lay across the trodden earth of the street, casting his shadow for a moment on ancient walls and dark windows.

Presently he caught sight of the sheen of water, and the street took a sharp turn before widening out—Jan could see— onto an open quayside which curled beneath the clustered houses as if it had been scooped out of them. In the moonlight he could make out the shapes of fishing boats nudging the harbor wall, rocking lazily. But it was a larger ship that caught Jan's eye, twin-masted, its sails furled, with two lanterns hung about the open deck and a dim glow of light that shone from the cabin. Curiosity led him toward it. No one appeared to be about; but then as he was within some twenty paces of the vessel Jan saw two figures emerge from the cabin and make their way across the deck toward the gangplank. They were talking—not loudly, but in that still, empty harbor their voices carried, and he realized with a shock that they were talking English. Jan was standing in the full moonlight and did not dare to move, but the two men were too intent on their conversation to notice him. Then he knew he recognized one of them: the second man was taking the gangplank with a more gingerly step than the first, and as he reached the quay he glanced up and for a moment Jan was looking at the old face of the English servant whom he had met with Jacqueline in the hall on his first evening in Goes three months ago. And at that instant Jan remembered Jacqueline describing how the man had once been Humphrey of Gloucester's valet—at Agincourt —and how he had chosen to remain with her when Humphrey left her.

There could be no doubt what he was witnessing. Jan could not understand what the two men were saying, but he knew that the second figure must be an emissary from Humphrey of Gloucester.

Still Jan dared not move. Thoughts crowded in on his brain too hurriedly for him to absorb them. The hint about Humphrey that Bona had let slip. The duke's talk of pressure from the English to hand over the Maid. Philip's keenness that Jan should return here and report back to him. And then—painfully—Jacqueline's determination to lead him away from Goes today rather than continuing with the portrait. And their lovemaking in the dunes. Was it all a careful scheme? Was that all it was? "I wish I were not who I am."

The shock of bitterness had barely ebbed before he saw the two men cross the quayside toward the darkened town, and as they did so a third figure emerged from the shadows to meet them. There was a shaking of hands and a huddle of conversation which Jan could not hear. But there was no mistaking the third figure in spite of the hood and the long surcoat. It was Jacqueline. And as the three of them moved away toward the silent town she turned her head for a second, and Jan knew that she had seen him.

The moonlight felt like an inquisitor in his room.

What ought he to do? When Jan made an effort to distance himself from Jacqueline his course of action appeared simple. He could feel no obligations to a woman who had deliberately tricked him: he would return to Bruges and inform the duke of what he had seen.

But Jan could not hold that distance. Always invading that space was Jacqueline herself—and the memory of a day like no other. He knew that she had never, from the first moment he had met her, behaved toward him like a woman employing her position and her charms ruthlessly for her own gain. She was . . . unlike any other woman; she was unlike any other lover.

"When I love, I love," she said. "All of me—my body and my thoughts and my hunger." Who was she—Jacqueline?

Jan looked out at the sleeping town veiled in moonlight. It was as if over the world there lay a giant web set to trap those who tried to fly free.

The portrait was nearly completed.

Jan had slept little, but by the morning it was clear to him what he would do. He would finish the portrait that day— without Jacqueline since the face and figure were now virtually done and only the background details remained. After that he would set off this very evening for Bruges. And after that . . . well, he would see.

He began work early in the high room overlooking the sea. The majestic figure of Jacqueline, in white, occupied the center of the painting, her face proud, sad, and beautiful. The room in which she stood required only a final glaze here and there; but the flowers, the carpet, the table, the small mirror on the wall—he was pleased with what he had done. The room seemed to breathe. Only the background vista remained sketched. He set to work on it in the clear light of early morning.

It was as though something unseen were guiding his hand, and his mind only a spectator. There before him Jan's hand was painting a landscape of white dunes like dry waves of the sea—hundreds and hundreds of them in shadow and sunlight to the farthest horizon. No life. No towns. No trees, flowers, birds. It was like painting Jacqueline naked—a portrait in sand, "You should paint me with those dunes around me, because it's what I am." Her voice seemed to echo from every dune as he painted it.

By evening it was finished. Jan returned to his room utterly exhausted and hungry. He had no idea where Jacqueline might be, but he recoiled from the idea of meeting her and made his way cautiously down the stairway and the dank stone corridor toward the entrance of the castle. Only a few servants were about, and they nodded to him respectfully as he passed. The guard, who knew Jan well by now, unbarred the heavy gate and he walked out into the street. Unlike the previous evening, it was raucous with life: everywhere was a market; everyone appeared to be trying to sell something to somebody else, and the cries of bakers, blacksmiths, peddlers, beggars, quacks, cobblers, fishmongers, fortune-tellers, and a score of other trades filled the summer evening. Curiosity drew Jan to the bend in the road from where he could gaze down onto the harbor: fishermen were seated barefooted and cross-legged mending their nets amid piles of glass floats; there were dogs, cats, children playing, women with baskets of fish on their heads. But the English ship had gone. Jan seated himself at a quayside stall and fed hungrily on grilled sprats that were served to him on a large wooden platter. If he had spoken the dialect he would have asked about the ship from England. Instead he held out a few coins to the stallkeeper, who wiped his red hands on a cloth before taking them with a grunt and a quick bob of the head. Then Jan walked back through the crowded streets to the castle. He alerted the young page in red to prepare his horse, and made his way back toward his room to collect his last belongings, rehearsing the message that he would leave for Jacqueline with the finished portrait. He hoped he would not meet her: he imagined he would not see her again. Sadness and relief washed over him.

Jan climbed the stairway to take a final look at the portrait of Jacqueline. That beautiful sad face. The slender figure in white. Her presence in that room was quite startling. And then his eye caught something on the surface of the painting: it was suspended on a slender chain and lay exactly where the wilderness of sand dunes formed the background to the portrait. Jan recognized his own locket, which he must have left in the wallet he could see lying beside his painting materials on the nearby table.

So Jacqueline had been here. Jan took the locket in his hand and immediately opened the clasp at the back, convinced that the strand of hair would be gone. But it was still there. He closed it again and stood holding it in his hand, wondering what he should do. Once more he opened the locket, and laid the coil of black hair in the palm of his hand. As he did so Jan was overcome with sadness. The black hair. The black raven. She had flown to him, enclosed him within her wings, and flown away. Jan turned over the locket. Of course, he realized, the raven carried a sword in its beak. Love was real, but love was transient, plucked on the wing and left as a carcass, a memento of its own death, while the sword thirsted for battle.

Jan had no idea how long he stood there. But suddenly he knew that she was in the room. He turned, almost frightened by what he might see. He half expected her to have a sword in her hand. Instead, she was standing there behind him, dressed in the same white gown in which he had painted her. She was lovely. She was still. She seemed to be waiting for him to speak. He noticed that in one hand she was holding a leather purse.

"I thought it would be better if I just went," Jan said quietly. "The portrait is finished."

Jacqueline nodded. "I saw. Thank you." Her eyes traveled to the purse in her hands. "I'd like you to have this for your pains, and for your skills." And she handed it to him.

Jan took it from her. It was heavy with gold. Then he laid it on the table beside her.

"The portrait is yours, from me . . . with love," he said. Jacqueline's serene, beautiful face moved not a muscle. "I should like to give you that love unbought," he added.

She said nothing for a moment, her eyes wandering past him to the portrait of herself in this very room against the landscape of dunes. Then, without any note of malice in her voice, she said, "Jan, I thought your love was already bought—by the duke of Burgundy."

He knew that she could see the anger in his eyes.

"In that case," he replied sharply, "why did you invite me here? And why did you choose yesterday to lead me away from Goes? Wasn't it so that I should go back to the duke and tell him you were living the life of a hermit—at the very moment when your plans were bearing fruit? Wasn't that it?"

Jan picked up the bag of gold and threw it at Jacqueline's feet.

"And you thought, if you could make me love you, and make love to you, then you could bind me to you; and whatever I saw and whatever I knew, I would never tell, because I'd be in your power. And then what would have happened to me? What would have been my fate when Philip discovered?" He glared at her. "But I don't imagine you gave that a thought, any more than you gave me a thought yesterday while I made love to you. You used me, Jacqueline. You used me."

Even while his anger burst from him, he knew he hated his own words. And when she spoke, her words cut right through him.

"I loved you yesterday, Jan," she said softly, "and I love you still."

If Jan had expected the collapse of a helpless woman, no behavior could have been more unlike that of a frail victim of her feelings. She gave him a look of intractable majesty, as if the misery of her life were something she had stepped beyond. She was the duchess Jacqueline as she stood there, and Jan could imagine how that same imperious stance would have confronted Humphrey, would have confronted Philip's victorious captains, and would one day, he felt sure, confront Philip himself.

"Listen," she said calmly. "I'll tell you everything—everything that it means to be Jacqueline."

She paused as if calculating how to begin, and her eyes moved from Jan to her own portrait, seeming to appraise it like an image of some other person. Then she looked back to Jan, and now her eyes seemed to be appraising him.

"Yes, it's true," she began. "I did want to trap you. I wanted to enchant you. I wanted to make you mine. Because you were the only hope I had." There was no note of self-pity in Jacqueline's voice. "Instead, I found I was the one trapped." Only then did she lower her eyes. "Maybe you don't believe that, but it's true."

Jan listened as Jacqueline continued, quietly, her voice almost detached. She explained how she had begged Bona to aid her. How Bona was unwilling because she liked Jan, who had never harmed anyone. But Bona was like a sister to her, and in the end she had agreed, trusting that he would find a way to survive the trap. It had all begun with a message from Humphrey of Gloucester, offering to return and help her reclaim her territories. Maybe, she added with a sardonic smile, the joys of a pretty lady-in-waiting had begun to pall, and Humphrey was remembering those rich lands he had lost for the sake of a wench. In any case, she had not believed him: Gloucester's brother Bedford would never permit it, she knew. But then, once the news came that the Maid was raising an army again in France, she had seen her chance. If she could only get Bedford on her side, then Gloucester would come with an army. The last time it had been Humphrey who had used her for his gain. This time *she* would use *him:* once she had regained her territories she would kill him. She loathed him, she said, and her face was tense with passion as she said it. She was sure the Maid would be captured: everyone knew she could not last. So she waited. And while she waited she summoned Jan here to paint her. She needed the duke's ambassador as her ally. The moment she heard the news of Joan's capture she rejoiced that it was the Burgundians and not the English who held her. This gave her the chance to write to Bedford asking for aid. At the same time she used what influence she had in Philip's court to persuade the duke not to hand Joan over. She had her friends there, she said: Jan might be surprised if he knew who they were. And they convinced him. Hence the long delay before she asked Jan back to Goes: she had to be certain Philip would hold the Maid; and she had to receive a reply from Bedford.

The rest he knew, she said. Except . . . and Jacqueline's face looked deeply tired . . . it had not worked out as she planned. The emissary from England was not expected while Jan was here. She had hoped to keep that a secret from him. But yes—this had been why she wanted Jan away from Goes all yesterday. And then . . . there had been something else unexpected.

The look on her face was one of helplessness.

"You must do whatever you need to do, Jan," she said softly.

The late sun had crept into the room and was bathing her shoulders and the curve of her breasts. Jan knew he had never seen her so lovely. How could he ever betray such a woman? He reached out his hands, and after a moment's hesitation she took them in hers.

"Don't go tonight," she said, her voice barely more than a whisper. "Make love to me tonight."

The dark ramparts of Bruges were like a prison that beckoned him on the horizon. The long journey from Zeeland had been through an unbroken mist of his own thoughts, a confusion of delight and dread that was sometimes stilled by a feeling of resigned exhaustion; and at other times it was enflamed by the recollection of Jacqueline's tearful hunger in the closeness of the night.

But then it was as if the approach of those familiar walls, with their reassuring crown of mill sails and their enclosing memories, began to disperse those mists of confusion in Jan's mind, and he surprised himself by the sharpness with which everything that had taken place in Goes presented itself to him. He saw those events before him as though they were scenes on a stage from which he had stepped down. There was Jacqueline, a woman quite unlike any other, peerless. Her passions were like awesome fires that drew him irresistibly toward the farthest frontiers of risk and danger; she was something brighter and more magnificent than he had ever imagined could be contained within the fragile body of a woman; she was a goddess who had entered his small mortal life for a day and shown him the fields of heaven. But she had also shown him destruction: he could see himself swept away just as a flood might one day sweep away the lands of the sea. Her passions lay in her body, but they also flew with her dreams. Yes, he loved her when he gazed at her and when he lay with her; then he saw her again, a hooded figure in the darkness of the harbor, and he saw her as the shrouded figure of death.

He would say nothing about what he had seen.

Chapter • Eight

It was as if the citizens of Bruges refused to let the summer go. Even while the first mists of autumn hung like webs between the gabled houses, the canals still resounded with a serenade of laughter and music, and on sharp brittle afternoons the waterways around the city were host to all those pleasures which the Flemings had grown so expert at devising. And if the sterner brethren of the church sometimes eyed what they took to be a festival of deadly sins in those rural creeks and glades, they must also have noticed how many of their own kind were numbered among the sinners. But then, Flemish churchmen were often especially proud of their resistance to the eighth Deadly Sin, *tristitia*—"thou shalt not be miserable"; and certainly there was no shortage of young ladies of Bruges well rewarded for helping them resist it.

The Englishman Hugo was not one to be troubled by any such distinctions between pleasure and sin: in his rubric all enjoyments received the blessing of a benign God, wherever he might be. Yet, being Hugo, no sport of love could ever quite assuage the pangs of love unsatisfied, and even during the sweetest dalliance his heart remained bruised with jealousy of the merchant Arnolfini—so ugly but so rich—whose mistress, Lysbet, Hugo would gaze at as upon a distant and golden star. Her heavenly twin, Marie, sometimes tortured his passions almost as cruelly, though even Hugo's imagination found it hard to dwell too long on a young maiden who lived perpetually within the cloister of a holy book.

Those two staid or too old for summer frolics exchanged pensive observations in the tavern. Jan de Leeuw (father of six), with his tankard of beer, and Godscalc Oom (bachelor), with his thimble of hippocras, sought satisfaction in their own wisdom as they watched yet another boat party of revelers pass beneath the sign of the Fallen Angel.

"Did you once do that?" De Leeuw inquired idly.

"I was always too large for a boat," came the grave reply. "And the ladies were of the opinion that I was too large for them." De Leeuw's calm handsome face exhibited a modest smile.

Their wisdom continued for a while in silence. It was Godscalc, indulging himself in a second sip of hippocras, who introduced a darker reflection on the revelry. What should one make, he asked, of a people whose two pastimes were merriment and murder? The Flemings, he expanded, were either marauding the countryside decapitating the duke's agents or turning the riverbanks into a brothel. The goldsmith's answer was to call the taverner for another tankard, and to press a further glass of hippocras on the rentmaster.

"So much wealth and so much waste," De Leeuw added cryptically, without feeling the need to explain.

In his house on the street of the Golden Hand, Jan was alone and despondent. As autumn mists blurred the clear light of summer he became aware of how much in his own life had likewise grown blurred: those sharp images he loved to paint no longer seemed appropriate to the world he knew. He had lost Margarethe, torn from him in a gale of violence and evil. The dream of Jacqueline filled him with a mixture of longing and dread: every path ahead of him was draped with a banner that said Betrayal—sooner or later there would be no other way. Betrayal of love. Betrayal of duty. Betrayal of himself. He was angry with Bona for having thrust all this upon him. Then he would stare at the half-finished portrait of the duke, so bold and confident, godlike almost, the steady features framed by a marble colonnade and soon to be outlined against a panorama of Burgundy and the sparkling towers of the new Jerusalem—oh, it was a splendid vision of which as a painter he had every right to feel proud, but where was the truth in it? And Jan's gaze would shift to the great altarpiece—Hubert's glittering landscape raked by the gold of heaven and peopled by figures of such radiant devotion; above it the benign majesty of God the Father; and surrounding it Jan's own images of

Adam, Eve, John the Baptist, the angel of the Annunciation,
the Virgin Mary: again how proud he had a right to feel.
Golden people and golden lands. And he could feel none of it.
He should be painting distant fires menacingly burning.

It was the merchant Arnolfini who shook him from his
dark mood.

"Why don't you go to Italy?" he suggested. "A man of
your skills and fame could live there like a prince. Venice.
Florence, Genoa. Siena. Rome. . . . Maestro Giovanni, you
would be."

And he gave a sardonic laugh. The Church, he explained,
possessed far more power and a great deal more wealth in Italy
than in Flanders. Here the Church was a mere tool of the duke:
there it ruled the rulers—as well as the people. It bled them
too, of course, in return for the promise of salvation, but that
was quite a high reward, and in any case Jan should not worry
himself too deeply about it since the bishops and abbots lav-
ished fortunes on paintings: hardly a wall or a ceiling of a
church or convent in Florence was left bare of some picture or
other. What was more, they had no one with any genius to
paint them: the only painter with a skill to match Jan's had
just died—Maestro Masaccio. Did Jan not know that? So now
was his chance. And the women . . . ! Arnolfini's lugubrious
face seemed to stretch itself in an ecstasy of wonder, and he
flexed his bejeweled hands as if the very air around him were
flesh.

"Why then, Giovanni, do you choose to live here in the
benighted north?" Jan asked with a wry smile.

"Ah!" he replied with a contented sigh. "It's one thing for a
painter like you, Jan. But for a merchant—a mere merchant,"
he added with a note of unconvincing modesty, "what the
Italians like to purchase is made here—or brought here." Jan's
eyes followed Arnolfini's glance around the room whose walls
were hung with the most exquisite tapestries from Arras and
Tournai, the furniture upholstered with the finest damasks and
the tables set with jeweled lamps. "All the traders of the world
come to Bruges," he went on. "If I like to be rich I have to be
in Flanders. And I do like to be rich."

Even had he not said so, Arnolfini's house would have been

evidence enough. It was a mansion that seemed to float in a dream of riches. Wonderfully wrought Venetian mirrors were so placed that the house appeared limitless in size, and those walking around it caught unexpected glimpses of themselves, near or far away, facing this way or that, like so many ghosts within an endless labyrinth. Then there was the mysterious accompaniment everywhere of the sound of water, to which Arnolfini never referred though it was rumored that once or twice visitors had heard the laughter of a woman's voice from where that insistent plopping of water seemed to come: and at the Fallen Angel a weaver from Ghent who had just delivered some fine scarlet cloth to the merchant's house swore that in one of the mirrors he caught a glimpse of a girl's body which for that instant became fragmented in a kaleidoscope of other mirrors everywhere. He was sure his face had betrayed his astonished delight, but Arnolfini had said nothing, and the weaver had not liked to ask. It was Bona who confirmed, in her offhand way, that Giovanni's tastes had extended recently to Moorish baths following a visit to Granada, and that she had arranged for him to install a similar device in her own house. As to the girl, Bona could only assume that if you had a bath in your house then people used it, and if that person was as pretty as Lysbet, then a man of taste such as Giovanni would see to it that her body could be appreciated in all its finer viewpoints. She herself was looking forward to enjoying the same experience with her lovers: imagine twenty different views of a body you were about to enjoy. It took an Italian, she explained, to apply such imagination to the pleasures of love. The Flemings would never have thought of it.

Jan came to the purpose of his visit.

"The regalia of the Golden Fleece," he inquired. "I need it, as you know, for the duke's portrait. The ducal herald suggests you are the person to obtain it for me."

Jan had no idea why Arnolfini should be in a position to lay his hands on ermine-lined gowns and gold-embroidered mantles, least of all the jeweled insignia of the Golden Fleece itself: at the same time he had grown accustomed to the Italian merchant's invisible empire of power, and it was no great surprise to him when Arnolfini—without a word or change of expression—unlocked a handsome carved cupboard in which hung the entire regalia.

"I shall arrange for it to be brought to you under special guard," he said in a matter-of-fact way. "He will have to stay with you while you paint it, I'm afraid. Not that I don't trust you, please understand, Jan. But there are thieves." Then his lips curled into a smile. "I should find myself rapidly back in Lucca should the duke catch sight of some master fishmonger in the marketplace adorned as a knight of the Golden Fleece."

Arnolfini smoothed the golden insignia of the fleece lovingly in his fingers, and Jan could detect the hunger on the merchant's face as he dreamed of selling such a rare gem to all the courtiers of Europe who had witnessed the noble ceremony during the duke's wedding festivities.

"Have you ever seen such a fleece, Jan?" he mused, holding out the jewel in his hand. "Certainly not on a sheep," he added, and Jan noticed a sly smile begin to creep over Giovanni's face. "You know, of course, that the master goldsmith was given a lock of human hair to copy?" He looked quizzically at Jan, whose expression was one of mild surprise. "Such beautiful golden hair," the merchant continued, his Italian intonation as ever growing more pronounced as the subject turned to female beauty. "How many of the honored knights of the Order are aware, I wonder, that they carry on their lordly chests a replica of one of the ducal mistress's locks? It casts an intimate light on the love of chivalry, don't you think?"

Jan was well aware of the merchant's fondness for salacious gossip and was at first inclined to discount the tale; but then he recalled Jacqueline telling him how the duchess Isabella had lost her unborn child when she learned that her own lady-in-waiting Louise had been the duke's mistress. Louise did indeed have the most glorious golden hair. Jan thought of the duke posing so nobly for his portrait in the robes of the Golden Fleece—speaking so movingly of his ambitions for the Order and the recapture of the Holy City: could such a man, newly married, really have chosen as the insignia of so lofty a cause a lock of his own mistress's hair?

It seemed that everywhere Jan turned there were voices snapping at the good name of the duke.

Arnolfini replaced the insignia and the regalia and locked the cupboard. He would have it delivered to him tomorrow morning, he assured his visitor. And then Giovanni once more surprised him.

"And what news did the duke's ambassador have to bring him from Zeeland?" he asked. There was an edge to the merchant's voice, and Jan wondered how he could have known of the duke's commission—and how much more he knew. It was as if every room in Bruges had ears.

"I brought him nothing," he answered as casually as he could. "There was nothing to bring."

Jan was sure from Arnolfini's expression that the merchant hoped for more, and he wondered why. Jan's meeting with the duke had in fact been brief and cordial: he had been relieved how easily he had erased from his mind the sight of the English vessel in the harbor at Goes, and the hooded figure of Jacqueline in the shadows. Thankfully the duke had seemed uninterested for once: there were other things on his mind.

Arnolfini was still gazing at him, but now there was a reflective look on the long sallow face.

"I used to see a lot of the duchess Jacqueline," he said. Again Jan was surprised and puzzled. "When she *was* a duchess, that is," he added. "Years ago."

Giovanni seemed to be turning something over in his mind. He picked up a finely engraved chalice that had been resting on the table, and began to examine it as though it held some secret. Once or twice he seemed about to explain, but continued to say nothing for a few minutes. Eventually he replaced the chalice almost abruptly and turned to Jan with a curiously intent expression.

"Let me tell you something, Jan," he said. "You're almost a newcomer here. I've lived in Bruges for more than fifteen years." There was a slight pause as he examined his slender fingers, flexing them one after the other and inspecting the fine rings that adorned each one. "I know the predicament you're in," he continued, not appearing to register the alarm on Jan's face. "I shan't tell you *how* I know; only that I understand this place as you don't. It's built on intrigue and on lies, and in order to survive you have to know that. You need extra ears—

and a good Italian nose." He gave a thin laugh, tapping his own prominent nostrils while his eyes narrowed cunningly.

"I knew Jacqueline because for several years I delivered to her all kinds of precious things. Tapestries. Silver. Gold. Jewels. Carpets. Silks. Damask. Always the finest. And do you know who paid me?" Arnolfini looked at Jan with that pale saturnine face. "It was Philip."

He was silent for a moment, allowing what he had said to sink into Jan's mind.

"He wanted Jacqueline," he went on in a quiet deliberate voice. "He wanted to marry her. I think he loved her. I even think he still does. . . . That is what you should know." Then he added, "So, you see, your situation is more complicated than you imagined."

Jan was stunned. He had once imagined that being a painter was a matter of painting people's pictures—of themselves, or for their churches or their greater grandeur. Nothing more. Now it felt as though a painter's life were located in the center of a tangle of knots, each being tugged tighter around him by determined people all pulling in different directions. Jan appreciated Giovanni's concern: he sensed not so much friendship—he doubted if Arnolfini was capable of that—as a softness of feeling toward a fellow survivor whose shell was as yet vulnerably thin.

Giovanni proceeded to tell him the whole story: it was another pattern in the tale of Flanders laid carefully over those other patterns which together were forming the carpet of this strange country.

"You have to understand not just love—Philip's love for Jacqueline," he went on, again examining the chalice as if it contained the very alchemy of Burgundy. "That would be too simple, and the duke is no simple man. It began, of course, with Jacqueline being the heiress to so much that Philip desired. All those lands. Rich lands. Hainault. Holland. Who could resist a lady—a mere girl at the time—who held all that in her grasp? So why not marriage?" Arnolfini's face took on an expression of mischievous delight and cunning.

"But Philip's father knew better—John the Fearless," Giovanni continued, carefully circling the rim of the chalice with a slender finger. "He wanted more. He wanted Brabant too. Then the Low Countries would be all Burgundy's—except a few sand dunes and swampy islands which are Zeeland." Jan's mind flashed momentarily to those very dunes. "So, instead, Jacqueline found herself married to the duke of Brabant—a wise enough move politically, and of course taking into consideration the feelings of none of those concerned; but then if marriage were to be guided by love the duke would have had no dukedom at all." Arnolfini laughed, clearly enjoying his exposition. "No, it was shrewd, shrewd of Duke John. For one thing, the lord of Brabant was sickly, a feeble creature, unlikely to live long if the duke could help it. And as for Jacqueline—well, the sight of a lovely bride of sixteen would certainly do nothing to stir his member: the duke had already tried every lady-in-waiting at court on him. And always nothing. It became quite a joke—the sleeping little worm of Brabant . . . And so, you see, there would've been no offspring from the match, and on the husband's conveniently early death Jacqueline would have Brabant too. And then . . . now do you see the plan? She would be for the duke's son Philip, and all hers would be his."

"And meanwhile"—Arnolfini's face crinkled like damp parchment—"the young Philip had himself set eyes on his cousin, the beautiful black raven, and his heart was carried away. Lost."

Jan was still too astonished to offer a comment, but Arnolfini was not expecting one.

"But then disaster struck. You know the rest. Jacqueline fled Brabant, and fell in love with Duke Humphrey of Gloucester, and married him. . . . And yet, even then Philip refused to give up. All that chivalry, you know"—Giovanni gave a mocking laugh—"staking your life and honor for a lady you can't have: how the Burgundians love it all. I think he really believed, once he'd beaten and bought off Gloucester, that the shapely Jacqueline would fall into his arms. Instead of which, of course, she fought him like a tigress, refused to give up . . . and *loathed* him. That hurt Philip most of all—her loathing."

Suddenly Jan perceived a quite different meaning to his

role as the duke's ambassador. Perhaps the news he really wanted to hear was not her plans for revenge at all, but the softening of her heart. His had been an emissary of love— could it really be? How ever more indecipherable the duke grew day by day.

"Tell me one more thing, Giovanni," he said as he was preparing to leave. "Supposing Jacqueline were to yield to Philip, perhaps in despair or self-interest, what would happen?" He could see Giovanni's small eyes beginning to crinkle again. "What would happen to Isabella?"

Arnolfini's laugh was not a joyful sound.

"Jan," he replied, his voice playful and patronizing, his long hands fingering the air, "the precious codes of chivalry are not about marriage. Marriage is a contract. Love is something else. Love is . . ." And at that very moment a door opened and the lovely Lysbet slipped into the room unannounced: her face and hair were shining with moisture and she wore only the lightest of wraps about her body. "Love is like this."

And with the air of a man casually drawing aside a curtain, he swept the garment from the naked Lysbet, who expressed not the slightest surprise.

"Love is what you desire; what you can afford; and what you can have."

Jan felt a wave of disgust at Arnolfini. And then he laughed.

"Is it also something you display like a jewel?"

Giovanni looked at Jan severely.

"Only to a man I would pay handsomely to paint her like this. Would you?"

Jan remembered the Italian cardinal Octavianni, who had asked Arnolfini for what he described as "cabinet pictures."

"I'm afraid you will have to disappoint the celibate cardinal," was all he could bring himself to say, so preoccupied was he with everything the merchant had told him.

Giovanni shrugged his shoulders carelessly and covered Lysbet with the garment again. Jan departed without a further word, his mind still grappling with the merchant's tale. As he closed the door he could hear the sound of female laughter behind him.

Unhappiness spread across the dukedom like an ugly stain.

In Ghent, wrote Joos Vyt, the weavers and cloth guild workers had set fire to warehouses—demanding rights, demanding pay, the lessening of taxes: his own family had been threatened; merchants, burgesses, councillors, aldermen, rentmasters, and other leading citizens were summoning the militia. There was blood, and hatred. There was sadness in Vyt's words: here he was, he said, the burgomaster of one of the wealthiest cities in all Europe, and the more money that flowed in, the more uneven was the distribution of it—or so it appeared to those who never had enough. Each guild master wanted to be his own duke, and who was to run the chaos of the state? Bishop Denis, Jan would be pleased to hear, had never been so happy now that his dark prophecies were burning around him. And when might the great altarpiece be ready? Perhaps the inauguration should be delayed until the city quietened. At least there was a good harvest, he understood: nothing calmed people's discontent more surely than a drop in the price of bread. He, as burgomaster, had already fixed the cost of flour: now he supposed he would have to deal with the fury of the farmers. Perhaps we should all retreat to a monastery, Vyt suggested: one that was far from the sulphurous fires fanned by Bishop Denis, he hastened to add. He personally favored the Augustinian house of St. Agnietenberg at Zwolle, where a man could live as he pleased (in other words, Jan understood, where good wine could be had): here, Vyt stressed, was a most admirable and kindly German monk from Kempen—his name Thomas Hamerken, known famously as Thomas a Kempis. Jan should read his remarkable book which Thomas had kindly sent him. *The Imitation of Christ.* Balm to a troubled soul, Joos assured him. This, for example; and Vyt quoted a phrase: " 'If there be such a thing as true pleasure in the world, the pure in heart enjoy it.' I like to think that you and I are pure in heart," Joos added. "But it was not a book likely to find much favor with Bishop Denis," he commented, and Jan could imagine the smile on the old man's face as he wrote it.

There were similar tales from other cities—Arras, Tournai, Liège; Bruges was still calm, and no reports of unrest came from Louvain, Jan was relieved to hear. Margarethe was never far from his mind. A sad glow in the memory. The loveliest of flowers which blossomed and was gone. Several times Jan had visited her uncle, the master weaver, now returned from Louvain. Always he hoped for news, for hope: but there was none. Only that Margarethe was in retreat, he would not say where, but good nuns were caring for her. She was free to come and go, but at present she preferred to remain in the *béguinage:* her mother was with her, close to death, the weaver understood, but she was cherished there. It was the right place for them both. Later . . . who could tell? The master weaver raised his shoulders sadly. There would be no point in Jan's going there: Margarethe would not see him, he felt certain. She would see no one. She was perhaps too frail for this world. Jan shook his head. He did not believe that, he said. She needs time.

But then so, Jan admitted to himself, did he. At present he needed to swim alone through these currents.

As for Margarethe, there were moments, in the half-awake hour after dawn, when she imagined Jan riding here through the forest and taking her with him; and in those moments she ached for him. But then, fully awake, she recoiled from the thought even though she still ached for him. The world beyond the high walls of the *béguinage* felt a haunted place in which the fires of Bishop Denis's vision flickered between the trees, and the branches took on the shapes of severed limbs. Before her eyes even the grassy bank where she and Jan had made love became a bed of torture to which she lay strapped naked while soldiers stood over her removing their clothes and laughing, boasting, pointing, jeering. And Jan was nowhere there—would never be there. Margarethe would cross her small cell and stare from the tiny window at the garden and the reassuring wall, with the small quiet houses of the *béguinage* secure among their neat plots of flowers, and only then would her spirit grow calm. It was not like being in a nunnery—the nuns were there, and the chapel, if she needed them; but what she needed most was the fact that they were there. That was enough. She worked in the garden, she cooked and sewed, attended to her mother, and dressed herself in her comforting gray. It was the shadow of a life, but the shadow held no fears.

Margarethe was not the only young woman immured within her own sad thoughts. For the duchess Isabella the new bright world of Burgundy had darkened. Since the loss of her child she had ceased even to try involving herself in the ducal court: she cared nothing for its colors and its ceremonies, and now that Louise was no longer her lady-in-waiting there was no companion with whom she could talk and laugh, even though laughter now felt like a language she had ceased to understand.

"I shall dine here alone, Beatrice," she announced to her new lady-in-waiting, as she said every evening.

"Yes, your ladyship," came Beatrice's reply, as every evening.

Beatrice was plain and dull, as Isabella had insisted. But oh! such plainness and dullness were no succor to the spirit, and beneath her own sadness Isabella knew there was a spirit still alive. But what would happen to it in this place? She often imagined herself growing old here, visited less and less by her husband the duke—occasionally by day, even less by night. She even wished sometimes that Louise were still with her, and she could ask the girl to suggest her a lover. How wonderful to *want* a man, to wait for him, dress and undress for him, glow for him: and how very short a time ago she had felt all those things for the man she loved. But the duke, Isabella knew now, was not a man any woman could love, because he loved all women.

She was wrong, of course, as Jan would have been able to tell her. Or maybe, after all, Isabella was not entirely wrong, since the beautiful Jacqueline had been the only woman in the duke's life to say no; and perhaps it was the Olympian disdain with which Jacqueline had received his courtship that hooked its barb into Philip's heart.

Jacqueline, too, was alone. As autumn dampened the parched fields and marshes she waited with the impatience of a chained creature for the gray seas to bristle alive with masts. When Humphrey of Gloucester would sail with his army and her hopes, she did not know: the emissary had conveyed only his intention to raise an army before the winter—to reclaim his lands. *His* lands, she noted. Her own anger seethed underground. It would remain unseen, she vowed, until the moment she prayed for: as duchess of Hainault, Holland, and Zeeland once more, she would take Humphrey lovingly to her bed and knife him through the heart. With *this* knife. And she held it in the palm of her hand—the very hand on which Humphrey had slipped her wedding ring so many years ago when her heart was young.

The swifts no longer screamed around the castle walls of Goes. They had departed for the south on the sea winds, leaving a silence in the evenings, broken occasionally by the cry of cranes that streaked the torn sky with skeins of slender wings that were black against the dusk. Southward again. Zeeland felt a lonelier place as the first gales whipped the dunes, tearing the sand into troughs between the plumes of stubborn grass: a wilderness that obliterated even the forms of yesterday. She would gaze at her portrait—it was a portrait of summer, and far, far behind her stretched the summer dunes. Sometimes when she looked at Jan's image of her it was as if the real Jacqueline were there in front of her, and she only a spectator of herself: she had given her nature and her spirit to Jan's brush, just as she had given his body hers. They felt like her last gifts.

Bona also gazed at the portrait of herself. It was Michault de Caron who remarked that it was like a portrait of a lover, and she detected in his voice a jealous inquiry. Bona said nothing. She was bored by jealousy, almost as bored as by the absurd poems Michault composed to her on every occasion, or no occasion: she desired him less with each offering of perfectly tailored passions. To make love to Michault, she imagined, would be like sleeping with a sonnet; she preferred her lovers raw and silent. He would stare at Jan's portrait of her as if it were an altar, while her own mind would drift to that other portrait of herself. Eve.

Bona had never been given to despising herself, but when

she thought of her treatment of Jan she felt ashamed. What she had done had been out of love for Jacqueline, her "sister." All through the long, bitter campaign with the duke, Bona had watched and listened with mounting anger as she saw everything that was Jacqueline's being taken from her—her love, her lands, her self-respect, even her freedom to find happiness. She detested the duke for his love of Jacqueline, and for the cruelty of that love. He would break her if he could: but Jacqueline would never break, she would just cease to be. A husk of herself, that was all Philip would ever have. But Jan—she had no right to have thrust him into this. It had been her own suggestion that he might help her, that he might be the only man who could help her, and Jacqueline had seized that frail hope like a drowning woman. But Bona had underestimated Jan: she had counted on his innocence without perceiving that no man of Jan's intelligence and skills would permit himself to be duped. He had seen straight through her, and she had felt disgraced, humbled, unworthy.

Then an idea came to her. She could help Jan. There was Margarethe. Jan loved her and had lost her. Perhaps she could do what he could not. If she could find Margarethe there was much that she could tell her—quietly, slowly, with care, gradually winning the girl's confidence and in the end, maybe, building in her that confidence in herself that had been so brutally shattered. It was something Bona wanted to try: suddenly her own selfish life took on a fresh color at the thought. It would be her reparation, and her gift.

How would she begin?

Since Jan was compelled to suffer a morose guard attending him while he painted the regalia of the Golden Fleece, he decided to make the man useful by asking him to wear it. He found it hard not to smile at the sight of so unlikely a knight of chivalry, concentrating on the splendor of ermine and gold rather than on the uncouth face in the midst of it.

In midafternoon his labors were interrupted by the arrival of the ducal herald. Lefèvre, himself the King-of-Arms of the noble order, at first registered some horror at the burlesque which presented itself to him, before commenting to Jan with a twitch of a smile that at least one of the twenty-four chosen knights he could mention looked no less ludicrous.

"And I am not referring to myself," he added. The herald was in good humor, and it soon became clear to Jan why.

"Since it is the ambition of the noble order to lead a crusade against the Infidel," he announced, "the duke has summoned the court to hear a proclamation he has received from the sultan of Babylon." The pale face, on which the summer had left no mark, took on an expression of weary surprise. "I was under the impression that Babylon had been expunged by God's wrath long ago, but it appears not to be so."

The herald then explained that Jan's presence was required, not merely to hear the proclamation of Mohammed's servant but to prepare himself to accompany the duke to Arras in order to portray the Maid, now imprisoned there.

So with the departure of Lefèvre the duke's portrait was further delayed and the regalia returned to Arnolfini.

The great hall of the ducal palace glittered with the nobility of Burgundy. Jan noticed the debonair figure of the first chamberlain, Anthoine de Croy, the glowering chancellor Nicolas Rolin, the bailiff of Bruges, Lodewijk van Haverskerke, the puffing Renier Pot, and the papery ducal chaplain, Guillaume Gilastre. The tough, swarthy form of Jehan de Luxembourg stood close to the duke. The court poet, Michault de Caron, looked spruce and handsome toward the rear of the hall, and beside him bulged the figure of the ducal rentmaster, Godscalc Oom. Jan noticed there was no sign of the duchess Isabella.

The duke was at his most relaxed and commanding, dressed as usual in black, which set off the prodigious adornment of jewels. He spoke easily as if addressing friends. He was departing tomorrow for Arras, he explained, with a few senior members of the ducal court. He thanked those who had assisted in the suppression of unrest in the dukedom, and stressed the costliness of the continued wars with France. Then he reminded those assembled before him of his promise to lead a crusade against the Infidel, and with an aloof smile on his face directed the eyes of the court to the ducal herald, who, he explained, would now read out a letter he had received

from the so-called sultan of Babylon, which—as he understood—had been written to all the princes of Christendom.
Jehan Lefèvre bowed toward his duke and proceeded to unfold
a lengthy scroll of parchment with his gloved hands. After a
preliminary cough or two the herald read as follows:

"Baldadoch, son of Aire, constable of Jericho, provost of
the terrestrial paradise, nephew of the gods, king of kings,
prince of princes, sultan of Babylon, of Persia, of Jerusalem, of
Chaldea, of Barbary, prince of Africa, and admiral of Arcadia,
master Archipotel, protector of Amazone, guardian of the islands, dean of the abbeys, commander of the temples, crusher
of helmets, splitter of shields, piercer of hauberks, breaker of
armor, lancer of spears, overturner of war horses, destroyer of
castles, flower of chivalry, a wild boar of courage, an eagle of
liberality, the fear of his enemies, the hope of his friends, the
raiser-up of the discomforted, standard of Mohammed, lord of
all the world: to the kings of Germany, of France, and of England, and to all other kings, dukes, and counts, and generally
to all on whom our courtesy may condescend, greeting, and
love in our grace. Whereas it is very commendable for all who
please to relinquish error, through wisdom—we send to you
that you may not delay coming to us to receive your fiefs and
inheritances from our hands, by denying your God and the
Christian faith, and laying aside your errors, in which you and
your predecessors have been too long involved. Should you
not instantly obey these our commands our indignation will be
raised and our powerful sword turned against you, with which
we will have your heads as a recompense, without sparing
yourselves or your countries."

There was many a smile around the great hall.

"Does our captain quake with fear, my lord of Luxembourg?" asked the duke; and then, turning to the rest of the
company, he added, "They say that Mohammed was mad: it
would appear that his malady has passed to his successors."

There was general laughter, though rather less of it from
Jehan de Luxembourg, whose soldier's view of Burgundian
ambitions rarely induced him to laugh.

"I think we might reply to Baldadoch, son of Aire and
provost of the terrestrial paradise," the duke continued in fine

humor, "that we in Burgundy intend to seize our fiefs and inheritances in our own time and with our own swords. Perhaps we should add our condolences to the sultan's no doubt many wives on their lord's imminent demise."

The laughter was now of a more polite kind, and there were many in that hall who reflected that the sultan's wives were unlikely to outnumber the duke's mistresses.

"In my opinion, Jan," said Michault de Caron later in the discreet recess of the tavern, "the bluster of the one is matched by the bluster of the other. I cannot believe Philip will ever ride in triumph to Babylon any more than Sultan Baldadoch will arrive with his hordes at the gates of Bruges."

But Jan's mind was on more immediate matters.

"Why do you think the duke is anxious for me to draw the Maid?" he asked, peering at Michault questioningly over the rim of his glass.

Michault looked surprised and took a quick gulp of his wine. Then he looked reflective for a while.

"I can only imagine," he said eventually, "that he thinks you may see something he has not."

"Or that she may tell me something?"

Michault shook his head.

"By all accounts she will tell you nothing. She rarely speaks except to rant against Burgundy."

"Then what?"

There was another reflective pause.

"I have only one clue, Jan." Michault refilled their two glasses and gazed into his own. "It may mean nothing at all, but I was with the duke shortly after the Maid was captured at Compiègne," he went on without raising his eyes at Jan. "And all he could speak of was the absurdity of her so-called voices. It seemed most important to him that Joan should be . . . how shall I say? . . . a fraud."

"And why? I wonder."

This time Michault raised his head and looked at Jan.

"Have you ever been able to fathom the schemes that go on in the duke's mind, Jan? At least you may be sure that, whatever it is, it's extremely devious and the outcome designed to make someone's life as uncomfortable as possible."

Jan heard himself give a deep sigh.

"That person seems rather often to be me," he said.

Michault laughed. "It's the price you pay for being a good ambassador, Jan. The price I pay is having to make up ludicrous poems."

Jan gave a shrug of resignation.

"So you mean, Michault, that the duke actually believes—because of some powers I'm supposed to possess—that as I draw the Maid I shall be able to detect whether or not the woman is a fraud. Is that it?"

Michault slowly nodded his head, and then a languid smile spread across his face.

"My dear Jan," he said. "I am the duke's sweet tongue. You are his eyes. You must be getting used to that by now." And he laughed again.

An hour after dawn the party of horsemen left by the western gate of the city. Ahead of them the road sped straight as a furrow through a scattered forest of mill sails and of willows leaning southward from the wind, their leaves already yellowing with autumn. The hard sunlight picked out the riders in their brilliant costumes like so many colored jewels against the silver of the flooded fields. There were some forty of them all told, led by the duke himself in his ermine hat and crimson surcoat. The duchess Isabella rode close behind, the mane of her white horse plaited with threads of gold, the bridle sparkling with rubies. Her tall headdress shimmered with opals. In the main group of riders was the duke's first chamberlain, Anthoine de Croy; his general, Jehan de Luxembourg; the chancellor of the Golden Fleece, Jehan Germain; and a host of other prominent courtiers. Jan kept a position modestly in the rear of the party alongside Michault de Caron. Around and behind them, maintaining a watchful cordon, rode fifteen or twenty armed soldiers.

Jan said little on that journey. At times his thoughts were so far from things around him that he was scarcely aware of the towns and villages they rode through, or of the panoply of splendor which drew the wonder of those they passed.

But gradually, as the hours stretched to days and always at

the same distance ahead of him rode the proud figure of the duke, Jan began to see that crimson surcoat as an image he was painting—bright as a flame burning before his eyes. Jan could even sense his wrist guiding the brush, the careful strokes, the slight darkening of the outline so that the image of the man seemed to vibrate against the expanse around him.

Suddenly, to his amazement, into that emptiness around the solitary figure of Philip there began to emerge—like ghosts at first and then real as flesh and blood—clusters of other figures; and they were armed, their faces fierce and brutal. Jan could feel himself painting those terrible faces, their bristles and their scars, and their rough clutching hands. Some wielded swords and spears, others carried chains. And now Jan saw that there were people being led by those chains, dragged, mocked, beaten. They were all of them women, but he could not see who they were: he could not give them faces. Now the figure of the duke in crimson had turned toward him and there was a look of cruelty on his face. He held a sword in his right hand, red with blood, and the red of his surcoat was nothing but blood. With his sword he pointed at first one group of soldiers, then another, another and another: four groups of jeering men, each of them dragging a woman in chains. Jan knew them now: he could paint their faces, and as he did so each one of them stared back at the duke with a look of such hatred that Jan felt a stab of horror. One was Isabella. One was Margarethe. One was Jacqueline. And the fourth was the Maid.

Jan knew he had painted his true portrait of the duke.

The fourth victim he had yet to meet. The duke was unusually silent, and that shadow which Jan had already noticed sometimes overcame him was now dark across his face as he stood apart from his courtiers in the draped hall of ducal residence in Arras. Jan was still shaken by the vividness of his own vision of the duke's portrait which had come to him while they had ridden here. Michault had inquired several times if he felt well, and had endeavored to cheer him with scurrilous tales concerning this or that member of the ducal court—tales which blew like chaff from Jan's mind as soon as they settled there. He realized ever more clearly that the change he had detected in the duke seemed always to be associated with the Maid—when he was thinking about her, whenever she was mentioned, and now when they were under the same roof. Jan thought about Michault's words in the tavern some evenings earlier, and he found himself waiting with a certain bleak curiosity to see when the duke would approach the subject of the Maid, and what he would choose to say.

The duke dined well that evening. He wore a robe of cloth of gold, and from his wrist flashed a bracelet studded with rubies. He extended warm courtesies to the duchess, who responded little, but there were those in the hall who noticed her eyes occasionally lift in the direction of a lady in blue velvet cut low to her bosom. It was Michault—of course—who whispered to Jan that she was the lady Peronnelle, wife of one of the duke's most chivalrous knights, who, it seemed, found himself constantly obliged to be elsewhere whenever the duke was in Arras. Michault did not imagine that the duchess would see much of her husband that night, and when Jan looked at Isabella's face there was a deadness in her eyes as of someone already well aware of that fact. The face of the lady Peronnelle, by contrast, wore a look of unassuming serenity, her small movements of the shoulders made with the air of one conscious that they were observed. She was palely beautiful, perhaps especially so, Jan thought, for the unspoken triumph of her evening.

The duchess rose and departed from the hall with much ceremonial bowing but without the company of her husband. Jan and Michault watched her leave.

"There goes a lady who has lost the game of love," said Michault quietly.

"If it were only a game," Jan answered, "there would not be such sadness on her face. She has lost everything."

"You take it all too much to heart, Jan. We live in a menagerie, and the creatures with claws tear at the ones with pretty feathers. That's the way it is."

Jan was glad at that moment that Bona had taunted Michault with her disdain, even though at that same moment he would have liked to wring Bona's neck.

"You know, Michault," he said, "I should like to get very, very drunk."

The poet laughed and placed an arm around Jan's shoulder. And then he withdrew it and muttered quickly in his friend's ear, "I think you may have more serious things to do."

Jan looked up and was surprised to see the tall figure of the duke parting the assembly of courtiers like so many bowing reeds and making for the table where the two men were seated. They rose.

Jan was annoyed to find himself so easily charmed. The duke led him to the privacy of his antechamber, talking lightly and easily all the while as if everything on this mission to Arras had hitherto been an unavoidable duty, and only now was Philip free to pass the time with the company of his choice. The long face was creased into the most amiable of smiles as he greeted one attendant after another while they held doors for the two men to enter, before courteously dismissing them. How gently, Jan thought, Philip could hold the reins of power; and at such moments how hard to believe the ruthlessness with which he could apply the spurs.

"I shan't keep you, Jan," he said warmly when they were alone. "You must be weary," The duke himself appeared fresh and quite unruffled by three days on horseback.

"As you know," he went on, "I have brought you here so that you shall draw the Maid. I would like you to do so tomorrow . . . and then show me," he added with a sudden note of impatience, "as soon as possible."

The duke must have detected a startled look on Jan's face. "You look puzzled," he added.

Jan could not help recalling Michault's words.

"Perhaps so, my lord," he replied. The duke was watching him intently. For his own sake there was something Jan felt he must ask. "Forgive me, but as your painter I'm anxious to give you what you need. You have met the Maid and I have not. Is there something in particular you would like me to look for?"

The effect on the duke was surprising.

"No!" he said abruptly. "No!" Jan saw that Philip was agitated. "I employ you to use your eyes." The voice was peremptory: it was the voice of command. Then he added in the same abrupt manner, "Yes, it's true I met the Maid once . . . but I shall not see her again."

Jan was surprised by the note of insistence. There were many other questions he would not risk the duke's temper by asking.

Then the moment of awkwardness passed, and as so often, the duke seemed to smile away the rough edges from his mind.

"I have to warn you," he went on, his voice recapturing the note of easy humor. "She will not talk to you as others do when you draw them. I fear the experience may be more like drawing a statue." He laughed. "But a statue, of course, that hears voices."

It was a strange interview. The conversation moved swiftly away from Joan as though the duke were anxious to dismiss her from his mind. He talked of other things. He talked of hunting and falconry: he hoped Jan would accompany him after their return—there were fine forests around Bruges with plentiful boar and stag, bears too. Then he joked about the letter from the sultan of Babylon. He was contemplating, he said jocularly, requesting Michault de Caron to compose a mock encomium to send to the preposterous Baldadoch which would incorporate the extraordinary catalogue of titles the sultan had awarded himself, but adding a number of further titles more appropriate to the ranting stupidity of the man, and perhaps implying in the most courtly possible language certain defects and inadequacies in the sultan's genitalia. The duke's good humor was entirely restored by the thought. Perhaps, he added, he might even compose such verses himself should the court poet find the task an affront to his dignity.

"It's one of the supreme pleasures of power, Jan," he explained, his eyes bright with pleasure, "to permit oneself occasionally to be outrageously rude to those who consider themselves to be important."

With that he bid Jan cheerfully good night. As he made his way to his own room two thoughts were lodged firmly in Jan's mind. First, that the duke's buoyant mood was inspired by the delightful prospect of the lady Peronnelle. Second, that Michault was right, and whatever the duke wanted from him was to do with the Maid's "voices." Philip, he felt quite sure, wanted Jan's eyes to tell him something about Joan's sincerity. But why?

And why, Jan wondered as he lay in bed enjoying the pallor of the moonlight, why was the duke so insistent that he himself would not encounter the Maid again? What could possibly have occurred during that first and only meeting between Philip and his captive to have induced such a determined resolve? It was as if—the thought surprised Jan—the duke were actually afraid of her. Could it be so? And would tomorrow cast any ray of light? More than ever the mystery of the duke's mind seemed bound to this figure of a girl in man's clothing whom he was about to meet—a girl to whom the angels spoke. Jan's last thought before sleep had nothing whatever—it seemed—to do with these entangled events. He was imagining himself painting the night sky. Why should it be, it struck him, that blackest night always lay in the mouth of the moon?

The first thing he noticed about her was her stillness.

She seemed not so much to occupy that gray cell of a room as to be a part of it. She wore a man's clothing, plain as the walls around her, and never once did her eyes turn to look at him. It was as though he was not there. The guard remained close to him all the time he drew her face, shifting from foot to foot, coughing, sighing with boredom, until Jan barked at him to be quiet. Those were the only words spoken.

It was some time before Jan noticed that her gaze was directed not at the gray wall but at a tiny crucifix that was pinned to it. He began to imagine in that colorless room a double thread drawn taut between the cross and her two eyes, along which her thoughts traveled. This made him peer more closely at her eyes, and as he peered he could feel his fingers tauten around the slim rod of silver in his hand. It was the eyes that were the key to her: he must not get them wrong, he must not miss the . . . What was it? It was the absence of a look, not a deadness at all, but a kind of blind awareness. Then as he tried to record those so very conscious eyes, Jan understood: she was not gazing at the crucifix, it was gazing at her. Her eyes were its object, its receivers.

Of course. Her voices. She received.

"Is there nothing you might have to say to me?" Jan asked when the drawing was almost completed. He did not know why.

There was not even a tremor of movement in her face. He wondered if she had even heard him. And yet she had spoken to the duke. Or had she? Had there been perhaps the same utter silence?

Jan looked at the finished drawing. And as he did so he understood something else. She had been like this for him in order that he might draw her as she really was.

"Show me," the duke said immediately.

For a long while he said nothing, holding the drawing sometimes closer, sometimes further away. They were in the same room as the previous evening, and again the duke seemed restless, tense.

"So she said nothing?"

"Nothing whatever."

Finally the duke took a deep, long breath and laid the drawing on the table. It was as though he had made up his mind. His fingers traced the profile of her face, then with a brusque movement of the hand he seemed to brush her aside.

"Tell me, Jan," he said, his voice less sharp now, "do you believe this is the face of a woman who hears the voices of angels?"

Jan hesitated for a moment. Joan had said nothing to him. He had nothing to go on but his intuition, and his own eyes.

"My lord, I cannot possibly know that," he replied. "But it's my belief that she does, or at least that she's convinced that she does."

The duke looked at him sharply.

"Hm!" He pushed the drawing toward Jan with a dismissive gesture. "Delusions is what you mean." He gave a contemptuous laugh. "I believe you've drawn me the face of a fraud without knowing it." Then to Jan's surprise he placed a hand affectionately on his shoulder. "Jan, you have a most commendable weakness for women. I wish I could afford to have the same—life would be a great deal softer and more full of pleasure. But I tell you, if Joan had been a man you would no more have believed in his voices than you would believe him capable of turning water into wine. Is that not so?" And he laughed, pleased with himself.

Jan found himself wondering if what the duke had said might be true. He doubted it.

"She was wearing a man's clothing," he said, unable to think of any other answer at that moment.

"Jan, you're being foolish. If I were to dress as a woman, would you regard me as a woman . . . or as a fraud?"

Jan was silent. But he gazed down at the face of Joan and felt certain the duke was wrong. And what, he wondered, would be the consequences?

The duke was anxious to leave for Bruges the following morning. He seemed his old brisk self again, joking with his courtiers, attending gently to the duchess Isabella, and teasing Michault about the interminable encomium he was expecting from the poet on the virtues and deformities of the sultan of Babylon. The party set off soon after first light, and again the bright calvacade threaded the forest paths and the harvested fields. The duke's good humor spread around him, and from the rear of the party Jan could hear snatches of song, with the duke's somewhat high-pitched voice leading the verses and the older courtiers making polite, unmusical attempts to join in.

The day passed. And then another. The mists of autumn gathered and dispersed around them. Stags darted across their path, and the duke's voice rose in excited anticipation of the hunting to come once they had returned to Bruges. The duchess Isabella rode silently, sharing little of the gaiety.

"You're very silent, Jan."

It was almost the first time he and Michault had found themselves parted sufficiently from the main party of riders to exchange more than idle comment. There had been no chance for Jan to tell Michault about his encounter with the Maid or his strange discussions with the duke. An uneasy load weighed on Jan's mind, and the brightness of the duke's manner as he rode some hundred paces ahead served only to deepen his own sense of disquiet. On this sharp autumn day it was as though they were riding into a storm. Jan wished he could understand what that storm might be.

"Let me tell you what took place," he said, "and then, Michault, you tell *me* what you think it all means."

It was comforting to talk as they rode through the peace of the forest. Michault listened attentively, occasionally glancing about him, and his face brightened or grew puzzled as he heard Jan's story. Jan described the duke's curtness on that first evening in Arras, his concern that Jan should draw the Maid as soon as possible—to use his eyes, was all he had said. Then there was the silent meeting with the Maid, and Jan's conviction that she was in a kind of trance controlled by the tiny crucifix on the wall. Finally he spoke of the duke's response to the drawing—dismissive, contemptuous—and Philip's certainty that Jan had drawn the Maid as a fraud without realizing it. The duke was convinced of it, unshakable, he explained, and his spirits had risen from that moment. Look at him now, Jan added. And the two men gazed ahead of them for a moment, listening to the sounds of singing and jollity drifting back toward them along the forest path as they rode.

The party dismounted by a river, and while the horses were being watered the duke and his senior courtiers attended to the duchess Isabella, who was fatigued from the long ride. Jan and Michault strolled along the riverbank some distance from the others. They were on the edge of Flanders now, and the familiar pattern of small waterways spread out around them, fringed by leaning willows. The autumn air carried with it the smell of the sea.

"I'll tell you what I think, Jan." Michault was staring pensively into the water, idly casting small sticks into the current and watching them spin and recoil in the eddies. "And it's the kind of thinking you acquire when you live at the court of Burgundy—I wonder if all courts are like this." The poet grimaced and then laughed. "First of all, why do you suppose the duke was so anxious that the Burgundians should capture the Maid and not the English?"

"Because she's a bargaining point—presumably," Jan answered.

"Right. Her capture gives him a certain hold over the English, because they want her dearly. And would pay him dearly for her." Michault looked hard at Jan as if to emphasize how important gold was to the duke.

"But she's also an embarrassment to him," he went on. "The Church is pressing him to try her as a heretic, and Philip wants no part of that. He would earn the hatred of all France; and—don't forget, Jan—Philip in his heart would love to be the ruler of France, or at least be in control of it. Why else do you think he is fighting this ridiculous war?"

Michault glanced around him again to make sure no one was within earshot.

"So," he went on, speaking more quietly, "he would be perfectly happy to hand the Maid over to the English: they want her desperately, he needs the favor of the English and he would like their gold. *But* . . . the duke will not do that if he believes it would earn him the loathing of France."

Jan was fascinated by the precise elaboration of Michault's mind. At the same time he could not help feeling shocked.

"You don't believe that the duke's sense of honor might compel him to resist the English and their ransom?"

Michault's face registered astonishment.

"You must be mad," he said quietly.

Jan looked at him sadly. Something told him that Michault was right, and he remembered Bona's mocking laughter. The duke has no ideals, she had said; only ambitions.

"All right, Michault," he said a little wearily, "now tell me what this has to do with the duke dragging me to Arras in order to draw the Maid, and then telling me I've got it wrong."

Michault looked at him wryly.

"Jan, you're too impatient. Wait." Irritatingly Michault went on throwing sticks into the water. "Now, try to follow me," he went on. "Suppose the duke hands her over. He receives his fortune. He gains the love of the English—who then have the task of trying her as a heretic. The bishop of Beauvais will do everything in his power to prove her so. What matters is whether or not Joan is a fraud: because if she is a fraud she will recant at the trial. Philip can then put pressure on the duke of Bedford to plead for her release under oath of keeping the peace, or something of that sort. And then—do you begin to see?—Philip earns the gratitude of France too. He will have it both ways—and the gold!"

Jan buried his head in his hands. It all sounded so brutally likely.

"But . . ." Michault continued, *"is* Joan a fraud? And will she recant? That is where Philip needed your eyes. Because if she goes to the stake as a heretic, it's farewell to France for the duke."

Jan said nothing for a while, absorbing the cynical scheme which Michault had unfolded. Then a look of puzzlement crossed his face.

"But I did not show him a fraud. I drew a woman who was in a trance: it was as if that crucifix was speaking to her. I told the duke so, and that she was sincere."

Michault placed a friendly hand on Jan's shoulder.

"Has it occurred to you, Jan, that since you told Philip nothing of value about Jacqueline he might have wanted confirmation that your eyes do not see as sharply as people say?"

Jan felt shaken.

"Perhaps. And yet I believe I'm right about the Maid, and that he is wrong," was all he could say.

"In that case, we shall see. We may soon know who is right."

They could see the riders remounting, and the two men walked back along the riverbank to rejoin them. They would be in Bruges by evening.

The long autumn was a time of waiting, and a time of tension. Jan tried to work, but his mind kept drifting away. He completed the painting of the regalia of the Golden Fleece under the baleful eye of Arnolfini's guard, but he was aware that the work was mechanical: his fingers and eyes were engaged, not his mind. When the guard had departed for the last time, there rested the portrait of the duke, nearly completed now except for those areas which would give it life and space and splendor —the vision of Burgundy, the spread of Europe, the new Jerusalem. And these Jan could not do. Instead he kept seeing his own "true" portrait of the duke that had risen before his eyes as he rode behind the ducal cavalcade through the forest: the duke dressed in blood, his soldiers dragging the chained figures of Isabella, Joan, Jacqueline, and Margarethe, as if they were being hauled to the stake, and the horizon flickered with fire. He wanted to draw his dagger and rend the portrait in front of him. Nothing would give him deeper satisfaction.

It was November already. The mill sails turned across the bleak polderlands. There were no sounds of laughter from the canals. There was no news of Margarethe, no news of Jacqueline. It was as if they had vanished with the summer.

Jan was pacing his studio listlessly when he heard the sound of footsteps and voices. Michault entered. His face looked composed and grave.

"The Maid has been surrendered to the English," was all he said.

Chapter ♦ Nine

No longer did Jacqueline look out each morning over the vast and empty sea. It was as if the light in those eyes died the instant she heard the news of the Maid. She would never again —she knew—hear from Humphrey of Gloucester; there would be no promises from Bedford; she had lost her inheritance forever. Her mind felt tired, her body old. There was not even energy in her to feel anger. Servants would enter her chamber soon after dawn to wake her, and find her awake as though she had never slept. In the evenings they would enter the small room where she dined to collect the remnants of her fish or game, and find she had not touched it. She would be seated gazing quietly at the dying flames in the fireplace, or aimlessly fingering some ornament that happened to be in front of her. Where once she had enjoyed encountering so many flattering reflections of herself in well-placed mirrors about the castle, now she had all those mirrors removed: the bleak prospect of stone walls as she passed by affronted her less than the image of some gaunt creature who was no longer the duchess Jacqueline. No finery or jewels brightened her appearance, and visiting merchants and burgomasters who came in awe of the regal figure of whom they had heard so much, imagined themselves at first to be confronting Jacqueline's maidservant. Only her portrait remained a witness to what she had been, and her attendants noticed that she would spend long hours silently regarding it. These were the only occasions when she would appear sometimes to free herself from the shroud of desolation in which she passed her days. At times she would touch it with her fingers as if searching for something that was once hers. Or she would shake her head. More than once she turned abruptly from the portrait after long scrutiny and was heard to

231

say beneath her breath, "He betrayed me." People grew anxious about her mind.

She did not know if weeks or months passed like this; only that the winter seemed like the winter of her life, without any prospect of spring.

But Jacqueline's was a spirit more easily bled than crushed; and there came a day when she called for a mirror. For a while she was not seen, but when she finally appeared in the long hall of the castle she was wearing a scarlet velvet dress no one had seen for many months, and there was a coronet in her hair —hair which she had oiled until its blackness glistened, and entwined in it were threads of pearl. She did not speak of the reason for this sudden rebirth of herself, but her chamberlain noted that one of her visitors the day before had stayed longer than was customary, only departing at dusk. No one seemed to know who it might have been.

In fact, the man was a Burgundian, an emissary, as it turned out, from the governor of Holland: hence, her servants soon understood, he had been permitted to ride to Goes unchecked. Jacqueline said nothing of the purpose of the man's visit; only that the following day she intended to ride from Zeeland toward Breda, and then northward to Leiden. A small party of soldiers would accompany her. She would be away perhaps several weeks. There would be no danger, she assured her attendants.

The emissary had brought Jacqueline news of no enormous consequence; yet it was the tone of kindness and concern that reached her withered spirits, and the fact that the governor had troubled to send his emissary at all. He was a man of whom Jacqueline had heard, a brave knight in the service of the duke of Burgundy by the name of Franz van Borselen, from his name clearly no French-speaking courtier—which pleased her. His message had been courteous. The lands for which he had been made responsible by the duke included, he learned, a castle which had belonged to Jacqueline's father and to which she was still entitled—the castle of Teilingen. He would be happy, he conveyed, to permit Jacqueline to visit Teilingen in his company and to discuss with her matters which related to her ownership of the place. In her unfortunate enforced absence, the governor's letter went on, he would hope to arrange with her that the fine castle be well cared for until such times as she might be permitted to stay there at her own wish.

She left Goes brightly, and with a sweet sadness in her heart, for Teilingen had been where she had spent many years of her childhood while her father was alive, and her memories of it were all of laughter and flowers. She could picture herself as a child playing there. It was where her father had taught her to ride—a dark-haired girl galloping along the lakeshores and the lonely dikes. Such memories were all that were left to her, and now she hugged them to herself as she rode through the winter landscape. Even the sight of children playing on the ice around the scattered villages brought smiles of pleasure to her tired face. She thought of nothing beyond returning to her own childhood.

At much the same moment the hooded figure of Bona was making her way eastward toward Louvain. With her rode a single manservant, who looked after his lady's baggage and safety, and a young page whose function was more intimate— to the annoyance of the manservant, who had once been of that same age and beauty. Bona declined to notice the tension between her two companions, being deep in thought. It had taken her nearly three months to discover the whereabouts of the *béguinage* near Louvain where the young Margarethe was in retreat. For much of that time she had grown despairing of success; it was finally the merchant Arnolfini who came to her aid, though typically he would not disclose how he managed to acquire the information she sought.

"Her mother has died," he volunteered languidly. "She lives alone."

"What else do you know, Giovanni?" Bona inquired.

"Only that she is at peace. The nuns are good to her."

Bona looked at the merchant sharply. She disliked having to wring information from a man she held in some contempt: besides, it annoyed her that his sources of knowledge should be so much more fruitful than her own. Against her will Bona felt compelled to inquire further.

"From what you know," she asked, "would you imagine the young lady might see me?"

Arnolfini's reply irritated her further.

"I should have thought," he answered, dragging out his Italian intonation as if it were gentle mockery on his tongue, "that any girl frightened of the world would quite likely be frightened by you. Your young page might enjoy greater success."

Bona snorted and departed with the most cursory of thanks, noting to her even greater irritation the supercilious smile forming on the merchant's face.

What should she say to Margarethe? The girl was overawed by her, which would be hard to surmount even without the present circumstances. And Bona herself was irritated by Margarethe, which she might find it hard to hide. She was not a woman inclined to be patient toward other women who lacked her own confidence to seize whatever she wanted. With the arrogance of someone born to privilege, Bona's instincts invariably led her to expect service, even if this meant the sacrifice of others; yet incongruously she combined this arrogance with an acute indignation at the selfishness of others. Hence her bristling disapproval of Arnolfini, who, in the eyes of those who knew them both, was in many ways remarkably like her.

It was the generous side of Bona which spurred her through the winter woods toward the high walls of the *béguinage.* She tried to set aside from her mind those quivering aspects of Margarethe's nature, and to recall her more positive traits which had made the girl more appealing and more steely than she had at first believed her to be. Bona remembered two incidents Jan had recounted, both of which had surprised her at the time. First, Jan had described how Margarethe had rounded on him in defense of the Maid when the Englishman Hugo had indulged in a gross burlesque of Joan during the winter carnival. Bona herself had no patience or sympathy for the Maid whatever: her male dress, her military excursions, her "voices," and her virginity were beyond Bona's comprehension of what a woman should be. Nonetheless, for Margarethe to have defended another woman against the drunken impertinence of a man was a spirited and admirable thing. The second incident she recalled still made Bona smile—Margarethe insisting on posing naked while Jan made tiny paintings of her for the lecherous ducal herald to peer at. If Margarethe could do that, all perhaps was not lost.

But it was something much more recent which occupied Bona's mind, and reflecting on it made her feel hopeful for Margarethe, though sad for herself. Her young page, after two nights spent in hostelries between Bruges and Louvain, already filled her spirit with a boredom verging on despair. It was difficult for her to believe the degree of lustful anticipation with which she had set out only two days ago: already she had determined to spend the nights on the return journey alone. Never had Bona been more aware that if the gods could only arrange it so she would take a different boy to her bed each night, the only fear accompanying so delightful an arrangement would be that there might not be enough boys in the world and one day there would be the most insufferable famine.

Bona found herself laughing at the sad absurdity of herself as the gates of the *béguinage* were cautiously opened to receive her. She had left her manservant and her unwanted lover at the inn in Louvain, and proceeded alone.

A nun calmly inquired the purpose of her visit; and Bona explained. She was a friend, she said, of the girl Margarethe, whose mother had recently passed away (she used the euphemism advisedly). Snow had begun to fall softly, casting a veil of silence over the tranquillity of the garden. Around it were dotted perhaps twelve small neat houses where those who came here in retreat spent their lives, and each house felt to Bona like a cradle.

She waited while the nun made her way through the snow to one of the little houses. Bona noticed that it was newly painted, and a thin plume of smoke was rising from the chimney set precisely in the center of the roof. As she looked and waited, Bona formed the image of a life of slow and neat precision, muffled against all irregularity and pruned of any danger of surprise. Yes, she could understand why Margarethe should want to be here: it was a place in which to be healed—

like a holy spring that would never cascade and never dry. And she imagined Margarethe old, smoothing out her last years here in quiet company and undemanding love. To be old, yes indeed; after life's battles and passions were over—a place to recollect the past without pain. But to be young and then grow old here: that could only be a sadness and a waste. To have no life to recollect in old age, no battles won or lost, no passions to savor, no children to remember, no lover long dead to shed tears for. What emptiness. Like an autumn that had followed no summer and scarcely any spring.

At first Bona did not recognize the girl when she emerged —shyly. Her lovely flaxen hair was lank and mostly hidden beneath a linen shawl. Another shawl, gray and rough-woven, covered her shoulders and arms and seemed to merge into the colorlessness of her dress. She wore clogs. For a moment Margarethe stood hesitantly by the open door as Bona approached, and then a suspicious, nervous look crossed her face and Bona wondered if she would suddenly disappear and bolt the door. But the nun was still lingering nearby, and her presence either gave her a little courage or restrained her from panic.

Hardly realizing what she was doing, Bona opened her arms in welcome, gradually lowering them as Margarethe failed to respond. And yet it seemed that the gesture of friendship allayed her suspicions, for she made a tentative movement of the hand indicating that Bona should enter.

Bona was surprised. The single room where Margarethe appeared to live was not like a nun's cell, as she had expected. It was bright and comfortable, and everywhere Bona noticed arrangements of dried flowers, plaids of corn and rush, colored pebbles, pretty tiles and gaily embroidered mats and kerchiefs. There were even paintings about the walls—trees and flowers done with a childish delicacy: as she glanced at these, Bona realized that Margarethe must have done them herself. There were no people in any of them, and there was never any sky. But the colors were lively and confident: the paintings were like sweet posies to be held in the hand.

"They're yours?" Bona asked.

"Yes."

They were the first words the two women had exchanged.

Bona wondered if it was the thought of Jan that had made her want to paint them.

"How pretty it all is," she exclaimed, gazing around.

Margarethe said nothing, but smiled; and Bona realized that the girl was happy here. Even the shyness had gone now that she was within her four walls.

"Aren't you lonely here?" Bona asked as gently as she could.

"Yes," Margarethe replied. "Sometimes."

Bona wanted to ask if she missed Jan, but thought better of it.

Margarethe had baked some small cakes, and without a word she vanished into the kitchen and re-emerged with a plate of them on a wooden tray which Bona realized she had also painted herself. There was a picture of a cat in the center of it, asleep on a wall, but on its face Margarethe had painted a smile.

"So you're content here," was all Bona could say.

Margarethe just nodded. Then she surprised her visitor.

"Why have you come here?" she asked. "Because if it's to persuade me to return with you, I shall not." Her voice was quiet but firm. Bona had not expected such calm or such resolve.

"Yes, I did," she replied. Bona would have liked to say something else, but no words came.

"Why should you trouble yourself, when you're not even a friend of mine?"

There was not the slightest note of aggression in Margarethe's voice, but her words pricked Bona like needles. Suddenly she felt able to come straight to the point.

"I *am* a friend of the man who loves you," she said, her eyes fixed on Margarethe's face. But if she expected the girl to flush she was mistaken.

"He will find someone else."

The reply was so flatly spoken, almost casual, that Bona felt a flush of irritation.

"And is that what you want?" she asked, and she could hear the brusqueness in her own voice.

For the first time Margarethe's composure seemed to

waver, and she hesitated for a moment before saying almost in a whisper, "It's what I accept."

Bona could see Margarethe's eyes begin to search about her as if for an escape, but she had not made this journey to see her escape. Bona knew she was prepared to wound her.

"You accept that another woman will share his life, share his bed, bear his children, care for him and love him, when all that could be yours?"

Margarethe turned from her and buried her face in her hands.

"Go away. Go away," she said.

"All right, I'll go away," Bona replied, her voice more kindly now. "But let me say this, Margarethe. I understand your shock, your pain, your fear. What happened to you was brutal. But it will never leave you if you hide. It will follow you—even here you'll never be free of it."

Margarethe was shaking her head. Bona tried to place her hands on the girl's shoulders, but she pulled away.

"Margarethe, listen to me," Bona went on. She knew it was her last plea. "You envy me because you believe I'm strong, I can get whatever I want, and people fear me. *You* fear me. But, believe me, you have something that causes much deeper envy in me. You can love. You can love a man. I can't." Bona saw Margarethe's face take on a perplexed look. "I've never loved a man in my whole life for longer than it's taken me to know him. I've wanted men, I've made love, and I've gone away. Think of that. And you who know how to love fully want to throw it away—the most precious thing in the world. I feel a cripple and would give anything not to be. Whereas you—you are choosing to be a cripple. You mustn't do that. You mustn't, Margarethe. You must take responsibility for your life."

Bona imagined as she spoke that the girl would crumble, and she wondered how a man as resolute and worldly as Jan could yearn for a creature so fragile. Instead she found herself confronted by a pair of green eyes whose look was quite steady. She took Bona's hand in her own and squeezed it gently.

"Thank you," she said; and then after a moment, "I've thought about those things. I've had a lot of time to think."

Margarethe's eyes took in the room where they were standing, settling on the pressed flowers, then the embroidery, and the plaids of corn. "You think of this place as a prison, Bona, but to me it's the world outside that's a prison."

Margarethe seated herself on a plain wooden chair facing the fire, and without looking at Bona she began to talk more freely—between pauses at first but then with confidence, even passion. Yes, it was true, she said, that she could love, and love totally; but it was not a world made for love, it was a world made for men.

"You ask me to take responsibility for my life, Bona, but don't you see that I'm not allowed to do that?" She looked up at her visitor, and Margarethe's face had a fierceness about it that Bona had never seen. "Out there I'm a slave to men. I'm their toy. I'm weak. I can be cursed by the Church because I'm beautiful. I can be raped. I can be killed. No man I love can shield me; he can only weep for me." She paused for a moment, gazing now into the fire.

"It's different for you, Bona," she went on. "You have wealth, position, influence. You can ride above the dangers of the world. I have nothing but what I am. Perhaps this place *is* a prison, but at least it's not a prison where I'm going to be violated. My body is safe here." Then, almost accusingly, she added, "Your body is safe wherever you go because you're powerful enough to make it so."

What could Bona say? She had failed. Slowly she turned to leave.

"Can I give Jan a message from you?" she asked in a voice that was quiet and sad. She saw Margarethe turn her head away.

"Tell him what I said," she answered softly; and then, barely audibly, "Tell him what you know."

Bona nodded. "One thing," she said by the open door. "You think it's different for me; and that's not so. It's no different for me, Margarethe, or for anyone."

As she rode back alone through the falling snow toward Louvain and her unwanted lover, Bona turned over in her mind all the things Margarethe had said. It perplexed her that she had not been able to answer, when the sacrifice of love for the sake of fear seemed so craven a crime; to construct such arguments against living in the wider world was like arguing that since we are all born to die painfully it is better not to be born at all. And yet Bona had not been able to answer her: and as she endeavored to search among her own thoughts for the reason, images rose before Bona's eyes. She saw Jacqueline on her windswept island, abandoned and defeated. She saw the Maid alone behind bars, awaiting trial and possibly death. And she saw the duchess Isabella, her baby lost, her husband romping in another bed, her own home a thousand miles distant. Was there, Bona wondered, no woman who had a key to the prison of the world?

And yet Bona would have been surprised had she known the effect of her visit on Margarethe at that moment. Her visitor's words had penetrated her solitude like arrows. Emotions she imagined she had lost already bubbled like blood around the wounds, and she could not wipe them away. Jealousy, loneliness, regret, anger: all was too confused for Margarethe to understand; and suddenly her own arguments seemed no more than a brightly painted shield behind which to cower. She saw the neat and pretty room that was her world—the care and love and toil with which she had created her domestic Eden: the walls of the little room, and beyond the window and the falling snow the walls of the *béguinage* were like an echo of that same room. And it was as though those enclosing walls were her own body, and her body was alive as she had quite forgotten it could ever be. Her eyes sought out the small mirror hanging between the plaids of corn and the paintings of flowers, and her hands seemingly of their own accord untied first the shawl around her head and then the larger, coarse-woven shawl about her shoulders. She did not know what guided her to the cupboard where the crimson dress had hung since the day she had arrived here; but now those hands reached for it and held it against herself before the mirror, and as she did so she remembered it was the dress she had worn when Jan's hands first touched her. In the mirror Margarethe could see the snow floating like soft tiny clouds past the window around her own reflection, and it was as if the flakes were Jan's fingers everywhere touching her. She gave a shudder.

It was the first time in half a year that Margarethe felt no need to block her ears to the sound of the bishop's words on that nightmare of an evening. It was the first time she did not need to veil her eyes from the vision of the soldiers stripping her on that riverbank, unbuckling their clothing, laughing, leering. It was with a sense of shock that she remembered, not the horror of that moment, but Jan's dagger killing for her. She saw the soldiers fleeing, and Jan lifting her tenderly onto his horse.

She looked out again at the walls of the *béguinage,* and through the snow she caught sight of one of the nuns throwing corn for twenty or so hens that were scuttling toward her across the open garden. Hurriedly she wrapped a heavy shawl around her and ran through the snow toward the woman.

"Could I do that?" she asked, out of breath.

The nun looked up, surprised, and smiled at her.

"Why?" she said, laughing, as she handed over the bowl with the remainder of the corn.

Margarethe knew why the moment the nun asked, but did not know how to say it.

"I'd like to do something."

The nun laughed again.

"Then you can do it every day if you wish. But you have to clean out the hen houses and collect the eggs too."

"All right," she answered.

It seemed foolish to be so happy about looking after hens, but Margarethe knew it was a beginning. She could hear Bona's words: "You must take responsibility for your life." She needed time, lots of time. To repair. To gain strength.

That evening she put on the crimson dress, just for herself.

But would Jan wait? She felt fearful. And then Margarethe knew that it did not depend on Jan. It was about herself. She would give herself the time she needed.

In the Fallen Angel there was an air of surprise at the continued high spirits of the duke. Godscalc Oom was in no doubt that this was due to the quantity of gold which Philip had received from the duke of Bedford in exchange for his captive, the Maid: a sum much needed, Godscalc added, in view of the cost of the war, particularly after the humiliating defeat in-flicted on Burgundy by the French on the Seine the previous December. The indignation of France at Philip's treatment of the Maid now knew no bounds, and seemed to have added a new sharpness to their swords.

"I suppose you're going to tell us this will mean fresh taxes," came the sour voice of Pieter van Orley from behind a tankard of beer.

"Yes," answered Godscalc, without bothering to look up from his glass of hippocras.

"The weavers won't put up with it," snorted Van Orley, smearing the froth from his lips onto the back of his hand.

"And what will you all do about it?" inquired the mer-chant Arnolfini with the air of a man accustomed to the blast-ings of impotent rage.

Van Orley glared at him.

"Revolt! . . . And put parasites like you out of business."

Arnolfini's lugubrious face bent into a cold smile.

"Put yourselves in a coffin, you mean. What bags of wind you all are."

Van Orley would have struck the Italian merchant had an enormous hand not swiftly appeared from the direction of the goldsmith Jan de Leeuw and grabbed the master weaver by the shoulder; which was perhaps just as well, since, had the blow landed, the weavers of Bruges might have found their business sorely disadvantaged in favor of the weavers of Ghent. Van Orley diluted his anger with noisy gulps of beer.

It was a dank winter evening, warmed only by the glow of the fire and the glow of good Bruges beer. The taverner at-tended to both conscientiously, keeping a cautious eye on the aggressive quantity of liquid being consumed by the master weaver. The Englishman Hugo broke the silence.

"Giovanni," he said, turning to Arnolfini, "why have you not brought your lovely Lysbet to brighten us all up?"

Arnolfini's reply had the effect of a small earthquake.

"Because I am to be married," he said, his voice no more emphatic than if he had said he felt tired.

Confusion was engraved on every face. Added to the sur-prise of the announcement was the uncertainty of how to react to it. Could it be that he was marrying Lysbet? An unlikely event; but if it were so, then why should this be a reason for the girl not being with him at this moment? And if it was not Lysbet, then who? And when? And why? These were the unasked questions on the faces of all who were at that moment staring at Arnolfini in astonishment. His impervious silence provided no clues. It was Michault de Caron who made the first guarded comment.

"Congratulations, Giovanni, but do tell us more."

The silence broken, other congratulations tumbled over each other. Arnolfini raised a slender gloved hand in a gesture both of acknowledgment and of warning.

"Thank you," he said. "I shall tell you more in due course. The wedding will not be for a year, when the girl is sixteen."

A further crop of speculations sprouted from this small revelation. So it could not be Lysbet, who was already twenty. Presumably this was also why she was not with him at this moment: perhaps the aggrieved mistress had been cast off, or departed in a huff. The court poet found it hard to believe Giovanni was proposing to remain celibate for a whole year, but felt it improper to inquire about the fate of the lovely Lysbet. Hugo's fecund imagination was already taking possession of the distraught lady, suddenly liberated from the merchant's grasp and why not therefore available for his own?

"Can you not even tell us the lady's name?" asked the silversmith Pontin, scratching the thicket of hairs on his hand as if Arnolfini's secrets might be buried there.

Arnolfini's long face creased into a cunning smile.

"No," he replied. Then he added with an air of satisfaction, "But I can tell you that she is Italian—of course."

"And beautiful?" asked Michault de Caron.

"I trust so, being Italian."

"You mean you have not seen her?"

The merchant adopted an air of grave composure.

"Not yet. But I shall soon. She lives in Paris."

A great deal of liquor was consumed in Arnolfini's honor, until Godscalc Oom was the only member of the party sober enough to raise a toast to the future bridegroom—a toast rendered the more solemn by the efforts of the others to pull themselves together for such an occasion.

One thought focused itself in the blurred brains of those who finally wandered into the winter street that night. Whoever the girl might be, there could be no doubt that Giovanni would not have waited twenty years to marry unless she was very, very rich.

News reached Bruges toward the end of February that the trial of the Maid had begun in Rouen, with the bishop of Beauvais, Pierre Cauchon, as president of the tribunal. The only surprise —except to a few—was the unflagging buoyancy of the duke. It had been widely put about that he never believed Joan would be charged with heresy; as for the charge that she insisted on wearing men's clothing, this had brought a scoff of derision from the duke, and members of the court noted how he reminded them—almost affectionately—that the duchess Jacqueline had fought him in men's clothing for nearly five years. It had not occurred to anyone in Burgundy, he surmised, to bring the lady to trial for it. And Philip had laughed at the thought. There were many, though, who were amazed by how little the duke appeared disturbed by the redoubled hatred of the French, and by the mounting vigor of their attacks on the Burgundian armies.

Jan's silent encounter with the Maid in Arras remained vivid in his mind. He could see the set, expressionless face, and could imagine the same unyielding look directed through and beyond the ugly stare of her accusers and their insistent barking questions. He felt even more sure than ever that Michault de Caron was right, and that Philip firmly believed the Maid to be a fraud who, any day now, would break, would recant, would beg forgiveness—and that would be the duke's chance. In the meanwhile what did it matter if the French hurled their hatred at him? Soon he would deserve their gratitude, having already enjoyed the Englishmen's gold.

Jan did not think it would be so. Neither did Michault, particularly since the court poet had paid a visit in homage to Christine de Pisan, the most celebrated poetess of the day, now elderly and in retirement. The poetess had shown

Michault what she vowed was to be her last work, inspired—
she explained—by Joan's victories over the English. Joan had
made safe the kingdom of France, Christine avowed; this was
"something that five thousand *men* could not have done," she
went on fiercely. Did the duke of Burgundy really believe—
she asked Michault—that such a woman would humble herself before the hated English just to save her own life, when
she had already risked that life a hundred times in the cause of
France and the cause of God?

Michault had been more deeply affected by the aged poetess than by anyone he had ever met, he claimed. She had made
him feel a small thing, he confessed sadly; a timeserver, not a
true poet.

Jan nodded. He did not believe this to be true, he reassured
Michault; nonetheless, he understood what the poet meant.

"Don't you imagine I often feel the same when I try to
paint this portrait of the duke?"

And he stared at the still uncompleted painting.

"But you're a master, Jan. Everyone knows that," Michault
replied.

"I feel a timeserver when I paint this," Jan went on. "My
portrait of Jacqueline was truthful. And *this* is truthful." He
indicated the many panels of the great altarpiece for Joos Vyt.
"And my drawing of Joan was truthful."

"Then it's the duke's blindness that he did not see the
truth in it," Michault commented. "I fear his eyes may be
opened too late."

The poet was peering closely at the ducal portrait.

"So what will you do, Jan?" he asked.

Jan explained with a wry smile how he had worked hard
on a fragment of the background, paying meticulous attention
to each tree and flower. And then he had stopped.

"At least, if the duke asks to see it I can show him the
wonderful intricacy of what I've done, and so bargain for more
and more time to finish it. And then . . ." Jan shrugged his
shoulders wearily. "I suppose I have to hope something unexpected will happen: maybe in the end he won't want it, or he'll
be satisfied with an incomplete portrait. He likes the idea of

genius being flawed: he told me so once. I encouraged the idea."

Michault laughed and clapped his friend on the shoulder.

"You're learning to survive," he said cheerfully.

Michault's frequent visits to Jan's house were in part friendship—more firmly bound since the visit to Arras—and they were partly in the hope of encountering Bona, or at the very least for the pleasure of contemplating Jan's portrait of her as Eve. The latter contentment invariably had to be enough since Bona now rarely called on Jan, having decided to say nothing about her encounter with Margarethe. The occasion had depressed her; she did not know whether or not to believe the girl. A voice inside her was still insistent that Margarethe would return, but meanwhile Bona had no wish either to raise or to dampen Jan's hopes. The best course was to keep away.

An even rarer visitor—since his humiliation over the story of Joan's capture—was the ducal herald Jehan Lefèvre. But one day in March he did appear at the house on the street of the Golden Hand. And after the customary scrutiny of various paintings, accompanied by a twitching of elegant fingers, he announced to Jan a summons from the duke—for that very day.

"A task to test your skills, Jan," he hinted, his face a mere fraction away from the bosom of Eve.

"Skills of what kind?" Jan inquired.

"Not at painting women, I believe. The duke is well aware of your skill at that. . . . Diplomatic, rather. Powers of persuasion, Jan." Lefèvre's eyes were now roving inquisitively over Bona's anatomy, a careful journey downward from one breast and then upward to the other, before standing back to compare the two. "But a lady *is* involved, you will find," he added.

That afternoon the duke was merrier than Jan had seen him for a long time. Again the charm of the man seemed to fill the room, and his welcome was warm. He looked relaxed and well; the tense, distant look had quite departed. He joked about the follies of the court—did Jan know that old Renier Pot had encountered a wild boar while hunting, and had been compelled to climb a tree, a most improbable sight? He even repeated a scurrilous tale about Abbot Eustache, who, it appeared, had undertaken a pilgrimage and returned with a most unclerical disease. Jan was accustomed enough to those moods of the duke to suspect that a sharp dagger might be disguised somewhere. But for a while Philip continued to allow his good humor to embrace all the thoughts that drifted into his mind. He inquired, in passing, about progress on the ducal portrait, to which Jan replied with a well-rehearsed explanation of its slowness. Then he asked about the altarpiece for Joos Vyt, and on hearing that it was well-nigh complete, the duke expressed his intention of being present at the inauguration—which he understood from the burgomaster was to be during the summer. He looked forward, he explained, to seeing his court painter honored for the finest church painting ever completed outside Italy. He trusted that ambassadors from Florence and Venice would be present to acknowledge the supremacy of Burgundy in a field which the Italians had for too long regarded themselves to be rulers.

"I shall enjoy observing their dejected faces," he added. Jan felt puffed with pride and not a little bewildered.

The dagger, when it was revealed, was more surprising than sharp. The duke had heard, he said, from the lord of Bedford, of Jacqueline's plot to enlist the support of Bedford's brother Humphrey of Gloucester: fortunately it had come to nothing, but it revealed that Jacqueline was still a dangerous woman. Jan noted that no reference was made to Bedford's own complicity in such a plot—presumably Bedford had carefully omitted the fact. Jan also wondered if the duke harbored any suspicions that Jan himself might have known about the plot: he might never know, he realized.

What followed filled Jan with astonishment; and as he listened to the duke he could not help believing that what Arnolfini had told him about the duke's love for Jacqueline was true.

"She's dangerous. I've always said so to you. I want to offer her a truce; I want to offer her my friendship. She is my cousin, Jan." There was a look of softness, almost of longing, on the duke's face. He paused for a moment while he poured out a goblet of wine for both of them.

"She hates me," he continued with a note of sadness in his voice. "But she likes you and she trusts you." Jan wondered how he knew, and indeed if it was true—he no longer felt certain. "I should like to offer her all the lands of Holland for her lifetime—as duchess," he went on. "And you are to be my ambassador who will deliver the letter to her, and speak for me."

Jan was too surprised to know if he felt troubled or overjoyed. So he would see Jacqueline again, and he would bear her good news. But how would she receive that news? How would she receive him? And what would he find himself compelled to report back to the duke?

He was to leave the next day. The duke embraced him, presented him with the sealed letter, and wished him well. A guard of soldiers would accompany him, he assured Jan. He would await his return eagerly.

"My trusted ambassador," the duke called him as he departed. There was just a hint of a reminder in his voice as he said it.

There were the earliest hints of spring in the color of the marshes and the softness of the air. Flocks of wintering birds on the salt flats were stirred by restlessness as if the urge to move to their breeding grounds were enough to stimulate loud circling flights but not yet enough to prevent them from settling again where they had come from. The wasteland of mud was a living sea of movement and excited sound as Jan rode with his party of soldiers along the straight, familiar dike that drew them closer and closer to Goes.

Jan had imagined he might never see Jacqueline again, and the prospect filled him with excitement and alarm. Seven months had passed since his last visit—since that long summer night of love—and not a word had reached him during that time. Even Bona had seemed not to know what might have taken place out there in those months, though when the news reached Bruges that the duke had delivered the Maid to the English, Bona had commented quietly, as a secret shared, that it must mark the end of Jacqueline's hopes. Bona's tired face had been the witness to her sorrow.

It always seemed to be dusk when Jan reached Goes. There had been the dusk of his first arrival, and the dusk of his return; and there had been the dusk that settled softly around them as they made their way back from the great bed of the dunes. And it was dusk when she had said in no more than a whisper, "Don't go tonight. Make love to me tonight."

Jacqueline. How would she receive him—unannounced—on the dusk of this new day?

There was a long wait in the courtyard of the castle as the light faded from the walls etched deep by the teeth of the sea. The same page in red greeted him—with a glance of surprise—and then disappeared, carrying with him the seal of Burgundy, which Jan had brought with him. The soldiers stood about with the blank looks of men accustomed to waiting and never being told the reason.

It was dark and cold before the page returned. There was no hint in his manner of how Jacqueline had received the news of Jan's arrival, only a few words to the guard at the gate that the soldiers be led to their quarters, followed by the familiar gesture to Jan that he accompany him into the castle.

All was as it had been before. The lamps along the stone corridors. The painted shields. The closed doors to the left and right as they made their way between the pools of lamplight. No sounds. The arms of the black raven with the sword in its beak. And there was the great door—which the page opened with no hesitation and not a word.

Jan entered, anticipating the dark hollow hall draped in shadows, and a fire blazing at the far end. Instead, what greeted him made Jan start. The hall was bright, and amid the glare of torchlight stood perhaps twenty figures all clad in crimson, their cuffs and collars white with swaths of ermine, on their heads tall hats of beaver plumed with feathers silver and red, and in the hand of each a staff mounted in gold. And as he entered they bowed—not to him but toward a figure who was standing in the center, furthest away from Jan some little distance from the fire. At the same moment one of the men in crimson stepped forward, and Jan heard the ringing solemn voice call out, "Duchess Jacqueline of Hainault, Brabant, Holland, and Zeeland"—and then after a pause as the man turned toward the visitor at the door—"the ambassador from the duke of Burgundy."

Jan found himself bowing; then, as he advanced slowly between the ranks of men in crimson, his eyes took in the figure of Jacqueline. She was robed in blue velvet that was almost black against the flicker of the fire, with a necklace of rubies and pearls suspended almost to her waist, and in her black hair a coronet ablaze with stones so large they seemed like points of colored fire.

"You are welcome," she said.

Only the deep, soft voice was familiar to Jan. He bowed a second time some three paces distant from her before holding out the letter with which the duke had entrusted him. She did not move, but the same man who had announced him stepped forward again, took the letter, and with a further bow handed it to Jacqueline. She did not even look at it, but passed it to the figure on her right, whom Jan recognized as the English valet he had seen before.

Then very faintly she smiled, and it was the smile of a duchess acknowledging the representative of her equal.

"You will be well looked after here," she said in that same deep and rather distant voice.

It was as if Jan had never been here before in this oak-beamed hall; as if Jacqueline had never set eyes on him, and even now was smiling at an ambassador whose name she did not know or wish to know.

"You shall hear from us tomorrow," she added.

With that, Jacqueline turned her eyes from Jan and proceeded gracefully toward the door. He found himself backing away behind the line of courtiers in crimson, who without a further glance at him followed their duchess stiffly out of the hall. Only the English valet remained a few moments longer, time enough to summon with a gesture one of the servants who remained lingering by the door. Then without a word he departed in the wake of the retinue.

The servant approached without haste, bowed, and indicated that the visitor should accompany him. Jan followed the man through the familiar small door into the smaller room where on so many evenings he had dined with Jacqueline alone in the intimacy of the firelight. And there indeed was the fire; and there was a table exquisitely laid—for one.

Only now did Jan begin to feel bewilderment at what was occurring. He remembered that when he had first arrived in Goes ten months earlier this was precisely the reception he had expected; instead Jacqueline had been alone and informal, enchanting. Now he had returned as—he imagined—a friend and a lover, and she was receiving him as a duchess. Not even Philip had ever welcomed him with such impersonal ceremony.

Dinner was laid before him with the same careful politeness. Hungry after his long ride, Jan consumed with relish the delicately prepared herring, the corn salad, fresh cheese and bread, cakes and savories, and he poured pale wine from the flagon set in front of him while servants hovered in the half-darkness beyond the lamplight until he had finished. Finally when he had eaten and drunk his fill one of them came forward and offered to accompany him to his room. Jan had the uneasy feeling that the servant understood a great deal more than he did. But he nodded without a word, and, appearing a little unsteady from the wine, followed the man into the long stone passageway toward the staircase.

Jan was a little surprised to find that he had been given the same bedroom high over the sea. There were no flowers, he noticed, but then in March there could hardly be, he realized. He felt mystified and tired. What, he wondered, might he expect tomorrow? Jan listened for a while to the soft rustle of the tide, then pulled the heavy fur over him and was soon asleep. He dreamed of the sea, and woke to the sound of the sea.

After lying awake for what seemed an age, he dressed, uncertain what he should now do. He had never known a place so silent as this castle. From his window Jan could see the far dunes, cold-looking under the March sunlight and the bluster of the wind. In a while there was a discreet knock at the door and the same servant entered with a tray of fresh bread and butter and a glass of warm milk. Again there was this feeling that all around him people knew he was there, and knew whatever was in store, but would say nothing. Jan ate his breakfast and decided to wait rather than venture into the unwelcome of the castle. He was the duke's ambassador, he reminded himself, and it was his role to attend patiently: what was past was another world—it was as if someone else had been here before, not him.

The summons when it came was delivered in the same deferential undertone by the same servant. He did not say where the duchess Jacqueline would receive him, only that she was waiting. He was to follow the man.

It was a room Jan had never seen. Not even when he had first been received by the princess Isabella in Portugal had he encountered such pomp. The walls were lined with damask and with tapestries in which threads of silver shone in the morning light; and all around stood precious things displayed as though they were the wealth of Solomon—caskets, chalices, golden dishes minutely engraved, goblets studded with jewels, bowls of porphyry or of crystal enmeshed in silver, enameled reliquaries, crosses, swords set with sapphires and rubies, and a hundred other treasures on which the sun danced. And there, on a high-backed chair raised as if it were a throne at the far end of this golden room, was seated the duchess Jacqueline. She was dressed in white satin from her high neck to her feet, and a coronet of diamonds and pearls was set into her hair. There were rings on every finger, and a necklace of rubies glimmered on the whiteness of her dress. Behind her, Jan noticed as he bowed and then looked up at Jacqueline, hung his own portrait of her.

Jan's eyes glanced from one face of Jacqueline to another: from the woman he had listened to and loved, to this face of majesty whose eyes, he realized from the hardness of them, believed him to be her enemy. And he knew that same moment that there was nothing he could say and nothing he could do. She was beyond the reach of his voice and of his reason.

She said little. Two of her councillors whom Jan recognized from the previous evening stood at a respectful distance on either side. She thanked him formally for the letter he had brought as the duke's ambassador, and to which she was preparing her reply. This would not be in the form of a letter, she explained; it would be a simple message to his lordship. There was a slight edge of bitterness in Jacqueline's voice as she said this; and then she added, confirming Jan's suspicions, "You have never found it difficult to report what I have said to you."

They were some of the coldest words anyone had ever spoken to him. And as their force stung him, Jan realized with horror that Jacqueline believed him to be responsible for her plight. She believed he had informed the duke of what he had seen that summer night by the harbor; and she believed it was this information which had persuaded Philip to surrender the Maid to the English. Even as he bowed to her, Jan could feel his indignation rising. How could she imagine he would do such a thing? She seemed to notice the anger in his face, because for a moment their eyes met like knives. Jan glanced at the two men flanking her, then back at Jacqueline.

"Madam," he said quietly, "I have never reported one word you have ever said or one thing I have ever seen." Then he added, his eyes still fixed on her, "At some great risk to myself." Jan could feel the muscles of his jaw tighten.

There was silence for a few seconds. Jan thought he detected a slight tremor cross Jacqueline's face. Then the hard look returned.

"I shall summon you this afternoon," she said, and rose.

Jan bowed again, and left. She made no gesture.

He walked out into the busy town, comforted by the ordinary bustle of the market and the sea smells of the fishing port. The two faces of Jacqueline kept appearing before his eyes. It was as if the new, proud face of the duchess were a second portrait he was painting: he could feel his brush tracing the stern lines of her chin and nose, the contemptuous eyes, the glittering coronet which no longer added beauty to that face so much as rank—the unapproachable authority of title. It was like painting a jeweled mask. The warmth, the laughter, the passion, the magnificent anger, the sudden tenderness; all these had shriveled away behind those hardened features. Jan imagined removing the mask and finding behind it a mere shadow of Jacqueline. Perhaps not even a shadow. Perhaps the face was a mask of death.

And yet—the offer: Philip's hopes for truce, and the promise of Holland. Might that not be enough even for so proud a creature as Jacqueline? How would she react? Jan stood watching the wind spinning the waves over the harbor wall; then he gazed back to where he had seen the English ship riding at anchor, and the hooded figure of Jacqueline emerging from the shadows. He realized he did not know how she would react; that he did not know her, he did not know her at all. He had painted the portrait of an unknown lover—an enchantress who had worn for him one of many masks. Perhaps it was the mask by which she wanted to be remembered: the woman she would have liked to be. "I wish I were not who I am"—once again those words returned to him.

Her gift for surprise did not desert her. Jan told the servant who had attended him that he would be in the high room where he had painted Jacqueline's portrait. He would await her summons, and while he waited Jan decided he would draw the roofs of the town and the long curve of the shore. Jan loved the shapes and the slant of roofs—it was like drawing the secrets of a town; but now, as the silvery lines began to grow alive on the paper, he found his hand guided to the distant wilderness of the dunes. And as he drew he could feel their warm softness underfoot, feel the sting of dune grass against bare legs, touch the sheen of black hair spilled over white sand. Nevermore. The day of a dream.

Jan did not know how long he remained lost in that dream, until—as once before—he became aware with a jolt that he was no longer alone. He spun around convinced for a second that he would find her standing there with a dagger. Instead Jacqueline was by the open door quite motionless, and Jan saw that she was wearing the same white dress in which he had painted her portrait. One hand fingered a gold necklace, and while he gazed at her in surprise she slowly extended her other hand toward him without a word, palm upward, fingers closed. It was an invitation to take whatever she was holding; and as he reached out his own hand—hesitantly—the fingers uncurled and in her open palm rested a gold ring.

Jan looked up at her as he took it, and her face was worn

and tired—but then a smile like the faintest sunlight passed across her face.

"I maligned you," she said quietly. ". . . Have this from me."

Jan looked down at the ring, and he saw that the gold was wrought in the form of a bird, its wings curled around until they linked. The bird was a raven, and as he slid the ring onto his finger the raven's wings enclosed it.

He fumbled for a few words of thanks and looked at her bewildered. Her eyes were very intent, and in those few moments the silence seemed to carry everything that had ever passed between then.

She broke the spell with a slight laugh.

"Be careful who sees you wear it. You've taken enough risks already. But then, of course, you like a touch of danger."

He smiled, and she reached out and touched his arm just as she had done so often by the lamplight and the fire. Jan caught the scent of roses from her skin, and he placed his own hand over hers. He could feel her fingers parting to enclose his—like the raven's wings.

Then she squeezed his fingers and withdrew her hand. She was looking at him with an expression Jan did not understand.

"I have something to tell you, Jan; something that you can tell the duke." She paused for a moment, still looking at him with those dark tired eyes. "Philip won't need an answer to his letter when you tell him that I am married."

Jan did not know whether it was jealousy that shot through him, but he was aware of feeling as though the room was being shaken around him. He said nothing, he could say nothing; and he was conscious of a numbness in his face. His mouth felt dry.

"Married!" was all he could say.

She was smiling, and her face wore a look both of triumph and of sadness. Then she walked slowly across the room, and as she did so she explained, quite calmly.

"I told you that I fought Philip because I was a woman," she said. She went over to the window and stared out over the town and the sea. "Then he denied me the right to be a woman," she went on, not looking around at Jan. And after a pause she added, almost under her breath, "But no one can deny me that."

Jan was no longer surprised. He might have known that a woman who had fled her first husband and married Humphrey of Gloucester could never be chained by Philip, whatever else he might do to her. This was her dagger for Philip.

"Who is he?" Jan asked tentatively.

Jacqueline's laugh was almost savage.

"Philip offers me Holland as a token of peace," she went on, "not knowing that I am already married to his own governor of Holland." And she turned to face Jan with that same triumphant look, except that now there was a wildness in her eyes. "I took him, Jan"—and the fierceness in her voice softened—"because I want a child."

Jan looked at Jacqueline bemused, grasping piece by piece what she was saying.

"A child, Jan," she went on. "I want a future, because myself I have none." Her face was intense, with a look almost of grief. "I know that I shall lose everything. My stars frown at me, and I can only shake my fist at the sky. But I could leave something behind me—some piece of myself on whom fortunes may smile as they have not on me. I should be happy if I knew that might be. I want it." Then, after a moment, she added, "I think you understand."

Jan nodded. Yes, he understood. And he feared for her.

She began to speak less urgently. His name, she explained, was Franz van Borselen. He was a Flemish knight in the service of the duke of Burgundy, and Philip had appointed him governor of Holland. They had met a month ago in Leiden— he had offered her safe-conduct to visit the castle of Teilingen, which had belonged to her father and to which she was now entitled. And he had fallen in love with her, she said in the same matter-of-fact tone. She had explained to him that she had been compelled to sign away her right to marry without the duke's permission, and to her surprise he had shrugged it off. A brave man. He did not believe that the duke, whom he had served faithfully, would keep her to her word. Philip would show compassion. He would not live without her, Franz had insisted.

"I do not know what Philip will do," she added, "but I know that I had to do it."

There was such defiance in her face, and such tenderness.

"I am a woman, Jan. You know me. . . . You know what I am." Again she touched his arm gently with her fingers. Then she lowered her eyes, and there was a moment of silence. "I wanted you to have that ring because what you have been to me is outside all this.

Jacqueline reached for his hand and turned the ring on his finger. Then she looked up at him and he kissed her. Nothing further was said, and with a final squeeze of his hand she turned and departed.

It was an empty room; and beyond the window clouds spread their ragged wings over the lands of the sea.

It was a subdued ride homeward.

"You know me. . . . You know what I am"—these had been Jacqueline's words. Yes, he might have expected something like this: he might have known that, defeated at every turn, she would play one last defiant card. And he had to carry it to Philip, who loved her. How this would wound the duke: a husband, a child perhaps. She could not have knifed him where it hurt more.

Jan tried to understand Van Dorselen. It seemed like suicide to defy the terms of a solemn treaty which Philip had made with Jacqueline, that she should not marry again without the duke's consent. Was there perhaps something Jan did not know, and which would make this impulsive act less foolish? He would soon find out, no doubt.

And Jacqueline. It was painful to envisage the scene, but Jan felt in his bones that he knew what had taken place. First the unexpected letter from the governor of Holland—considerate, kindly, offering safe-conduct so that she might visit her own property. Then the meeting in Leiden, in the governor's house. Jan knew how Jacqueline would have behaved: here was a man she needed—far more urgently than she had needed Jan. She would have dressed for him: oh, how she would have dressed! The bare skin, the eyes, the velvet voice, the teasing laugh, the little touches of the arm, the shadow deepening between the breasts. It hurt Jan to picture the scene. And the tale of her life, her injuries, her misfortunes. Her talk of love, and all it meant to her. Then the ride to Teilingen through the winter landscape, all in furs, all in laughter. The blaze of firelight in the evenings. Just the two of them together, he listening enchanted, she casting her spell. Only more so than on Jan because here was not just a painter, a man of skills; here was a knight, a man of title and position. How could he not have longed to marry such a woman? Her presence would have drugged his senses; nothing else would have seemed to matter but that he should possess her utterly. Her awareness of her own body must have enveloped him in a scent of skin and roses; and yet she would not have let him so much as touch her until . . . Such a short time it must have taken.

The small flowers of spring by the pathway brought no comfort to Jan as he rode, hardly aware of the soldiers before and behind him. He bore no letter of reply for the duke; only a few words. And something Philip would never see. Jan removed his glove and gazed for a moment at the ring on his finger. The raven embracing his own flesh, as she had embraced him, and as—she said—she had loved him. It had been something else, something outside this defiant dance, something that in another world might have been.

Jan felt older, and sadder. And the spring seemed like a time of dying.

Chapter ♦ Ten

There is a range of kings and princes more furious than that of lesser mortals long accustomed to misfortune as they stumble along the road of their ambitions. Philip, duke of Burgundy, was not a man who recognized that success may be no more than a happy casting of the dice or the sudden shift of a wind at sea. Philip ruled—and neither winds, nor dice, nor one single act of chance found credit in his mind for any goal he reached or any battle won. All was by the sole command of his authority and the exercise of his unchallengeable will. With such temper of man and steel was the duchy of Burgundy carved, and in his eyes nothing could stand in opposition to that ordained course except through his own merciful forbearance. Even patience rested within his command. In time he vowed he would have it all. Philip's opponents fell—in his chosen time. One day he would stand before his maker and proclaim—modestly—"I have won."

And so it might have been that this Burgundian Achilles had chosen one opponent he could never defeat—for all his triumphs of arms—because he loved her, and because she loathed him. Philip of Burgundy and Jacqueline of Hainault were locked in a combat from which there could emerge no victor. The prize she valued was her stolen inheritance which he would never return. The single reward he sought was her submission to his love, which it was not in her heart to offer. He would always crush her, and he would always lose. She knew his vulnerable heel, and her aim was deadly.

So she was married. And not even, this time, to an English duke and brother of a king, but to a member of Philip's own court, his own governor appointed to oversee on his behalf the lands of Holland, which by right belonged to Jacqueline. And she had married him, as if in stealing him she had taken back what should be hers.

The rains that lashed the roofs and canals of Bruges that early spring were like summer breezes compared to the rage of Philip, duke of Burgundy.

Jan was still shaken as he grasped the tankard of beer pressed on him by the silversmith Michaut Pontin. News of the ducal tempest had already reached the Fallen Angel by the time the court painter entered, but no one present on that rainswept evening understood the cause. A single glance at Jan's face told them they would know very soon.

"Sit, for God's sake." Michault de Caron pulled up a chair for him by the blazing fire. The silversmith called the taverner for instant refreshment while the others gathered around Jan as if protecting a wounded comrade. "What happened?"

Jan began to revive as the rain dried from his clothes and the beer warmed his belly. The faces of Pontin, De Caron, Jan de Leeuw, and Godscalc Oom peered at him in anxious curiosity. Nothing, he assured them, had been actually hurled at him personally, though the duke's aim was none too reliable in his enraged condition and one or two chalices and candlesticks had hurried closely by.

"Jacqueline is married," he explained.

There was no one around him who failed to record the magnitude of such a piece of information. Michault de Caron, who alone among Jan's friends knew the depth of the duke's attachment to Jacqueline, emitted a long whistle.

"The lady certainly knows how to kill," he muttered. "And to kill herself."

Jan then told the whole story: at least, not entirely the whole story, omitting—just as he had to the duke—Jacqueline's desire to have a child. He related how the duke had received him eagerly, his face bright with anticipation. Jan could see from Philip's expression that he was expecting a favorable reply to his letter. Where was her response? he had asked, his eyes searching Jan for signs of any letter he might be carrying. When Jan had explained that there was no letter, the duke looked perplexed at first, and then his brow furrowed in irritation. There had been a painful pause while Jan had mustered the courage to deliver his brief message: finally he spoke quickly and as confidently as he could. For a moment the duke had not appeared to understand, and there was another pause while Jan waited for the storm to burst. Even so, he had not expected quite such violence. He was aware of servants rushing in: Jehan Lefèvre was there, cowering, until a gold box struck him and he retreated bleeding behind a screen with whimpering cries. Others appeared and retired hastily. It was Jehan de Luxembourg who finally calmed the duke in some measure by the bold procedure of grasping Philip around the shoulders and arms and holding him in his soldier's grip. Servants meanwhile began to scuttle around retrieving the objects thrown and the tables overturned. It was Luxembourg who indicated to Jan by a nod of the head that he should make his departure, and he had gratefully left the two men together—the duke and his captain. Lefèvre, his brow split and blood-soaked, preceded Jan bent low and moaning woefully.

There was silence after Jan had completed his story.

Finally Michault de Caron cleared his throat. Only he among the company at the Fallen Angel knew Franz van Borselen. A brave and silent man, De Caron assured them.

"A brave and silent fool," added Godscalc Oom weightily, mopping several chins from the heat of the fire.

"Why do you think he did it, Jan?" inquired Jan de Leeuw, who had said nothing so far, but now turned his sturdy face toward the painter.

"For love," was all Jan could say. It was all he could imagine.

A silence fell on the group of men around the fire. It was as if Jan had introduced a thought none of them had entertained, or could quite grasp.

"Love!" exclaimed Godscalc after a moment or two. His mouth had drooped toward his upper chin and his prominent eyebrows pushed his forehead upward into a sea of furrows. "Love!" he repeated in a puzzled voice. "People don't do things like that for love."

The others looked at Jan.

"If you had met Jacqueline you might not be so surprised," he answered. He had no wish to talk about her, and his own heart was full of dread after witnessing the outburst of the duke that afternoon.

It was Michault de Caron who brought some sharpness to the discussion.

"She is a lady who knows men's weaknesses." It was a remark that meant more than he said, and the poet glanced knowingly at Jan, looking away again before he should cause his friend any embarrassment.

Jan wished Bona were hear, but he had scarcely seen Bona for many weeks. It was said that she had been away. There was no one else with whom he could confide his fears for Jacqueline: there was no one else who might cast some light on an act of such apparent madness.

Later, alone in his house in the street of the Golden Hand, Jan waited.

In the early days after the duke's eruption of rage those around the ducal court were inclined to keep their heads low and wait for the tempest to pass. Lefèvre's head was seen to be dramatically bandaged, but he never appeared now at the Fallen Angel, so no information could be extracted from him about events within the palace, and his special barrel of Beaune gathered dust. Michault de Caron, who saw more of the ducal palace than anyone at the Fallen Angel apart from the herald, reported an uneasy silence: people walked more quietly than usual as if floorboards might give way should they proceed normally. He also reported the sad state of the duchess Isabella: it appeared that the duke rarely visited her, and even the news that her former lady-in-waiting Louise had been dismissed from the court to return to her errant husband did little to raise her spirits.

Michault was of the view that something was about to happen; he did not know what. His view was shared—more savagely—by the master weaver Pieter van Orley; but the events to which the weaver referred had nothing to do with the marriage of Jacqueline, about which he seemed unaware or unconcerned. The guildsmen of Bruges, he assured all who would listen, would before long rise in arms against the duke.

Godscalc Oom continued to shake his head and murmur the word "folly" into his small glass of hippocras.

It was four days after Jan had delivered the news of Jacqueline's marriage to the duke when further events were seen to take place. A party of soldiers left the eastern gate of the city with Jehan de Luxembourg at their head. They spoke to no one as they departed, but the old soldier wore an expression of grimness on his scarred face which those who saw him said reminded them of his look when he had ridden out to make Joan the Maid his captive.

When he heard this Jan was sick with dread. He thought of the Maid, in irons at Rouen, her inquisitors pressing her relentlessly toward the stake with no sign of the capitulation which the duke was anticipating. Would Jacqueline become another victim? The thought of her carried in chains—to be tried, mocked, imprisoned—stirred a vision of such horror before Jan's eyes that he vowed he would flee the country rather than witness it. Why not go to Italy? Arnolfini had suggested, half jokingly. Perhaps this was what he should do?

He found Arnolfini at dusk in his fine house of treasures, standing in the midst of numerous iron-bound chests and dressed in a long velvet surcoat which seemed to elongate the merchant's slender, lizardlike figure. Jan did not know what had drawn him to visit Arnolfini, whom he did not like much: but then no one much liked Arnolfini and yet everyone was drawn to him. Was it wealth? Or perhaps the tantalizing aura of hidden wisdom? It was eerie how often, when dire problems arose, people's thoughts turned to the wily Italian. No one knew more about the dark workings of the world than Giovanni, and that knowledge had made his fortune. There was an uneasy comfort about being in his company, and it was this—Jan realized as the merchant greeted him with a kind of smile—which had drawn him here. It was not really to do with Italy at all.

"I am about to depart tomorrow, as you can see," Giovanni explained. His eyes appeared to be counting the massive chests amid which he stood like a dark priest among coffins.

"Business," he added contentedly. "Paris." His small eyes crinkled slightly as he said it. "Business of a personal kind."

Suddenly Jan realized that Giovanni was about to meet his future wife for the first time. Impulsively he offered the merchant his hand, which Arnolfini took.

"Yes! My wife," he said; and a look of such pleasure passed over his pallid face that Jan shook his hand a second time, more vigorously. And suddenly he felt almost cheerful: Giovanni was the one person he knew who at this moment was not sunken under the grim events of Flanders. He was that rarity—a happy man.

"I wish you well, Giovanni." And Jan realized that he meant it.

"All *will* be well, Jan, because I have arranged it so."

To Jan's surprise he found himself listening to the merchant, and in the course of listening all but forgot that he had come here to air his own woes. Arnolfini was in a mood to talk, and seating himself languidly among his chests of treasures, he gave Jan a lesson in philosophy.

He had waited many years—too many, he said—for a lady with the right combination of qualities for him to undertake the bond of marriage. These were: beauty—naturally; as a man of refinement he could not be expected to tarnish his surroundings with plainness, especially since his own appearance displayed quite enough of it. Then, intelligence: even Venus herself would surely pall if she could not discourse upon worldly matters with some sharpness of wit. Wealth: well, a man of his years and standing could reasonably expect his partner to enhance his position in the world as richly as he would hope to enhance hers. Lastly, though he considered himself to be emancipated from pride of nationality, he nonetheless nourished a sentiment which rendered it impossible for him to consider a woman who was not from his native Lucca. They were the best.

"And you have found such a paragon, Giovanni?" Jan asked, a smile of pleasure on his face at the merchant's lucid and touching vanity. "Even though you have never set eyes on her?" he added, a touch caustically.

Arnolfini made a favorite gesture by touching his nose knowingly.

"I am acquainted with people who are aware of precisely

what I like," he explained in the neatest of voices. Jan imagined that he could easily have been referring to a fine length of damask. "Certainly I have found her," he added.

After many years of patience, he went on—made bearable, he was happy to admit, by the accommodating ladies of Bruges—the ideal creature was now known to exist. Her name —he would confide this to Jan—Giovanna Cenami; she was the daughter of a merchant from Lucca like himself, though unknown to him since Cenami was long resident in Paris. Approaches had been made through the ambassador of Lucca in attendance on the duke's wedding (how weddings beget weddings, he chuckled): a certain Francesco Lombardi, cousin of Cenami and a frequent visitor to his house in Paris. The girl was—no other word for it—a jewel. What was more, Cenami was a widower devoted to the memory of his late wife and therefore certain to have no more children. Giovanna was his only child. Giovanni paused to make certain Jan grasped the full weight of what he had just said. Jan had no difficulty in understanding that Arnolfini's "jewel" possessed many rich and desirable facets.

"Giovanni, Giovanna: is that not suitable?"

Jan nodded, still smiling.

"And, as I have always promised, you, Jan, shall paint the wedding portrait . . . in time," he added with a note of caution.

Jan found himself trying to imagine the complexity of contracts which the two merchants would doubtless require before the love match could be sealed. Besides, he remembered, the girl was not yet sixteen. And what, Jan wondered, might this "jewel" of a young girl be thinking of the arrangement herself? Perhaps the ambassador of Lucca had done his work just as skillfully in Paris as in Bruges, and the dreaming Giovanna had before her eyes this very moment an image of Adonis. He hoped the jewel would not find her setting to be of too base a material.

"Good luck," he said, shaking the merchant's hand a third time.

Jan departed without having spoken a word of what he had wished to unburden on Arnolfini. Yet he felt a cheerfulness settle about him as he walked back through the rain and the lamplight toward the street of the Golden Hand. It was the first time in many days that he felt able to separate himself a little distance from the storms around the duke and whatever storms were about to strike a marriage less blessed than that of Giovanni and Giovanna.

They seized him from her bed.

Jehan de Luxembourg was not a cruel man, yet he had spent his life inflicting pain, and it showed in the weathered shield of his face. It was he who had taken the Maid into captivity; he who had hounded Jacqueline into submission; now it was he who at dawn dragged Franz van Borselen to prison.

The soldiers smirked at Jacqueline naked as she struggled to hold her husband from them. They pushed her away, and the knife when she grasped it was too late. The door slammed and she was alone.

Later that day the soldiers led her back to Goes and stood guard over her castle. She looked at the dagger she had reserved for Humphrey of Gloucester, and as she turned it in her hand she prayed that Philip himself would bring the ultimatum. To kill him, and then herself: there seemed no other way of ending it. There was no child in her womb: her body was empty; and before her eyes only nothing.

But when it came it was the lord of Luxembourg, once more, who delivered her fate—by command of the duke. She listened without looking at him. She scarcely heard. After Luxembourg's departure it was her councillors who repeated the conditions she was offered. They were simple. A choice. She could surrender her remaining lands and titles—in perpetuity—save only the castles of Teilingen and of Goes. Or, if she chose to refuse . . . her chief councillor found it hard to pronounce the alternative and Jacqueline had to order him to continue . . . she would be taken to Leiden and there compelled to witness her husband's execution. She had two weeks to consider the offer—two weeks to choose between her titles and the life of Franz van Borselen. Should she decide to spare his life—and here the duke's clemency seemed like the tiniest rose in the wilderness of her life—she would be permitted to live with Borselen as husband and wife in the peace of anonymity.

Day after day the people of Goes watched her ride out alone along the dunes and the spring marshes. They had seen the Burgundian soldiers depart with the lord of Luxembourg and imagined their duchess to be free and herself again. They did not know that Jacqueline was paying her last visits to her villagers as their ruler and protector. She held her godchildren in her arms, distributed silver, embraced her friends and bid them goodbye. Fishermen raised their caps to the lone figure riding by along the dike among the flowers of spring. They could not see her face.

In Bruges the mood was dark. The duke was locked within himself, the long face drawn as if wires of pain were pulling the flesh from within. Sometimes he thought of the triumphant portrait Master Jan was painting, and he had no wish to inquire after its progress; he had no wish to be reminded of his own days of radiance. His ambition to acquire all the Low Countries was almost complete at last, yet for once he could feel no joy. Of course, Jacqueline would sacrifice her titles and her lands—of course, because, he thought ruefully, she would always put her heart first. So why had he not executed Van Borselen as a traitor on the spot? Why had he not given that order to Luxembourg? Because he could not do it: he could not kill a man whom Jacqueline truly loved. If she hated Philip now, she would hate him in eternity for that. The grain of happiness left to her he could not steal.

Philip tried not to think of the Maid. His councillors had visited her in Rouen: they were there to hint tactfully, out of the hearing of the English, what he might do for her should she recant. But Joan would not even look at them. She had turned her back. She would not hear the voices of traitors, the duke was given to understand. Memories of his meeting with Joan kept returning to plague him, and they would not go away. Supposing Jan had been right, and the Maid was not a fraud.

Two women he had conquered rattled their chains at him, and haunted his sleep.

A third woman he had conquered slept alone. The duchess Isabella dreamt of home, and awoke in Flanders as if her heart were falling into a pit.

"What day is it, Beatrice?"

"Thursday, my lady."

Sometimes it felt to Isabella that such information was all that was accessible to her in this gaunt and silent place. She dressed for nobody, and undressed for nobody. There was nothing for her eyes to dwell on except closed doors, and the timid bustle of servants tidying her little life as if it were a vase of flowers.

One morning she stood gazing by the window at the familiar dullness of Flanders; and there far beyond the walls and ramparts of the city her eyes spotted a man plowing. It felt like the only event in her day, to watch the tiny figure leaning on the plow and slowly crossing and recrossing the field behind the plodding ox. She hoped he would not finish his task too soon so that she would be compelled to search for a further diversion from her embroidery. And then suddenly she saw the man collapse over the plow, fall sideways onto the turned earth. The ox ambled on a few paces, and stopped, swishing its tail. No one came. The man lay there. Isabella realized that he was dead. She was horrified. By the next morning the man, plow, and ox had gone. No one ever completed the plowing, and after a while the weeds obscured where he had been.

She could fall like that, she thought. Someone would carry her away—like the dead plowman, like dead flowers.

"What day is it, Beatrice?"

"Tuesday, my lady."

And so the burgeoning of spring passed her by like a stranger in the dark.

Isabella was not alone in the despair of that springtime. Bona received the news of Jacqueline's marriage and the duke's ultimatum with a feeling of helpless dismay. She had always feared for Jacqueline: her capacity for taking majestic risks was a quality that filled Bona with admiration and awe— to aim for everything, nothing less. But never until now had she considered her to be a fool. Perhaps had Bona known of Jacqueline's urge to bear a child she might have tempered her judgment; but she did not know. The marriage to Van Borselen seemed nothing less than suicide on both their parts. Van Borselen she could understand—an infatuated young man closing his eyes in love, senselessly in love with her very power over him. But for Jacqueline to have *married* him—a woman who had ruled the hearts of dukes and princes. There was fear in Bona's mind that her dearest friend, her "sister," had been driven insane by the battering of fortune, and that the vengeance she had hoped to wreak on the duke had finally turned its knife on herself. Of course, her marriage must have wounded Philip more deeply than any other woman could ever wound him: powerless, Jacqueline had not been able to resist that single passionate hold she had over him, the one weapon he did not possess.

But he had all the other weapons, and he would use them.

Unlike Bona, Jan had heard Jacqueline's words, and had witnessed the duke's rage. Now he could feel little beyond a resigned helplessness. He gazed at the ring Jacqueline had given him before his departure, turning it until he could see the bird's wingtips entwine like fingers. Then he removed the ring and placed it in a small leather box. He knew he would never wear it. If so many things had been different he would have worn it all his life. But the raven had flown. There was nothing more: only the shadow of a woman whose splendor had shone on him for an hour.

Jan did not know what drew him out of the city at first light the following morning. But as he rode through the spring pastures under the early sun he could feel an unexpected peace settle on him. It was as if a spell were broken. There was such beauty here; the forests closing around him in their silence, the dew on the bluebells like a million sapphires. The altarpiece for Joos Vyt was finished—a long journey completed—and now suddenly it was as if he were riding through Hubert's golden land blessed with flowers. The landscape of the Holy Lamb. For so long Jan had felt alien to that bright vission of heaven on earth: everything before his eyes had been deformed, ugly, burning, the landscape of death. Now that image of the lamb was vivid before him. But why the lamb? he wondered. How strange, incongruous, Jan reflected, that all around him were men of the sword—who killed, imprisoned, maimed, tortured, betrayed each other—and yet all of them yielded in their prayers to a god who stood before them as the meekest of all creatures on earth—a lamb. A lamb raised upon an altar. Violent men worshipping a humility they did not themselves possess.

Perhaps, Jan wondered, this was the meaning of it. He thought of Philip and of Jacqueline. How alike they were, he realized. Both had requested him to paint them, to give back to them a vision of themselves by which the world would know them after they were dust. What they had both desired from him were visions of splendor and of peace; yet in their lives they sought only the glory of battle. They were two people obsessed with one another, locked together in struggle, each holding the other hostage. How very alike. Both of them searched for love, but for each of them love in the end was only an interlude, the fairest of dreams; love was a lone wayfarer who once in a while raised its golden head as they hurried by on the road to some irresistible destiny; then forever became just a shimmer of sweet memory in the haze.

He did not want to live and love like that.

On impulse Jan turned his horse toward Ghent. He knew he wanted to tell Joos Vyt that he had finished the altarpiece. He wanted to see the pleasure on the old burgomaster's face. Jan felt a surge of relief that he belonged to Joos's world, not among the visions of princes and the tyrannies of their destiny. How happy he was to be a painter, who worked with the skills of his hands, just as Joos as a young man had dug channels, built dikes, with his hands. The world was what you touched, what you molded, what you embraced—like land that you dragged from the sea, like a painting you coaxed out of an empty panel, like love.

The thought surprised him. If he ever loved again he knew there would be no battle in it: it would be the grounding of his life, and out of it there would flow a love of all things.

Jan could not remember a morning more beautiful. A

weight of pain had lifted from him, and he could feel lines of
pleasure on his face that he had forgotten existed.

It was with a shock that he recognized the place by the
river where Margarethe had been attacked. Jan dismounted
and led his horse to the water. Nowhere, he thought, could
look more innocent than this. Flowers were strewn across the
fields like Hubert's landscape and the trees were splashed with
young green. He found himself longing for Margarethe to be
here to see the healing of this place. Would she ever return?
Perhaps that too was only an interlude. He would do nothing
—he knew—to find her, coax her: she would come or she
would not. He would not wait for her. Then, even as he vowed
this, Jan remembered her face, her laughter, her movements,
her body—and at that moment he hoped more than he dared
to hope. Jan picked some flowers as if for her; then he re-
mounted and rode on.

He reached Ghent well before midday. To his surprise Joos
himself opened the door; the smile on the burgomaster's face
filled the doorway and the old man's arms embraced him like a
son.

"Jan. Jan," he kept repeating. And then amid a flurry of
indecision he thrust out his hands in several directions before
calling excitedly to his wife.

"Elizabeth!" And more loudly, "Elizabeth!"

Jan could make out the cautious figure of Vyt's wife peering toward them from the end of the shaded corridor.

"It's Jan," Joos called out.

Sounds of surprised pleasure accompanied the old lady as
she advanced toward them a trifle awkwardly, as if some ceremony were being called for to which she was not accustomed.
Her mouth moved in and out of a smile, and her eyes darted
nervously between the visitor and the floor.

Their welcome touched Jan deeply. The ordinary humanity
of it. Vyt's round, eager face was bright with pleasure, and his
wife's quiet attentions to her visitor caused plates of small
delicacies to appear every few minutes at Jan's elbow. Then
she vanished in the direction of tempting smells from the
kitchen, and within a minute of her departure Joos was leading
him into the large paneled room hung with paintings and was

taking down a familiar dark bottle and two heavy green goblets.

"So, tell me." Joos's hand trembled a little as he handed Jan one of the goblets. The protruding eyes, somewhat bloodshot, gazed at him shrewdly.

"It's finished," Jan replied.

The old, round face folded into a hundred wrinkles. The mouth fell open.

"I came to tell you that," Jan added.

For a moment Vyt could do nothing but raise his goblet toward Jan and nod his head with grave bewilderment between sips of wine.

"Thank you," he said finally, very quietly. And all his gratitude sounded in those two words.

Recovered from his surprise, Joos began to talk excitedly. When might he arrange to have the altarpiece delivered? He understood from the ducal herald that the duke himself intended to be present at the inauguration. This should be soon. June. Why not? Everything was prepared. Even the bishop. (Joos gave a cunning laugh.) And how long could Jan stay? Tonight at least, he hoped. (Jan nodded, and thanked him.) Then this afternoon they would go together to the cathedral, and Jan would see the chapel where the painting was to rest—above the altar. He had donated everything in the chapel himself: the painting would be his crowning gift to the city.

"To God's glory," Joos added gravely. "And a little bit to mine," he went on with a smile. "To yours too, of course, Jan. They'll remember you long after I'm dead and forgotten . . . unless my portrait is so overwhelming in its piety that even God the Father is overshadowed."

He folded his hands before him exactly as Jan had painted him, and then laughed, clapping Jan warmly on the shoulder.

"Portrait of the donor masquerading as a good Christian," he chuckled.

"No less convincing than some of my friends masquerading as Adam and Eve and John the Baptist," Jan retorted with a smile.

"And no wine stains?"

"No wine stains."

"Good." Joos poured out a second goblet of Burgundy for Jan and himself, and a look of deep contentment settled on his face.

"I joke, Jan, most blasphemously," he went on reflectively. "It's the effect of Bishop Denis on my spirit." He paused for a moment as if collecting his thoughts. "But I must tell you, there is nothing in the world I have wanted more at my great age than to offer to God some small thanks for all that he has given me." There was a further pause before he continued. "I'm a man of true faith, Jan." And then with a laugh and another gulp of good wine he added, "The trouble is, it doesn't show."

That afternoon the two men made their way at Vyt's careful pace along the quay flanked by tall, brick merchants' houses whose gables cast pointed shadows over the water. They crossed the little bridge and made their way through the tangle of market streets until the dark bulk of St. Nicholas's church rose above them. Suddenly before them stretched an avenue of spires, one ranged behind another as the churches seemed to stride across the city, each gesturing to the heavens. They passed beneath the huge bell tower surmounting the cloth hall, and there before them across the open square rose the gaunt mass of St. Bavon's cathedral—larger, Jan thought, than any requirement might have imposed, like everything else in this city of wealth and appetites.

The burgomaster was enjoying the respectful salutations of those who turned as they walked by. Jan glanced at the shrewd old face with its shadow of a smile, and wondered how many rivalries, how many hatreds, lingered behind the watchful looks that followed them.

Inside the cathedral a huge vault of gray light diminished them as their steps resounded across the expanse of stone. Jan could hear the soft regular wheezing of the old man's breath. Two figures loitering beside a column broke off their conversation as they passed. Jan caught a glimpse of a scarlet bodice unbuttoned low and realized that the woman was a prostitute. She had a small dog with her, on a long lead, a red bow round its neck. It had urinated against a pillar.

"There," said Vyt. And he swung open the iron gates of a side chapel.

All was new in the chapel—the stained-glass windows, the tapestries, chairs, the long altar flanked by heavy candlesticks, the embroidered altar covering in deep crimson, the polished rail.

"My chapel," he added proudly, looking around him. "And that wall . . . that's yours."

Jan felt moved. They stood in silence for a while, facing the blank stonework. He could see the painting here, folded like a book, then unfolding to reveal Hubert's golden landscape and the altar of the lamb. Adam and Eve. The Virgin. John the Baptist. The crown of God. The choir of angels, playing, singing. He would fill the chapel with silent music, Jan thought. Perhaps there would never be a painting he would do like this again. He would put his name to it, and Hubert's. Jan could already see the words inscribed modestly along the base of the altarpiece: "The painter Hubert, than whom none was greater, began it; Jan, second in art, having completed it at the charge of Jodocus Vyt, invites you to contemplate what has been done." Perhaps it should be a verse: Michault de Caron could apply his wit to the problem.

How very proud he felt. Vyt's hand was resting on his shoulder.

"In the end, Jan," he said quietly, "it's only what you leave behind that matters. I wonder what they'll be saying five hundred years from now—if there's still a world."

They made their way back to Vyt's house. Jan promised Joos he would have the altarpiece crated and ready to be transported within two weeks, before the end of May. The ceremony in Ghent would be the greatest of occasions, Joos assured him.

"The bishop will be on his best behavior," he added solemnly. "And so shall I. . . . No wine stains."

And he chuckled as he produced the large iron key to the burgomaster's house.

The evening was at the pace of the old people. Vyt and his wife moved and spoke with economy, leaving long pauses in which the room seemed warmed by their presence. They ate well and slowly, and the wine descended steadily under the watchful eye of Elisabeth, which Joos studiously avoided. Finally she left the two men to their talk by the fire, first restoring to the cupboard the second bottle of Burgundy, which Vyt promptly reclaimed after her departure.

"She says I drink too much," he commented, pouring a fresh glass for them both. "I say she complains too much."

Joos settled himself carefully in the large chair. His watery eyes shone in the firelight and for a while he said nothing, but the corners of his mouth twitched from time to time as if a thought had crossed his mind which he was not quite agile enough to catch. Then his eyes rested on Jan for a second or two before flickering away toward the emptiness of the room; and Jan was aware that he was thinking of the last time Jan had been here—with the beautiful Margarethe. He knew what had occurred: Jan had informed him by letter, and Joos had replied in sorrow. Now he was too discreet to inquire, for which Jan felt grateful.

It was Jan who broke the silence. There was something about the sharpness and wisdom of the old burgomaster which drew him to talk about the ducal court, about his portraits of the duke and of Jacqueline, about his journeys as ambassador. He did not feel, he said, fitted for that shining world: he preferred humbler things, more real things.

Vyt was looking at him intently. He was nodding his head gently.

"I can imagine," he said at last. "Certainly it would not suit me." He savored the aroma of his wine and took several small sips before replacing the glass on the table. "But then I am a man who has lived in a practical world. My skills are that I make things work for me . . . and for Ghent, which is why they made me their burgomaster. I have no visions of glory: I suffer no pains of deprivation. I do what I can do, and God has rewarded me for it." He stroked his stubbled chin. And then he chuckled. "Or perhaps I have rewarded myself and have attributed it to God just in case I should be guilty of pride."

And then a thought came to him, and with some difficulty Vyt rose from his chair. With small steps he crossed the room.

"I'll show you something," he said. "I promised it to you in a letter. A book that has helped me understand a lot: it might interest you in view of what you've said." And from a table at the far end of the room Joos picked up a volume and carried it back toward the fire. "Do you remember," he went on, "I talked of my friend the German monk, Thomas a Kempis? His book which he sent me is a jewel of good sense in our mad times."

Jan went over to the small table where Joos had laid the book under the lamp. He could see the title, *The Imitation of Christ.* The old man was turning the pages, and Jan saw that the monk had inscribed the volume to Vyt—"my friend and fellow lover of wisdom," he had written. The book itself was in a neat scribe's hand.

"This, for example." Vyt's finger followed one of the passages. "Your Latin is certainly superior to mine, Jan, but I'm not ashamed to try." And he read, slowly: *"If you cannot sing like the nightingale and the lark, then sing like the crows and the frogs, which sing as God meant them to."*

"How good that is, Jan. Now, you may be a nightingale for all I know, but I am certainly a frog—I even look like one. And yet I think I've sung as well in my own way as those with sweeter voices." He paused, and then added, looking wisely at Jan, "the trouble with kings and princes is that they believe the power they are given makes them better than other men; and when they hear themselves squawk and croak like the rest of us they cannot bear it, and we all have to suffer."

Vyt was turning the pages again, absorbed.

"Here too," he exclaimed. "Listen to this, and think of your courtly world: *It is a very usual thing with us to have a mighty confidence in ourselves, when, alas, the lack both of abilities and performance reproves our vanity and folly: for how small is the proportion of our gifts in comparison with our own imaginations concerning them."*

Joos sat back and drained his goblet of wine.

"It seems to me, Jan," he went on, "and you may say it's good wine that induces such ideas in an old man; but when I read thoughts like these I feel certain that the future belongs to men like us—to people who work and think and care—and not to your strutting princes with their absurd visions of glory."

Jan had never heard Vyt speak like this, but he understood more clearly than ever why he warmed to the old burgomaster. He knew that he would rather have spent his life draining sea marshes and building a city than dreaming of Jerusalem.

"Mind you . . . !" Joos was chuckling again, and contemplating whether or not to pour a final glass of wine. "Thomas a Kempis is a churchman, and there are many men of his own calling who have much to learn from him. How would you care to remind Bishop Denis of this?" And his fingers turned another page of the book by his side. Joos pointed to a passage Jan saw had been marked with an emphatic cross.

It was six words. *God is the small still voice.*

Jan did not know why that phrase resounded so deeply. But he thought of the rantings of Bishop Denis, and of Margarethe departing in tears. And suddenly he had an understanding for the first time why she had fled from him, why she had sought a place of retreat. She needed to hear that small, still voice. The God of peace. The God of love. The voice that gives strength. The voice denied to kings and princes. Peace of mind. It was what he had felt that morning riding through the spring meadows. Call it God, or not, it was the same voice.

If she found it, that peace and that strength, she would return. Jan felt sure. If not . . . then there was nothing he could do.

Joos gave a caverous yawn and rose.

"I'll tell you one thing to ponder on," he said as he shuffled toward the door. "There are not many small, still voices to be heard in Flanders. There will be trouble in Bruges, Jan: take it from me. The duke is not loved. I know the mood of it because I've dealt with it here." He placed a hand on Jan's shoulder, and his face was anxious. "Should you need to come to Ghent you're always welcome. You know that." Then he added with a tired smile, "Among the crows and frogs."

Jan lay awake a long time, his mind turning with unquiet thoughts.

It was a matter of hours after his return from Ghent when the sound of voices downstairs announced the arrival of Michault de Caron. He burst into the room and threw his hat on a chair.

"Thank God you're here," he announced with a dramatic sigh.

Jan had just begun to make a final examination of the many panels of the altarpiece, and had laid out his smallest brushes ready to add small dabs of varnish here and there where the surface seemed uneven. He looked up with pleasure and surprise.

"Michault."

"Oh!" groaned the poet. "How lucky you are you weren't here this morning. The duke's been summoning all to hear the news. I don't imagine you even know."

Jan shook his head. His mind was too occupied with his visit to Joos Vyt to spare much interest in the duke's affairs at this moment.

"Joan has recanted," Michault went on. "The duke is unbearably overjoyed. Laughing. Bubbling. Throwing his arms about. Oh God, I see more poems glorifying his wisdom—I've only just disposed of the sultan of Babylon. As for you, Jan, the duke kept saying he wished you were there so he could rub your nose in it. Crowing, he was. I've never seen him so pleased with himself."

Then Michault grew more serious.

"It seems a messenger arrived from Rouen yesterday evening," he explained. "It's a terrible thought, Jan; the executioner's cart was actually waiting. Joan could see it there. The crowd was beginning to throw stones. And she recanted."

Michault let out a long breath between his teeth.

"She said she would rather sign than be burned."

Silence filled the room as the spectacle of that scene in Rouen formed before the two men's eyes. The Maid, beckoned by the torture of death, recoiling in terror of the flames. It made the duke's joy a tasteless thing, Jan reflected. He had put her through this ordeal deliberately, callously, for his own mean ends. Another sacrifice to his greater glory. Jan remembered Vyt quietly turning over the pages of the book by Thomas a Kempis and pointing to the words *God is the small still voice.* How vividly he could imagine the shrill, cruel voice of Joan's inquisitor, the bishop of Beauvais—a voice neither small, nor still, nor that of God. He shuddered.

Michault went on, speaking quietly. Joan had submitted, he said, to the judgment of the Church. A document had been prepared—a simple one in essence. She was requested to disavow her "voices," and to renounce the male dress she had insisted on wearing. That was all. Joan had signed, and then added a cross. Her excommunication was to be lifted, and her punishment was to be perpetual imprisonment.

Jan winced. But Michault went on.

"From which the duke, no doubt, believes he will be able to free her. That will be his next move."

"And if he fails?"

Michault gave a short laugh.

"Have you ever known him to consider such a possibility?" The poet gazed around the room and his eyes settled on the ducal portrait, its background still just as unfinished as when Michault last looked at it.

"I suspect," he went on, "now the duke's spirits are on high again he will be pressing you for that glorious vision of Burgundy you promised him."

Jan nodded wearily.

"I fear so."

The two men sat and talked for the best part of an hour on that warm afternoon in late May. Beyond the open window the sounds of summer were beginning to stir, and boats passing along the canal carried with them the voices of men and women singing and laughing.

"Why aren't we doing that?" asked Michault with an air of resignation. Then, without waiting for Jan to reply, he added his own answer. "Because we've both caught the Burgundian disease of being in love with unavailable women. Isn't that so?"

Jan raised his eyebrows quizzically.

"Perhaps we should all be like Arnolfini and treat love as fruit to be plucked or as a contract to be drawn up."

"Do you see me plucking Bona like a fruit," Michault replied, "or tying her to a contract?"

"Then you've picked the wrong lady. If you chose some pretty creature brought up to sit around waiting for love, then

I'm sure you could spend every afternoon singing your verses to her along the canals while she gazed at you adoringly."

"And I'd be bored after a year and take a mistress."

"And she a lover. That's the normal way of it. And is that what you want, Michault?"

The poet did not answer but rose and looked moodily out of the window.

It was in that silence that they heard the noise of a commotion outside. There were excited cries and the sounds of feet running on cobbles. There followed a loud rapping at the front door—insistently. Jan hurried to the head of the staircase in time to see his housekeeper open the door to the familiar figure of Jehan Lefèvre. But the herald was not his usual aloof self; he hurried past the housekeeper in an agitated fashion and, noticing Jan looking down at him, threw his arms apart in a gesture of dramatic alarm.

"The duke," he announced breathlessly. "The duke is here."

And even as he spoke, a tall composed figure in black stepped into the hall and, taking no notice whatever of the fluttering Lefèvre, slowly peeled off his gloves and looked around him with a thin smile on his face. Half a dozen soldiers took up hurried positions around the hall while the petrified housekeeper pushed the door closed and stood with her back pressed against it as though anticipating an instant execution.

"Master Jan," said the duke in the mildest of voices as he began to mount the stairs, "I know you enjoy surprises, so I thought I would give you one." And as he reached the open doorway to Jan's studio he paused and gave the painter the warmest of smiles. "I heard today from Vyt that you were back from Ghent and that the great altarpiece was completed. I thought I should like to see what has kept you from painting my own portrait so long."

He walked slowly into the room.

The twenty-six panels were arranged along two walls of the room, waiting for the wooden frames into which they would be set and hinged. Recovering from his surprise, Jan stood silently to one side while the tall figure in black moved slowly around the room, inspecting one panel after another.

Michault, whose presence Philip had scarcely acknowledged, stood awkwardly next to Jan, while Lefèvre fidgeted by the door. The soldiers remained downstairs under the housekeeper's terrified eyes.

It felt to Jan as if painful hours were passing. Not a word was said. The duke would pause, peer closely, stand back, pause again: then a few quiet steps and he would pause, peer again, pause, and move silently on—further and further around the room. His expression never changed; it was as if he were storing in his mind a host of thoughts which he felt no need whatever to impart. Even when he came to faces he knew he registered no surprise or pleasure; only the same searching gaze and firm set of the mouth. He gave not even a glance at his own portrait which stood on an easel in one corner of the room, but appeared entirely engrossed in the altarpiece.

Finally, when he had completed his inspection of each panel, he stood in the center of the room while his eyes swept slowly across the whole display before him. And still he said nothing. For perhaps three or four minutes he went on contemplating the work in this fashion; and then suddenly, without turning his head toward the others in the room, he said in a slow, quiet voice, "This is the loveliest thing any man ever painted."

And to Jan's astonishment the duke turned, came toward him, and embraced the painter.

Then it was as if he removed a mask from his face. The intense expression melted, and he laughed, turning as he did so to the ducal herald.

"Lefèvre," he called out, a note of affectionate mockery in his voice, "you've told me so much about this painting, none of it of the smallest relevance. You told me that the angel of the Annunciation was a whore, that Eve looked pregnant, and that our court poet here was hiding his genitals as though he might not possess any. I can only conclude, Lefèvre, that you are as poor a judge of painting as you are of everything else— except, of course, of ladies espied through windows."

The duke's laughter filled the room and flooded the herald's face with confusion. Jan glanced at Lefèvre coldly. The louse, he thought.

Jan was too touched by the duke's response to the altarpiece to find Philip's mood of euphoria as intolerable as Michault had described it. Once again he was aware of how easily the duke's charm and apparent sincerity could dispel the horror he felt at his treatment of those who opposed him.

But suddenly Jan's attention was forced back to the realities of the duke's ambitions. "You'll have heard, Jan," he said, "that Joan has renounced her 'voices.' So, you see, I was right," he went on, his eyes gleaming with self-assurance. "It's often the most fraudulent of people who are the most stubborn. Your vulnerability to women, Jan, is an appealing flaw, but it's as well I didn't listen to you."

There was such benign superiority about the duke's manner that Jan felt unable to reply. But as he acknowledged the gentle reprimand with a nod, Jan thought of Philip's vulnerability to Jacqueline and wondered how he reconciled the contradiction. Then, even as the discrepancy crossed Jan's mind, the duke triumphantly produced another ace from his sleeve.

"Since we're talking of women," he announced more gravely, "I can tell you that Jacqueline has agreed to give up her titles and her lands." There was a brief pause as the duke enjoyed the expression on the faces around him. "All that for a foolish marriage. Do you realize, gentlemen," he continued with an air of supreme contentment, "that all the Low Countries are now part of the dukedom of Burgundy? This is something my father fought for, and my grandfather. I feel deeply proud."

The duke did not remain more than a few minutes longer.

"Perhaps, Jan," he added with a wry smile as he prepared to leave, "now that God has been well served, a mere duke might reacquire the good services of his painter." And for the first time Philip glanced at the portrait of himself on the easel. Then, without a further word, he briskly left the room.

There were sounds of hasty activity in the hall below, and the shuffling of soldiers' feet, before the front door closed on a house silent with surprise and relief.

Neither Jan nor Michault said anything for a while. Jan gazed pensively out of the window toward the canal, from where further sounds of voices and music rose on the warm spring evening. It was the shrewd Michault who broke the silence.

"It makes it hard, doesn't it, when so dislikable a man likes and admires you so much?"

Jan gave a slight laugh as he turned to face the poet. He was right, of course.

"You know, when he says things like that about what I've slaved over for a year, I want to forget everything else he's ever said or ever done. I feel like a prince. And the moment he's gone I feel like a traitor for being so easily bought with praise."

"Ah, that's real power, Jan," added Michault; "to be a tyrant and yet be the most civilized of men. Philip renders us all helpless by filling us with gratitude and fear—in equal measure. It's very clever."

Jan filled two glasses of wine and handed one to Michault.

"So we dance in the palm of his hand. And now he believes he has it all—both Jacqualine and Joan within his power. . . . And yet, Michault," he went on, gazing thoughtfully down at the wine, "I believe both of them still have more power over Philip than he has over them."

Michault looked surprised.

"What makes you so sure?"

Jan raised his shoulders in a gesture of puzzlement.

"Perhaps it's only a hunch," he answered, "but when I saw Joan I couldn't believe I was looking at someone who could ever betray her faith. She wasn't quite of this world. As for Jacqueline, the duke can take everything from her and she'll never be his. Never."

"So what do you think is going to happen?" Michault sipped his wine and looked questioningly at the painter.

"I don't know . . . What I really want to know," Jan went on, "is why those two women have this power over him. It's as if Jacqueline has the key to his heart, and Joan the key to his fortunes."

Michault smiled knowingly.

"Don't you think that a man who believes so strongly in chivalry, as the duke does, has to believe that women hold the key to everything?"

Jan looked at the poet sharply. As usual, he realized, Michault had put his finger on the truth.

"I'll tell you something else," Michault went on, his fingers idly tapping the glass in his hand. "When the duke went to see the Maid, shortly after her capture at Compiègne, he took with him his chronicler Enguerrand de Monstrelet, who, as you know, is a quiet, decent man devoted to compiling the glorious history of Burgundy, and in particular the glorious achievements of Duke Philip." Michault paused, and his fingers continued to tap the glass. "Now, you would have thought that few occasions would be more glorious to record in full than the noble duke's encounter with the savior of France, whom he had just captured. What pages of eulogy you would have expected from so loyal a chronicler. And shall I tell you what Monstrelet's chronicle contains about that historic occasion?"

He looked up at Jan quizzically, and paused again to add emphasis to his story.

"Nothing at all!" Michault flicked a last loud tap on the glass with his forefinger. "He writes only that *he does not recollect what was said* . . . Think of that. What a remarkably diplomatic lapse of memory."

The poet rose to leave. But before he did so he glanced toward the duke's portrait on the easel.

"I should have thought that if you are really to paint the 'true' portrait you say the duke has asked for, then you would need to know just what the Maid said to him that was so shocking it had to be deleted from history. But you will never never know, Jan. Monstrelet, I assure you, will go to his grave a loyal servant of Burgundy, if not of the truth. . . . And now I must depart, my friend, to compose a poem about the latest ducal triumphs—which will also not be in the service of the truth, I assure you. Good day, Jan."

Accompanying his footsteps down the stairs came the sounds of a song which Jan recognized to be a hymn of praise to no less celebrated a divinity than the penis of Abbot Eustache.

The air of euphoria surrounding the duke was almost as bewildering as the rage that had preceded it so short a time before.

Nor was it a mood shared by anyone around him, except by those lesser courtiers whose role it was to act as small mirrors of their master's whims. The duchess Isabella was more surprised than overjoyed at her lord's sudden attentiveness: he even visited her bed on several occasions, which made her feel that Philip was keeping in practice for the next mistress, whoever she might be. His lovemaking only reminded her of the joy she used to feel barely one year ago when he would come to her—all the promises, the hopes, the dreams with which he would regale her, intoxicate her. It reminded her of how she had loved him, and how she could not imagine that love ever fading. Now when he entered her it was like the reopening of a wound, an invasion of her pain. She waited for him to withdraw and depart quickly, hoping that his vigor had not become weakened by the demands of Louise, or Peronnelle, or some other fancy. Isabella did not hate him: she felt nothing for him at all beyond a kind of grief.

Outside the walls of the ducal castle the duke's mood was likewise shared by none. Alone in her house, Bona gazed at the mirrors which Arnolfini had recently supplied at her request: but instead of contemplating with appetite the prospect of so many fragmented views of her lovers as they disrobed before her, she contemplated only herself, and her face and form seemed to age before her eyes as the cruel glass threw back at her every fold and wrinkle of her body. She thought of Jacqueline, imprisoned with her husband, inaccessible, her anger turning gradually to poison and despair. And there was no help to be given, no comfort, no love that could reach her. Jacqueline, Bona knew, was doomed. When, and how, would it end?

In the Fallen Angel the company was stunned by further news—brought by the Englishman Hugo—that the duke had forbidden the sale of English wool within the duchy of Burgundy. Hugo was distraught. He was ruined. He would leave for home in a few days. They would miss his laughter, and his hopeless obsessions with beautiful women out of reach.

Godscalc Oom, seated massively before his minuscule

glass, explained that—as he understood it—the duke's decision was because men like Hugo were simply too successful, and Flemish sheep farmers were unable to compete. Their wool was inferior—that was why, Godscalc added, gazing about him like an overfed owl. The folly was, he continued, that the weavers of Bruges relied on English wool to produce the best cloth: Pieter van Orley would vouch for that if he were here. The reason he was not here was doubtless because he was stoking up his anger in the company of his fellow guildsmen: they were all of them longing for a storm that would blow everyone away including themselves. Godscalc was shaking his head sadly.

Then, with an unexpected gesture of warmth he placed a meaty hand on Hugo's shoulder. Perhaps we should all come to England, he suggested: it could not be worse than here.

"The duke may be in his heaven," Godscalc pronounced, "but his new Jerusalem could turn out to be Jericho. You may be well off away from it."

Hugo's familiarity with the Bible was none too fresh, but he liked the sound of Godscalc's sympathy. For once he did not stay at the Fallen Angel until the beer carried him into the street on a tide of song. Bruges would be a quieter city without him, the others reflected sadly as they watched him depart. Hugo with his bluster, his good heart and his dreams. Jan de Leeuw, Michaut Pontin, and Godscalc Oom turned their chairs toward the unlit fire and sat in silence.

Even as the three men sat there, another of the ducal messengers was hastening across northern France from Rouen. It was the thirteenth of May. For the whole of the gentle summer day the duke would remain unaware of what that date would soon engrave on his memory. It was perfect weather for hawking, and in his sable hat and surcoat of white ermine he rode jauntily out of the city gates at the head of his party of courtiers, his saker falcon on his wrist.

Meanwhile the messenger was riding hard, changing horses, scarcely sleeping. He had been a witness to it all.

At first he knew only that an excited crowd was gathering. He watched a scaffold being raised—high—and on top of it a stake. He inquired anxiously. The Maid, they said: it was to be today. Her voices had prevailed. Suddenly she was led out in a cart, wearing a black shift, a kerchief around her head, and he could see that she was weeping. English soldiers were pressing closely around the cart—there must have been two hundred of them armed with staves and swords. How they jeered, and leered, shouted obscenities. The crowd grew excited.

He watched them chain her to the post, roughly, and as they did so he heard her call on St. Michael several times, raising her eyes. Then she called out, "Rouen, Rouen, shall I die here?" and she gazed about her with so terrified a look the messenger could hardly bear it. Her arms were still free and she asked for a cross to hold. It was one of the English soldiers who came forward with two pieces of stick bound together, and she kissed it before placing it beneath her shift.

It seemed interminable. Sermons. Prayers. The soldiers were growing impatient, and one of them called out, "Priest, will you make us dine here?" The others laughed. Then a man appeared with a processional cross from the church nearby, and Joan took it from him, embracing it until they seized it from her and bound her hands.

They lit the pyre. The flames seemed so slow at first, just wisps. Then the smoke thickened and began to rise. The crowd cheered as Joan became almost hidden. The flames followed the smoke, and still she was alive. He could her her calling out again and again—St. Michael, St. Catherine. He had never seen anyone burned at the stake; but he had heard that someone would climb up and dispatch the prisoner before the final agony. A man next to him explained with a grin that because of the crowds the scaffold had been built too high: so she would be left to the fire. That was better, he said. The pyre was blazing now, all around her: she was a burning shadow. He heard her call out for holy water. Then a gasping cry: "Jesus!" And he saw her head drop.

It was over. The soldiers dispersed for their dinner.

The duke was enjoying the hunt in his surcoat of white ermine.

Jan heard the news from Michault de Caron, and returned

to his studio horrified. So Joan had died for her faith: was that it? Or had she perhaps believed in a miracle which never came? Or could it be that this, only this, would unleash the vengeance of France against the English and against the duke? But what did it matter why? A political move had turned to burning flesh.

Jan looked about him. All around stood this huge altarpiece he had painted to the glory of God; the angels, the saints, the worshippers, the Holy Lamb. Here, painted with all the love and skill he could muster, was the story of the Bible, and people would say with gratitude that he had opened their eyes to the scriptures. And yet . . . was the Bible not full of prophets who heard the voice of God and the angels? Like Joan. And they were honored for it—Noah, Job, Jeremiah, Isaiah, Moses from a burning bush, Jonah from the belly of a whale, John the Baptist from the wilderness. The Virgin Mary herself. Jan looked at his own painting of her. Then from a drawer he took out the small drawing he had made of Joan on that day of silence. So what was the crime this courageous woman had committed that she should be tortured to death?

Jan reached for the finest of his brushes, and to the figure of the Holy Lamb on its altar he added a few drops of blood from the creature's heart trickling into a golden cup.

Chapter ♦ Eleven

The sunlight poured through the windows of Vyt's chapel and threw colored patterns across the paradise garden with the Holy Lamb raised upon its altar. Jan glanced at Joos while the bishop was intoning his blessing on the altarpiece, and there was a look of benign contentment on the burgomaster's face. The old man's eyes were fixed on the figure of the lamb, and Jan knew that he had noticed the bright drops of blood dripping into the golden cup, and that Joos understood their meaning. Not even Jan had imagined that this service of dedication would become a requiem for the Maid. The bishop's face was grim with piety. How appropriate, Jan felt, that the man who had so harshly condemned Joan on that fateful evening should now unwittingly be conducting a mass for her soul.

They were all of them on their knees in the small chapel: Joos and his wife, perhaps twelve members of the Vyt family, a few aldermen, a few priests, several representatives of the local guilds. Then, as the bishop turned and extended his blessing to the congregation, two vergers moved quietly forward and closed the two wings of the painting. Joos and his wife, both in red, became mirrors of their kneeling portraits which now faced them; and Jan saw that the expression on the old burgomaster's face exactly matched the one in the painting. He smiled as he remembered how this morning Joos had practiced that expression.

"Was this how I did it, Jan?" Vyt had looked nervous. His wife had already locked the wine cupboard. But he had not been able to resist a creasing of the eyes and a slight twitching of the mouth.

"You painted me so impossibly pious, Jan," he sighed. "I shall never be able to live up to it. On the other hand, I shall not live very long, and after I'm dead people will always think of me the way you've painted me."

He had appeared quite content with the arrangement, as if a few years of incongruity were well worth an eternity of respect.

The two vergers again unfolded the wings of the altarpiece and now the bishop was kneeling in silent prayer before that vision of paradise. Jan gazed at Hubert's landscape raked by bars of golden light; then he looked at his own portraits of Adam and Eve, at the choirs of angels, St. John the Baptist, the Virgin Mary, and he thought of the people he had painted in these roles—the stories they had told him, the gossip and laughter in the tavern, the lust and the intrigue. It was like gazing at the story of his own life in Bruges. Except that there was no Margarethe in the painting, and no Jacqueline: the two women he had loved and lost. Here was a paradise of Burgundy with only the blood of the lamb as witness to the pain.

The service proceeded in a murmur of Latin. Neither Joos nor Jan, kneeling in front of the altar, saw the figure of the duke—in black—move silently into the rear of the chapel. He, too, saw the bright spots of blood and understood what was meant. No one saw him lower his head and close his eyes for a moment. By the time the service was concluded, the duke had gone.

They all moved quietly into the empty nave of the cathedral and out into the sunlight of that June morning. Jan, the burgomaster, and his wife made their way across the busy square.

"So the lamb bleeds," said Joos after a while.

Jan nodded and said nothing. He was wondering why the duke had not attended the dedication as he had promised. Had he too, perhaps, sensed the meaning of the sacrifice of the lamb, and as the agent of that sacrifice had stayed away?

"It's hard to imagine, Jan," Joos went on, speaking quietly as they passed among the bustle of the market stalls, "but those devout figures of Hubert's around the altar of the lamb are probably no different from the churchmen who sentenced Joan and then enjoyed watching her being burned at the stake."

They walked on. It was not until they were inside Vyt's house that anything further was said. Joos retrieved the key to the cupboard and began to sip his good wine with thoughtful care.

"It's finished, then, Jan."

Joos looked old and tired. Jan knew that he was referring to the altarpiece, but the way he spoke made it sound as though he was thinking of his life. Jan realized that Vyt had made his peace with his city and with his God: what was there left?

"It's finished," he said a second time, more emphatically. And then he looked at Jan with those sharp, moist eyes and the hint of a smile. "It's good to have completed something. Something that will last. You and I have done that. I wonder if the duke, for all his schemes and his ambitions, will ever be able to say such a thing."

There was a pause while Vyt continued to contemplate his wine. Then he gazed about him as if testing his thoughts against the paneled walls.

"I fear the duke's in much trouble," he said suddenly.

Joos did not explain for a moment, but returned his gaze to his glass before raising it to his lips.

"He believes too much in glory," he went on, "but the reality is all too often humiliation. He struts where he should bow."

Between sips of wine Vyt began to speak about that "reality" while Jan listened, attentive. Of course, Joos explained, the duke had been horrified by the execution of the Maid— perhaps only a little horrified by the thought of her painful death, admittedly, but certainly a lot by the blow it had dealt to his own plans. At the very moment when Philip had been plotting the most skillful interference at the tribunal in Rouen, and the gratitude of all France was within reach, his hopes had been dashed. And now the French were after his blood. Less than a week ago, Joos went on, the Burgundian army under Louis de Chalon had been ambushed and slaughtered near Lyon. This was the worst defeat, but it was not the only one. Everywhere the armies of Burgundy were being routed, so he had heard. And the reason? Vyt's eyebrows caused a dozen ripples to cut across his forehead. Philip's armies had no heart for this war, and why should they? They were Frenchmen, like the duke's enemies whom they were supposed to be fighting. The Flemings would not fight for him: what was his glorious vision of Burgundy to them? The Flemings only wanted to be left alone to make money, make love, eat and drink.

"And what better?"

The thought seemed to lift the old man's spirits, and he gave a chuckle. They might not be a very imaginative race, the Flemings, he went on, but this did have its advantages. When a Fleming dreamed, he assured Jan, it was not of the new Jerusalem but of a pretty girl and a fine haunch of venison.

"But then, as a Fleming yourself, you would understand that." Joos laughed. "Certainly, that was all I ever dreamed of as a young man."

And he extended his hands as if one of them held a woman's buttock and the other a hunk of flesh to eat. Then he poured another glass of wine and drank it liberally: Jan saw purple stains on his lips but made no comment. He had grown to love the old burgomaster.

"So what the duke needs is a truce with France," Joos added. "Desperately."

He looked thoughtful again.

"Meanwhile, he's incensed the weavers by forbidding them English wool. He's taxing them to the hilt for his armies —which then get slaughtered."

Vyt gave another deep sigh before refreshing his thoughts with a further sip of wine. Then, all of a sudden, a look of concern clouded his face.

"Take care," he said suddenly. And he placed one hand on Jan's forearm. "There will be trouble in Bruges: I've told you that. Take good care. And remember you have a home here." After a moment he added, brightening, "Tomorrow, before you depart, let us go and see our painting again. The two of us. No larks and nightingales; just a frog and a crow."

As if to refute the dark omens, it became a summer in which Bruges shed her burdens more joyfully than ever. With the absence of the duke and his court—far away in Dijon—discontent locked itself behind hidden doors, while those with a

Flemish appetite for pleasure took to the rivers and the forests. At moments the very air seemed to whet the senses, and the old city grew young again admiring itself in the softness of summer water. It was a way of forgetting. It was a time of forgetting.

On quiet mornings Jan would pass a little time adding small and irrelevant details to the background of the ducal portrait in order that he would be able to demonstrate its progress should the sudden need arise. Often these were the only moments when he would work at all: after the completion of the altarpiece he felt squeezed dry, and sometimes wondered if he would ever be roused to paint anything so ambitious again. Michault de Caron, much relieved to have been excused attendance at court, likewise complained that even two lines of verse were beyond him at present; and the two men would ride out of the city at noon and pass the long day talking, drinking wine, and bathing in the seclusion of the forest. It was a season of laughter and languor.

A few surprises drifted past in the long days. The sadness of Bona was suddenly lifted, so it was learned at the Fallen Angel, by an unexpected arrival. Just as it was believed that she had at last exhausted the supply of young lovers, or else had grown permanently immune to their charms, it became known that she was in love. She was obsessed; she would scarcely allow the young man from her adoring sight. He was of a beauty unimaginable, it was said, and of a prowess unequaled. It was unclear whether Bona's unwillingness to appear at the tavern was out of fear that he might cast a beautiful eye on some maiden, or whether there was simply no time to be spared from lovemaking.

It was Jan de Leeuw, usually so withdrawn and familial, who decided to seek out the truth on behalf of all who lived around the street of the Golden Hand. The goldsmith paid Bona a visit unannounced at a sober hour, and at a less sober hour reported to the company in the tavern that he was indeed the most beautiful of boys and that he was as black as night. Only Godscalc Oom registered no astonishment, pointing out in the most offhand way that in his younger days it was quite normal for highborn ladies with a taste for pleasure to take a black lover, or several: it was well known that the tropical sun did a great deal more than darken their skin, and that the pallid Flemings could no more offer comparison in vigor than they could in complexion. It had been no accident that the Church, perturbed by such goings-on, should have preached that the devil himself was black, and that he was equipped with a member of indescribable proportions and insatiable activity. Bona could consider herself most fortunate—in Godscalc's opinion.

A silence of surprise filled the tavern, less perhaps at Bona's revelation than at Godscalc's knowledge of these matters. The rentmaster stroked the uppermost of his chins, sipped his glass of hippocras, and appeared uninterested. It was Jan de Leeuw who added that if the jewels which adorned the young man that afternoon were rewards for his services, then indeed he supposed Godscalc must be correct and the man was a truly remarkable devil.

"What language does he speak?" inquired the silversmith Michaut Pontin.

De Leeuw, with no change of expression, expressed the view that Bona certainly did not employ him to talk. A severe lady with the unnecessary name of Constance, who rarely visited the tavern, by now had the face of one who was unlikely to visit it again. Michault de Caron was the only other member of the company to look displeased by the revelations. He was shaking his head sadly, quite unable to grasp how the lady of his heart should prefer a dumb African slave to the splendors of his own person. It was Pontin who, understanding the reason for the poet's misery, suggested unkindly that had Master Jan not painted Adam with so modest a fig leaf his Eve might have preferred him to a black servant.

"Servant or serpent?" he added with a laugh.

De Caron departed with a ruffled dignity amid the smiles of all except Constance.

"Did you ever have a black lover in your youth, Constance?" continued Pontin even more unkindly.

He was rather drunk, and seemed unaware that Constance was still striving to preserve a youth she had never had. The others looked on a little embarrassed as Constance left in some haste, her throat taut with choked-back tears.

But the summer soon presented Michault de Caron with a more healing surprise. The poet had taken to moping away his evenings at Jan's house, to the latter's vexation. Jan found it hard to understand how a man so shrewd in worldly matters should be perpetually so inept in matters of love. It seemed perfectly clear that if Bona had a taste for black servant boys there was absolutely no point in Michault reiterating his own superiority, since he was neither black nor a servant nor a boy: that was the end of it. Michault did not appear able to think like that, and continued to draw out the long maudlin evenings with tireless re-examinations of the tragedy until a threshing floor could not have been more thoroughly trodden.

"I cannot understand," asserted Michault for the tenth or one hundredth time that hour. The two men were seated in Jan's garden by the edge of the canal on what should have been a quiet and scented evening. Jan sighed.

"I know you don't," he said unsympathetically. "Why don't you go and write a poem about it?"

But Michault was as oblivious to Jan's weariness as he was to good sense.

It was at this moment when rescue appeared quite unexpectedly. Jan noticed a boat approaching, laden as he imagined in the half-dusk with yet another enviable couple on their way to the secluded waterways beyond the city. But then he saw that the boat was being paddled by two young women, one of whom was pausing to wave in their direction. And as they drew closer he realized to his amazement that the two figures were none other than the heavenly twins, Lysbet and her sister Marie.

What followed was nothing less than salvation. The two women pulled up to the wall below them, and within a minute it was as if every dart in Cupid's quiver had struck the bewildered heart of the court poet. Lysbet, who had previously always ignored De Caron, now turned on him her lovely smile and tilted her head of golden hair in the evening light. From the look on Michault's face it was clear that the unobtainable Bona could have plunged forever into the darkest pit: he was a spirit reborn; the wings of love had gathered him in one swoop.

"Come with us," called Lysbet, laughing.

Michault leapt into the boat even before the laugh had finished, and grasped the paddle as if his whole future would be guided by that fragile craft. Jan shook his head at the invitation a little regretfully, unwilling to compete with Michault's fervor and even more unwilling to be left in the bewitching darkness with the saintly Marie.

He watched Michault paddle his lovely cargo into the gathering dusk, relieved to be rid of the poet's self-pity and marveling at the speed with which a mortal wound could heal. By the time the boat was out of sight Jan had decided that the turn of events was altogether perfect: Lysbet, presumably now abandoned by Arnolfini, would keep Michault in adoration and in poetry at least for a breathing space. And Jan could not help reflecting with a smile, as he sat enjoying the last of the light, that doubtless no young man had ever before paddled a boat of love containing both the Virgin Mary and the angel of the Annunciation.

It was only a few days later that the last of the summer surprises overtook the street of the Golden Hand. This was the news that Giovanni Arnolfini had returned from Paris, and was unrecognizable. He, too, had fallen in love.

Even those who had resisted astonishment at the condition of Bona and the helpless capitulation of Michault found it impossible to restrain looks of bewilderment. Arnolfini in love! It was Jan who confirmed the phenomenon because it was in Jan's house where the merchant delivered the news. The wedding was to be in the new year, and Jan was to be chief witness —if he would agree—and was to paint a picture of the occasion just as the merchant had always promised. This was what Giovanni had called to ask him.

Jan had expected a man who had agreed to a satisfactory contract. He had not expected a man who looked as though he had discovered the Holy Grail. Giovanni's normally lugubrious face wore an expression of incredulous delight which did not appear to know where to put itself, so unfamiliar was it to the wearer. He struggled to be mundane.

"She is, of course, what I expected, what I had been given to believe . . . most suitable." Giovanni's thin hands fluttered like wings that had forgotten how to fold themselves. And then his joy broke through. "She is . . . wonderful, Jan. Entirely wonderful."

Jan could see already in the merchant's eyes that gleam of adoration which he had noticed before in Italians who have discovered in some shy fawn the image of the Madonna reborn. How they loved to worship untouchable perfection. He was happy for Giovanni, who had never until this moment seemed entirely human. Now it was as if the flawlessness of all those beautiful objects which had passed through Arnolfini's hands in half a lifetime were brought to flesh and blood in the form of this creature who had consented to be his wife. He will wear her like a jewel, Jan thought, and stifle her with tendernesses.

"I have already purchased her a little dog," Giovanni explained, "which you must paint too."

And to Jan's surprise Arnolfini produced from the sleeve of his surcoat a minute ragged object whose nose shone like a truffle and whose tail beat frantically at the rings on the merchant's hands as he tried to hold the squirming thing.

"Only a puppy," Giovanni explained unnecessarily, lowering the creature to the floor, where it wandered unsteadily, leaving a thin trail of urine to mark its course. "Pepe." Arnolfini bent down to stroke the errant puppy fondly. "Giovanna loves dogs."

Jan looked down at the leaking bundle and reflected that if Giovanni's madonna could love something as ugly as Pepe, then she should have no trouble loving her husband.

"I'm very happy for you, Giovanni," he said. "A marriage portrait would be the happiest of pictures to undertake. Thank you for asking me." Then, watching his housekeeper following Pepe with a mop, he added, "If I'm to include the dog, am I also to include its libations?"

Giovanni retrieved Pepe with some embarrassment and restored it to his sleeve.

"He will be trained by then, I assure you. My apologies.

And I'm so glad you will agree. You are a good friend, Jan." To his surprise Jan realized that Giovanni meant it.

It was a summer of unlikely love—as though the waterways threading the old city had become distorting mirrors bewitching those who gazed into them, the ripples inventing irresistible bonds. Perhaps the departure of Hugo also played a part: Hugo, the very spirit of impossible and unrequited love, no longer present to cast a despairing spell and mock all liaisons with absurdity. Perhaps, too, it was the absence the entire summer of the duke, whose presence was the curse of love.

Jan often wondered how the duchess Isabella was enduring her living widowhood—transferred now from the lonely polderlands of Flanders to the warm pastures of Dijon: what new Louise or Peronnelle taunted her solitude with glances of pity and triumph across the lamplight and the echo of distant laughter in the night?

And Jacqueline? What of her marriage and her love—imprisoned within that stone tower of the sea winds? Jan sensed that before long he would know. When the image of Jacqueline rose before his eyes he no longer saw the softness of the dunes her summer bed; instead he saw pale hands stretched tense across cold sheets and no one to look into those sleepless eyes.

It was Bona who told him. She did not explain how she had managed to make her way to Goes undetected, what guise she had adopted, or what purpose drew her there in defiance of the duke. But she had seen Jacqueline, she said, and Bona's face was drawn with sadness. Van Borselen had departed, and Jacqueline was alone. She had chosen to be alone, she had told Bona: the man she had believed she loved was already repellent to her. His timid gentleness that had once seemed like balm to her wounds soon became the most craven subservience. She wanted to kick him. She could not stand his longing eyes, his hopeful attendance, his apologetic self-abnegation; she could not stand his flesh. And there was no child in her womb.

She did not even want to bear his child, Jacqueline had told Bona. She would rather everything of hers ceased to exist.

"I fear it will," Bona added, looking sadly at Jan.

"How did she look?" he asked half fearfully.

"Beautiful, of course . . . but a beauty from which something has departed. The spirit. Herself, even. It was as though she were not there, and she had left her beauty behind as a memorial."

Bona crossed the room very slowly, her face that familiar sullen mask. She was gazing out toward the canal.

"She gave me a message for you." Bona did not turn her head. "She said, 'Tell him he is my painter, my ambassador, my lover.' "

It was disturbing to feel how many things were reawakened by what Bona had said. Something private, and long past, had become a secret shared, a living thing. What he heard from Bona's lips seemed to Jan like an invitation suddenly to tempt danger, to risk everything just as Jacqueline had risked everything, to go to her—regardless.

"Could I see her?" Jan asked, aware of an urgency in his voice.

But Bona was shaking her head.

"No! No, Jan!" Then she came toward him and with unexpected tenderness took both his hands in her own. Surprisingly she gave a laugh. "She said she hoped you would want to do that, and that if you had not I was to tell you. But she forbids you to. She said you had risked enough for her already, and you had your life you must lead."

Jan looked hard at Bona, who had released his hands and was now gazing expressionlessly at the ducal portrait.

"But if *you* can manage to visit her undetected, why can I not?"

Bona turned her head, and a faint smile formed on her lips.

"I never said I was undetected," she answered.

"And yet you managed it. How?" Still there was that smile on Bona's face.

"I am a woman," she said. Then there was that laugh again, taunting, mocking this time. "Remember, Jan, I am Eve."

Did Bona really want him to believe that she had offered herself to the soldiers? She would not do that. As always, Jan thought, Bona liked to guard her secrets.

"Besides," she went on more seriously, "I have nothing to lose. You have everything. Jacqueline is right: you have risked quite enough already."

Bona was preparing to leave. And as so often, she left for the last a thought which smothered everything that had preceded it.

"She loves you, Jan, in her way. But I must tell you that since Humphrey of Gloucester, Jacqueline has yearned for one thing more than any man. And that is—an end to it all. Something died in her when Humphrey left her."

Bona departed. Jan felt bruised. Could it really be so? He remembered Jacqueline in the reed village holding her godchild in her arms. He saw her embracing the villagers, cherishing them, laughing with them, taking the hands of the blind old man. He saw her riding through the lands of the sea with a look of such contentment, the sun anointing her. He saw her face in the lamplight, her eyes searching, inviting. He could smell the scent of roses on her skin. He could feel her hair slipping between his fingers, her body moving beneath his in the sand. And he could hear her sigh. How could a woman so in love with living yearn for an end? For death? Jan did not believe it.

Beyond the window Jan could hear the first rains of autumn.

The blow when it struck was like a wound on the lovely face of Bruges.

Joos Vyt had predicted it. Jan had only half believed him. There was nothing in his life which could have prepared him.

It began quietly. Messengers arrived from Dijon announcing the return of the duke. What seemed strange was that every guild in the city received a command to turn out on the afternoon of his arrival, unarmed and in their best clothes. They were to greet the arrival of their prince.

The leaders of the guilds met at the entrance to the cloth hall, puzzled and suspicious. The duke normally came and went as he pleased: it was only on occasions of triumph when a ceremony was made of his arrival, and this was no such occasion. There were no tableaux of heroes and sirens being prepared, no order to ring every church bell. Nothing. Only this command that he be greeted by his people. Why? The guildsmen felt no need to greet the duke, nor had any wish to. He had already squeezed them with taxes, and he had cut off their supply of English wool. Bruges was their city, and he was crippling it. They did not want him here; least of all did they want to cheer him. Nonetheless, they would obey.

A little before three o'clock in the afternoon the sound of bugles could be heard some distance beyond the southwestern gate of the city. In every street it sounded faintly. Jan opened his windows and listened. The company in the Fallen Angel put down their beer and strained their ears. The bugles had an unfamiliar, military note.

Before long there was a stirring of watchmen on the ramparts. Meanwhile, within the houses people were preparing to obey the duke's orders and were brushing down their best clothes: there was an air of excitement amid the suspicion. The people of Bruges liked to dress up. There were flags being hung from the houses and the streets were swept. Faces were beginning to peer expectantly from gabled windows.

But what they saw first were figures running toward the marketplace and the cloth hall, and there was only one word being shouted as the men passed. Soldiers! Now those on the ramparts could see them—thousands of them. They were Picards, people said. Nobody liked Picard soldiers: they were Frenchmen; and what were they doing here? Anxiety overtook the faces peering from the windows as they heard the news. The duke was bringing an army to Bruges.

By the time the messengers arrived from the ramparts the various guilds and societies of Bruges had already assembled— as sprucely turned out as they were able—and were preparing sluggishly to form a procession that might look welcoming. There were several thousand citizens gathered in the marketplace amid a hubbub of voices that expressed the pervading mood of civic pride blended with indignation. A perceptible tension divided those who were positioning themselves to lead the procession. Merging easily with the crowd were the deans and magistrates, all of whom had been elected by the guildsmen. Awkwardly to one side stood the duke's men, the city councillors like pallbearers in their black robes, the un-smiling burgomaster, Morissis van Varsenare, and the lean stooping figure of the bailiff of Bruges, Lodewijk van Havers-kerke.

The bugles were clearly audible above the surge of voices. The duke had entered the city. The procession began to move in the direction of the southwestern gate to meet him.

It was at this moment that those who were watching the proceedings from their windows noticed that something was wrong. They saw the messengers arrive running from the ram-parts, and they saw the leading guildsmen speak earnestly to the deans and magistrates even as the procession was already on the move. Several figures immediately broke from the ranks of the guildsmen and began running with the greatest haste down the narrow side streets which were the most direct means of access to the southwestern gate of the city. The councillors and the burgomaster were looking about them anxiously as more and more men broke from the procession and followed those who had taken to the side streets. Soon there was hardly a procession remaining: people turned their heads and passed the word to those walking behind them—and so on in a ripple of heads turning, followed by splinters of figures abandoning the moving crowd and vanishing within the maze of houses and hidden alleys.

The message in the heads of all who ran was the same: the duke was entering their city at the head of a mounted army of Frenchmen. Why, no one knew; no one had time to inquire, or the opportunity. They ran, and with a common purpose—the gate must be closed. All the gates must be closed. There was an echo of running feet along a thousand narrow streets. The city was in mutiny.

The southwestern gate, the Boeveriepoort, rose like a double tooth from the ramparts, and from it a drawbridge stretched across the encircling canal to where the road to Lille approached from the open polders and the forests beyond. At one moment an unbroken phalanx of horsemen was pressing across to the lowered bridge and under the twin towers of the Boeveriepoort. A moment later a swarm of figures on foot had surged from the ramparts to the left and right and had cut that moving thread of horses. Unarmed men seized bridles, stirrups, saddles, feet. Animals were rearing, swords flailed, men were falling like swatted flies into the water, screaming. But in swarms they kept coming, unarmed men armed with their anger and with no time to feel afraid. And the riders were helpless in so narrow and perilous a place: the horses panicked, bucked, knocked each other over the edge, their legs pawing the air before the water seized them; then suddenly the drawbridge began to rise, jerkily higher and higher, and as the planks caught the sun they glistened with blood.

The city was closed. All nine gates. Outside, two and a half thousand soldiers remained on the farther bank of the canal. Inside, fifteen hundred men rode toward the marketplace, none except those few at the rear with the least idea of what had already happened. They rode serenely through the city, led by the duke himself and his general, Jehan de Luxembourg. In every upper window as they passed there were people wearing their finest clothing: they also knew little what was happening except that they were here to wave their hands in greeting to their duke.

Within minutes everyone in Bruges would know.

There was no stopping it. Mistakes have their own relentless momentum, and there are no tears or pleas that can check their course.

The duke was leading the pageantry he loved. He was a man who ruled by display. He liked parades, and to know that a mounted army was parading behind him was a tonic to the certainty of his power; His armor was black, and the hilt of his sword gleamed with rubies. He was proud to be riding through his own city with all the ceremony of strength upon which the world gazed in awe. Shortly he would exchange greetings with the guildsmen, with his councillors and his bailiff, the bond of loyalty would be sealed, and tomorrow he would lead his army northward toward Holland, where there was unrest to be quelled. He was here in Bruges to see his people, and to be seen. Bruges, the bright gem of Flanders, would be polished by his presence.

The duke smiled graciously at the faces in the high windows. All was as it should be.

He was relieved to see the marketplace ahead of him full of common people unarmed, as he had instructed, and dressed suitably in his honor. A respectful silence seemed to fill the great space under the shadow of the bell tower as the crowd moved back to let the Picard horsemen ride into the open square, their bows across their shoulders, swords at their sides, reins loose. The only sounds were the ring of hooves on worn cobbles and the tense murmur of the crowd.

Then everyone saw the Picard captain ride forward toward the duke and his general, Jehan de Luxembourg, and nobody there knew why. But they saw Philip draw back, startled, and in the next minute he had drawn his sword and wheeled his horse. Jehan de Luxembourg did the same. A tremor seemed to pass through the crowd in that marketplace. Then, even as some of those closest to the duke began to draw back in fear, they saw him turn his head vigorously this way and that, his sword raised as if to strike someone who was not there. And they heard him cry to Jehan de Luxembourg: "Shoot!"

(Philip, lord of Burgundy, greatest of princes, you went to hell with that single word.)

A master baker, Race Yweyns, was shot dead with an arrow as he stood before the duke doffing his hat in welcome. His wife threw herself toward him in horror and was trampled by a Picard horseman. Everywhere there was the rustle of bows being swiftly handled, the rush of arrows, the stumbling of feet, a thousand unarmed hands raised in terror against the swarm of death, and a cry of panic and pain rose from that slaughterhouse under the sky and swept across the city. But the streets were too narrow for flight, and the horses were swifter, the arrows of their riders swifter still. Every alley was spiked with the dead and the dying. The archers looked up as they rode by and saw faces at open windows: their arrows struck people who had been leaning bareheaded to greet their prince: arrows hung quivering from dormers, gables, tiles, window frames, doors, and from the slumped bodies of their owners. And onward the horsemen rushed—over bridges, along quays, into courtyards, churchyards, gardens. Nowhere was safe, and all the city was a cry of terror and a crashing of glass.

(Philip, lord of Burgundy, where now was your vision of the new Jerusalem?)

It was only the beginning. As death passed by, another cry rose up among the gabled houses and across the canals. "Arm! Arm!" People were rushing to their homes: men buckled swords around their belts, drew axes from their cupboards, knives, daggers, sticks, poles, whatever they could grasp and wield. Some of the guildsmen dragged small cannons on to the bridges and began to fire wooden missiles at the Frenchmen. Suddenly down every street advanced furious men, and the sound of running feet began to drown the clatter of hooves and the yells of pain. The horses wheeled, and men were still advancing toward them. Stones rained down from windows, and not only stones—bricks, pokers, chairs, tables, hammers, cooking pots, basins, clogs. A storm of vengeance broke over the soldiers. They fled through every alley and yard, through water, over walls—leaving their panicked horses. They rushed in small bands of terror from one city gate to another, and all of them were closed. The people of Bruges spared none they could lay their hands on, and with their bare hands they tore them like so much cloth.

Outside the city gates two and a half thousand Picard horsemen heard the cries of the dying, and could do nothing but wait for silence.

The duke stood pale with terror in the marketplace, with him Jehan de Luxembourg and a bodyguard of some twenty knights. Their swords trembled and their eyes glazed with horror. It was the burgomaster who came to their aid. With him they rode in an armed pack out of the open square toward the ramparts. Near the moat and the southwestern gate was the house of Jacob von Hardoye, the chief watchman. The burgomaster slid from his horse and battered on the man's door while two of the duke's knights forced it open with the shoulders.

They grabbed the man by his arms as he cringed from them, and with a knife to his throat he handed to them tools that were used to repair and secure the gate—hammers, pincers, chisels, saws, iron bars. With these the party rode to the Boeveriepoort, and while some of the knights formed a cordon around the gate others set to work to break it down.

It was seven in the evening, as darkness began to fall, when the drawbridge was lowered and the duke and his lords rode out of Bruges toward Lille.

Five hundred citizens had died within a single hour. More than three hundred soldiers perished at the hands of those who had survived.

Then silence settled on the wounded city, broken by the cries of the bereaved and the cries of the dying.

Bruges was like a city raped. No laughter rose from the canals at dusk. The taverns were empty. Even the street vendors seemed to trade in a whisper. If the city still gazed at its own beauty in the water it saw the ripples as its own tears. The lament of church bells drifted across autumn fields where nothing appeared to move. The gaunt mills stood in mourning.

Nobody said why they gathered at the house of Arnolfini. Possibly it was because Giovanni was a foreigner, and his presence among them brought a reminder that there were warmer lands which at that moment did not bleed. Or else because he alone among them possessed something fecund in his heart: he was in love, and the dreams he wove lifted the others from the shock of pain and brought them balm—a little.

By now everyone knew who had died in that hour of murder. Pieter van Orley was dead: a Picard sword had cut him down in the midst of his yell of hatred. They had disliked him but they would miss him: he was one of them. Jan de Leeuw had lost a brother, Michaut Pontin his father. Jan knew that Margarethe's uncle, the master weaver, had also died, shot through the stomach as he dragged his wounded wife back from the horsemen.

And Bona was blind. The horror of that news silenced them all when Jan told them.

Her black servant had called at his house, on Bona's orders. He was distraught. It had happened suddenly. Three Picard soldiers had fled in panic into her courtyard. They burst into the house just as Bona appeared, roused by the din. She had a dagger in her hand which she plunged into one of the Frenchmen as he rushed past. The others were concerned only to make for the open quay which they could see beyond the far window. But it was not the quay: it was a mirror. Everywhere there were mirrors. The soldiers saw only themselves fleeing in terror—so many faces thrown back at them. A party of guildsmen were following them into the house, brandishing swords, clubs, staves before them in their fury. In despair one of the Picards toppled a huge cupboard toward them: it caught Bona as it fell. The guildsmen killed the two remaining Picards, but when they carried Bona to a couch her eyes were closed, and when she opened them she could not see. "I am blinded," she had murmured.

The black boy had gazed at him helplessly. Through the shock, Jan could only think at that moment of how cruel a joke it was for Bona to have been blinded because of the very mirrors she had set up in order to be able to see.

Later, Jan had called to see Bona, but she was sleeping. Her servant was seated beside her, holding her hand.

"I wish the duke in hell," muttered the goldsmith Jan de Leeuw.

Some of the others nodded. Rain beat in flurries on the windows of Arnolfini's house, and the city was heavy and gray. There was a grunting sound as Godscalc Oom shifted his position heavily on his chair. He had said nothing, but now he breathed deeply and looked about him at the tense faces.

"The duke's not the only one who should roast," he said "The guildsmen share the blame."

The others threw Godscalc a hostile look, but the old rentmaster was unperturbed. He looked down at his massive hands.

"It was a clash that was bound to happen," he went on. "So much suspicion has to be paid for. Belligerence finds its victims—usually innocent ones."

The duke, he emphasized, had harbored no thoughts of using the Picards against the citizens of Bruges: he was merely —and the corners of Godscalc's mouth described a downward curve—indulging in a little display of strength; perhaps it was to warn the guildsmen not to press their grumbling too far; perhaps to demonstrate that not all the Burgundian army had been routed by the French; perhaps most of all because the duke enjoyed the opportunity to parade in full armor through his favorite city at the head of several thousand men. He was like a child with his toys, Godscalc added wearily. As for the guildsmen, it was suicidal folly to have closed the city gates against the duke's own men.

Godscalc looked around him grimly; then, seeing that he had an attentive audience, he offered a lawyer's cold judgment on the guildsmen.

"They think they want justice from an unjust duke. What they really want is his power to be as unjust as he: then they can squabble and knife each other till everyone is ruined."

Jan de Leeuw turned his long, sad face toward the rentmaster.

"So you would keep power in the hands of tyrants rather than run the risk of sharing it with fools."

Godscalc's expression of gloom changed not a fraction.

"I would prefer one tyrant to a thousand fools."

Jan was growing irritated by the debate, which seemed to decorate grief like unwanted weeds.

"At present what we have is one tyrant *and* a thousand fools. And it's people who are neither who bear the brunt of it."

"Then what would you have?" asked Godscalc.

"Only that those who seek power should keep it in the shadow of their humanity."

Jan realized as he said it that he was thinking of Joos Vyt, and of course of Jacqueline.

He was weary of the company and took his leave. The rain had stopped, and a mellow autumn sunlight polished the orange roofs and the dark gables. He wandered without really knowing where, or why. How unreal it seemed, this beautiful city. A damaged pearl. Some of the houses where he walked still had banners draped from high windows in honor of the duke; and there above them Jan could see arrows lodged in the eaves like spines. No one had removed either. Joy and grief both left behind, side by side. There were few people in the streets, but ahead of him he noticed two children playing with a leather ball. They were laughing, throwing it from one to the other. Then, as he approached them, the younger of the two threw the ball too high and it rolled across the cobbles onto the quayside of a canal, where it continued to roll before disappearing over the edge into the water. Suddenly the laughter stopped abruptly and the elder boy cursed and struck the other child in the face. Jan saw that his nose was bleeding, and he began to scream while the other boy delivered him a sharp kick and walked angrily away. The child with the bleeding nose ran into a nearby house, and the street was empty again. Jan could see the leather ball bobbing in the water.

He walked on. The incident seemed like a miniature of what had happened two days earlier. This city, so full of play and laughter; how easily it turned to blood. How civilized it could feel. The duke, with his love of beautiful things—books, paintings, clothes, beautiful women, beautiful visions, the new Jerusalem. And he, Jan, preserving those visions, gilding them, offering them to all eyes as the truth of the world. He thought of his friends, Godscalc, a lawyer skilled in justice. De Leeuw, maker of the finest jewelry. Michaut Pontin, whose hands shaped and engraved silver. Arnolfini, his life carpeted with beauty. Michault de Caron, composer of songs and poems to please all who read and sang them.

Such civilization, so skillfully and devotedly created out of the rough material of humankind. And yet, how fragile a membrane: tear it and the ugliest passions burst like pus.

Jan realized he was near the eastern gate of the city. He looked up and felt a chill pass through him. A man's head was impaled from the highest tower. From the ramparts he could see the next gate, and above it the silhouette of another head. The watchman grinned at him with black teeth.

"Nine of them, master. One for each gate." The man laughed. "Guildsmen," he added. "The duke's command."

The sun was low. It was an evening in which one would have longed for a nightingale to sing. Jan could hear the deep, timeless gong of the cathedral bell. The city from here was a jeweled crown of spires—Jan had often painted it like that—

but around it, instead of diamonds, were set the heads of dead men.

"If it had been my command, the duke's head would be among them," Jan replied.

And the watchman laughed again.

Chapter • Twelve

Bona stretched out a hand when she heard that her visitor was Jan.

"Let me touch you. It makes it easier to imagine I can see you."

There were tears in Bona's sightless eyes, and tears in Jan's as he gazed at her. The black boy looked on with an expression of devotion and grief on his face. Around them rose the mirrors which had been the instruments of her blindness; they transformed the house into a labyrinth in which fragments of its contents appeared unexpectedly here and there as if hurled by some earthquake. The image of Bona lying on her couch seemed tossed from wall to wall, each glimpse and angle thrown back at her in mockery of her sightlessness.

Already her face had acquired that blankness of someone looking inward, who had lost the awareness of her own appearance and of its effects on others' eyes. It was like a wall behind which she lived, and through which she talked.

"It's hard to believe my body still exists," she said. And she touched her breast and her cheeks as if surprised to find them there. Then she gave a tired laugh. "Perhaps it's my punishment for being Eve."

There had been so much anger within Jan during the long days since the riot, and nowhere that he could lay it. Autumn hung in a gray shroud over the city and around the shoulders of those who walked the narrow streets and quaysides, their heads and their voices lowered. Only gradually did the shock begin to heal, and in its place people's faces showed only the resigned helplessness of the righteous. Nobody had done more than nod as Jan passed.

Bona wanted to know who else had suffered, who had

died: a twitch of pain marked her face as Jan told her of the friends and relatives she knew; and when he talked of the heads impaled above the city gates she gave a shudder and her mouth grew tense. Her servant came forward and put out his hand, and as if she sensed it she groped in the air before grasping it and drawing the boy to her. He placed his dark head on her breast like a child while she ran her fingers through his hair.

"Who else?" she asked.

Jan told her of Margarethe's uncle and aunt—both killed, he explained. They had done only what they were commanded to do, put on their best clothing in order to greet the duke in the marketplace: he had never been one of the troublemakers among the weavers, unlike Pieter van Orley. They had waved their hats, and the next minute both of them were dead.

"And Margarethe?"

"I don't know," Jan answered. He realized that he had almost forgotten Margarethe. It was more than a year now.

"Have you found nobody else?"

Jan shook his head, and then remembered that Bona could not see.

"No."

She seemed to be looking hard at him even though she was blind.

"Then you must be waiting for her." Bona seemed so assured that Jan was taken aback. He wondered if it was true. He could not even recall the sound of Margarethe's voice. Did she remember him, think of him?

"So what am I going to do with my life, Jan?" Bona asked suddenly. She had raised herself to her feet and was taking a few cautious steps, one hand grasping the black boy's arm, the other held out before her. Then she stopped and turned her head this way and that. "You know," she went on, "I'm just aware of the light. That must be the window. How tantalizing."

"Is there something I can do for you?" Jan asked, taking her other hand. She gripped it warmly, and again she turned her head as if she were looking at him.

"Come here. Let me touch you," she said. Her fingers moved slowly across his face. "Be my friend—and be my eyes. That's enough. No one ever had sharper sight than you. Share some of it with me by telling me what you see. . . . And make me laugh," she added. "I want to know every piece of scandal you hear. Every day, preferably."

Bona seemed cheered by the thought.

"Yes," she went on, feeling for the couch and cautiously seating herself on it again, "you must tell me what Arnolfini's madonna is like when she arrives from Paris. Whether she is as ugly as he is. Whether he really loves her. And how rich she is. And you must tell me about the cast-off Lysbet and the ridiculous Michault; whether she eats him alive as he deserves. Do ask her what lies curled up under Adam's fig leaf. He was always trying to show me, but I declined the offer." Bona laughed mockingly, and Jan could imagine how she must have treated the unfortunate poet. Blindness seemed to have sharpened her tongue. "And of course, *you*. I always used to know when you desired someone by the way your lips moved; but now I can no longer see, you will have to tell me. No secrets: it is a woman's privilege to have those; one of the few defenses we have. Will you promise?"

Jan found himself laughing too.

"No," he said "Of course not."

Bona's mouth descended at the corners.

"So you don't trust me. How unkind. I'm the most moral of people." She sighed and lay back against the head of the couch. "But perhaps you're right," she added. "I may be moral, but my morality is rather porous." And again she laughed.

After a while Jan departed, finding it hard to believe he had been in the company of a woman struck blind. There was such bravery in Bona's laughter. He wondered what she was like when she was alone.

He could never have imagined the thought that rested in Bona's mind as she lay there listening to the rain. Her servant was preparing her a meal. She was just conscious of that smudge of light where she knew the window was. But she could not lie here all her life—being fed, being tended, dressed and undressed, making love. She liked Jan: it still hurt her to remember what risks she had imposed on him in Jacqueline's cause. He could have lost his life. There was a debt that remained unpaid. It rankled that she had been unable to persuade Margarethe to leave the *béguinage* and return. Bona had felt surprised by the girl, impressed by her spirit and by her arguments. Bona had failed where she had not expected to fail.

Suppose she were to try again. The challenge filled her with a kind of fierceness which her blindness quickened rather than subdued. She would go to Louvain: why should a blind person not ride? It was as if dangers were less now that she could no longer see them. And if there were dangers, what of them? "It's different for you," Margarethe had said. Bona remembered the girl's words clearly. "You have wealth, position, influence. Your body is safe wherever you go because you're powerful enough to make it so." She would show her it was not true; that it was no different for her, or for anyone. This time the girl would not be able to answer.

When the boy returned with her food she told him. He was terrified. Bona grew angry. He submitted. And later he made love to her as if it were the last time. Bona imagined the beauty of his body caught in the labyrinth of mirrors, and she thought she had never made such love.

The next morning two figures rode out of the city gate and across the polderlands as a gale tore at their clothing. They were a strange pair—a youth whose skin was black as night, and a woman for whom the whole world was black as night.

It was a gale from the sea. The mill sails were furled tight; farmers threw ropes over the straw stacks and secured their shutters with iron bars. Fishermen moved along the exposed dikes bent at the same angle as the flailing trees, and from a mile distant you could hear the anger of the waves. From horizon to horizon the air was a glowering purple even at noon, as if the wind were blowing out the flames of the sun. There were dark prophecies in the villages, and screams of terror in the night as trees began to fall. People huddled in their houses for the winds to abate, but day after day the gale drew breath only to strike again more ferociously than before. Prayers were blown away unheard.

In Bruges there were stories told. A man who had traveled from the port of Sluis spoke of waves tearing away the jetty and hurling it into the town like flotsam. In the harbor no one knew whose boat was whose since they lay crushed all together against the quay. He explained how one day, in a moment of luminous light during a lull in the storm, he had caught sight of the distant dunes which marked the islands of Zeeland far across the estuary; but the next morning during another break in the storm he could see only the white tumble of water.

Michault de Caron looked anxiously at Jan from across the fireplace in the Fallen Angel, and from the painter's expression he knew they shared the same thought. No one spoke for a while.

They all understood. Elsewhere, whenever the sea blew angry, people turned their backs and went on with their lives. But here in the Low Countries it brought fear: from childhood everyone knew that their land had been fought from the sea, and it was a fight that the sea could always win—just as years ago, it was said, there was land from here to England until the fury of the north wind drove the waves like a giant wedge between the two nations. Fishermen told tales of church bells sounding beneath the water on silent evenings, and of nets that dragged up bones from sunken graveyards. The hunger of the sea was God's sword of punishment, priests said, just as it had swallowed up the sons and daughters of Cain. People sneered at the priests, yet when the winds blew they still lived in terror of the sea.

It was a measure of the mood in the Fallen Angel that evening that no one chose to joke about Godscalc Oom and the likelihood that he would survive a flood as successfully as any whale. Nor did anyone suggest that Abbot Eustache would be building an ark and filling it with his offspring two by two.

A week passed. Anxious eyes from the ramparts looked out thankfully each morning to see the broad polderlands still raised above the surface of the swollen waterways, and the scattered farms standing on their low hillocks among the debris of trees and broken fences. Then, on the eighth morning, people awoke to an unfamiliar silence. They gathered in the streets and the marketplace in bewildered relief, and from the ramparts a band of blue lay stretched across the northern horizon.

It was the following day that messengers arrived from Antwerp and Breda. Much of Zeeland, they said, had vanished—dunes swept away, fields and villages sucked into the sea, fragments of houses washed up amid the froth of the shore.

Jan felt as cold as ice.

The news of the flooding of Zeeland reached the duke in the courtyard of his palace in Lille. He was dressed for hunting, a feathered cap of ermine at a jaunty angle on his head, leather gloves reaching to his elbow, on one of which dangled a golden chain to which the court falconer was about to attach the duke's favorite saker falcon with its bell and ducal arms around its neck. The bird was hooded on the falconer's wrist, its head flicking from side to side as if aware that a partridge or a hare would soon be before its eyes. A party of courtiers was waiting nearby in their velvet and furs, and among them a number of young ladies in scarlet or blue surcoats with embroidered collars. The duchess Isabella was not among them.

It was Jehan Lefèvre who brought the news. The duke saw the tall elegant figure of the herald cross the courtyard toward him and bow. The message was brief. The duke's reaction was instantaneous: he made an agile leap from his horse, discarded his gloves impatiently on the cobbles, and without a glance at the assembled company, hastened into the palace with Lefèvre close behind him. The hunting party waited all morning, but their lord never returned.

No servants were admitted to the ducal antechamber while the herald solemnly recounted all that he knew. The duke's long face wore an expression of tension all the time Lefèvre spoke, and when the herald had finished only a few curt words passed from Philip's lips.

"And the duchess Jacqueline—where is she?"

Lefèvre could not help noticing that the duke addressed her by her former title. The herald could only shake his head.

"I do not know, my lord," he answered. The duke's response made him start.

"Why do you not know?" he shouted, and his fist on the long table rattled the golden cups and candlesticks which decorated the length of it.

The herald recoiled in a dignified cringe, but the duke was no longer paying attention to him. He had risen swiftly to his feet and seized the bell cord by the huge carved fireplace. A servant hurried in even before the sound of the bell had died away.

"Send for the lord of Luxembourg instantly," the duke ordered.

The servant was hastening for the door even as he bowed. The duke turned to Lefèvre as the door closed, and his manner was suddenly gentle.

"Jehan, if Jacqueline is safe, we must bring her here." Then he added, more to himself than to Lefèvre, "I forgive her everything. I wonder if she will ever forgive me."

The herald was surprised by the change of mood, and by the sadness in the duke's voice. He was aware of Philip's feelings for his rebellious cousin, but had imagined that after the last rebuttal those sentiments would now be dry. Clearly it was not so.

It was the next morning when the duke's captain, Jehan de Luxembourg, was seen riding northward from the city in the company of a party of twenty soldiers.

Few people among his court saw the duke during the days that followed. He summoned no councillors, no secretaries; he dined alone. He passed much time in his library, but the librarian made it known that the lengthy romances normally so beloved by Philip lay open, unread; even the legendary exploits of the duke's forebear, the Flemish knight Gilles de Chin, failed to engage his attention. And in the evenings there were no minstrels, there was no dancing, no flow of wine, no flutter of women around the ducal presence. He slept alone. Visitors to the ducal court, anticipating pleasure that would outshine a sultan, departed wondering what sickness had darkened the sun of Burgundy.

Those who knew the duke only at a distance attributed his mood to a longing for a truce with France; and they were right that the matter was much on his mind. Since the death of the Maid nothing in the war with the French had gone right, and not being a man attracted to lost causes, Philip was now seeking every opportunity to heal the breach with France. It would happen: he was sure.

But those who knew Philip rather better sensed that it was not a political ailment afflicting the duke. It was well known among Philip's closest councillors that even the most disastrous political event never affected his appetite for pleasure, in particular the pleasure of women's company. Indeed, there were a number of lords who owed their high position to no achievement more lofty than ensuring that their wives were in attendance at court while they themselves were conveniently not. What was remarkable at the present time was that there appeared to be no women—neither the duchess nor any other favored lady—whose company Philip either sought or enjoyed. Clearly there was a canker in the heart of Burgundy. The duke was like an alien within his own realm.

Alone, the duke lived among the splendid ghosts of his dream of Burgundy. Around his paneled walls hung tapestries representing the legend of the Golden Fleece, the labors of Hercules, and of himself in armor poised to crush the Grand Turk, or riding at the head of his army toward Jerusalem while the infidels fled as if blinded by God's glory. Everywhere Philip looked his eyes rested on magnificent gifts of gold and jewels, silks and ivories, swords, chalices, goblets, robes, crosses, and reliquaries—offerings from envious princes to the noblest Christian of them all in whose glorious presence they paled. Yet before his eyes rose only unglorious things. He saw his beloved city, Bruges, roused in hatred against him. He saw the Maid, her face proud amid the flames, gasping the name of Jesus before her head dropped. He saw the sad, accusing eyes of Isabella, who had loved him and to whom he had promised the world. And he saw the fierce disdain on the face of Jacqueline, heard her mocking laugh which echoed louder and louder until the winds caught it and spread laughter across the land.

He felt alone with the savagery of his own power.

"Lefèvre."

The herald approached cautiously, hands clasped before him.

"When did the lord of Luxembourg depart?"

"Three days ago, my lord."

"And how long a ride to Zeeland?"

"Three days, my lord."

The duke merely turned toward the window. Lefèvre stood waiting for a long while, then coughed pointedly, and since there was no reaction or movement from the duke, slipped quietly away.

It was an impulse so powerful that Jan had no time to consider the dangers or consequences. He only knew he must go to Zeeland. He told nobody: there was no opportunity for that either. It was scarcely dawn as he left the city by the northeastern gate and took the road in the direction of Antwerp. A few carts passed him laden with market goods, and in the half-light their owners glanced up in curiosity at the lone figure riding by. Before long the bleak polderlands gave way to forest, and ahead of him the palest rays of sunlight began to catch the bronzed leaves, and the damp cobwebs were like a frost of pearls strung between the branches.

Jan did not even know if he would be able to reach Zeeland. But he would ride hard, and he was determined he would be within sight of Goes by midday tomorrow. He was breaking the duke's command, but this mattered little to him. At least the cordon of soldiers around the approaches to Zeeland were unlikely to be still there after the gales and the floods; and if by chance the causeway was still guarded, then he would bribe them or talk his way through.

But all the time a dread weighed heavily within him—that as the forests gave way to marshland he would see before him only driftwood and the sea, as if Jacqueline had never existed. Now, as he rode, the image of her seemed to haunt the path ahead, always moving a little distance before him, glancing at him, then turning away. Dark hair. Dark eyes. Sunlight on white shoulders. The scent of roses. Laughter. A hand outstretched. Jan felt bewildered by the power of Jacqueline: what had seemed all past—melted away—returned with such pain at the thought of what he might find. And yet, along with the pain there was almost a hope in him that he would be confronted by nothing at all, that it would all have ended, the past be unanchored to float away forever. Then tomorrow could begin without that dark, enchanting shadow of what might have been.

Jan rode all day. He changed horses at Antwerp and continued northward into the evening for a further hour. Then exhaustion overtook him and he gratefully made for a low wooden farmhouse by the edge of a creek where a dog, chained to a boat drawn up among the reeds, barked frantically at his approach. The farmer appeared at the sound, bearing a long stave before him suspiciously. Jan dismounted and spread his open palms before the man as he bowed. The farmer still looked at him uneasily, but grunted something Jan did not understand and beckoned him inside. A thin light of candles revealed a single room with a few plain chairs, a small table, and a wall lined with hoes, spades, rakes, reed scythes, saws, interspersed with skeins of nets and fishing tackle. A large pot steamed on an open fire.

Jan laid a purse of coins on the table. The man stared at it before weighing it in his hand; then he did the same with the other hand as if mistrustful of the first. Finally he loosened the cord and carefully tipped the contents onto the table and moved a candle closer. Rough fingers felt the coins and turned them over several times. Then he scooped the coins into one hand and replaced them in the purse.

"Are you a soldier?" he asked gruffly. His accent was throaty and thick.

Jan shook his head.

"Only a traveler," he answered.

The farmer looked relieved and pocketed the purse.

"And what do you want?"

Jan explained that he had hoped for food for himself and his horse, and straw to sleep on. The man gazed at him for a while without replying, and for a moment Jan wondered if the farmer was contemplating killing him for his clothes and his horse, and the probability of further coins. He unobtrusively moved his own hand to within reach of his dagger, and wished he had chosen to stay at the tavern in Antwerp instead of risking his life in this godforsaken swamp. Insects whined and swooped in and out of the candlelight as the two men assessed one another in silence.

Then the farmer seemed to make up his mind, and nodded. Jan was suddenly aware that there was cold sweat on his own brow. He watched as the man crossed the room, and Jan saw him reach for a large pitcher on a shelf, and two wooden beakers which stood close by. Without a word he beckoned Jan to follow him outside where a further table and a long bench were set beside the wall. He motioned Jan to sit, and poured out beer into the two beakers. Having done so, he seated himself heavily. Beyond them the last of the light stretched across an unbroken wilderness of marsh and reeds, and the only sound was the squawk of unseen waterfowl.

"If you had been a soldier I would have killed you," the man said without looking at Jan, his hands clasped around the beaker in front of him.

Jan's suspicions had not been wrong. Suddenly the farmer gave a sharp whistle. The dog stirred, and after a few seconds there were further sounds of movement somewhere behind the house. Jan waited, a little apprehensively; then the figure of another man appeared. Even in the dusk Jan could see that he was scarcely more than a boy.

"My son," the farmer said.

Jan noticed that the boy was hobbling; and as the figure drew closer he realized that one leg ended in a wooden stump. The boy nodded to his father before staring uneasily at Jan. There was silence for a moment before the boy turned and hobbled into the house. Sounds of a pot being stirred were followed by a dull thud of wooden bowls being laid on the table.

"The soldiers did that."

The farmer sipped his beer, still not looking at Jan. There was another pause. The marsh was almost in darkness, and only the faintest light from the window rested on the man's face.

"They killed my wife, my father, and my brother," he went on. "Now there's just the two of us—my son and I."

Jan felt a stab of horror.

They sat in the cool autumn evening until the light had drained away. Nothing further was said, and only the invisible creatures of the reeds interrupted the silence. But later when the two men seated themselves at the table by the fire and began to eat their bread and soup the farmer began to talk, briefly at first, then in a lonely man's intensity and pain. The boy made himself busy elsewhere—Jan could hear him tending to his horse, and there were scraping sounds of a rake on stones.

They had always been happy here, his family, he said. Trouble had always passed them by in this remote place. Even in the wars between the duke of Burgundy and the duchess Jacqueline they were hardly aware of the sieges and the battles. The duchess had been here once not so long ago, the farmer explained: by boat from Zeeland. And he pointed in the direction of the marsh. A most gracious lady, he assured Jan, and dressed almost like a peasant. She had never said why she came, but when she left she gave his father a golden cross. The farmer rose and went over to the far side of the room: Jan could hear the sound of a box being opened; then the man returned holding the cross in the palm of his hand. Jan took it and held it to the candle. It was set within an enamel plaque, all blue except that at the base of the plaque was a band of gold, and as Jan turned it in the light he saw that the gold was engraved with the image of a bird, a sword in its beak. Jacqueline's insignia.

He wondered why she had made so fine a gift to a man she had met only once. Then he remembered how Jacqueline had told him of her visits to all the islands, however remote, and how she had godchildren in every village in Zeeland.

He longed to ask the farmer if he knew what had happened to Jacqueline. But as he replaced the golden cross he began to talk of the soldiers, and his voice quavered as he spoke. They were the duke's men, he said. They were guarding Zeeland, they told him. A boat had been seen leaving from the islands. Why? No one was allowed to go there. His father had shaken his head: it was no boat of his, he had assured them. They killed him. Then his brother had come to their father's rescue. They were laughing, jeering, even as they hacked him with their swords. And then . . . the farmer broke down in tears; his son . . . and his own wife. He would not tell Jan what they did to his wife. They knocked him unconscious when he tried to save her.

Jan had his arms around the man and clasped him close.

Little sleep came to Jan that night. The horror of the farmer's story kept turning within him like a knife. And he thought of Margarethe pulled off her horse, her clothes torn from her. And Bona blinded. Jan wished that every soldier who had entered Bruges on that afternoon of the duke's return had been murdered, and the duke with them. There was a powerless longing in him to rid the land of all soldiers and all rulers. This, he thought as he turned sleeplessly on his bed of straw, was the reality of Philip's glorious dukedom, the new Jerusalem which he—the duke's court painter—was supposed to color with the sparkle of God's radiance as if it were heaven on earth. This slaughterhouse. This river of blood on which Philip's vanity sailed beneath the banners of chivalry, honor, noble deeds, and a love of Christ. What a carnival of deceit, and was he not himself one of the masked figures in the parade?

Jan's anger melted into a sleep that seemed only a minute. When he opened his eyes a purple dawn hung over the room like a veil. The farmer was already about, and there was bread and cheese on the table. Jan could hear the sound of cows, and presently the boy hobbled in with a small churn of warm milk, which he set down before them.

"So where are you bound?" the farmer asked.

Jan explained that he was heading for Goes, fearful even as he said it that the farmer would shake his head. But he said nothing. His knife cut another hunk of cheese and he dipped his bread into the milk, stuffing both into his mouth. The two men ate in silence for a while. Then the farmer rose to his feet and led Jan outside. He gazed down at the creek, now scarcely more than mud.

"Go quickly, while the tide is low," he said. "The causeway was washed away." Then, with what was almost a smile, he added, "And so were the soldiers."

Jan embraced him, and as he left pressed a further handful of coins into the man's hand. The farmer nodded. There was no need for thanks. By the time Jan had mounted and turned his horse onto the path that skirted the wood along the fringe of the marsh, he had gone.

Before long he was on a familiar road. The sun rose behind him, and the gentle autumn morning made it hard to imagine the ferocity of the storm that had lashed this land so short a time before; though every now and then he came to a swath of woodland that had been cut like corn, the trees snapped jagged at the base, their bronze leaves already limp, branches tangled across the track. His horse picked its way carefully through the debris. As if they were following the long strip of sky above, a trail of migrating storks passed overhead, their formation rippling and re-forming like patterns in water. Soon, Jan knew, the forest would become thin and stunted, tree trunks ragged with lichen, branches thrust forward as if hurrying from the wind. And then suddenly there would be the end of the land. Already he could smell the marsh. What, he wondered, would he find of the long raised dike which had carried him across that vast abandoned bed of the sea?

He scarcely recognized the place. Instead of the careful patchwork of polders stitched by narrow channels and reed banks, now there seemed nothing between Jan and the horizon except a glistening surface of gray slime. The detritus of the sea. A giant hand might have smoothed everything away—the labor of ten, thirty, a hundred years, dissolved as though it had never been. Jan reined his horse. There was not a boat, a fence, a ditch, not even a tussock of grass which might suggest that a man had ever been here.

Somewhere out there were the lands of the sea. Or was there only the sea?

He led his horse slowly along the edge of the marsh, searching for signs of the old causeway. The farmer had hinted that it was possible to find a way across. "Go quickly, while the tide is low," he had said. So he must have believed there was something out there beyond the mist and the gray desert of mud. But perhaps he did not know. Jan would have taken a boat had there been a boat, and had there been a channel; but there was neither. He tried to remember where the causeway had once been, but all the familiar landmarks had been swept away; it was impossible to recognize the place.

At that moment the shadow of a cloud began to roll across the marsh from the north: it passed before him like a dark cloak, and as it did so for just a second or two it picked out a long curving thread that seemed to lie across the surface of the mud. Jan fixed his eyes on it as the cloud slid away and the sun returned. With an effort he could still see it, but at first he could not grasp what it was that he saw. Then he realized: a line of low stakes marked out a course—running straight ahead for some distance, before turning sharply to the left and vanishing into the mist. Jan remembered that was exactly the shape of the causeway. Someone must have been there— someone from Zeeland had felt his way along the foundations of the invisible causeway, probing the mud for solid ground beneath, driving in stakes as he went—day after day at each low tide, gradually extending a lifeline to the mainland.

Jan felt afraid. He must try. If only there were someone, some living soul, in that wilderness, some footprint even. But there was nothing. Only a line of stakes and a horizon of low tide. Jan guided his horse through the fringe of sedge and reed, and gradually coaxed the unwilling beast to take steps gingerly into the cloying ooze. The first stake was perhaps a hundred paces from the shore.

He nearly turned back. Jan was aware that probably nothing he had ever done was more foolhardy than this. Supposing the stakes marked not the former causeway but a channel, where as the tide rose boats could safely cross without the danger of currents and hidden mudbanks. And supposing, when he was a mile or so from shore, the tide should begin to advance. He had not even inquired from the farmer at what hour the tide would turn. Supposing his horse should slip, break a leg, drown—a mile from shore! No one would ever know, except the farmer. He would just have disappeared.

The horse stumbled two or three times, but on the third occasion, as Jan locked his knees onto the creature's flank to steady himself, he could feel to his relief the vibration of the horse's hooves slithering on stone. The beast seemed to understand, and placed its feet carefully into the mud, feeling for solid ground beneath. After a while horse and rider fell into a steady rhythm, and Jan could feel the tension gradually drain from him. Progress was slow—stake after stake after stake— the emptiness expanding around him, and always the squelch and sucking of the mud. It was as if he were the only man alive, alone above a sunken world. Jan kept an anxious eye on that smooth expanse of gray for the first sight of the advancing tide. But there was only the marsh.

From the angle of the sun it must have been close to midday when the mist began to disperse. The horizon slid further and further from him, broadening the emptiness of gray until it seemed that it could never end.

Suddenly Jan could see it. Like an isolated ship rose the walls and castle of Goes. Jacqueline's last bastion. It had survived the storm. Relief and anxiety flowed through him. Where was she? And why had he come? His fourth journey here, and his last—he knew that. Maybe he would not even see her: he would ask at the gate, be told she was safe, and return the way he had come. There was nothing to be said: it was all in the past. Now he could make out the familiar contours of the town, embraced by the sea; except that the pine trees and the billowing dunes which had shrouded the place had vanished. The bare marsh licked the very walls; the line of stakes ran right up to the stone gate of the town. Even as he looked about him Jan could see the first silent ripples of the incoming tide, slithering across the mud. He knew the speed of these tides. Within half an hour he would have been caught. He felt a thrill of exhilaration as he realized that he had escaped the sea by a matter of minutes. Only a dozen or so stakes lay between him and safety, and Jan deliberately slowed his horse in order to savor the narrowness of danger averted. Around him the marsh was already water as far as he could see, and behind him the long line of stakes vanished toward the low fringe of land from where he had come. He imagined himself just one mile back from here, standing as he stood now, but waiting for death.

The watchman let him through. There was no expression on his face, and within the walls of the town a stillness lay over the streets, so unlike the bustle of midday Jan remembered. The scrape of his horse's hooves echoed over empty cobbles. A few faces peered from windows and doorways, but no one spoke. Before him rose the castle—small dark windows like closed eyes under the brow of the battlements.

He heard the bell jangle and fade away. After a few moments there was a clank of bolts and chains, and the castle gate swung open but only wide enough for a face to appear, and below it a hand brandishing a sword. Jan was taken aback. All was as silent as a prison. The guard recognized him, but even so seemed of two minds about permitting him to enter. Jan waited, one hand on the bridle of his horse, the other poised near the hilt of his dagger. He knew something was wrong. The man's face looked drawn and grave.

"The duchess Jacqueline," Jan said. "A messenger from Bruges," he added, realizing as he said so that it was unnecessary.

The guard answered not a word, but hesitantly allowed him to lead his horse into the courtyard, making it clear with a look that he was to stay where he was. A second guard appeared; the two men exchanged glances, then with a blank stare at the visitor the second man hurried away and disappeared into the castle. Jan waited. Still not a word was said. He glanced about him at the pitted walls and the overbearing grimness of the place. Jan froze his mind from imagining what he might hear.

Finally, it was not the familiar page in red who emerged from the castle, but the old man whom Jan recognized as the English valet he had seen with Jacqueline, and on the harbor that night with the English emissary. The man nodded at the guard to take Jan's horse, then nodded again for Jan to accompany him into the castle. He followed the old man slowly into the long hallway. There were the shields with the emblem of the black raven, the ranks of closed doors, the cold walls dimly patterned with light from narrow windows. Where was the man leading him? Where was she?

The old man opened the doors of the great hall, and Jan followed him. There was no fire. A chill wrapped itself around Jan as he entered. She was not there. The hall was empty. The valet closed the door and turned to face him.

"She's dead."

Two words. Only two words. Jan's hands were covering his face.

Jacqueline was dead.

The emptiness of the room seemed like the emptiness of his heart. Jan did not know at that moment what had flown from him, but he knew that it had taken on its wings all color and all joy. What remained was sunless, hollow, barren. Only shrunken and sour things inhabited the earth, and the world was drab. He gazed about him—at the portraits, the crests, the table, candlesticks, fireplace—all were Jacqueline's, where he had known her and loved her, and Jacqueline was nowhere. It felt to Jan like the day after his own death, and he watching with dead eyes.

The old man's voice cut into the silence.

"She was the finest lady I ever knew . . . and there was no man ever like her."

Jan nodded. The valet's face was lifeless with sorrow. He too had loved her, Jan knew; had left his country for her, his family perhaps; everything. He placed his hand on the old man's shoulder.

"Tell me, if you will."

There was silence for a few moments. Then the old valet led Jan slowly from the room and out into the long hallway toward the staircase.

"I'll tell you what I know."

They climbed the stairs, saying nothing. After a while the stone corridor led toward a narrow window high in the castle, and when they reached it the old man stopped. Before them lay the huddled town, and the tiny harbor all but enclosed by houses. Jan could see no one. Beyond stretched the long calm shore, the sea almost asleep, barely stirring on the sand.

Then Jan noticed. Where the dunes used to rise in tall plumes flecked with green tussocks there was now only a smoothed curve of sand cut here and there with ravines in which rivulets of tide were being sucked out of sight. Jan's eyes moved inland, and instead of fields and dikes and tiny villages set among the reeds he saw . . . nothing. Only water. To the farthest distance there was only the gentle slither of the tide as it crept in along a thousand veins of naked marsh. It was as if it had always been so, and no man had ever trodden or tilled there.

"It was out there," the valet said softly, his finger pointing. "She died out there."

Of course. It would have had to be like that, Jan thought. Jacqueline of the lands of the sea. Her last possessions robbed by the sea. There could have been no other death.

He looked at the old man, whose eyes were still fixed on that waste of sand and water as if in a trance. Finally he drew a deep breath and turned away from the window.

"We all saw her go. No one tried to stop her. We knew she would never come back."

After a while—haltingly—he began to explain, while Jan listened without saying a word. It had been at the height of the storm. Beyond the walls of the town you could not tell which was wind and which was sea: the air was full of water. There was no sky. Day after day. The castle was like a rock amid the fury of the ocean. People huddled in terror: they whispered that it was the end of the world. But Jacqueline was calm. She gave comfort; she distributed bread, water, clothing. She smiled; held the frightened in her arms; scarcely slept. But then no one slept. In the castle there was hardly space on the floor between those who had fled from their torn houses. Jacqueline had passed to and fro between them, dressed as one of them. Then, one morning, she appeared in a long black cloak and a hood over her head. She greeted all those clustered in the hallway and the courtyard as usual. Her chamberlain was following her with an anxious look. Suddenly she turned to him and spoke just two words: "Distribute everything." He put out his arm to stop her, but she brushed it away and strode briskly to the stable, where she saddled her black mare and leapt astride it while the stableboys stood back in helpless alarm.

"Then she was gone. She never looked back. From the town walls you could barely see for the spray and the wind. She disappeared toward the dunes. . . ."

The old valet was staring past Jan at the peaceful ocean.

"The next morning the wind had dropped, and there were no dunes."

He turned toward Jan, his face weary.

"That was the longest of days," he added. "There was nothing to wait for, but we all waited." Then, as they retraced their steps quietly toward the hallway, he glanced again at Jan. "All her life was a storm," he said. "And she ended it that way."

It was over. There was nothing left to be done. Jan was swamped by a sense of grief and at the same time of liberation: one life had ended, and now another could begin. But it would always be clouded by the memory of Jacqueline: the raven's wings would filter the sunlight. The death of someone loved, he knew, takes with it part of everyone's life in order that the rest may flourish.

He wanted to leave. From the town gateway Jan watched the tide beginning to ebb, the ribbed current sliding across the hidden marsh toward the sun. It would be dusk before the stakes marking the drowned causeway would rise clearly above the water. It was too late to return to the mainland tonight.

There was perhaps an hour of daylight remaining. It had always been evenings when this place cast its spell around him, and there would never be another evening for him here. He knew there was one final journey he wanted to make. Jan returned to the castle and hurriedly saddled his horse—the same stable from which Jacqueline had departed to her death. He rode out in the direction she must have taken—through the city gate, along the fringe of the marsh, then up onto the scoured dunes white with sea salt where the storm had churned and carved the sand, smoothing its features away.

He rode on. Of course she was not here. Once, a dark

shape in the distance caught Jan's breath, and he urged his horse faster: it was a tree stump beached on the sand. Heaven knows where her remains drifted now, sucked deep somewhere under that peaceful ocean: who could have imagined so placid a sea whipped to such anger? No, of course she was not here: and yet this was the last place that saw her. It was like returning—but to her grave. Jan wheeled his horse and looked back to the distant town; then he gazed at the emptiness all around him. This was where they had loved. This was where she had died.

Now it was all over.

He left at first light. Strapped behind him on the saddle was a package which her valet had pressed into his hands the evening before.

"She would have wanted you to have this," he had said quietly.

Jan knew it was his portrait of her.

The marsh glimmered gray, and flocks of marsh birds streaked low in and out of the thin carpet of mist, their cries rippling as they passed. There was no other sound except the suck of the mud against hooves and the gentle flurry of the wind. Jan pulled his hood over his ears against the chill of the morning, and drifted into his own thoughts. It was like riding between one life and the next—a life that had ended and another that was uncharted like the marsh around him. He realized he had no idea what it would bring, what he would do. He should go somewhere new, let that new life be born where the sun might shine on it; go somewhere alone, with his skills, his courage, his luck. He would trust to those. There had been enough death, enough pain. Italy? France? The world around him seemed tired: there was no vigor in it. He was still young; he could forget all this. Be reborn. Rekindled.

Bruges was dying. Why did he feel this so certainly? Jan thought of his friends. Hugo—gone. Bona—blind. Godscalc—old. De Leeuw—resigned. Michault—disillusioned. Joos—nearing death. And Margarethe; how far and long ago were those bright days of hope and laughter. And the duke; so tarnished a prince, so monstrous a hero, his new Jerusalem a land of graves.

He must leave.

Jan did not realize, in his dark musings, that the land he was approaching was crowded with figures. Soldiers. He gave a start, then tugged the hood lower across his face. They were waiting, watching him approach. With a shock Jan recognized the captain in his scarlet surcoat and long sword buckled at his side. He knew that face well: Jehan de Luxembourg. For a moment he wondered if they were waiting for him on the orders of the duke; waiting to take him. There was nothing he could do. In any case, what did it matter? Jacqueline was dead.

Jan rode toward them as nonchalantly as he could, deliberately slowing the pace of his horse. He watched them out of the corner of his eye.

"What are you?" It was Luxembourg's voice.

"A merchant," Jan replied gruffly. "From Goes."

"Is it safe?"

Jan just nodded, and rode on. No one had recognized him, and no one cared. They had been watching him only to make sure that the marsh could be crossed. Once he had passed them Jan glanced back cautiously and saw the long line of soldiers moving slowly across the low tide led by their captain. Only after he had ridden out of sight, and the forest closed around him, did Jan understand. The duke must have sent them. They had come to fetch Jacqueline.

Again, and for the last time, Jacqueline had thwarted the duke. Jan found himself laughing aloud. He felt proud, and sad, and free.

He took his time returning. The woods were sweet with autumn, the ground damp with golden leaves. His dark mood had lifted, and his spirit felt released. Grief had bred euphoria: there seemed nowhere he could not go, nothing he could not do. Before him rose bright images of journeys he would make, works he would achieve, women he would desire. The world was an adventure, just as it used to be: all was refreshed, renewed, fecund.

Bruges welcomed him with its spires polished by the sun.

It draped its beauty before him in its dark canals. He was home.

Jan stood for a while in the empty studio. The altarpiece had gone; there was nothing of his past around him. He poured himself a goblet of wine and gazed about him, light-headed. Then, without knowing quite why, he unfolded two easels and set them side by side in the center of the room. From the cupboard where he had thrust it angrily before departing for Zeeland he drew out the unfinished portrait of the duke and rested it on one of the easels. This done, he unpacked the portrait of Jacqueline and placed it on the easel next to it. Jan's eyes moved from one to the other. Here was a man who loved himself: here was a woman who had destroyed herself. A man who loved her—and a woman who hated him. Yet they were a match. They belonged together.

He looked at the portrait of Jacqueline. That proud, noble face poised between triumph and despair. The greatest of women. Jan could still hear her voice: "I wish I were not who I am." And as he heard it the pain returned. He crossed the room, took out a small key, and retrieved the ring and locket she had given him. He slipped the ring on his finger and twisted it until he could see the two wings entwine. Then he looked down at the locket in the palm of his hand and turned it over, opening the hidden compartment with his thumbnail.

The coil of black hair shone just as when she had cut it for him on that evening in the dunes. Jan gazed at it in sadness, touched the hair with his fingers, and closed the lid. Again he looked at the beautiful proud face. Oh, Jacqueline—what a loss! She was not for him; she was not for Philip. She was not even for herself: she had preferred to die. Such waste!

And Philip. The shrewd, vain face. The robes of the Golden Fleece. The jewels. The power. The dreams. Now Jan knew why he could never finish it. The duke had wanted a portrait of the "real man." But he had not caught the real man. Philip stood before him as an ideal, not a man of flesh and blood. And Jan had wanted to believe him. But the real man was the Philip who had loved Jacqueline—and who had destroyed Jacqueline.

It was as if Jan watched himself do it. He would perform Jacqueline one final service. He drew his dagger—the dagger that had killed the duke's soldiers, that had cut the lock of Jacqueline's hair. He saw himself raise the blade before him and slash the duke's portrait in one stroke.

Chapter ♦ Thirteen

Half awake, he felt uncertain if he had really done such a thing.

The house was silent in the early morning, and Jan wrapped a coat around himself and made his way to the studio, apprehensive of what he might find. As he opened the door, for a moment he expected to see nothing at all—an empty room. The studio was cold. A mean light of dawn invaded the bareness. But there it was: everything just as he had left it the previous evening—the two easels, two portraits, the long diagonal wound across the figure of the duke which had cut deep into the panel, tearing at the paint on either side.

To Jan's surprise he felt no regret, only relief. He lifted the damaged panel from the easel and stood it against the wall, noticing that his dagger had cut right through the insignia of the Golden Fleece across the duke's chest. Then he crossed the room, and from the tall cupboard reached for the drawing he had done of the Maid. Jan propped it where the duke's portrait had been, and stood staring at the two easels.

So they were both of them dead—the Maid and Jacqueline: the two women who had held keys to the secret of the duke, one to his fortunes and the other to his heart. No, Philip had not exactly killed either of them—not directly, with the knife. Both had died in their own chosen way, in spite of what the duke intended, and in doing so they had both defeated him. In Philip's bright vision of Burgundy it would have been quite otherwise—in that new Jerusalem which he, Jan, had been unable to depict and was now slashed beyond repair. But if that vision had come true after all, how very different the duke's world might have been. Jacqueline would now be duchess of Burgundy, breeding future dukes, princesses, kings even—

who knows? The most feared, most adored woman in Europe. What a couple they would have made: their jewels and their power would have dazzled the world, and the sun anointed their brows.

And Joan? There lay a deeper secret. Her voices. Her prophecies. Where might she have been in that golden world of Philip's dreams? He could have been her savior. She could have delivered him the love of all France. Joan's voices and Philip's visions might have met in triumphant unison.

What a failure lay before Jan's eyes.

And what should he do?

Should he leave Bruges—leave Burgundy altogether—wipe it from his life? Begin again somewhere far out of reach of Philip's hand of death?

It was midmorning. Jan had dressed and eaten, and for several hours had imagined he was preparing himself for the decision he had to make. But each preparation had led only to a further preparation: he had readjusted his dress, walked in the garden, studied the ripples in the canal, contemplated many items of furniture, and on more than one occasion had opened the door of his house with a view to seeking advice from De Leeuw, or from Bona, Michault de Caron, or Arnolfini. Then he had closed the door unable to decide whom he should ask first. And now, once again, Jan found himself upstairs in the studio, hoping that further contemplation of the damaged portrait would spur his mind to that desired state of certainty.

Instead, quite another question was foremost in Jan's mind as he gazed at the painting: why had he persuaded himself to destroy so much fine craftsmanship? He became quite indignant as he recollected the care and skill with which he had rendered those jewels, silks and velvets, the stone columns, the brilliant light, the vista unfurling into a blue haze. All spoiled because . . . well, because he had allowed himself to be more than he was trained to be. He was—he tried to remind himself—a painter, not a judge. Jan thought of Michault de Caron, most skillful of poets: would Michault ever have completed a verse had he first weighed the justice of every line? Would anyone ever do anything—except be a martyr or a hermit? Then Jan's eyes moved to the portrait of Jacqueline, and he shook his head. No! He could not have painted Jacqueline's portrait if only his skills had been in play. Jan looked at that proud, painted face. He had painted the truth—about her, and about himself face to face with her. He had painted what lay within. And after all, was this not why he was First Painter to the duke of Burgundy? Had Philip himself not asked him for a portrait of the "real man"?

He had destroyed the picture because he had not found the "real man."

Jan knew then that he must confront the duke with his own failure. He no longer had to prepare himself for the great decision. The decision was made. He would stay.

While he was still contemplating the wreckage of the portrait Jan heard sounds below. Women's voices—his housekeeper and someone else. He only half paid attention. Then there were footsteps on the stairs, and the door opened. Standing there was Margarethe.

In those first few seconds Jan did not know if he was looking at a stranger or a lover. Neither spoke. She quietly closed the door behind her and stood gazing at him without shyness, almost boldly. For Jan it was like searching for familiar landmarks in a forgotten place: he did not know where he was or where he should go. Then he saw her lower her eyes, and in her face he could feel the fear of being turned away. He noticed she was wearing the crimson dress he had always admired, and the necklace he had given her. The long flaxen hair was pinned back. His eyes lingered on the curve of her shoulders.

After so long, there she was. Waiting. Older. Lovelier, he realized. But the same Margarethe—with whom everything had once seemed possible, before . . . and Jan's eyes instinctively moved for a moment to the portrait of Jacqueline. Margarethe's eyes followed his glance. How could he respond to her after the storm that was Jacqueline? In that instant he wondered if he might be cruel, and watch Margarethe go. He did not even know if he wanted her. But . . . and he looked at that young, hurt face: she wanted *him*, and would he have had the courage to come back if he were in her place? Suddenly he could not bear the thought of her going.

Jan held out his hands toward her. She took them, and the absence between them seemed to shrink away as he touched her. They had both of them been away, he realized: far away. They had journeyed to the farthest extremes of their own natures. Was it possible, now, that they could return and meet, knowing where those far boundaries lay? Jan found himself smiling, and he noticed her lips part as she gazed at him.

"Are you sure?" she said at last, very quietly.

Jan took her in his arms. He had forgotten the smell of her skin and the color of her hair.

"If there's no one else," she whispered on his shoulder. A note of anxiety had crept into her voice.

"No one!"

Jan took her face in his hands, tilting it back to look down at her.

"I'd forgotten," he said.

"Me?"

She looked sad.

"No! I'd forgotten how much I'd been waiting for you."

There was a look of wonder in her face as he said that. The green eyes wide, searching. The mouth. He kissed her, and her body moved as he ran his hands down her.

"Let me stay, now," she said. "I belong here."

"Are *you* sure?"

She nodded vigorously.

"How do you know?" he asked.

She looked startled for a second, as if fearful that he might not believe her.

"I'll try to tell you."

For a moment she said nothing, and Jan saw her eyes turn to the two easels, the drawing of the Maid and the portrait of Jacqueline.

"They're both dead, aren't they?"

Jan wondered why she had said that, and how she knew who they were.

"And Bona's blind," she added.

Jan looked surprised.

"Tell me what happened to bring you back," he said.

There was a knowingness about her which Jan did not recognize. The fragility was still there—and the little starts of fear. But a hardening had taken place, and as she talked she seemed to bear the pain of the last year and more almost lightly. Listening to her now, Jan could see that she had been a child when he first met her, a girl when they became lovers, and now she was a woman.

She told him how Bona had visited her—twice. The first time, Margarethe had sent her away. But after Bona had gone it was as if things began to melt within her. It was the first time she had been able to hear the bishop's terrible words without blocking her ears. It was the first time she could see the soldiers stripping her on that riverbank without covering her eyes. Instead, she had remembered Jan's voice, soothing, caressing: and she had remembered his dagger killing for her, and Jan lifting her tenderly onto his horse. But still she could not bear to return. "You must take responsibility for your life," Bona had said. But how could she do that when it was not within her power? She was not like Bona, who could ride above the dangers of the world. For herself the world was too powerful: she would be given no choices, no options.

But then Bona had returned. And she was blind. Margarethe was appalled. That such a thing could happen even to someone like Bona, who had position, influence, money. Blinded. And still she had traveled to the *béguinage*—through the storm, with one boy for a servant. That was courage. Bona had said very little, but had embraced her. Had laughed. How could she have laughed? Why had she come? Margarethe had asked her. For Jan's sake, Bona had answered; not for hers.

It was then that she knew she had to leave the *béguinage*. That very day she had said goodbye to her friends. She could not remain here simply because the world might be too powerful—because it might offer her no options. Already she had lost a mother, an aunt, an uncle; and Bona was blinded. The world was so dangerous, she realized, that there might never be any options, and if she waited for them it would be too late. And she thought of the day when Jan might not be there, and suddenly she could not bear it: she wanted the chance of a life with him most of all—if he still wanted it. Without that there would be nothing; she would grow old alone behind those walls, and die never knowing what might have been hers.

"I was too young, Jan, for all that happened."

He folded his arms around her, and she wept as if for all the time she had been away from him.

Then she drew back and smiled at him through her tears. He placed his fingers against her lips, and she closed her eyes. He pressed her head to his shoulder.

Many thoughts became clear in those few moments. Around him stood his own images of Philip, of Jacqueline, and of the Maid. All of them in their ways had bound threads to his life; all of them were people of great events. But he, Jan, was not one of them: he was a man of small events, a painter of small precise things, precious things. There were no great visions, no battles, no dreams to die for. It was with Margarethe that he could have those small rich things. A place in which to love and be loved. Marriage. Children. A life which had a center to which he would always return whatever the drag of the currents or the tug of the wind.

Margarethe saw him looking at the image of Jacqueline, and felt only a little ashamed to be happy she was dead. The day Bona arrived at the *béguinage* the news had just reached Louvain, she had said. Margarethe had wondered then why she had mentioned it. Now she understood. It was as if Bona had said, "Come back, it's all over."

She was no longer frightened that Jan would disappear into the world. He would come back to her, just as she had come back to him. She looked at that beloved face.

"Make love to me, Jan," she said very softly.

Michault had seen the duke. No one had set eyes on him since the rebellion. There were rumors that he was contrite about the slaughter; others reported that he was angry and blamed the guildsmen. But until now no one had actually claimed to have seen him. It was Michault who told them at the Fallen Angel that the duke was back in Bruges. He was a hated figure, but there was still much curiosity over what he might feel toward the citizens of Bruges, and in particular over how he had taken the death of Jacqueline. Considering Philip's habitual swing between euphoria and fury, it seemed reasonable to expect that any man summoned to his presence at this moment would be putting his head in a lion's mouth.

So at first, when Michault entered the tavern, the company seated around the fire were quick to imagine from the poet's expression that a gale equal to the one which had destroyed Zeeland must have torn the poor man in shreds. A goblet of wine was pressed hastily into his hands, and a chair pulled up for him.

But far from it.

"It's very strange," Michault began to explain, shaking his head in disbelief as he seated himself among them. "But I've never seen the duke so subdued or so gentle."

They all stared at him in disbelief—Jan, Margarethe, De Leeuw, Pontin, Godscalc, Arnolfini. It was a chill, blustery evening, and their faces looked red as they huddled close to the heat of the fire. After a moment Michault leaned forward to warm his hands before the blaze, and went on.

"It's as though the death of Jacqueline has released him from his own anger."

"She haunted him," said Jan in a quiet voice. There was a sharp, knowing look on his face as he turned his head to glance at Margarethe. "Perhaps now she's dead he can love her in peace."

There was puzzlement on several faces. But Michault was looking at Jan thoughtfully. The poet nodded. Then his bony face broke into a cryptic smile.

"Peace!" he said. "Yes, we could all of us do with some peace. I have to tell you, my friends, there'll be little of it for me. You can imagine what the duke wants from me."

This time Jan laughed.

"A poem. A very long poem."

The mood of the company began to warm. There was relief that for once the conversation was not sinking into gloom.

"Worse," replied Michault. "Not just a long poem. A great many long poems—all to the glory of the duchess Jacqueline, whom I never met. Worse still," he went on, amid some laughter, "I am to compose them in conjunction with the chronicler

Monsieur de Monstrelet. He is to compose an official account of events in his own inimitably dull style, while I am to provide the fancy and the verse. God help me."

Arnolfini, without raising his small keen eyes from the fire, made a reflective sound into his wine as if he doubted the Almighty's assistance would be much use.

"Why don't you exercise your fancy on celebrating the return of this beautiful lady?" he said, glancing appreciatively at Margarethe, who was looking radiant. She and Jan were lovers again. They were to be married: there was a happiness in her soul that she had imagined to have gone forever.

"Lovely women," Giovanni went on, warming to his favorite theme, "are the fountain of poetry and the mistress of the imagination: they should be showered with the richest compliments and the rarest jewels."

Margarethe began to feel sated with the Italian's words, yet found herself pleased by the attentions.

"And when, Giovanni," inquired Godscalc Oom heavily, "are we to have the pleasure of meeting the mistress of *your* imagination—if, that is, she can endure the journey from Paris under the weight of all those jewels?"

Only Arnolfini did not smile. Ignoring the rentmaster's gibe, he said, quite casually, "Tomorrow."

As always, Giovanni's quiet revelations abruptly stunned the conversation.

"Tomorrow!" The bearlike hand of Michaut Pontin lowered his flagon of beer, and even the forest of hair on the silversmith's face could not hide his astonishment—which he shared with all around him. "Giovanni, will you never cease to surprise us? And when is the wedding?" He gave a chuckle. "The day after?"

"No," the merchant replied in the same matter-of-fact voice. "A week after."

There followed an uproar of congratulations in the tavern, which Arnolfini received with good-humored ease. So accustomed had they all grown to Giovanni's dedicated evasions of marriage over the years that this nonchalant rush into wedlock seemed inexplicable. At least, it seemed so at first: what became evident after more careful consideration was that Jan had been right, though no one had been quite prepared to believe him until now. Giovanni was in love. He had found his madonna. Whatever were the magical properties the lady possessed, they had clearly enslaved the merchant. He could hardly wait to become a husband.

And the company frequenting the Fallen Angel could hardly wait to see what she was like.

"Jan," he said as he took up his hat to leave, "the wedding portrait: I trust you will have your colors ready. I shall wear maroon velvet trimmed with fur, and a black hat. Giovanna will wear green—the color of spring; with a white veil, of course." Then the sallow face broke into a half-smile. "The color of Giovanna's dog, you know, as well as its habits."

He had thought of everything. They watched him leave, drawing on his fine gloves and adjusting his features to confront the humdrum world and the golden prospect of tomorrow.

Jan and Margarethe departed soon after.

"And when I'm your wife," said Margarethe, laughing, as they stood by the warmth of their own fire, "shall I also be the mistress of your imagination? And will you shower me with the richest compliments and the rarest jewels? I shall expect them."

Jan kissed her, and she curled her body against him.

"I rather fear, my lover," he said, his fingers playing across the skin of her shoulders, "that after the duke sets eyes on what I have made of his portrait we may be selling every jewel we possess."

He unlaced her dress and let it fall.

"But compliments you shall have—in plenty."

The news of the return of the duke passed through the city like a flame, rekindling hatreds and memories that had only just begun to cool. Even though it had been made known, through the burgomaster, that the mutiny and the massacre were regarded by Philip as a regrettable mistake on both sides, those guildsmen who had lost brothers and wives in the slaughter found small comfort in such an admission; no one found it hard to point out that the heads impaled above the nine gates of the city had not been the duke's men but their own innocent kinsmen. Meanwhile, in the shadow of the duke's disfavor, they all sensed that Bruges was in decline. The prohibition on English wool was crippling the weavers: long accustomed to wealth and privilege, they now found themselves struggling to survive, their warehouses empty, their customers drifting elsewhere. They were angry, while those bold enough to defy the ban soon found that merchants were being given a favored welcome by other cities—Sluis and Antwerp—as if Bruges were a victim of the plague. More than this, the storms of the autumn had ripped the dunes from Zeeland and, like a subversive hand, spread an invisible tilth beneath the waterway linking the city with the sea. Strangely, people muttered, all endeavors to dredge the channel mysteriously foundered. Boats had been holed, laborers spirited away to more lucrative employment. In Bruges the looms grew silent, the meetings of the guildsmen noisier and more bitter— not only the cloth weavers but those whose trade depended on their prosperity; painters, glaziers, saddlers, joiners, locksmiths, cutlers, butchers, fishmongers, bakers, and many more. Bruges was being squeezed by the throat, the beautiful city gasping for air.

It seemed unforgivable that in the midst of this discontent the duke could stand in his splendor watching his beloved city crumble—by his own hand, by his own fear of its anger and its power.

"He does not understand," muttered the goldsmith Jan de Leeuw gloomily.

"I think he understands very well," replied the rentmaster Godscalc Oom. "All too well." The two men had halted on the little bridge that spanned the canal behind the street of the Golden Hand. They were watching the silent movement of people in the direction of yet another meeting in the town hall.

"What he understands is that Bruges is only one city," Godscalc went on. He spread out a large hand and with a little finger seemed to remove a tiny speck of dirt from the palm of it. "No bigger than that in his dream of things. The duke may love Bruges, but he would rather crush it than let the weavers rattle their threats at him. In the end, what's Bruges to him compared to Burgundy, to Europe, to Christendom?"

"I believe he's wrong," De Leeuw added, his eyes continuing to follow the small groups of silent men as they passed by. "Because every city is like Bruges. The duke's power is his wealth, and his wealth comes from people like these. If their purses are empty, so will his be. And if their lives are threatened, so will his be."

"You underestimate him. He's cleverer than us all." Godscalc again gazed at his large hand, this time appearing to notice that what it lacked was a small glass of hippocras. "And he learns more quickly. You wait and see."

De Leeuw accompanied the huge figure of the rentmaster in the direction of the Fallen Angel.

"If you're right, Godscalc, he has a lot to learn. He's lost the love of Bruges. He's lost the Maid. He's lost the duchess Jacqueline. By all accounts he's lost the love of Isabella. And his armies lose to the French by the hour."

"That's *why* he will learn."

The tavern was almost empty.

The town hall was almost full.

There was no one who understood why the duke had returned, least of all those who had reluctantly returned with him under the cover of dusk—the duchess Isabella, the first chamberlain, Anthoine de Croy, the ducal herald, Jehan Lefèvre, and Philip's captain, Jehan de Luxembourg. Each of them, and many others, had advised him to remain in the safety of Lille: it seemed an act of dangerous perversity to be entering Bruges so soon after the events of the early autumn. They pointed out that the duke had already adopted an expedient policy of subduing the belligerence of the city by placing its trade at some disadvantage: the cloth weavers, it was felt, would soon bend to his authority once their purses and their bellies grew slacker. He should now wait, his advisers assured him: before long there would no doubt be an obsequious delegation pledging loyalty and pleading for a restoration of trading privileges. All would be his in time.

But the duke was not in that frame of mind. He had turned

abruptly from his first chamberlain, and treated the lord of Luxembourg as though he were not there. Instead, he had taken Isabella by the hand with surprising gentleness and said, as if no voice of opposition had ever been raised, "We shall go to Bruges."

Philip took the precaution of wearing the most modest of clothing, and insisted that others in the party do the same. They must enter the city discreetly. A small guard of soldiers accompanied them. And there were no bugles. On arrival, only the city watchmen recognized the tall bowed figure in a gray hood, and gave him a scared look. They saw the glint of Jehan de Luxembourg's sword, and the hard glare in his eye.

The word soon spread.

It was the duchess Isabella who received the first intimation of why her husband had returned. She had already noted his unaccustomed softness of manner: then, on the morning after their arrival in Bruges, he had appeared unexpectedly in her chamber before she had risen and had seated himself almost shyly on the corner of her bed. She was aware that there was something weighing on his mind.

"Do you think I am to blame for what happened?" he asked in a subdued voice.

He had never once before raised the subject in her company, and she did not know what to say. Besides, she had not been in Bruges when the mutiny took place.

She had looked at him in surprise, saying nothing.

"Isabella"—suddenly his voice sounded like an appeal—"everything that I stand for has brought me back here. I cannot skulk. I will not be frightened in my own city." Then he added, "I love this place. It pains me when people say I cannot even walk the streets in safety."

The duke had hesitated as if there was more he wished to say. But, sensing a certain strangeness between the duchess and himself, he had risen and departed. Later, Isabella was told that Philip had sent for the court poet, Michault de Caron, which mystified her further.

What Isabella could not see—she was not close enough to see—was that the duke was a wounded man. He had never thought that he could bleed. Pain was a small, near thing to be despised: Philip preferred to keep his eyes on the farther, brighter vision. But now it was no longer so. First there had been the death of the Maid—which had hurt and shocked him; furthermore, he had known all along what would be the end of it, but he had not listened; in dismissing her "voices" he had grown deaf to his own voice. Then there had been the rebellion in Bruges. How could it have happened? How could he have understood his own people so little? How could his own vengeance have been so heartless? And then the death of Jacqueline. Perhaps, he realized, it was the horror of that event which had unlocked in him so many tendernesses he had long denied. Jacqueline. There were no failures in Philip's life to equal the helplessness with which he had endeavored to batter her scorn. And now it was too late. He would have to live with that scorn, and her death.

It was on the second morning after his return that Lefèvre reported to Philip how, in the square beyond the ducal palace, a current of men was passing toward the town hall—a constant flow. The herald's manner was uneasy and his eyes kept shifting to the window of that long chamber lined with tapestries and glistening with gold. The duke was in black, as usual, and to Lefèvre he appeared on that morning to have the calm of a priest. He had never seen him so little perturbed, as if there was nothing whatever to fear. He himself longed to be back in Lille: it seemed another world, where he had felt able to partake—albeit surreptitiously—of the life of the city, strolling easily through the streets, sipping the most excellent Beaune at the tavern in the company of friends and such very pretty women. Now he felt imprisoned. There was hatred in the streets.

At midday the duke ate alone. He seemed in no mood to talk, and in no hurry to attend to matters which his secretaries were anxious to bring to his notice. He drank only water—as usual when he was alone—and those who observed him reflected on the contrast between this frugal scene and the splendor of the ducal feasts for which Philip was renowned. There was no one who made the mistake of thinking the duke a modest man, but the stillness and pensiveness which filled that small room carried with it an air of seclusion, as if the glories of Burgundy did not really sit upon the private man. It was hard to believe this figure strode the world. People realized they did not know him at all.

It was Jehan de Luxembourg who roused him.

"My lord, there is trouble. It's as I warned you."

The duke appeared to pay little attention. But after a minute he rose and without any sign of haste followed his captain along the heavy stone corridor leading to the western part of the palace. There, assembled in an antechamber overlooking the cathedral square, stood clusters of people, the duchess among them. Through the anxious whisper of their voices rose the murmur of an invisible crowd.

There was the crash of broken glass. And a cry.

The clusters of figures withdrew further from the windows of the antechamber, and eyes turned nervously toward the duke—who ignored them.

There was another crash of glass, and the noise from the square deepened into a growl through which individual voices could be heard, shouting.

Jehan de Luxembourg had his hand on his sword hilt.

"I'll lead the soldiers out," he said curtly, and turned to make for the door. But the duke grasped him by the arm.

"No!"

"My lord . . . we must!"

"No!" he said a second time.

The duke and his captain faced one another for a moment, and there was not a sound or movement among the others in that room. They watched with apprehensive faces as the duke walked slowly toward the window. Luxembourg tried to compel him to stand back, but Philip brushed his hand aside. He stood by the open colonnade some thirty feet above the massed crowd, and gazed down on the scene below with an expression of thoughtfulness on his face.

Here and there in the square men caught sight of him standing between the stone columns above them. People nudged each other and pointed. Within a minute everyone had noticed him, and the sound of the crowd changed: a note of fear and of anticipation softened the growl of voices. But then, as he continued to stand there neither moving nor attempting to speak, bolder voices burst out from the mass of guildsmen. "Traitor! Butcher! Murderer!" they shouted. And still the duke did not move. A stone rattled against the wall below where he stood. Soon others struck the colonnade and the low parapet. People could see figures trying to pull him back, and they saw the duke resist, shrug them away. A stone struck the column a mere foot from the duke's face, and he scarcely flinched. Again the mood of the crowd changed. Voices cried out, "He's unarmed!" There were scuffles among groups of figures. A woman was seen to beat her fists against the face of a young man raising his arm to hurl a stone. Several people were pushed to the ground. Gradually the square fell quieter, and there was only a low murmur of expectancy—broken by the deep gong of the cathedral bell.

The duke did not know how long he stood there by the window, so many thoughts were flooding through his mind. It was as though he had never looked at people before; and now he saw down there below him not just ugliness and hatred toward himself but men who were living in an entirely different age from his own. It came as a shock when he realized that it was they who were the men of the future. Always until this moment the duke had seen himself as the man of tomorrow. His vision of Burgundy spread across Europe like a brilliant carpet—the majesty of the Golden Fleece—the laws and dreams of chivalry—the urge to crusade, to raise the banner of Christendom: suddenly all these bright peaks no longer seemed to be what the world was straining to reach. They were no more than unlit torches in the dark; they were mere tales told about yesterday. Even the colonnade where he stood mocked those dreams: he thought of Master Jan's portrait of him, standing before just such a colonnade with the new Jerusalem spreading beyond his gaze; except that now, what did he see before him? No golden land upon which God smiled. No mirror of heaven. No new Eden. The spires were not the pinnacles of a holy city; they were the spires of a city of guildsmen whose angry voices even now rose in protest against everything he could offer them. Stones rattled against the very window through which he had wanted to show them heaven on earth. It was with a shock of sadness that he realized he was not the ruler for them. He had expected men who would follow him to Jerusalem, who would join in the pageant of glory. But they were not like that: they did not care about chivalry, crusades, about visions of the greatness of Burgundy. They wanted . . . an ordinary life; they wanted peace, money, trade, beer; they wanted to be left alone. Small pleasures. Small joys. A life that stretched no further than the grasp of their hands.

No, he was not the ruler for such people.

A stone struck the column close to his face. He forced himself not to move.

The battle—he knew—was not between him and the guildsmen; it was between two worlds which could never meet. Except . . . the square was crowded with men and women who were risking their lives: if he had let Jehan de Luxembourg have his way there would have been another slaughter, and this they all knew. They were in danger, and so was he.

Perhaps, then, they could meet in courage, at least. He would show them.

The duke stepped back from the window and, without a word to those waiting apprehensively around him, brushed past Jehan de Luxembourg and began to descend the stairs toward the courtyard of the palace. He was almost by the gate before people realized what he intended to do. By then it was too late. The duke gave a sharp order for the stout wooden gate to be opened, and before the horrified eyes of those within he stepped out into the crowd.

It seemed for a moment like a man walking to his death.

Jan was standing with Margarethe on the steps of the cathedral overlooking the square. She felt his hand grow tense and he gave a gasp.

"Good God!"

Jan watched transfixed as the tall, unarmed figure in black walked slowly toward the crowd. He had never seen the duke's face so composed: it was as if he were strolling among friends. The crowd fell silent. They fell back: some were hastily pulled back to make room for him. He continued to walk slowly into their midst. Hard, bewildered eyes followed him.

Hands holding stones were lowered. Then he stopped and looked around him, his eyes traveling quietly across that sea of intent faces. Jan saw the duke raise one black-gloved hand. He was going to speak. A murmur rose and died away around him.

He called out four names—with no note of an order; more a request. Jan recognized the names of the four city magistrates. There was a pause, and much turning of heads in different directions. Then, reluctantly as it seemed, figures began to move forward toward the duke. Several hands tried to restrain them, but they continued to move forward until four elderly men in long gowns broke through the crowd and stood in the space surrounding the duke. They were elected from among the guildsmen, Jan knew: they were hostile to the duke.

Jan heard Philip speak again, addressing them only just audibly.

"You are the representatives of the law," he said. "I committed some injustice which I intend to repair."

He then requested the magistrates to submit to him a list of all those families who had suffered loss—through death or injury—in the recent disturbance. Jan noticed that the duke used the mildest of words to describe the mutiny. He paused for a moment before raising his voice to address the throng. He wished, he said, to offer whatever handsome compensation he could to those bereaved or injured. This would be done immediately: he gave his pledge.

That was all. The duke turned away and walked toward the gate as slowly as he had come, without once glancing back. There was a numb silence in the square. The gate closed behind him. Only then did a wave of sound spread across the crowd—voices of astonishment and perplexity.

Margarethe noticed a look of bemusement on Jan's face. He turned to her after a few seconds.

"That was the duke I should have painted," he said. "I never knew that he was brave and I never knew that he was human."

It was some time before anyone remarked on how clever the duke had been, and by that time the tide of anger had ebbed and people were drifting away to their homes. The magistrates had repaired to the town hall to begin their task of drawing up a list of families who had suffered. Only then was it pointed out that the whole city had suffered, and was suffering still. The duke had said nothing about their grievances—their loss of trade, the drying up of the waterways, the taxes. But by now it was too late. People's fury had been stilled. The duke had outmatched them by being more cool and more courageous: he had risked everything. They could have killed him; they could have stormed the palace. It would have been the end of Burgundy.

They had allowed Philip to rule as he thought fit.

Within the palace the faces of those in the courtyard expressed amazement and relief. Jehan de Luxembourg stood awkwardly to one side, his hand still on the hilt of his sword. The duke's first chamberlain, in his finery, stepped forward as if to greet Philip, but then paused as if uncertain what he should say. Instead he coughed into his hand. The ducal herald was mopping his brow and blinking, a dazed look on his face. The only person who seemed to know what to do was the duchess Isabella: to everyone's surprise she hurried toward Philip and threw herself in his arms. The duke embraced her, and those around him caught a look on his face which they had never seen. He was overjoyed—not triumphant, not proud, but tender. His arms folded around Isabella, and without a word he led her into the palace.

When they were alone he spoke to her as she could hardly remember him ever speaking: he was a man she had never known. When he looked at her it was almost with surprise, and he held her hand, not wishing to let go.

"I have been through a fire," he said.

For a while he said nothing more, his eyes searching around him and every now and then returning to the still figure of Isabella. Her hand remained clasped in his.

"It's curious," he went on. "Only when I knew I could be frail could I find the courage to walk into that crowd."

He was speaking almost to himself, not looking at her. There was such tiredness in his face, and his head seemed to droop.

"You're my wife," he said suddenly, gazing up at her.

It was a long while before they left that room. No one dared enter. Isabella listened to him talk of things he had never mentioned, and which she had never dreamed he would say. Several times he talked of the fire which had burnt him, and it was only after some time that Isabella realized it was the fire of the Maid which kept returning before his eyes. Joan at the stake. He would shudder as if in horror. Suddenly he looked at Isabella earnestly.

"I'd expected a peasant girl," he said. "Someone I could intimidate." The duke paused, and a bewildered look crossed his face. "Instead, I found a woman of vision. And what's more, I realized that if I hadn't been what I am I could have followed her."

There was another pause while the duke looked reflectively along the wall of gilded mirrors and tapestries depicting the labors of Hercules and the legend of the Golden Fleece.

"When I spoke with the Maid I understood what it was to *believe*," he went on. "I knew that she could go to the stake for her faith, and I knew that everything I believed in was like chaff compared to that. And yet I did not expect her to do it."

The duke rose and crossed the room toward the window from which she had so often seen him gaze proudly over Flanders. Isabella's eyes followed the tall figure in black whose splendor was suddenly so dimmed; and to her surprise she wanted to reach out and touch him.

"I'll never forget what she said," he added, and his face as he turned wore a look of haunted pride. "She said I was only half a man. That I was a fraud. That I was a Frenchman who had betrayed France for my own small glory. . . . And I couldn't answer. . . . Later I told Monsieur de Monstrelet to make no record of what had been said. And when I said that I knew that she had been right."

Isabella had never imagined she would see her husband so humbled. And then she remembered his courage only an hour before and wondered how many men could have done what he did.

"It's not half a man who braves an angry crowd unarmed,"

she said. "And it's not a fraud who loves a woman he can't possess."

There was a startled expression on the duke's face as he realized that she was referring to Jacqueline.

"How did you know?" he asked in a bewildered voice.

"I've always known that you loved Jacqueline," she answered. "If I hadn't I should have imagined you to be incapable of love."

He looked at her as though not quite understanding what she had said. Then he nodded.

"Yes, I did love her. And now she's dead, I feel freed."

Isabella turned her head.

"For whom?" she asked.

There was the briefest pause.

"For you—if you still have any love for me."

Isabella did not know if she wanted him to hold her. There had been so much pain, and she had learned to shield herself with the distance grown between them.

"Tell me," she said after a moment. "What was it you loved so deeply about Jacqueline?"

He looked startled, but her eyes felt very close and suddenly very dear to him. He knew the answer.

"She was beyond my reach," he said.

Isabella gazed quizzically at him, and then smiled. She knew it was perhaps the most honest thing he had ever said to her.

"So must I go far away for you to love me?"

Again Philip seemed not quite to understand, and did not reply.

She looked at him, and as she did so she reflected on all the women he had possessed who were not beyond his reach— possessed and discarded like so many pretty ornaments. Jacqueline was the one ornament he had never been able to wear. And she realized that the man in front of her—uncertain of her—was someone whose life was the pursuit of a dream. She thought of his grand vision of Burgundy, his love of chivalry, the Golden Fleece, his promise of a crusade. And she thought again of Jacqueline. All of them dreams. And here was she, within reach of him: he could have had her love, all of it. But she was not a dream, and now she knew with a painful sadness that he could never give her the same love he had felt for Jacqueline. It could never be hers. And at the same time she knew that she no longer searched for it, no longer wanted it. She would guard that distance which protected her. For the moment he was here close to her, needing her: so many of his dreams had collapsed that he had fallen—like Icarus, his wings burnt by the sun. But sooner or later he would take wing again: there would be other women, other dreams. She could not love a chaser of dreams.

Nevertheless, she thought, there is now; there are these moments, and they are not nothing.

She smiled at him and extended her arms. He held her close, and gratefully.

"Tonight we'll dance," he said.

And as the sounds of music alerted the owls in the night city, hooded figures carrying lanterns were drawn into the streets like winter fireflies. It was as if the unexpectedness of such gaiety soothed so many wounds until Bruges began to remember that even the most unlikely love could look possible in the deceiving mirror of its canals. The merchant Arnolfini was seen to pay a late visit to the church of Our Lady, where he was shortly to be married. Accompanying him was a slim fair-haired creature whose hand Arnolfini was holding rather as though she were a flower. Afterward the pair of them stood for a while on the bridge by the hospital of St. John, and had Giovanni's friends from the tavern been witnesses to the occasion, one at least of them might have commented that the place he had selected to admire his lady's reflection was at the precise point where the street of Our Lady becomes the street of St. Catherine—where virgin becomes martyr. Further along the Dijver canal, where the gaunt belfry shaded the moonlight and disguised the rapture on the face of Michault de Caron, the lovely Lysbet was being awarded the tenth or fiftieth poem in honor of her perfection.

Near the church of St. Giles, a little to the north of the street of the Golden Hand, a black boy was leading a blind woman lovingly by the arm. She stopped as if to look around

her, and he waited silently. Suddenly she turned to him, and
in the moonlight the boy could see that she was smiling.

"Isn't it strange?" said Bona. "In the darkness I can see."

The boy gazed at her in wonder.

"I can see your face," she said, touching it with her fingers.

Chapter • Fourteen

Only Jehan Lefèvre could make a knock on the door sound pompous. Jan knew it must be the ducal herald, and in spite of his anxiety about Lefèvre's mission he smiled as he imagined the slender gloved fingers grasping the knocker as if it were something that had fouled his shoe. "Monsieur Elégance" would be waiting in the persistent rain, his beaver hat low over his brow, a black surcoat so long and slim that it might appear to be enclosing a mere twig.

Jan waited. The housekeeper's footsteps could be heard downstairs.

He sensed that at last there was no avoiding it. Lefèvre had no other possible reason to come: the confrontation with the duke was about to take place, and what on earth was Jan to say? He had slashed the ducal portrait in anger. He had been commanded to paint the "real man," and had failed. Even the *un*real man still remained incomplete, savaged—what was more—with the point of Jan's dagger.

He listened to the slow footsteps on the stairs, aware that very shortly his position as First Painter to the duke of Burgundy was likely to be plucked rudely from him. At the very least he would soon find himself earning his daily bread painting the sallow faces of magistrates squeezed into black, or vacant Madonnas receiving usurious bankers to the court of heaven. At the worst, ducal disfavor might be so dire that Jan would be compelled to hasten from Flanders under sentence of banishment. Thoughts of Italy once again drifted into Jan's mind.

But at least it was a relief not to have to wait any longer.

As he entered, Lefèvre appeared paler and more lofty than ever. Once in the privacy of Jan's studio his features assumed

357

that familiar stretched look which invariably preceded a formal command from the court. Margarethe had retired, an anxious expression on her face, though not before Lefèvre had awarded her a beady stare which reminded her—blushing—of the drawings of herself naked and how the herald had peered at them lengthily. She felt his close-set eyes peeling her like a peach.

There were few moments of silence. It was some time since Lefèvre had been here, and the break seemed to widen the distance between the two men. The space was occupied by a distinct chill—and eventually by a well-prepared cough.

"As you might expect, the duke is anxious to see the portrait," he announced coolly, his eyes probing the bareness of the studio in search of some new delicacy of flesh upon which they might rest.

So Jan was right. There was to be no chance to explain that the portrait was still unfinished; no time even to attempt some repair to the wound he had inflicted on it. He felt paralyzed. He had rehearsed what he would say, and now no words came to his mouth and no thoughts to his brain. There were only seconds in which to act.

"Of course," he heard himself reply. "But I need time to make the final touches."

Lefèvre had by now located a small silverpoint drawing of flowers and trees, and was gazing at it with apparent disgust that it contained no female matter, however closely he peered and from whatever angle.

"Quite unnecessary, Jan," he said airily, still searching the foliage for a hidden breast or thigh. His tone of voice was amiable suddenly, and Jan dreaded the salacious observation which this usually heralded. But none came.

"Quite unnecessary," he repeated. "In whatever state, he wishes to see it."

Jan closed his eyes for a moment and searched in the darkness for some reprieve. In whatever state! Little did Lefèvre know what that state was.

His closed eyelids offering no avenue of escape, Jan resolved to brave the worst. If this was to be the end, let him approach that end truthfully and with some self-respect.

"When?" he inquired.

"Today. As soon as possible."

Jan nodded mechanically. Then into his numbed state floated words from the herald which made him raise his head in puzzlement. Lefèvre had abandoned the drawing of trees and was speaking again in that wry tone, his hands flexed behind his back and his head jerking from side to side like some marionette.

"You will understand," he was saying, "the duke was much affected by his cousin's death."

For a few seconds Jan failed to understand why Lefèvre had suddenly introduced the subject of Jacqueline. He looked at the herald blankly. The thin, lofty voice was continuing.

"He was—how shall I say?—deeply attached to her, for all her extreme behavior toward him." Lefèvre's head began to jerk affectedly as if he felt embarrassed by what he was required to say. "The duke says he would like to see her again," he added.

An ocean of relief swept over Jan. Why had the herald not explained that it was the portrait of Jacqueline the duke wished to see? He felt for a moment a quite unreasonable affection for the absurd Lefèvre. He wanted to call out to Margarethe that it was all right; they were rescued. He wanted to open a bottle of the finest wine. At the same time he resolved that he would risk no further agonies of this nature. Agony or no agony, anger or no anger, he would see to it that the ducal portrait was repaired within a matter of days, and if he had to invent a gleaming vision of the new Jerusalem in which to enshrine the duke, then he would summon up every cold, hard skill at his disposal *and do it.*

"Of course," he said lightly. "If you wish me to accompany you, I gladly will." Jan found himself making the kind of elaborate gesture of the hand with which Lefèvre always accompanied the least statement.

The herald perceived that he was being mocked, and turned toward the door with a similar gesture.

"You have a man who will bring it?" he asked coldly.

"I shall bring it myself."

It was the first time Jan had set eyes on the duke since he and Margarethe had watched the tall figure in black walk with apparent unconcern into the angry mob gathered in the cathedral square. It was the first time he had been in the duke's company since before the mutiny and slaughter of the guildsmen, and since the death of Jacqueline.

Jan was carrying the wrapped portrait under his arm. He saw the duke glance at it, and then look away. He began to talk in that easy, casual way designed—Jan often felt—to lower the guard of those he was addressing. It occurred to Jan how suspicious he had grown of Philip. All the admiration he had once felt for the man—scarcely a grain of it now remained.

At the same time, he might have known that Philip would surprise him.

"The altarpiece is a triumph," he said, smiling. "Even Bishop Denis feels compelled to admire it, and you know how he detests everything that gives pleasure." Then he gave a laugh. "As for Jodocus Vyt, I never knew he could look so pious."

The duke was gazing at Jan, watching the pleasure on the painter's face. Jan could feel himself being drawn toward the man again, responding to his charm.

"It was a dignified ceremony," he went on. "I was careful not to intrude on it. It looked like a family occasion, and I left you to it."

For the first time Jan understood that the duke had after all been present at the inauguration, just as he had promised. He felt a wave of pleasure. But before he had a chance to reply Philip delivered another surprise.

"So your lady has returned, and you're to be married." He was smiling again. "My warmest congratulations. We shall have to honor the occasion."

"Thank you, my lord," was all Jan could say.

He could feel a deep irritation with himself that so much anger and contempt for the duke should so easily begin to melt. Around him lay the familiar room of splendor—the golden ornaments, the jewels, the tapestries in which threads of silver glistened. It was as if nothing of Philip's grandeur had been touched by the events of the past months: deaths, defeats, rebellion, tragedy—all of them had drifted past like clouds on the wind. And the duke had survived as he would always survive, around him the blood dried and crumbled, the ashes blown away. Amid so much affirmation of his glory it was hard to think of Joan at the stake gasping out the name of Jesus, or of Jacqueline driven to her death among the lonely dunes.

At last the duke's eyes seemed to settle on the package containing the portrait. How, Jan wondered, had Philip known he had brought it back from Goes? He realized Jehan de Luxembourg must have told the duke he had been there. As always, Jan had the feeling of being watched. There was little that Philip did not know: it was only a matter of how much he was prepared to admit that he knew.

Jan unwrapped the package. There she was, the haughty, sad loveliness of her face as real as life against that huge sky—the black raven raised in majesty over the lands of the sea. For a moment it was as if her dark eyes were gazing at these two men who had loved her, compelling them to silence. Jan was aware of the great golden room where they stood, and of the stillness of the duke as he contemplated that proud face.

Finally he seemed to break the spell.

"Such wildness in her," he said; "how well you've caught it." He bent down and picked up the portrait. The duke's eyes appeared to Jan even more heavy-lidded than usual as he looked at it. "It was a wildness that turned almost to madness in the end," he added.

The duke set the portrait against the wall in the sunlight which had broken through the rain, and continued to gaze at it with a hollow expression. How very different from the imperious look Philip had adopted for his own portrait. Jan wondered what was passing through the duke's mind. Sadness? Anger? Recrimination? Remorse?

"She wrote me a letter," he said suddenly, "a half-crazed letter."

The duke paused. It was as if he were unsure whether to continue. Jan was aware of being no more than the duke's painter. But he was conscious too of a bond, and he could sense that Philip felt it—that in having painted Jacqueline, Jan was offering the duke something they both shared. Perhaps there was no one else to whom Philip could talk about this woman who had obsessed him.

"It was a letter she wrote shortly before she died," he went on. "The lord of Luxembourg brought it to me." There was another pause, and Jan could see lines of tension in the duke's face. He was sure that Philip had never spoken about the letter to anyone.

Jan waited. Eventually the duke's eyes left the portrait and wandered about the room as though Jan were not there at all.

"Crazed," he said again. His mouth was suddenly very thin. "She wanted to say how she'd fought and schemed to destroy me for so many years, and it was only now—in defeat —that she knew how to do it." The duke's voice fell to little more than a whisper. "And that was to kill herself."

Jan felt shocked—by the letter, and by the fact that the duke was telling him these things.

"She wanted me to know, when I heard of her death, that she had done it deliberately—that she was determined to destroy herself in order that she might haunt me forever, she said." Jan saw Philip swallow and reset his mouth. His fingers were extended as if reaching for something that was not there. Jan knew he was witnessing a man in pain. The voice continued—flat, faltering. "She wanted to blight my life with her death, she said, just as I had blighted her life with *my life.*"

Jan's eyes met the duke's, and what Jan saw was a terrible loneliness. It was the loneliness and impotence of power. He had no weapons against her now she was dead: Jacqueline had plucked them from him. Jan was standing before one of the most powerful men in the world, and what he saw in front of him was helplessness. The velvet and jewels which adorned the duke might have been rags, and the slender hands extended toward the portrait might have been begging for alms.

Quite unexpectedly he gave a laugh as if to clear the pain, glancing at Jan as he did so.

"I remember saying to you that people you painted seemed to talk to you—as though you opened them like a box and looked inside. You did it with Isabella. With Jacqueline. And now, it seems, with me."

He laughed once more—another painful laugh. Then he looked at Jacqueline's portrait again.

"I can imagine what she must have said to you while you painted her. I can almost see the loathing on her lips." He turned away from the portrait as if he could not bear to gaze at it any longer. "We fought for so many years," he went on. "For me it became almost a game of love and hatred: I don't think I believed it was entirely real. I realize now how very real it was. It's appalling to know she hated me so much that she'd give up everything to wound me—even her life."

The duke's face seemed to crease like parchment.

"Her life," he said again, his voice little more than a croak. "To haunt me."

There was the kind of silence from which some violent action might at any second burst. But at the same moment Jan saw that Philip was not a violent man. And then he said something which took Jan's mind back to that scene in the cathedral square when the guildsmen were hurling stones.

"The worst time was when I walked unprotected into that crowd," the duke was saying. "They were calling out 'murderer.' I thought I was the one who would be murdered." Jan remembered the serene look on the duke's face that extraordinary afternoon—the stark bravery of the man. "I knew I was courting death. But I was indifferent. I would not have minded. And then it seemed that I could hear Jacqueline laughing. A haunting laugh. For a moment it was as though she had won—she had made me not care even about my own life. That was the only time I felt anger—with myself. To have allowed that to happen to me. 'Jacqueline is dead, and I am not,' I said; 'nor will I be.' And I raised my hand and addressed the guildsmen. They lowered their stones."

The duke looked at Jan, then at the portrait. His face seemed quite different, as if the pain had passed.

"I think that freed me," he said.

He picked up the portrait almost casually.

"I should like to keep this. There'll not be another woman like her." Suddenly the familiar amused look returned. "Perhaps I should be thankful for that," he added.

It seemed the moment for Jan to leave. He was aware that

he said nothing at all. He bowed and turned toward the door, but the duke stopped him.

"And when may I have the pleasure of seeing my own portrait at last—before some other woman intervenes?"

There was a flicker of a smile on the duke's face.

"Within one week, my lord," Jan replied. "You have my word."

Jan walked back through the winter streets with a sense of bewildered relief. He knew that he had witnessed the "real man" the duke had asked him to paint. Already he could see the finished portrait. There would be no new Jerusalem behind the stone colonnade. Philip would be standing there much as Jan had watched him that afternoon above the cathedral square—a brave and aloof figure, and below him the tangled roofs and streets and little fields of Flanders with people going their own way, perhaps hating or respecting their duke but in the main indifferent to a ruler who was not of their world and with whose private passions they were entirely unconcerned.

Jan found himself wondering if the duke would hang his own portrait near that of Jacqueline so that they would gaze at one another forever, bound by their own impossible dreams.

As if the dark days were over, the gradual return of Bona's sight seemed like an augury.

In the Fallen Angel they spoke of how the black boy had come running into the tavern with his face awash with tears calling out, "She can see . . . she can see."

At first it was only shadows and silhouettes—soft echoes of the outer world. Then one morning Bona had announced, "I know that color; it's yellow." She was aware of the sunlight on a golden curtain, and the boy drew it across the window to protect her eyes. Bona kissed him tenderly. And when he stood up to fetch her a glass of water she said, "Isn't that red you're wearing today?"

She began to receive visitors like a queen.

"You look a little thinner," she commented as Jan approached the couch where she reclined. "But perhaps it's because I still can't see you clearly enough, and in reality you are very much fatter," she added with a laugh. "I shall have to wait until Godscalc calls, and then I shall know if I can tell the difference."

"It's a miracle, Bona." It was all Jan felt able to say as he took her hand and kissed it.

"No, not a miracle. Luck."

And she laughed again. Not for a long while had Jan heard real laughter from Bona. She began to talk of those who had visited her. Never had she felt so courted, she said. People felt compelled to be solicitous, faced with an invalid, she explained. They approached her rather like priests. She, on the other hand, found her condition the most delightful pretext for plain speaking. (Jan felt surprised that she should need any pretext.) Michault the poet, for example, she continued: it was such a relief that he had found a new recipient for his poems and his amorousness; he no longer seemed so entirely ridiculous to her. But was he a good lover? she inquired of Lysbet. She herself had always avoided the comedy of finding out, she had explained: besides, there had invariably been a poem in the way. Even with her half-sight Bona had been able to make out the mortified look on Michault's face as he listened to these remarks. As for Lysbet, she had made no answer, and Bona formed the impression that she was more interested in assessing her beautiful black boy. Doubtless the flighty Lysbet was already tiring of love in the sonnet form. Bona hoped the girl would not repeat the visit: she had no wish to resort to violence in order to protect her rights.

"At my age a woman cannot afford to be generous," she said firmly.

Then Bona screwed up her eyes to gaze at Margarethe.

"You should remember that, my dear," she said loudly. "Jan likes women a little too much. You must make it clear from the start that if he strays you'll cut his prick off; then you'll have no trouble."

She could not see Margarethe blush, but she heard Jan chuckle and squeezed his hand.

"I am his Eve, remember. I offered him the apple and my goodness, how he did eat."

Bona was beginning to enjoy herself a little too much for Jan's comfort. To his relief she switched the conversation to

Arnolfini and his wondrous madonna. Bona began to describe their first meeting with some relish.

" 'Giovanna,' I said in my best French, 'I assume you're a virgin?' And do you know, the tender creature almost ran from the room. 'Don't be so timid, girl,' I called out. 'You're in Flanders now, where people are frank about these matters. Besides, there aren't many virgins in Bruges and you may be the object of some curiosity. You'd better get used to it. It won't be for long.' "

Arnolfini, Bona explained, had assumed a look of pride mixed with flustered indignation. She wished her eyesight had permitted her to scrutinize this paragon of a girl to discover what precious attribute she possessed which had reduced the licentious merchant to such a state of adoration. Bona assumed that three qualities were probably enough—that Giovanna was beautiful, she was wealthy, and her family was from Lucca. Perhaps, Bona thought, other, lesser qualities might have played their part—silence, pliability, domestic orderliness, an inclination to lower the eyes when gazed upon, a disinclination to possess opinions or to challenge his own.

"I think he's quite simply in love," suggested Jan.

Bona looked surprised, and Jan noticed her glance at the black boy with an expression that was suddenly tender.

"I suppose it could be," she said reflectively. "It had never occurred to me."

The thought seemed to change Bona's mood like the drawing of a curtain.

"You know, I'd begun to believe there was no such thing as love. Only what people searched for and could never find."

Bona had a way of looking beautiful suddenly when she spoke about the heart. The sulkiness vanished, along with the contempt, the malice. Jan understood why people were loyal to Bona even while she frightened them. He watched her take the boy's hand and unselfconsciously lay it on her breast. He thought how much he would enjoy painting her like that. The touch of love. One moment which caught everything. He would paint Arnolfini and Giovanna at such a moment, so that they would forever remember it and feel its pulse.

She was lying there, her half-sighted eyes seeming to

assess the two of them as they stood in attendance at the end of her couch. The winter light was bleaching the wooden panels around the room.

"Being able to see again," she said, "it's like having lived in two worlds. The old one's died; everything is starting afresh. I like that." She laughed, and the look of Eve returned to her face. "You're reborn, you two. Goodness, what a life there is for you. I can see it in the way you touch one another."

It was as if those few words opened a door into a garden. They were walking homeward through the quiet city, the pallid sunlight flickering in the canals. Margarethe squeezed his arm.

"What Bona said about two worlds—that's what I feel," she said. "It's as though I had to go away to Louvain and close my eyes on what happened. As though I had to go blind, like Bona. Do you understand?"

Jan nodded. He understood, and he felt the same. In his mind was the garden Bona had shown him, and he seemed to be painting it. Bright flowers. Birds. People in sunlight. And suddenly—he laughed—Arnolfini's little dog. Behind him the old world lay in shadow. It was all storm and battle, victims and heroes, a place where love was always fleeing, and people eternally questing. He did not tell Margarethe that he had thought immediately of Jacqueline when Bona had said that, but he knew that her death felt like the dying of that old world.

"Bona says I should cut your prick off if you stray." Margarethe's face wore an expression of mock solemnity, and her eyes looked very wide and liquid. "I should hate to do that."

"What would you do, then?" he asked with a grave expression to match hers.

The green eyes scanned his face. It was a moment before she spoke.

"Weep," she said.

She pressed very close to him, and he could smell the warmth of her hair. In the dark canal their faces gazed back at them. Margarethe dropped a pebble into the water, and the two images shattered until gradually the ripples settled and drew them together again.

"That was like us," she said quietly. Then, still watching their twin faces stirring in the canal, she pressed her cheek against his to see them join in the water.

"Do you remember, we used to swim in the forest stream in summer? Shall we do that again when summer comes?"

Jan nodded and smiled at her. He had never seen her face more lovely or more loving.

"We'd make love in the grass," she went on, "and hope no one would come by."

"And once we thought they did, and when I looked up it was only a deer." He laughed.

"And once you laid flowers around my breasts, and you said you'd like to paint me like that. Will you do that, Jan?"

"Yes."

And he kissed her.

"I'll paint you in flowers, Margarethe. I'll paint you in water. I'll paint you in sunlight. And I'll paint you asleep." There was such a look of delight in her face. "The only thing is, when I paint your body I shall want to make love to you, so perhaps none of them will ever get finished."

Margarethe shivered a little as they walked into the shadow of a gabled street. Then she laughed again.

"Supposing I say no until you *have* finished?"

"Then I shall have to learn to paint very fast."

She looked thoughtful.

"And where shall we put all these paintings of me?" she asked. "I should be embarrassed."

It was Jan's turn to laugh.

"Oh, we'll have one big room, always locked. No one will ever enter but us. Your body will be all around the walls, and in the center will be a big bed where we'll make love."

"And when we have children, what will you do then, Jan?" She was gazing at him with that radiant face. "Because I want lots of children."

He looked at her with a wry smile.

"That's easy. I'll paint a Bible story on the back of each picture, and then we can turn them all around."

The two of them wandered along the quayside toward the little bridge which led past the Fallen Angel toward the street of the Golden Hand. They passed Jan de Leeuw's door, and for a moment through the window he caught sight of his friend seated at his workbench by the light of a lamp, a glass squeezed to his eye. De Leeuw's huge fingers were setting tiny stones into a golden brooch with the delicacy of a spider spinning its web. The jeweler was entirely absorbed, and never noticed Jan peering in at him as he passed.

What struck Jan in that moment was that he could paint that brooch with just the same minute sureness of touch. His, too, was a world of infinitely small things perfectly understood. The glitter of light on gold. The look in an eye. The curl in a strand of hair. The touch of a shadow on a woman's face. It was with these tiny, sharp perceptions that he understood the world. He did not need dukes and princes to show him their dreams of what the world might be.

Jan remembered what Joos Vyt had once said—that their time was already passing, and that he, like Joos, was one of the new men.

Jan had not expected that to paint Arnolfini and his bride would be so joyous an affirmation of that new world; but never had he set about a picture with so much confidence and pleasure.

The church wedding was over. The bells of Our Lady had scarcely died away before the merchant in rich and somber clothes had led his Giovanna to the small room draped in scarlet for the civil ceremony. And there they stood while the registrar stumbled over a few plain words. Then they signed— Arnolfini in the florid hand that had witnessed so many bills of dispatch to the courts of Europe, Giovanna minutely as if her identity had just crawled out of a little box unseen.

"And now, Jan, you must work fast." Giovanni was smiling for the first time. "This is no way to be spending the first moments of one's marriage."

Jan wondered what the silent Giovanna was thinking about it all as Arnolfini led her to the center of the room and carefully positioned her by his side, his hand holding hers. How delicately their fingers touched, Jan noticed; like doves' wings. The merchant wore a large black hat which almost embraced his long sallow features. Giovanna, as he had promised, was in white and green. Virginity and spring. The dog, Pepe, took up his position before them and with an air of curiosity cocked his head but not—to Jan's relief—his leg.

He began to draw swiftly, adding touches of color along with notes to remind him of textures, shadows, highlights. The atmosphere of silence and intimacy he would remember. As he worked, Jan became conscious that he could be recording a rehearsal of his own marriage—especially because of the mirror on the far wall behind the bridal couple. It was a convex mirror which bent the whole room in which they stood, stretching it far away to the far-distant point where Jan and Margarethe could be seen as witnesses to the marriage. This time he was painter and witness, Jan told himself; not—mercifully—painter and ambassador. There were no messages to relay, no secrets to withhold. Neither Arnolfini nor, certainly, Giovanna would tell him anything about themselves. He was here as craftsman and friend.

Jan carefully sketched in his own small figure in the mirror, adding a touch of scarlet for the hat Arnolfini had insisted he wear. Then just the outline of Margarethe by his side. She was very quiet all the time he worked, and he knew she was thinking of the day, only a short time from now, when she would be standing in such a room holding his hand and taking just such a vow.

In a bold, elegant hand Jan inscribed above the mirror in Latin the words "Johannes was here"—*Johannes fuit hic.* He would have liked to add "and Margarethe," but since he was the sole witness and Arnolfini would accept no inaccuracy, he left it at that.

Finally Jan took special care over the eyes and hands. Again it was as he wished his own marriage to be—his own life to be. The implication of trust in that touch of fingers. The dignity of the glance they gave one another. The light on their faces just as it would fall each ordinary day—no blaze of heaven raining gold upon a new Jerusalem. While Jan was drawing them, catching the exact set of the lips, the precise tilt of the head, he was surprised how easy it was to forget the unlikelihood of this union; instead, he was aware only of its simple realness.

His portrait of them would be about that—nothing else. And even as he drew that quiet room, and the two figures standing there touching hands so tenderly in the midst of their vow, Jan thought of the portraits of Philip and of Jacqueline as he had set them side by side in his studio. Such contrast. There stood the duke, and there the woman he loved. Each stood like fierce monuments to their own grandeur, separated by a rage of longing and of hate.

Jan looked again at the tenderness of those two hands touching, carefully modeling the fine shadows between their fingers.

He had done enough. He would work on it in peace.

"She's pretty," Margarethe said as they made their way back toward the street of the Golden Hand. "I wonder if she ever speaks."

Jan glanced at her.

"Madonnas aren't supposed to speak."

"Why not?"

"Can you imagine the Virgin Mary telling the child Jesus it's time for bed?"

Margarethe laughed so that people turned to watch them as they passed by.

"I'm glad I'm not your madonna." Then she looked at him with a tenderness that almost overwhelmed him. "Jan, I do love you," she said.

"And we shall be happier than anyone we know."

Jan unlatched the door. His housekeeper hurried forward in a state of excitement, and beckoned them to follow her. She opened the door of the studio, and there before them on a table lay six tall silver cups.

"The duke sent them," explained the housekeeper in a tone of wonder. "For your wedding."

Jan and Margarethe looked at one another, bewildered. The housekeeper kept glancing at the cups as though they might disappear. Jan turned to her and ordered some wine.

"The storm is over," he said, smiling at Margarethe.

They raised two of the duke's cups, and gazed over them at one another. How impossible it was at that moment to believe there had been so much pain.

It was a while before Jan realized that the housekeeper was still standing there. She was holding a letter.

"A messenger brought this for you, too," she said. "From Ghent."

Jan broke the seal. He was puzzled. Then Margarethe saw his face grow solemn.

"It's Joos," he said quietly. There was a pause while Jan finished the letter.

"What is it, Jan? Read it to me."

The housekeeper discreetly retired. He began to read aloud. " 'My dear Jan, I heard your news and I'm so happy. Will you give me the further happiness of seeing you both again? But please make it soon—before winter is over. I feel I shall not have very long to live. In case I've gone, remember—we did great things, we frogs and crows. We sang well. God be with you. Joos.' "

That was all. Jan's face had a lost look, and Margarethe placed her arms around him.

"I've loved him," Jan said at length. "I should like him to see us together again . . . before it's too late. . . . You know," he added, "I scarcely know him, and yet no one has taught me more."

Margarethe said nothing for a moment. Then she took Jan's hands in her own.

"Tell me," she said.

"Oh . . . !" As he thought about it, there were so many little things. Perhaps that was it—that they were *little* things. "Most of all, that in the end it's not grand ideas and grand visions that count: it's ordinary people, and what they do, what they achieve, how they love, how they treat each other. It's as Joos said—the crows and the frogs, not the larks and the nightingales."

"And what are we?"

He smiled at her.

"Lovers."

The winter carnival always invited the snow. It fell gently like a million flowers, pale against the canals, dark against the torchlight, bandaging the ancient city in white petals; and as the evening lengthened into night a chain of bonfires was lit along the ramparts, burnishing the tall mills dimly gold between fire and fire, laying a coronet of flames upon the city. And as if to mark this coronation of fire, from the cathedral of St. Donatian, from St. Saviour's, from the church of Our Lady, the church of Jerusalem, St. James's, St. Anne's, St. John's, the chapel of the Holy Blood, and from the church of every parish across the city, rose a tremendous clamor of bells.

So there she lay, Bruges. Girdled by water and crowned by fire. It was two years since the duke had led his bride here by ship to a salute of torches and a fanfare of silver trumpets. Now, once again, as the snow fell, the streets had become a revelry of masks and it was another night of forgetting. Down there before the ducal palace, figures stood clustered around a brazier, drawn toward it by the smell of mutton and pork ribs, chestnuts, sausages, and hot spiced wine. From time to time they lifted their elaborate masks and ate with their fingers; then they raised pewter goblets and their laughter filled the dark spaces between the torches. The one with the headdress of a lion was the jeweler Jan de Leeuw, his lion's tail acting as a support for an unsteady Michaut Pontin the silversmith. The rentmaster Godscalc Oom was dressed plausibly as a bear, the poet Michault de Caron less probably as Hercules, an arm around each of the heavenly twins. Bona was no less than magnificent as a snow queen in a shimmer of ermine, her black prince on her arm. Arnolfini was looking somewhat absurd as Lancelot, though his Guinevere appeared serenely contented with her knight and champion. The jester, complete with cap and bells, was none other than Master Jan, his Queen of Hearts by his side.

For a moment the pair of them were seen to gaze beyond the warm pool of laughter around the brazier, as if aware of another figure invisible out there who had once ridden through the falling snow in this carnival of dreams, her eyes on fire and her hair black as a raven's wing.

A final blare of trumpets drew the masked faces toward the opened gates of the palace. Two mounted figures were riding slowly into the torchlit square. One was a tall man in black with the headdress of a stag; beside him his lady was veiled in white and crowned with the helmet of Minerva. They reined their horses for an instant, and both acknowledged Master Jan with a wave before riding by. He in turn removed his cap and bells and bowed to the duke and his lady; then he watched them until they melted into the darkness as if they too only haunted the carnival as ghosts, before turning back with a smile to the warmth of the brazier and the laughter of friends.